To Sandra,
Enjoy!
Allie Marie

HEART OF COURAGE

The Red Ruby Story

Allie Marie

This book is a work of fiction, and does not represent real events. Characters, names, places, and incidents are works of the authors imagination and do not depict any real event, or person living or dead.

HEART OF COURAGE
The Red Ruby Story

Published by Nazzaro & Price Publishing

Published in the United States of America

DEDICATION

In loving memory of my dad
I miss you every day, Daddy.

.

THE PROPERTIES

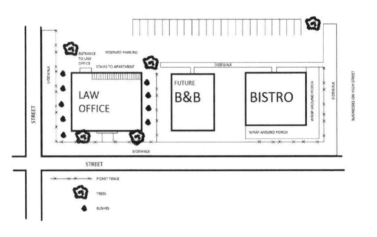

ACKNOWLEDGMENTS

There are so many people to whom I owe deep gratitude for supporting my writing adventure in some way. Thank you to the following:

To my husband Jack, love of my life, for all you do for me.

To my sister Kathy, with love. (That Steve Perry/Journey reference is just for you, Sis.)

To Sandi Baum, for the overwhelming support and encouragement you give me during our almost daily critique sessions. I'll be forever grateful. Get ready for the next book!

To Laura Somers and Janice Philbin, for reviewing my drafts and encouraging me to press on.

To the men and women who have served, or are currently in the Armed Forces. To my Marine husband and son, and my Navy SEAL dad for their past service. There aren't enough words to say thanks for protecting our country and our freedom. And to my ancestor Captain Antoine Paulint for his service during the American Revolution.

To the "Breakfast on Tuesdays Bunch"—from what other source could I have possibly come up with a name like Briley Gavin? You guys will all be in a future book.

Although the businesses in my story are fictional, there are a number of delightful places in Olde Towne that exist for real. I truly appreciate the help from Dawn Richardson, of the Mermaid's Porch and Deon Foster of The Kitchen Koop for answering my many business-related questions.

To Audrey Lassiter and Nettie Fischer of the Little Shoppes on High for your welcome and encouragement, and the Olde Towne Business Association.

To the following businesses for your support: Dodd RV, Dominion Coin, Doris and Roger's Kitchen, Jalapeños, and Leigh Allyn Jewelers.

To my publishers, Helen Brown Nazzaro and James Price,

for your faith—and patience! Another beautiful cover, James. And special thanks to the editing and proofreading staff: Elizabeth Garrett, Julie Graham, Kelley Vinton. It's my keyboard, I tell you.

To my roadies, Sidnie and Carmin, and to my "colonial" girl Elayna. Love you girls.

PROLOGUE

MARIE JOSEPHÉ
On the way to Yorktown, Virginia, July 1781

I huddled with my sisters under the heavy canvas covering the cumbersome wagon. We were already bruised from the many bumps and jerks caused by the constant jolting. Every new crack of the driver's whip caused another painful lurch as the animals responded.

At the driver's shout of "Easy!" the horses' pace slowed. We scrambled into upright positions. Theresé and I sat protectively on either side of our baby sister Nicole, who now slept fitfully, dried tears smudging her cheeks.

I rose to one knee to ease Nicole's curled form from my lap to Theresé's, and then groped my way toward the rear gate of the wagon. Another jolt when the wheel crashed over a rock sent me tumbling. My shoulder struck the sideboard with a loud crack. A crate overturned and raked the side of my arm. I bit back the cry of pain, but could hear my sister's gasp of concern.

In spite of the horses' slowed gait, I slid from side to side until I reached the back and pushed the oilcloth covering to the side. Rainfall from the earlier storm had gathered in the fold, fat drops plopping on my head as I peered into the night.

A bright moon and crystal stars lit the open field to my right, the thrashing of the storm long since passed. White rocks stood out like flat sentries, but their path of travel followed close to a tree line that cast shadows on the wagon. The air was thick with humidity and pungent with the smell of wet grass and dirt. Small pools of mist swirled low to the ground. The stench of tidal marsh soon overpowered the other scents.

I scuttled backwards and settled beside Theresé on the hard floor covering. At the slower pace, my sister and I could now talk with ease. We leaned our heads closer together so only we could hear our whispers.

"The storm has passed." I broke the silence first. "The thunder only rolls far in the distance now."

"What did you see?"

"Tis dark, but the moon lights the way. No one follows. We ride

vii

alongside a range of trees, perhaps to conceal the wagon. I can smell the river nearby."

Theresé arranged the scant coverlet across Nicole's shoulders and said, "The driver has slowed his pace. We must be far enough away from Portsmouth. How much longer do you think it will be before we reach Father's camp?"

The sigh escaped before I could prevent it. "I know not. Mayhap hours."

We fell quiet, swaying in unison with the horses' gait. Only hours earlier, we had fled our grandfather's house in advance of British soldiers. We'd had no time to ask questions as we raced through pouring rain to the waiting wagon.

Neither of us mentioned the crack of gunshots or the awful confusion that ensued as our party was confronted by two soldiers. Muzzle flashes matched lightning strikes, and the boom from the rifles deepened the thunder that drowned our screams, as both our mother and grandfather fell wounded to the ground.

Two more shots echoed, muzzle flashes searing the night as the soldiers fell.

From the shadows, our brother Louis emerged, pistol in hand. Disguised as a British soldier, he pushed us into the wagon and shouted to the driver, "Go. Now!"

We older sisters obeyed without hesitation, fearing any delay could compromise his cover. Little Nicole screamed for her doll, left behind in the chaos. She is only four; it is understandable that the toy is the most important thing to her young mind.

Theresé's voice broke through the dark. "Sister, I worry so about our mother. I fear for what happened back there."

"Louis will do what he can to protect her and our grandfather." I spoke in a voice strong with courage I did not feel. I wondered if my sister experienced the same clutch in her chest as I did, not knowing whether our loved ones had even survived.

I reached into my sleeve to retrieve the small pouch I had tucked away in the confusion of our departure.

It was gone!

"Theresé! I cannot find the pouch with the necklace Mama gave me!" I ran my fingers along the material covering each arm. "I did not have

time to give it back to her, so I pushed it inside my sleeve. I thought the cuff would hold it in."

"Are you sure?" Theresé ran her fingers across my dress sleeves. "We had to leave in such a hurry. Mayhap it fell out when you pushed Nicole inside. Let us hope Louis will find it."

"As I hope he also finds Nicole's doll. She left it in the room."

Theresé dug fingers into my skin, her voice thick with tension as she whispered hoarsely, "Louis' message..."

I interrupted. "His message is safe. I did not leave it in the doll's dress this time. Some odd feeling overcame me and seemed to warn me to take it." I peeled a layer of cloth from my dress cuff and touched the small flat papers hidden in the false hem.

Warm air brushed my cheek as my sister sighed in relief. A rumble from deep in my belly made us both giggle, as we had not eaten for hours.

Suppressing her laughter, Theresé whispered, "We must soften your hunger growls or it will lead the British right to our wagon."

"I should be happy to have a firecake right now." We muffled our nervous snickers at mention of the tasteless bread made with flour and water. "I long for this war to be over and we are in our real home again. I will prepare such desserts and treats." I have never liked to cook, but I loved to bake fancy pastries. "What shall I bake for us when we are in our own home again?"

"Crusty bread baked the way Mama made it." At mention of our mother, we fell into sad silence.

"We should rest now, sister," Theresé suggested, and we settled in the uncomfortable space.

As I rested my head against the wooden crate on her left, I touched my dress sleeve. I again lamented the loss of my mother's gift, but quickly banished the selfish thought.

My family faced grave danger over the next few days. We knew the importance of the mission that Louis and our father were conducting, and willingly obeyed our brother's orders. How I wished I could have remained behind, to fight alongside my brother! He was a soldier, however, and I a mere girl.

But I was doing my part. I fingered the cuff of my sleeve, once again satisfied the hidden flap protected the vital secrets I was trusted to deliver.

As slivers of moonlight sliced through rips in the canvas, my gaze drifted to the wagon floor. Hidden in a false bottom beneath us, firearms and ammunition were crammed in every space.

If the British army stopped the driver and discovered the smuggled weapons, we would all be taken prisoner—or more likely shot on the spot.

If we could reach the James River's edge where a boat would ferry us to the north side and our father's camp, we should live to see the sunrise.

CONTENTS

Allie Marie

CHAPTER ONE

MARY JO
Portsmouth, Virginia, present day September

Hurricane Abby showed her full fury, leaving local residents to feel her wrath for days to follow.

From atop damaged homes, roofing crews tossed wood and shingles for disposal. Below, carpenters' hammers pounded, and saws buzzed around splintered building exteriors.

Mary Jo Cooper carried an armful of sawed wood limbs to the waiting wheelbarrow, carefully picking her way over broken pavement. The larger of two trees had toppled squarely onto the roof of her new café. Tree trimmers worked furiously to dislodge the boughs that had broken through part of the roof and back wall. She and several friends had pitched in to assist the tree crew clearing debris while construction teams tackled the damaged buildings.

On one side of the driveway, her friends stacked wood cut into logs for burning. On the opposite, a worker used a wood chipper to grind up the more scraggly limbs. When things returned to normal, firewood and mulch would be in high demand.

Over the steady drone of a generator and the squeal of chain saws, a shrill whistle penetrated her ears, followed by shouts. She turned in the direction of the commotion and frowned. Another whistle pierced the air, followed by more shouting, not the ordinary noise of workers raising their voices over the din of construction, but one of alarm.

At the base of a fallen magnolia that had once stood at the far corner of the parking lot, a foreman waved, crossing and uncrossing his arms. Mary Jo caught sight as his windmilling arms knocked his hard hat to the ground, and he stepped away from the gaping hole left by the uprooted tree and pointed. He shouted, waved, then put two fingers to his mouth and repeated the piercing whistle. He caught the attention of a man cutting limbs from the magnolia's base, who stopped his saw and whistled to the other men at work.

As the signals reached the crewmen, the whine of chainsaws silenced, as did the tattoo of hammers beating on the back of the house where the tree had landed. Metal clangs pierced the air when construction workers dropped heavy tools and listened.

In the reduced hubbub, Mary Jo heard the panic in his voice as he shouted, "My God! Come quick. Hey, somebody!" She threw down the firewood and ran.

From the opposite side of the storm-ravaged yard, Chase Hallmark, the construction company owner, picked his way through debris and cracked pavement to reach his foreman first. Mary Jo watched Chase's body stiffen and his eyes widen before he held up his hands and waved other workers away.

He commanded firmly, "Everyone stay back." His men retreated a few feet back, several craning their necks to see.

Mary Jo's long stride closed the gap seconds behind Chase. Her foot kicked a clump of dirt, sending it cascading into the hole. She regained her footing and straightened to her nearly six-foot height.

Chase glared but said nothing.

She cut her eyes in return, but asked, "Is someone hurt?"

She was part owner of the damaged property, but knew

well that the rapid cleanup following the hurricane had more to do with her business partner than her. She wasn't going to jeopardize the quick response from Chase's crew with a petty squabble—this time.

"No, ma'am." The crew chief ran his hands through his unruly blond hair and pointed.

Mary Jo traced her gaze along his outstretched arm to the fingertip pointing to the base of the fallen magnolia. Rope-like roots stretched from the hole like gum to a shoe. Less than two feet deep, the diameter of the hole spanned well over twelve feet.

It took a second for her to distinguish the outline entwined in the snake-like tentacles, and she gasped. The upper torso of a skeleton lay exposed in the dirt.

Dislodged when the tree fell, the human frame appeared to be sitting in an awkward position, roots curled around and through the rib cage.

Chase punched numbers on his cell phone and smacked it in frustration. "I'm trying to call nine-one-one. Cell service is still out."

Shade fell across the makeshift grave as Mary Jo's best friends joined her. The three women, two tall and one short, formed a single jagged shadow as they stood together.

Terry Dunbar tried her phone and shook her head.

Petite, brown-haired Stephanie Kincaid reached into her back pocket and tossed her old flip-phone to Chase. "Try mine. I just had a call come through a few minutes ago, but service has been intermittent."

Chase held the phone to his ear and nodded. "Got a signal," he said. With an incline of his head to his foreman to follow, he took wide steps to the side and poked the three emergency numbers. He turned his back, one finger to his exposed ear.

"We heard the commotion," Terry interjected, peering at the tree. "What happened?"

Mary Jo pointed, keeping her arm angled until both women cast their sights on the bones.

Like Chase, their bodies stiffened, and their eyes widened. She imagined she might have reacted the same way.

The skeleton shifted suddenly. Dirt clods skipped in the shallow incline as one bony hand jutted forward through the tangled roots, index finger pointing in their direction. The skull tilted and came to rest on the shoulder of the unknown person, eye sockets staring straight at the three women. Instinctively, the trio moved as one to step back a pace, casting sideways glances at each other.

Stephanie brought her fingertips to her lips to cover the small "o" her mouth had formed as she inhaled a ragged gasp.

"I got through to the police," Chase said. In two steps, he returned to the small mound of debris where the women stood. "They have a patrol car on the way." He handed the phone to Stephanie with a grim smile. "That ancient phone sure worked better than my supposedly super smart one, Steph." He stared at her pale face. "Are you alright?"

She nodded, her hand now resting at her throat. None of the women mentioned what they had just seen.

Terry leaned forward to peer in the dark hollow. "Those bones look old. Does it look like there are any others down there?"

"None that I can see. Could it be a burial plot?" He mirrored her stance, his movement causing another rain of pebbles to cascade into the recessed space.

"It's highly possible," Terry answered. "This section of Portsmouth was established in the mid-seventeen hundreds and a lot of American history took place here. Significant events occurred during the Revolutionary and Civil Wars, as well as a deadly yellow fever epidemic. I can recall one or two instances of a skeleton uncovered during excavations and later found to have come from long-forgotten family burial plots."

Mary Jo scanned the area. The parking lot serviced three buildings, each over one hundred and fifty years old, and each had sustained varying degrees of damage. Once homes owned by or connected to Terry's family, they were now commercial endeavors. Terry had inherited one house from an elderly great-aunt and converted it into a law office on the first floor with an apartment above. Mary Jo and Terry had jointly purchased the middle house with plans to convert it into a Bed and Breakfast. Although the exterior suggested the appearance of a newly restored Colonial house, the inside was still a shell. The remaining building, her crown jewel, contained her French bistro *Pâtisseries à la Carte*.

"The police just got here," Mary Jo announced, jutting her chin toward the road where the blue and white car stopped on the street outside the small parking lot. Two officers emerged, police radio conversations squawking from their collar mikes. The pair, a black female and a stocky white man, picked their way over the tree branches and debris blocking the entrance.

Terry walked over to greet the officers she recognized from mutual court cases. "Hi, guys. I don't know what we have here, but it looks like Hurricane Abby has uncovered a body in my backyard."

After introductions and an initial assessment, the female officer strode over to the patrol car and retrieved a black case from the trunk.

The male officer pulled a notebook from his pocket. "Terry, this looks old, but we'll have to start an investigation."

"I know. We'll do whatever you need, Jonathan. What are you guys doing in uniform? Did you leave the bureau?"

"No. Most of us in the detective bureau were sent to supplement the uniformed guys. We're on twelve hour shifts because of the hurricane and 'Nessa and I are covering eight a.m. to p.m. We'll be back to the homicide desks Tuesday."

Terry gestured to the house furthest from the tree. "My law office is right here. We've been using it for the construction crew, but you can use the conference room to do what you need."

"Thanks. Like I said, I don't think we have an active crime scene here, but we'll have to interview everyone before they leave."

"How are things elsewhere around town?" Mary Jo asked.

"Lots of downed trees and power poles, a few on cars and

houses, like those two." He nodded toward the fallen trees.

"That's my café. I just opened for business a little over a week ago," Mary Jo explained as she pointed to the far end of the lot.

"Ouch. Tough break. We made it by for lunch. Last Thursday, I think. Good food."

"Thanks. Hopefully we'll be able to recover quickly."

"Hope so. Good luck. Terry, I'll need to talk to the person who found the body first, after 'Nessa and I cordon off the area."

Terry nodded. "I'll make the room ready. Here's the owner of the construction company and his foreman now."

Chase shook the officer's hand. "My foreman discovered the skeleton, officer, when he checked the base of the tree." He patted the man's back and gestured toward the building. "Go on in, Paul. Settle yourself."

"Appreciate it, boss." Paul glanced toward the tree and visibly suppressed a shudder.

"I'll see if Terry needs any assistance," Stephanie said and turned to follow Terry's retreating figure.

"You gonna be okay?" Chase asked, walking beside her.

"No. Yeah. I just…" She shivered in spite of the warm sun.

"I know." He patted her shoulder. "You'll be fine. I better go handle my crew. I think some of them are pretty shaken. We all are."

He stopped abruptly. Mary Jo, bringing up the rear, had turned her attention elsewhere and bumped squarely into his back.

"Excuse me," she said curtly.

"Entirely my fault," he responded, equally curt. He stepped into the dirt as Mary Jo passed on the narrow walk, then turned and spoke over his shoulder, "My crews can't work on removing the rest of that magnolia now, but they can take care of other repairs. I'd like to get things done as soon as possible, so I can redistribute them to other customers."

"Thank you." Mary Jo ended the strained dialogue. She caught up to Stephanie, who held the door open.

"*Asshole*," Mary Jo muttered under her breath. When she observed Stephanie's raised eyebrow, she merely shrugged as she passed through the door. "Long story."

Activity bustled inside. In the aftermath of the storm, the law firm had closed for business and now served as a family emergency operations center, where the extended Dunbar clan, including childhood friends Chase and Mary Jo, had gathered to discuss the damage.

The law office converted from operations center to a police interview room. Workers rotated in and out quickly, as no useful information could be shed on the old skeleton. A forensic team spent several hours sifting through the dirt for other remains and clues.

The medical examiner arrived, conversing with the officers and Terry.

Although curious, Mary Jo and Stephanie remained in the background, lugging debris to the street. The atmosphere was more somber as work resumed with less intensity. Even the saws and hammers seemed quieter, as if in respect for the unknown dead.

"I wonder what they're discussing," Mary Jo muttered as she watched the medical examiner gesture to the police officers, who bent to look where he pointed. She stopped to press her hand to her back.

Stephanie pulled off garden gloves and flexed her arms with a grimace. "Wow, I ache." She looked toward the base of the tree. "It doesn't seem right, does it, to continue on normally while some poor soul lies out there."

"I know, Steph. But things are never normal after a hurricane, and these trees and debris need to be cleared."

"I hope it's just old bones and not a recent crime," Stephanie said. She stiffened as a black hearse rolled up to the piles of debris blocking the driveway. "But I don't think I can watch them remove it. I'm going to my apartment to fix lunch. Do you want to come?"

"Sure. We need to catch a break. I might even stretch out on your couch and take a nap. It's been a long twenty-four hours."

The two women stepped over tree debris still littering the path and studied the makeshift staircase. When a thin pine had fallen behind the building, its upper branches crashed through the stairs and balcony leading to the apartment Stephanie had moved into only days before. After the storm had passed, Chase had built a temporary set of stairs. Although she had navigated the improvised stairway several times since the storm cleared, Stephanie still eyed the structure warily.

"It's sturdier than it looks, but I'd still rather we go up one person at a time," she suggested.

Nodding in agreement, Mary Jo waited until her friend touched the top step, and then followed. Before she closed the door behind her, she glanced back at the upended magnolia that had once stood sentry in the back of the parking lot. At its base, the police officers and Terry peered as the medical examiner stooped and made a sweeping motion toward the hole. The two funeral home attendants in black suits stood a few steps away, in a respectful stance.

With nothing else to do, she stepped into the apartment.

"Bathroom is…" Stephanie pointed over her shoulder.

Mary Jo nodded. "I know."

After scrubbing grimy hands, she returned to the kitchen to find a plate with deli meats and cheese on the dining table.

"What can I do to help?" she asked as Stephanie walked back to the refrigerator.

"Can you get the paper cups and plates from the cabinet?" Stephanie buried her head in the refrigerator and came out with condiment bottles. "I'm so grateful Chase brought that generator last night. I don't have to worry about my food or lights."

After placing the condiments beside the deli tray, she reached for the remote. "And let's take advantage of it and check the noon news." She clicked buttons. The television set, mounted above the fireplace in the living room and visible from the dining area, flickered to a broadcaster stepping to the side of the weather map.

Stephanie fiddled with more buttons to find the volume as a wall map of the Mid-Atlantic section appeared behind the weather forecaster turning to trace the storm's path. She and Mary Jo glanced toward the screen occasionally while they finished setting the table.

The only human voice came from the television broadcaster. "With much of the east coast braced for Hurricane Abby, the storm teased the viewing area by dancing around the Atlantic for six days. As the storm veered east and away from the Mid-Atlantic seaboard, it seemed the coast would be spared the brunt. However, during early morning hours it made a rare and unexpected one-hundred-eighty-degree loop, slamming into the coasts of Virginia and North Carolina as a strong Category Two."

The weather forecaster ran his fingers back and forth in an arc along the map's coastal region. The map in the background switched to a close-up of the Hampton Roads area. "Abby uprooted trees, downed power lines and disrupted cell phone service but caused no deaths or serious injuries. Minor flooding has occurred in some areas. Since hitting land, Abby has been downgraded to a tropical storm as it continues to travel further inland."

Footsteps on the staircase grew louder as someone reached the door. After two light taps the door opened, and Terry peered around. Her face brightened as her gaze dropped to the table.

"Oh, goodie, I saw you guys head up here, and I was hoping for lunch."

Stephanie muted the television. "You're just in time. We want the scoop."

"Let me clean up first." Terry pulled off dingy leather gloves and tossed them beside the door, then headed to the bathroom.

She returned and dropped wearily to a chair. "Well, the good news—if that's the right thing to say—is that this is not a recent burial. The medical examiner believes the bones are well over one hundred years old. It's an adult, but due to age and condition, he can't say for sure whether it was male or female until they've conducted some examinations in which they measure the pelvis. Most likely the skeleton came from a family grave. He ordered the remains transported to the crime lab in Norfolk, but we probably won't hear anything back for a few weeks."

Stephanie shivered and pushed her half-eaten sandwich aside. "It's kind of creepy."

Terry nodded. "After the police finish, they'll allow the construction crew to cover the hole with plywood. Chase placed orange mesh fencing around the perimeter, which they then draped with more yellow crime scene tape. We should be cleared in the morning to continue removing that tree." She looked around and turned to Stephanie. "Has Gage been sleeping through this entire ruckus?" Her brother Gage was a fireman and heavily engaged in the city's disaster relief, working twelve-hour shifts during the aftermath.

"No, he's not here," Stephanie said as she pulled her plate back and picked up the sandwich. "He got off at eight, and his crew went to help one of their friends, whose house got damaged pretty badly. He'll probably then go to your parents' house to sleep before his shift."

"See what you are getting into, marrying a firefighter?" Terry asked as she scooped potato salad onto her paper plate. Gage had proposed to Stephanie the night before. She had shone the sparkling engagement ring to Mary Jo and Terry that morning and then put it away for safekeeping just moments before the bones were discovered.

Stephanie looked at her bare left hand and pouted, then brightened. "Why don't you guys stay the night here? You'll avoid the long drive home after this exhausting day, and keep me company while Gage works the night shift."

"I like that idea, but we don't have anything to sleep in."

"I've got plenty of t-shirts and yoga pants, even if they hit you guys at the knees." Stephanie was at least four inches shorter than Terry, and six shorter than Mary Jo's six-foot frame.

"I'm game." Terry jumped to her feet. "Right now, I want to see how things have progressed."

Mary Jo jumped up. "With that tree still piercing the café, we're going to be set back on repairs. I think I'll go through the front door again and see if the damage is as bad as it looked last night."

Mary Jo scrambled down the steps. A quick glance to her left revealed the hearse had left. The two officers still worked at the tree's base. The female knelt on one knee as she put items back in a black canvas bag, the male wrote on a clipboard. Occasionally they spoke, but Mary Jo could not hear over the hammering.

Stepping over limbs scattered on the narrow strip between Stephanie's apartment building and the next, Mary Jo reached the sidewalk and turned to face the three buildings nestled side-by-side. From the front, the only signs that a storm had passed were a few scattered tree limbs.

Local residents long whispered the center house was haunted. In fact, rumors swirled about all three properties, but most seemed to center on the old house in the middle. Tales of strange happenings had been passed down through generations of Terry's family, and other Olde Towne homes had similar histories. She'd hoped the facelift to the dilapidated exterior would dispel such rumors in the future, but worried the skeletal discovery would only renew them.

Moving to the front of the structure, Mary Jo studied the building she considered to be the crown jewel of the trio, and sighed. The very day the old house went up for sale, she'd put a contract on it and began planning for her French bistro and pastry shop. On the day she closed the deal, she received notice her Reserve unit was activated. In ten days, they would depart for a one-year deployment to Afghanistan.

With no choice but to conduct business via email and Skype, her dream came to fruition in her absence. Terry acted as the middle person between Mary Jo and Chase Hallmark as designs were drawn, revised, and debated in emails. *Pâtisseries à la Carte* soon emerged from the shell of the old building.

Terry's sister-in-law Beth Dunbar had then prepared the café for a two-week trial run to work out kinks prior to Mary Jo's return.

But before Mary Jo even had the chance to whip up a soufflé or croissant, Hurricane Abby struck with the fury of an angry woman and side-railed the business.

Fingering the key in her pocket, Mary Jo braced herself at the bottom step and stepped onto the covered porch, which wrapped around the building's front and sides. The veranda would have created the perfect setting for guests of the future B and B to enjoy tea. A string of white lights had worked loose from their clips and now dangled on one side over the door. She tucked the end into a notch and stood poised with her hand above the lock.

Aware of the chaos inside, she faced the reality that neither dream might come true.

The mumble of male voices and thumping footsteps resonated from the side of the wraparound porch. She leaned far enough to the right to peer around the building, where she observed Chase stepping on boards, testing the stability with each bounce. When he turned his head toward the man behind him, she used the opportunity to scramble down the steps and out of sight.

She'd had enough of hurricanes, fallen trees, and skeletons for one day.

And of Chase Hallmark for a lifetime.

On the way back to the apartment, she once again passed the B and B building. This time, a movement in the upstairs window caught her eye.

A waif-like face she had not seen since she was a teenager stared down at her and then faded away.

As a shiver coursed through her, she shook her head and stomped toward the apartment.

She could add ghosts to her list as well.

* * *

They planned to get a good night's rest and start early the next morning. But three friends sharing common hardships did what friends sometimes do instead. They chucked the idea of sleep and broke open a bottle of wine.

Although the generator provided energy to light most of the apartment, Stephanie lit candles around the room to conserve fuel. They tossed cushions around the coffee table and nibbled on a cheese platter while they relaxed and chatted.

As Stephanie reached for her wine glass with her left hand, the marquise-cut diamond on her ring finger flashed in the flickering light. Terry squinted and gripped Stephanie's wrist.

"You're wearing your engagement ring! Did you have it on during all that yard work?" she asked.

"No. I wouldn't dare!" Stephanie laughed, looking again at the ring and wiggling her fingers to create dancing sparkles. "I hate to do it, but I leave it in my jewelry box."

"Have you set a wedding date?" Mary Jo stretched her long form and rested her head against the couch.

"No. That storm threw everything for a loop. I've never been through a hurricane before."

"Hurricane Abby sure showed what a bitch she was," Mary Jo interjected. "I've been away from them for so long I've forgotten how bad they can be."

"It's the worst storm to hit this area in years," Terry agreed.

"Well, without the storm, I might never have discovered that box with all of those letters, or the diamond necklace." When Stephanie had originally visited Portsmouth in the summer to explore family tree connections, she had taken a temporary lease on Terry's apartment to continue her research—and be closer to her new fiancé. She moved in just days before the hurricane crashed into the area.

"I don't know about that," Terry disagreed. "No telling what else you are going to find as you go through all those old family documents."

"That's true." Stephanie agreed. "Since arriving here at this house, I have had one adventure after another." She shook her head. "First, the ancestry search leads me here. Gage and I meet and fall madly in love. Your mom has old documents that hold more clues. Then ghosts appear. The hurricane hits, another ghost attacks me, and I find that box with the old doll and the diamond necklace." She paused with a cracker midway to her lips, and her eyes grew wide. "Do you think those bones belong to one of the ghosts that supposedly haunt these three buildings?"

The women grew silent. Before the storm, the three women had carried on lengthy discussions about whether or not the place was haunted, with Terry and a reluctant Mary Jo admitting they had seen similar apparitions when they were young girls.

Now, as an adult, Mary Jo distanced herself from the possibility that ghosts existed, unsure if she was being pragmatic or just cynical.

And in spite of her own recent sighting—or perhaps because of it—she rolled her eyes skyward.

A hurt look slid over Stephanie's features, emphasized by the low candlelight.

"Stop it, Mary Jo," Terry snapped. "You saw the marks on her arms where the specter tried to pull her from the attic window during the storm, overshadowing everything else that happened to her."

Mary Jo raised her hands in surrender. "Look, I know strange things have occurred over the years, especially in the Bed and Breakfast. And now there's a skeleton buried in the backyard. I don't want to talk about it anymore. I'm going to bed." She softened and patted Stephanie's hand. "But, Steph, your ghost Nicole appeared as a child to you. Remember, the coroner established this was an adult."

"I know." Stephanie sighed. "I don't know why she appeared as a child to me. Since she's my ancestress, it's obvious she lived long enough to have children."

"Maybe something happened to her as a child, and she can't rest," Mary Jo offered.

"Well, listen, ladies." Terry stood and tossed a cushion on the sofa. "Ghosts or no, we have another day of work ahead of us. I'm headed for bed...and you are sitting on it." She yanked the cushion from under Mary Jo, sending her sprawling.

The laughter that followed provided a welcome relief for the somberness of the day.

CHAPTER TWO

The rattle of heavy machinery thundered in the parking lot, waking the occupants of the small upstairs apartment and signaling another day of recovery in the aftermath of Hurricane Abby. As the backhoe's incessant beep penetrated her eardrums, Mary Jo groaned and stuck her head under the pillow, which did little to eliminate the sounds emanating from outside. She opened her eyes and looked around the unfamiliar room. She had to think for a moment before remembering she had stayed the night at Stephanie's.

Knowing she still faced the chore of clearing storm debris, she pushed the pillow to the side and stretched her nearly six-foot frame, wincing as she moved. Although she frequently worked out and was in good shape, the strenuous exertion of the past two days had strained muscles she never knew existed. They had made excellent progress on clearing the downed tree limbs. That is, until the skeleton was found, and police halted the work to investigate.

The bones!

Jolted by the sudden memory, she scrambled out of bed and stumbled toward the kitchen where Stephanie moved in a stiff and reluctant manner at the sink while filling a coffee pot with water.

"Make it double strong, will you, Steph?" Mary Jo begged.

"That noise is horrible."

"Yes to both," Stephanie replied. She poured water into the coffeemaker reservoir and set the pot under the drip. "I've been up most of the night thinking about those bones they found yesterday afternoon and who might be buried out there. I was glad you and Terry stayed the night, otherwise I might not have ever fallen asleep."

"Me too, I just hope it turns out to be an old burial plot and not something more sinister."

"How are you feeling this morning?"

"Unknown muscles are literally screaming at me." Mary Jo stretched gingerly.

"Oh, mine too. Even wearing gloves, I got blisters on my hands."

"What about your engagement ring?"

Stephanie held up her bare left hand. "Back in the jewelry box." She sighed as she looked at her splayed fingers. "As soon as I'm finished cleaning up after Abby, I'm putting that ring on, and it's never coming off again."

"Will you two pipe down?" A muffled rebuke emanated from the direction of the couch across the room.

Mary Jo and Stephanie looked at each other in amusement, and then glanced back toward the mountain of covers on the couch.

"Half a dozen machines are outside thumping and beeping, hammers are banging, and chainsaws are grinding. And she tells *us* to pipe down?" Mary Jo marched over to the sofa and yanked the covers off Terry's huddled form.

"Bitch," Terry mumbled, trying to pull them back.

"Snot," retorted Mary Jo, turning to Stephanie and grinning mischievously. "I've done that to her since we were kids. It's always fun."

"Shut *UP!*" Terry leaned forward and glared grumpily.

"Okay, girls, truce called." Stephanie rapped on the table for attention. "Coffee's almost ready. We've got a long day ahead of us again."

"Don't remind me." Terry sighed in resignation, got up

from the couch and shuffled to the table. "We can't do anything in the parking lot until the police give the go-ahead, but maybe we can remove broken stuff from the café." An attorney more accustomed to tackling difficult court cases than grueling yard work, she looked at her hands, each sporting three broken fingernails and shook her head. She plopped in a chair and wriggled her ragged fingertips, adding, "I've got a big case this Friday. How can I show up with these claws?"

"It'll suit your reputation in court," Mary Jo said with a smirk. "It's only Sunday. You'll have time for a manicure, Miss Glamour Queen."

"You always amaze me, Terry," Stephanie interjected. The youngest and newest member of the trio, she strived to keep peace around her. "Even in baggy sweats and wild hair spilling out from a loose headband, you exude glamour, in spite of six broken nails."

"Don't mind us, Stephanie." Mary Jo smiled. "We've been needling each other since we were six."

"I'm not used to it," Stephanie admitted. "It comes from being an only child, I guess."

The three women sipped their coffee in silence, until Terry spoke, swirling her almost-empty cup. "Is this that special blend from the Kitchen Korner?"

"It is," Stephanie confirmed. "I don't drink much coffee but I first tasted it at *Pâtisseries à la Carte* and fell in love with it." She got up to start another pot and called over her shoulder, "Terry, the master bath is available. And Mary Jo, everything you need is in the main bathroom. I'll whip up some omelets while you guys get ready. I'm not much of a cook, but I can handle eggs."

The other women mumbled thanks and carried their coffee cups with them.

By the time they returned to the kitchen, Stephanie had breakfast plates ready. As she set them on the table, she spoke in a low voice. "All night long, I kept seeing the face of that poor foreman, the one who discovered the bones in that hole." She shivered. "I've never seen such a look of terror on a person's face in my life."

Mary Jo answered grimly. "I have." Only a week back from a year-long deployment in Afghanistan with her Army reserve unit, she had already seen the face of fear too many times in her life. The chime of the doorbell interrupted the conversation. Closest to the door, she reached for the knob, glad for the distraction—until she opened it to find Chase Hallmark standing there.

The familiar feeling of irritation hit her stomach, and she was torn between slamming the door in his face—or just slamming her fist into it.

From the annoyed look on Chase's face he obviously had not expected to see her and she enjoyed a moment of satisfaction. Anything she could do, however slight, to contribute to the aggravation of that bastard gave her great pleasure indeed. Ten years had not healed old wounds.

As always, however, he recovered smoothly and looked past her, saying icily, "I'm looking for Stephanie."

Without answering, she turned her back on him and moved so he could see Stephanie at the table.

"Hi, Chase," Stephanie called over her shoulder. "Come on in. Would you like some breakfast, or just coffee?"

He remained at the door. "No, thank you." He nodded in greeting toward Terry. "I just wanted to give you a heads up on a couple of things. We're gonna be turning the generator off now. The power crew is starting to work on the transformer. Electricity should be restored in a few hours."

"Okay, that's no problem. The generator's been a blessing. We've finished cooking and were getting ready to come down to work."

"Well, that's the second thing I wanted to prepare you for. With the discovery of that body—bones or whatever—you've got news crews and curious gawkers gathering outside."

"Oh, really?" Stephanie moved to the window overlooking the back lot, pulling the curtains aside at the exact moment a cameraman had his lens trained in her direction. She let the curtain drop as if it singed her fingertips and backed up.

"Oh, dear. A cameraman just panned the back of the house."

Terry stepped beside her, and they both peeked through the curtains. Over her shoulder, she called, "Mary Jo, there are at least a dozen bystanders around the vicinity of the fenced lot, watching the cameraman, who's standing on the fallen pine."

"I'm staying out of it," Mary Jo continued to drink coffee.

Terry glanced again. "Now, he's aimed toward the base of the magnolia. They're outside the area roped off by crime scene tape, but a reporter is gesturing like a windmill toward the hole where they found the bones."

She turned abruptly from the window. "Well, we can't prevent them from filming, but I sure as hell can kick them off our property. Come on, Mary Jo."

Mary Jo shook her head. "You better deal with them. I'm liable to lose my cool. But I'll be on the sidelines if you need me."

Chase said, "That's all we need, more sensational news coverage. That skeleton already unnerved some of my guys. Three of them asked to go to different job sites today."

Terry paused at the door, hand on knob. "Chase, can you put more of that orange mesh fence all around the property line? I think we're going to need to cordon off more than just where the police put their tape." Before he could answer, she flounced outside, Chase on her heels.

Rolling her eyes skyward, Mary Jo stood up and followed. Stephanie brought up the rear, locking the door behind her. They stood near the bottom of the steps and watched as Terry maneuvered into the media frenzy. Roofers and yard workers alike stopped work, tools in hand, as they watched the scene unfold, the air noticeably quiet.

In spite of her earlier annoyance, Terry displayed nothing but consummate professionalism as she approached the news crew with a polite smile.

"Good morning, folks," she said. "I'm happy to cooperate so you can do your job, but I'm sure you'll understand we have to ask you to film from across the street. There is simply too much damage in this area, and we don't want anyone to risk injury."

"Are you the owner here?" The reporter asked. "What can you tell us about the discovery of the body under the tree?" She waved a microphone under Terry's nose, but Terry smiled with a shake of her head.

"I simply can't answer anything standing around all this debris and broken pavement. I'll be glad to talk more if we get out of this area." She deftly stepped over loose bricks and a section of tree trunk and headed toward the sidewalk. The news reporter scrambled beside her, still asking questions and poking the microphone at Terry, the cameraman in hot pursuit.

"If someone shoved a mike at me like that, boy, I'd..." Mary Jo growled between clenched teeth and shook her head in exasperation, smacking her fist pointedly into the palm of her hand.

"Me, I'd just stand there, stuttering and letting them walk all over me while I babbled answers to questions they had no business asking." Stephanie cast admiring eyes as Terry maneuvered the news crew precisely where she wanted them, and only then allowed them to ask her questions.

"Assholes," Mary Jo muttered. "I got my fill of reporters during my deployment. And speaking of assholes..." Mary Jo glared toward Chase but clamped her mouth shut.

"Alright, Mary Jo, I'm buying more wine, and tonight you are going to tell me what's going on with you two." Before Mary Jo could respond, Stephanie shouted, "Gage!"

Rounding past the mounds of debris, Fire Battalion Chief Gage Dunbar, brother to Terry and fiancé to Stephanie, scooped his bride-to-be into an exuberant embrace.

"Hey, babe," he said, nuzzling her neck before he set her down. Over Stephanie's shoulder, he caught Mary Jo's eye and nodded. "Morning, Mary Jo."

"Hey, Gage."

Stephanie slipped her hand through the crook of his arm. "Terry just came down to face the news crew, and Mary Jo and I are in the audience. Are you hungry?"

"No, I just stopped by to see you before heading out to Connor's house. He's on the night shift too so we figured his place would be the quietest today." Connor, a firefighter in Suffolk, was the younger Dunbar son.

"How much longer will you be on these twelve-hour shifts?" Stephanie asked.

"At least three more days. Things are slowly returning to normal."

"I'll walk you back to your truck," she offered.

"I had to park three blocks up because of the repair trucks."

"It's okay. I want to walk with you." She took his hand and pulled him toward the street.

"Okay, okay. Mary Jo, see you later. Tell Terry hi."

Mary Jo watched the happy couple nuzzle while navigating through the debris and averted her eyes, tamping down a little twinge of jealousy. She drew her attention to her other friend still capably dealing with the news crew, and watched as Terry maintained control.

Before long, she tired of the news event and walked around to survey the havoc wreaked on the streets of the quiet old historic area. Almost as soon as the storm fizzled, residents had started recovery efforts. Neighbors pitched in to help each other remove trees so the roads could open to traffic and allow repair crews to reach the area.

The sidewalks were blocked by piles of tree limbs and storm debris, so she cut her walk short and returned to the parking lot to find the news crew gone. Construction work had resumed, and the pounding on the roof and whirr of chainsaws gave her hope that much would be accomplished before day's end.

She observed Terry's mother, Joan and distant cousin, Hannah entering the law office's back door, which opened to the staff kitchen. Each woman carried a huge cardboard box. She quickened her step in hopes of finding the box full of Hannah's home baked goodies.

Hannah, Joan's cousin, had moved in with the Dunbar

family when she was taken ill years before. After recovering, she insisted on repaying the kindness by keeping house and caring for the three young offspring while the parents worked. Mary Jo and Chase, each with their own turbulent childhoods, had grown up with the siblings and felt as close to the family as blood relatives.

Mary Jo considered both Joan and Hannah as surrogate mothers in the absence of her own mother. Raising a child alone and forced to work late shift, Patricia Cooper often had to leave Mary Jo alone. Tenants discovered the unattended child after they were roused by a fire in another apartment and began checking the building. The authorities were about to put her in child protective custody, but the twelve-year-old Mary Jo had raised such a fit that the caseworker asked the Dunbars to take custody of Mary Jo for the night. They eventually became her permanent foster parents.

Both women greeted Mary Jo warmly. She hugged Joan first and said, "Good to see you, Mom Joan."

"Hey, honey. How are you? We've called in reinforcements today. Let's see what we can get done at the café to get you back in business." Joan returned the hug and then rummaged through a cooler on the counter.

"Thanks. We're gonna need it." Mary Jo kissed Hannah on the top of the head. At six feet, she towered over the spindly thin, older woman. Only five feet tall, Hannah sported snow-white hair cut in short spikes poking out in different directions. A chain-smoker with deeply tanned skin wrinkled like a prune, she favored wild outfits. This day, she chose jeans, a baggy orange sweatshirt with a scowling pumpkin on the front, and purple tennis shoes.

Mary Jo reached for the cardboard box in the center of the conference table, sniffing appreciatively. "What have you got in here, Hannah?"

"A little of this, a little of that," the craggy old woman's voice croaked in reply. A nomad in her youth, she had learned the art of European cuisine and specialized in baking French pastry delights, a skill she later taught Mary Jo.

"Oo-la-la!" Mary Jo cried, peeking under the lid. "*Canelé, bichon au citron*, croissants —and éclairs! Oh, Hannah, I can't wait until we are baking together in the café." She hugged the diminutive baker.

Hannah scowled, although her eyes twinkled as she stretched her arm to pat Mary Jo's shoulder. "We will, baby girl," she said. "We will. These desserts are guaranteed to win those workers' hearts through their stomachs. They'll be so grateful they won't want to stop working." She let out a scratchy chortle.

Mary Jo straightened and looked around. "Where's Terry? And Stephanie?"

"Terry's in her office," Joan called over her shoulder. "And Stephanie went up to her apartment for something."

"I'm going to take a look at the café again. I'll be right back."

"Do you want us to come too?" Hannah rasped. She reached for her cigarettes.

"No, thanks, I just want to look at something. I'll be right back. And, Hannah, those things are going to kill you," Mary Jo admonished. She didn't mention she herself had picked the habit back up while in Afghanistan.

"Yeah, well, something's gonna," came the scratchy retort.

Mary Jo shook her head as she grabbed a pen and paper from the counter and headed out the door. She noticed small clusters of people gathered on the property's outskirts, pointing to the tree and trying to peer around the workers at its base.

Word was getting out.

The sidewalk was cleared completely of the smaller pine tree, but workers blocked the path with debris from the broken porch of the café. She turned onto the tiny pathway between the law office and the Bed and Breakfast to reach the front sidewalk, and nearly ran into Chase. Her foot slipped from the narrow stepping-stone as she tried to move to one side, stumbling. Chase caught her by the elbow, and she steadied, placing one hand on Chase's sinewy chest.

"Heads up, Coppertop," he said, using an old nickname he had given her.

Mary Jo bristled, but only said "Sorry." She knew she benefitted from the rapid repairs only because she was co-owner with Terry, so bit back the sarcastic comment she was about to add. Chase made the work his top priority because of his long-standing respect for the Dunbar family, not because of anything she might have once shared with him.

She stepped on the grass to walk past him, then paused. "Chase, I'm grateful for all you are doing. I'm not saying it enough, but thank you."

Chase touched the tip of his hard hat and nodded, continuing on his way.

Mary Jo continued the few steps to the sidewalk. With all her willpower she refrained from looking back at Chase.

Once she rounded the corner she wished she had glanced back—just to see if he had done the same.

Turning her face upward, one fleeting look toward the top floor of the B and B confirmed a now empty window where the face had appeared the day before. Her long legs covered the steps two at a time, and she opened the front door to the pastry café. The familiar peal of the entry bell tinkled overhead, in competition with the pounding of hammers on the back of the house. She peered around the glass case that separated the kitchen from the dining area and smiled politely at the handyman assisting with a window replacement.

Rain had seeped in through the windows broken by tree limbs, but the water damage was confined to the building's rear. With the help of her friends immediately after the storm, Mary Jo had cleaned up the initial disorder.

In the center of the kitchen, the barely-used appliances and cooking surfaces stood pushed together, covered in heavy plastic to prevent more damage. Counters bent under the weight of the intruding tree limb, which had also dented the two industrial stoves. Flying debris scratched the glass-fronted refrigerator, but it had escaped the brunt of the destructive branches.

Debris tossed by the wind had shattered glass pedestal dishes designed to hold enticing pastries and desserts on top of the antique display case. With a red-and-white striped awning hanging over it and a ceiling painted to resemble a sky with billowy clouds, the image had once created the impression of a French storefront café. The sad remnants of the canvas fluttered like shredded pennants.

Mary Jo brushed her hands over the rounded glass front. Remarkably, the cabinet remained unscathed. She smiled, remembering the joy in her fiancé Jay's voice when he called to tell her he'd discovered it in an antique shop in Smithfield.

"I've found the perfect case for your café, Mary Jo!" He shouted with excitement. "I'm with my mom, and I can bum the cash from her so we can get it right now."

He sent a picture over his cell phone, and she knew the antique wooden framework with rounded glass front would be the perfect way to display the café's delectable desserts.

"It's just perfect, Jay. Tell your mom thanks, and I'll have a check waiting for her," she promised. A week later, Jay had died unexpectedly of a heart attack at age thirty-two.

Tears fell at the memory, and she shook her head, turning her gaze toward the red-striped awning. She ran her hand down a tattered remnant. Her emotions immediately changed from sadness to annoyance as she remembered the email arguments she had with Chase over that awning.

Chase: *I don't think your indoor awning idea is going to work.*

Mary Jo: *We have to put it inside, Chase. It won't meet the building code on the outside, but I still want the feel of a French café. This is how I'll achieve it.*

Chase: *It seems silly to me. Putting the display case where you want it and then extending an awning over it inside takes up space in your dining area where more tables could go.*

Mary Jo: *It's what I want.*

Chase: *All right already. It's what you're paying me for. Consider it done.*

She rolled her eyes and clenched her teeth. That exchange of messages was only one of many they'd had during her deployment. Chase usually won the arguments that involved sound structural advice, but she knew what she wanted aesthetically and dug in her heels on this one.

Subconsciously she ground her heels on the floor. Despite the initial emergency cleanup, glass still crunched under her boots as she strode back into the dining area. Tables, including her beloved ice cream parlor sets, were shoved into the center of the room, chairs balanced precariously on top or pushed haphazardly toward the front door.

Mary Jo shivered in spite of the warm sun and dropped into one of the parlor chairs. Although she tried to suppress the images, her mind drifted to the moment when she'd heard the anguished cry resounding across the parking lot after the foreman discovered the skeleton. Following that incident, she had seen the face in the window. Memories of the events triggered a succession of shivers as goose bumps pricked her skin.

She'd seen that apparition several times when she was a young teenager, during visits to Terry's great-aunt, who'd owned the old home where the law office was now located. When the elderly woman died and Terry had inherited it, the two friends began to plan their future ventures.

At the thought of ghosts, Mary Jo sprang to her feet like bread popping from a toaster. She glanced at her watch and realized she had been daydreaming for nearly a half-hour. *Enough reflection!* She had a clean-up job to do.

She retrieved a broom and dustpan from the utility closet, laughing inwardly when her gaze dropped to the mop stuffed in the corner. She'd heard the story of how Stephanie had come to the rescue and helped Terry during a staffing emergency. Hannah, the craggy old baker, had mistaken Stephanie for a burglar and held her at bay with a mop. Terry arrived in time to explain the situation and calm the irate older woman down. The story brought chuckles every time it was told.

Mary Jo filled the dustpan with shards of glass undetected during the first clean-up efforts. She stepped into the kitchen to find it empty, and realized the crew had already left for a lunch break. She carried the dustpan to the trash, the sliding glass chinking melodically as it slid down the sides of the metal can. When the jingling continued, she looked down at the empty dustpan, before she registered the sound of the bell over the front door.

Frowning, she walked back into the dining area. The room was empty, the door shut. She checked the small side rooms and found nothing amiss.

"Must have been something outside," she said out loud. The distinct whiff of freshly baked bread reached her nostrils and she strode to the kitchen, expecting to see workers carrying lunch bags inside.

There was no one in the room.

She finished sweeping with furious strokes. *It's bad enough we have to deal with the reality of the bones and the hurricane.* She dumped the last of the fragments in the trash can. *Now it's compounded by ghosts.*

She refused to think about the recent strange happenings that had occurred to Stephanie, where the spirit of the small girl had appeared several times or the more menacing apparition that tried to pull Stephanie out of a window during the storm.

It didn't matter if some *very* credible stories were told about the latest sightings.

She didn't believe in ghosts.

And it didn't matter if *s*he herself had imagined she'd seen specters years before…or even yesterday.

She would still not believe.

A buzz from the refrigerator, coupled with a flash of light, told her power was restored. A loud cheer emanating outside confirmed it. Mary Jo locked the front door and walked along the wraparound to the back step. The noisy generator sputtered to a halt. A man's voice called, "Power's restored," earning more applause from the spectators gathered around the site of the mystery. Some of the bystanders were residents of Olde Towne; most, however, were simply the curious.

She leaned over the rail and spotted Stephanie and Terry in the back of the parking lot. Although the steps had been demolished by the tree, she easily scooted over the railing and strode to her friends.

"The crowd has grown," she remarked. "It's too bad the café was so badly damaged. I could be making a killing selling to all those people."

Terry crossed her arms and made a face. "Word of the discovery spread fast. I think people are already bored by news of the hurricane, and in its aftermath they've discovered a new topic of conversation to check out. With Halloween only seven weeks away, this just adds to the mystery around here."

Stephanie shivered and said, "I hope I don't sound like a needful baby, but I was kind of hoping you two might stay the night again. Gage won't be home tonight."

"I don't mind at all," Terry and Mary Jo said in unison. "Thanks."

Noisy laughter emerged as Chase stepped out of the law office, holding the door open for Hannah, who passed under his outstretched arm with a foot to spare. He held a half-eaten éclair in his other hand, and bit it as Hannah lit a cigarette.

Mary Jo stiffened and narrowed her eyes. A new pang of jealousy bit her. Although she and Chase had always been treated as if they were members of the Dunbar clan, Hannah had always had a soft spot for the two outsiders, Mary Jo in particular. Mary Jo had always considered Hannah her rock, and she didn't like sharing her with Chase.

As if reading her mind, Chase shifted his gaze directly onto hers as he popped the last bite of pastry into his mouth. With a hint of a smirk, he drew his sunglasses over his eyes with one hand. With the other, he drew Hannah close for a hug.

Mary Jo knew that *he* knew he was getting under her skin.

"Asshole." She thought she said the word in her mind, but the word hissed out under her breath.

"Mary Jo!" Stephanie admonished. "Why do you give him

29

such grief?"

Ignoring the question, Mary Jo asked, "Did we drink all the wine last night?"

"I only had the two bottles. There's probably a half carafe left."

"Let's get another bottle for tonight," Mary Jo said.

Chase walked in their direction. "Hello, ladies." He shoved his hardhat back, raised his sunglasses and tugged Stephanie's bangs. "Have you decided to dump that loser fireman and run off with me?"

She laughed as she wiped a dab of chocolate from the corner of his mouth. "I'm afraid he's a keeper, cowboy, but thanks for asking." She leaned close and sniffed. "Do you know you both wear the same cologne?"

"He copied me. I wore it first." With another affectionate tug on her bangs, he turned to Terry. "The last of the tree will be gone tomorrow and all of the debris cleared. We'll start digging out the broken pavement and get it ready for new surfacing. I'd like to talk to you about that."

"All right. We can use my office."

Chase dropped his sunglasses over his eyes before he angled his head toward Mary Jo. She crossed her arms over her chest and stared at the tinted glass.

"Mary Jo, Hannah mentioned you wanted to extend that porch all the way to the back. Now's the time to do it. Can you give me an idea of what changes you want by tomorrow?"

"Well." Mary Jo paused. Voice dripping with false sweetness, she added, "I emailed ideas to you a few weeks ago, but I'm sure *I* kept a copy."

"Then *I'm* sure we'll get it all worked out tomorrow. See you later, ladies." Chase tapped his forehead without really looking at any of the women and sauntered toward the crew working on the back of the café.

Terry glared at her friend. "You can be such a bitch sometimes, Mary Jo."

Mary Jo merely shrugged. "We've got work to do." She turned to Stephanie. "I'll fix dinner tonight, but I need to make a store run. And we can pick up that bottle of wine."

"Bottle?" Stephanie asked. "Ha! I'm buying a whole case."

CHAPTER THREE

LIZZIE
Portsmouth, Virginia, July 1781

Lizzie the maid had an unfortunate life. Her mother, Victoria, the impoverished sister of wealthy Abigail Weldon Roker, had fallen on hard times in England and needed to borrow a large sum of money to keep her farm running after her husband was injured. Unable to obtain a loan from a bank, she had turned to Abigail, who had loaned them the money at a high interest. When it came time to collect, Victoria could not pay.

Fourteen year old Elizabeth—nicknamed Lizzie—was sent to Portsmouth, Virginia to work for Abigail to pay off the debt. By agreement between the sisters, she would work for four years to pay off the family debt, one more to cover the cost off the passage to America and her room and board, and Abigail would consider all debts paid.

Lizzie was not treated as a niece by the matriarch of the household, but as a servant. She addressed Abigail as "Missus" or "the Missus," but never Aunt Abigail.

She looked at her rough, reddened hands, evidence of years of harsh labor to meet her aunt's demands. Yet in spite of the shapeless faded dress and the ever-present apron that identified her as a servant, she'd caught the eye of the handsome soldier Louis.

At last, her debts were paid, and she was entitled to leave.

But before Abigail would release her charge, she forced Lizzie to accompany her on the week-long trip to Richmond to visit an ill cousin.

Lizzie could ascertain no reason for her aunt's demand to accompany her to Richmond, other than spite. Abigail ordered her to help the cousin's household maid with mundane tasks and spent several hours every day out of the house.

After a particularly lengthy day outside of the manor house, Abigail returned at dusk and announced they would return to Portsmouth a day earlier than planned. Lizzie was elated. Soon enough, she would be out of her aunt's control forever.

They started the arduous journey at sunrise. Shortly after they began the trip south, they encountered a tremendous storm that lasted the rest of the journey. By the time the carriage lumbered along the High Street of Portsmouth, darkness had fallen.

The carriage driver swerved abruptly to avoid a covered wagon passing in front at top speed, the horses' hooves flipping up chunks of mud that splattered along the glass windows of the carriage. As the wheels fell into the ruts left from other wagons, the lurches threw Abigail and Lizzie from side to side and nearly unseated them several times.

Abigail screamed at the driver as though it was his fault, demanding he drive straight to her home without delay. He finally shouted "whoa!" and Lizzie gathered her skirts, indeed glad the ride was over.

At the sight of two English soldiers standing over two more outstretched on the ground, Abigail scrambled out of the carriage before it rocked to a complete stop.

"What has happened here?" she screamed.

One of the uniformed men stepped forward and answered, "Robbers attacked a man and woman here, and shot these soldiers who came to the rescue."

When Abigail demanded to know who had been attacked, he merely shrugged, and she tore into her house, Lizzie behind her. They followed a trail of muddy footsteps up the back stairwell, meeting a soldier just starting down the top step.

"Who are you? Look at all this muck and mud!" Abigail cried. "I demand to know what is going on in my home!"

"British soldier, madam," the soldier answered. "We brought the gentleman and lady inside. They were accosted by robbers and have been shot."

"Who was shot? Is my husband here? Lizzie, see this soldier out and then come upstairs immediately!"

"Yes, missus." As Abigail thundered up the stairs, the tiny maid turned abruptly and led the soldier back down the staircase to the rear door. Without exchanging a word, the two embraced quickly. Then Louis whispered, "Hide the doll," before stepping out into the rain.

A hand to her mouth, Lizzie closed the door and scurried upstairs.

Two of the upstairs bedrooms resembled operating rooms in an army camp. Muddy footsteps marred the usually pristine wood floors; bloody strips of cloths littered the areas around the beds; small bed tables were shoved against the wall to make space for the doctors attending the two victims in separate rooms.

In the larger room, Abigail knelt at Phillip's bedside. He was on his stomach, and she took his limp hand in hers as the doctor rattled instruments spread out on the bed beside the stricken man. He groaned, so he was still alive.

A soldier Lizzie recognized as Louis' friend James stood near Phillip's shoulder. When they made eye contact, he made the slightest shake of his head in warning. Understanding she must not show recognition, Lizzie dropped her eyes and backed out of the doorway without a sound.

She peered in the other room. Clothiste was already in ill health when she'd arrived at her father-in-law's home, seeking shelter with her daughters. Now the frail woman lay motionless. However, though the doctor worked furiously with a neighbor woman at his side, Lizzie wondered if the French woman was already dead.

Her gaze drifted across the room to the window seat, where a cushion partially hid Nicole's abandoned doll. She knew the secrets the doll often carried, and fear gripped her.

Could she retrieve it before anyone else discovered it?

MARY JO
Portsmouth, Virginia, present day September

When Mary Jo and Stephanie returned from the store, people had crowded the sidewalks, peering at the barricaded area where the construction foreman had discovered the bones. Stephanie parked her car in front of the building, which required the two women to walk back through the crowd to enter the apartment.

Mary Jo jumped out of the SUV and headed to the back to grab two grocery bags.

"I hope this curiosity doesn't last long," Stephanie said. She withdrew the fragile carton containing six bottles of wine and braced it on her hip so she could pull the hatch down. Together they walked around the left side of the building.

Mary Jo merely shook her head in disgust and said, "I counted at least twenty people milling by the driveway, though I think those piles of debris create more of a psychological barrier than physical to keep the crowd at bay."

Some spectators moved aside so the two women could pass, but when Mary Jo and Stephanie entered the yard, the buzz started and catcalls began.

"Look, they're going into the building!"

"Aren't y'all afraid?"

"Can we have some wine?"

Mary Jo and Stephanie ignored them, and hurried toward the stairway. Someone started singing, "*Lizzie Borden took an axe...*" and the crowd burst into laughter, some adding to the chant.

"Assholes," Mary Jo whispered to Stephanie at the top. "I don't need this shit tonight. By the way—in case you haven't noticed, I'm designating that as my new favorite catchword these days."

"Well, let's get inside and have a glass of wine while they stand out here looking like idiots." Stephanie giggled as she set the wine down and fumbled for her keys in the waning light. She opened the door and pushed the box in with her foot.

Mary Jo followed, setting the grocery bags on the table and plopping into a chair.

"That's the first time more than one of us has been on that temporary staircase at the same time, so it's obviously safe." She threw back her head and laughed, then stretched. "If nothing else, Chase is a master craftsman. The asshole."

"I know you've been a lifelong friend of both Chase and the Dunbar family, but what happened between you two?" Stephanie asked. Immediately, she held her hands up. "I'm sorry. I had no business to ask you that. I've only known you a short time. I'm sorry." Blushing, she grabbed a grocery bag and took out fresh produce.

"It's okay, Steph. It's just..." Mary Jo paused, torn between opening up and holding in her long-kept pain. She shook her head and jumped to her feet, reaching for the other grocery bag.

"Mary Jo, I am so sorry. I really shouldn't have said anything. I..." Stephanie wrung her hands.

Mary Jo set aside a bag of rice and threw an arm around Stephanie's shoulder.

"It's really okay, Steph." She repeated and hugged her friend. "It's something I'm trying to come to terms with, now that I'll probably be seeing him on a daily basis for a while." Then she threw back her head and chuckled. "I just realized how short you are, you peanut."

"Yeah, I am. You've got me by at least six inches."

"More like eight, but who's counting?" Mary Jo added, and Stephanie's laugh filled the air. "And you have the most infectious laugh. I love to hear it."

"Thanks. I love laughing."

Through the open window over the kitchen sink, the strains of "Ghostbusters" drifted across the evening air as a passing car paused, and the driver turned up the volume. Someone in the crowd whooped, the cry followed by the crash of a bottle.

"You know what I wish?" Stephanie plopped a can on the countertop with a forceful thud. "I really wish Nicole or one of those other ghosts would materialize and scare the crap out of them."

Mary Jo nodded, then pointed to a tripod holding a flipchart with pages marked in colored ink and asked, "How are you coming on your family tree?"

"The storm halted my progress. I hope to get started again soon." Stephanie stood in front of the easel, running her finger down a column of names. "Kyle is coming back down tomorrow and we'll start back up." She pushed the easel back against the wall.

"Kyle?"

"Kyle Avery, the professor from Maryland. Joan hired him to research her family tree."

"Oh, yeah, I remember now. Gage called him the Indiana Jones look-alike, right?"

Stephanie laughed. "That's Kyle. He looks like Harrison Ford when he first played that role. He's nerdy cute. Can't you picture him in a classroom full of awed students? We had such poor reception when he called the other day, but all I know is he is coming with some big news for the family."

"I wonder what that could be," Mary Jo mused, as she washed a red pepper. After they set out ingredients to prepare dinner, the two women drifted into silence.

In spite of her efforts to put ghosts out of her mind, Mary Jo's thoughts drifted to Stephanie's "ghost."

In recent weeks, Stephanie had encountered the spirit of a small girl dressed in colonial garb in the apartment and the attic. At a family gathering after the storm, she revealed the increasingly spooky encounters she'd experienced. The spirit seemed to communicate through Terry's four-year-old nephew Tanner, asking Stephanie to find Nicole's teardrop.

Later, in the middle of the hurricane Stephanie had a harrowing encounter with a malevolent spirit that tried to drag her from a window in the apartment. She'd managed to break free and fell back into the room, her shoulder striking and breaking a wood panel that revealed a secret compartment. Inside, she discovered a box containing an old doll with a diamond necklace shaped like a teardrop concealed in the skirt.

After that, Stephanie had not seen the ghost. Through letters she found in the box with the doll, clues led her to believe the ghost belonged to her ancestress Nicole. In spite of extensive research, she had not yet discovered what might have happened to the child in this house.

Mary Jo shook her head to clear her mind of ghost stories

and return to her cooking. Nicole was a benevolent spirit that caused no fear.

But that night, the evil that lurked in the attic above the B and B was not yet strong enough to give the curious onlookers—or the women in the apartment—something to really talk about.

Yet.

* * *

By the time Terry arrived thirty minutes later, the aroma of peppers and pineapple greeted her. Mary Jo was in the process of preparing a Hawaiian-based chicken dish—with the help of the culinary-challenged Stephanie, who sliced vegetables and set the table.

An appreciative Terry sniffed the air and sighed, then headed straight for a wine decanter on the counter. She poured a glass, took a gulp and turned to her friends.

"Did you guys see those people out there?" She motioned toward the window.

"Yeah, they were there when we got back from the store." Mary Jo chugged back a big sip of wine herself.

In solidarity with her friends, Stephanie did the same. "Now, we'll all feel better," she said brightly, wiggling the glass in her hand.

"It was a good idea to have Chase and his crewmen fill in that hole under the tree or we might have found two more corpses in there tomorrow morning." Terry lifted the cover of a steaming pan and sniffed approvingly with a thumb up. She turned toward Mary Jo and Stephanie, who both stared at her with puzzled looks on their faces. She explained. "Just now, I found two people out there poking around so I called nine-one-one to see if they can get the crowd moving. Can you imagine if someone fell in that pit before it was covered? It was quite deep."

"I don't understand what brings people out to gawk at things like this. By the way, I thought you handled the news crew well this morning," Stephanie said as she reached for the remote. "Which reminds me—we should be able to catch it. The six o'clock news is starting now."

Mary Jo sipped wine, then stirred the pots' contents. "When we got back from the store and walked around the building, we were treated to chants of 'Lizzie Borden…blah blah blah.' How about you, did the gawkers serenade you, too?" Mary Jo arranged the chicken on a platter, surrounded it with the sautéed peppers, onions and pineapple while Stephanie brought out the rice pilaf.

"No, I just heard murmurs as I came up the stairs." Terry dropped into a chair and sighed. "I'm glad the tree limbs block most of the entrance to the parking lot. Along with the mesh fence and the 'No Trespassing' signs, we may get through this without too much aggravation."

"We're hoping Nicole or one of the ghosts makes an appearance and scares the hell out of them." Stephanie laughed. When the beam of a red laser light danced across the wall, she rolled her eyes skyward. She spun on one heel to face the curtains. With a crisp snap, she pulled the two panels together to block the prankster.

"Asshole."

Stephanie's use of the now favorite word of the day elicited an "Atta girl!" from Mary Jo, who raised her wine glass in a toast, and added mischievously, "'Bone' appetite, ladies."

This prompted a groan from the other two as they lightly touched glasses together.

Then they listened to the news, volume low until Terry's interviewer appeared on the screen.

The reporter started her delivery accurately describing the chaos left behind by Hurricane Abby and the severe damage to some areas of Olde Towne, ending her coverage with, "In the aftermath, fallen trees continue to litter the region." Then the cameraman panned to the uprooted tree, and the reporter became dramatic, waving her arm behind her as she gripped the microphone.

"But this fallen magnolia behind me revealed something

sinister under its roots. When construction crews prepared to shore the earth around the gaping hole to prevent a cave-in, a worker discovered human remains, and the property owner called police.

"No one knows how long the body has been buried there or why. The remains were taken to the Crime Lab in Norfolk, and police are investigating. Preliminary reports indicate the bones are more than one hundred years old.

"These old buildings are located in the heart of Olde Towne, which has had its share of ghostly claims in past generations. Some of these fabled events are even recounted in the 'Olde Towne Ghost Walk' held every year in the historic district. You can click on our link for more information." The camera switched to footage shot in the daylight, aimed at the back of the buildings, at apparently the time Stephanie had looked out the window that morning. The cameraman had caught her movement dropping the curtain, and the timing couldn't have been worse. From the angle it was taken, the motion created an ethereal appearance.

"Oh, great," Terry fumed. "That will bring the ghoul-seekers out."

"She didn't even show your interview, Terry," Stephanie said.

"Probably too rational to use on the air," Mary Jo griped. The scene with Stephanie dropping the curtain was too like the actual vision she had observed in the window of the Bed and Breakfast.

"I'm just afraid there will be even more people showing up to gawk and wait for ghosts to appear." Terry stood and stretched.

"We should be able to finish the inside of the café tomorrow." Mary Jo abruptly changed the subject as she started clearing dishes from the table. "I've got to get that place up and running again. Every day it's closed I lose money."

Exhausted, they agreed to call it an early evening. Tomorrow would be another long day.

"We'll make good progress tomorrow," Terry promised as she cleared the dishes. "We're all that much stronger for this storm. Abby hasn't beaten us."

In the attic of the house next door, an angry mist formed, hissing as it swirled around the stored objects. The room took on a dirty silver glow, haze filling the air; a trail of black ice crystals momentarily formed in its wake.

Then, in a blink—the film disappeared, and the room returned to normal.

CHAPTER FOUR

Once she fell fast asleep, the movies in her mind started.

The dreams were not those that appeared most often in Mary Jo's adult sleep, the ones with war, battlegrounds, explosions, and gunfire.

This time, she suffered through dreams that repeated every nightmare of her childhood, segueing from scene to scene like a bad horror movie. These dreams weren't as intense as the ones with the war scenes, but they evoked even more unpleasant memories.

The images started with the Christmas dream, where none of the presents under the tree bore her name. A young Mary Jo ran from room to room of the house, searching until she found more gifts towering on a shelf in the closet. No matter how high she climbed or what she stepped on, the brightly wrapped boxes stayed just out of her reach.

Then the segment morphed into an Easter egg hunt, as she ran with other children in search of the colorfully dyed eggs. But while the other kids quickly filled their baskets with eggs they found easily—tucked in tree branches or on windowsills—for some reason she always had to dig in the ground for hers.

This scene transformed into the rain dream, where a heavy downpour drenched the egg hunt participants. The other children ran to escape.

All except for Mary Jo who, crying and drenched to the skin, continued to dig—dig—dig in the mud to find a prize she could never uncover, despite her tears mixing with the pelting rainfall.

For as long as she could remember, her dreams were frequent, vivid, and rarely pleasant.

As a teenager, after reading a biography of Molly Pitcher, she often dreamt of loading cannons on a Revolutionary War battlefield, dressed in colonial garb. She never understood why, but storms during the night always brought on the war dreams as the sounds of thunder outside transformed into the boom of gunfire in her sleep.

She never screamed or thrashed, no matter what devastating images her subconscious created. That had stopped long ago, back when she was a child, back when comforting arms were seldom there to hold her until she recovered.

On a few occasions, she had been able to force herself to wake up.

Somewhere in her subconscious, she was aware of the root of this flashback and could deal with it. But she had to wake up first and did as she always did. She struggled through the flashing imagery until she reached the point where she could force herself to wake and escape it.

Bolting upright, she cleared her mind, comforted in reality. She remembered glancing at her watch when she flopped on the bed earlier, revealing the time was ten-thirty. Now when she squinted at the tiny dial, she found it hard to believe it was only midnight. The combination of wine at dinner and sheer exhaustion should have knocked her out until morning.

Waking up this abruptly after less than two hours of sleep meant she had too much time on her hands and too many memories in her brain. She would be awake until sunrise.

She punched her pillows and wondered if she should hate her life right now.

The recollections spilling from her mind should have been enough to convince her.

She was the daughter of a single mother who had shown little maternal interest in her child. Patricia Cooper never physically or verbally abused her daughter, but affection was rare, especially after she was forced to work an evening shift to keep her job. Since childcare facilities were not open nights, she'd often had to leave her nine-year old daughter home alone.

Self-reliant and obedient, Mary Jo learned how to cook her own dinner while her mother worked evenings. She would clean up, do her homework, check to make sure the doors were locked, and then go to bed. At first, when the house creaked and groaned, she would pull the covers over her head. After a few nights, she learned to ignore the strange sounds that sometimes occurred and slept well—except when she had the dreams.

She packed her own school lunches. Most mornings her mother slept, and it was the little girl who played caretaker, leaving a plate of food in the refrigerator for her mother to find during the day.

Now and then, Mary Jo came home to find a snack on the table or a meal already prepared and waiting in the refrigerator. And to her mother's credit, she was always home on her one day off each week. That one day a week was a highlight for Mary Jo. Her mom fixed dinner and sometimes asked about school. They shared popcorn and watched a video. It wasn't like a mother and daughter relationship, though; it was like a friendship.

Mary Jo tossed and punched at her pillows again, trying to force that memory away. But her mind continued to play a slideshow of her life as the next memory shoved its way into her head.

Three years later, a fire in the apartment building exposed her mother's carelessness. Mary Jo had just turned twelve and a frigid winter had gripped the area. Already huddled in bed, fast asleep, she was unaware of the power outage due to a raging ice storm.

If Patricia Cooper had gone straight home, she would have

been with her daughter. But she had gone to a friend's house first, and in the short time she was there the ice had built up and made travel too dangerous.

While Mary Jo slept, the elderly landlord who lived upstairs knocked over a candle and couldn't control the spreading flames. He and his wife called 911 and hurried downstairs, alerting the occupants of the other two apartments. They were aware that the little girl was sometimes left alone in the second apartment, but they hadn't interfered. The mother paid the rent on time; the child stayed inside and never caused trouble. When no one responded to the door, he used his key. He raced inside, located the little girl buried under a mound of covers and scooped her up, to wait together outside in the icy rain for the fire department.

The Fire Department called Child Protective Services as soon as it was determined that her mother wasn't home and could not be located. Mary Jo adamantly refused to go to a stranger's home and begged them to contact Mr. and Mrs. Dunbar, the parents of her best schoolmate. When they agreed to let her stay for the night, the caseworker released Mary Jo to their temporary custody.

Child Services allowed Mr. and Mrs. Dunbar to act as foster parents and soon after they qualified, the arrangement became permanent. The Dunbar family and their distant cousin Hannah helped her live a more stable life. From Hannah she learned the secrets to making pastries, croissants and petit fours, and fanned her passion to someday open a little French café, with Hannah behind the counter to help whip up tasty treats.

For years Mary Jo had meticulously saved half of every dollar she ever earned or received as a gift to realize her dream of opening that little shop, which she proudly named "*Pâtisseries à la Carte.*" Although she had to settle for its transformation in her absence during her deployment to Afghanistan, she had ruled the renovation with an iron fist via email.

She tossed to her other side, reminded of how many

arguments she'd already had with Chase Hallmark over design issues—most of which he won in the end because he provided sound construction reasons for his decisions that far outweighed her quest for aesthetics.

Terry's sister-in-law Beth was her café manager while Terry acted as a "silent partner." Beth had gotten the menu up and running, working out the many kinks of operating the small restaurant while Terry concentrated on business issues.

Mary Jo was ready to roll up her sleeves and plunge into her enterprise as soon as her enlistment was up. She'd only had one chance to visit the completed bistro on her return and see it in all its shining glory.

Then that bitching Hurricane Abby hit, she thought with bitterness as she stirred restlessly and got up to pace. Her long-awaited dream was now in tatters. In fact, her whole world was in tatters. For a second time, she wondered if she hated her life.

But Mary Jo Cooper was a fighter. She decided that for the rest of the night she would allow herself a good sulk over everything that had gone wrong in her life. She would wallow in her misery from beginning to end.

Then she was coming out swinging.

Maybe Chase Hallmark's chin would be one of the targets.

Hmmm. She felt better already.

* * *

Mary Jo never went back to sleep, and at six slipped out for an early morning jog. She ran for thirty minutes but cut short her usual hour because tree limbs still littered the path, breaking her stride as she dodged them. She returned to the apartment planning to start a pot of coffee but found Stephanie already showered, dressed and at the sink drawing water.

"Morning," Mary Jo mumbled. She needed her dose of caffeine to jump-start her morning conversation. She could hear the sounds of the shower in the hall bathroom. So Terry was already up—and startlingly early, too.

"Morning. How'd you sleep?" Stephanie asked as she drew a store-bought quiche out of a box.

"Oh, that pains me to see." Mary Jo pretended to cover her eyes in mock protest. Quiche—the real kind—was one of her specialty dishes, and she had looked forward to serving a "quiche du jour" in her café.

Stephanie grimaced guiltily. "Oh, sorry, I shouldn't have insulted you with this. It's just something I grabbed for a quick start."

"Oh, it's okay. It's fine. I do, however, appreciate that you recognize your disrespect to culinary excellence."

"I bow to the cuisine queen." Stephanie made an exaggerated curtsey.

"I had such dreams last night," Mary Jo said suddenly, surprising herself that she even mentioned it. She shook her head in memory, frowning. "They were dreams I used to have when I was a kid."

"Do you want to talk about it?" Stephanie placed the frozen quiche in the microwave, punched the buttons and went to her friend's side.

"Talk about what?" Terry shuffled down the hall, her hair turbaned in a towel.

"Mary Jo just mentioned she had some dreams last night. I was about to pump her for more info."

The comment backed Mary Jo into a corner. She rarely discussed her personal life, but felt so at ease with Stephanie that the words just popped out.

"Let's get breakfast on the table first," she said. "This will take a while."

The combination of two curious minds and three pairs of hands had the table ready in record time.

For a few minutes, Mary Jo pondered her options, tempted to tell her friends that she realized the dreams were silly and nothing worth talking about. But she reconsidered—maybe it was time to talk out some of her issues after all.

So between bites of acceptable frozen quiche, she described

the montage of dreams so vividly that Stephanie and Terry both stated they actually felt like they were experiencing the dreams as well.

"Wow," Stephanie added when Mary Jo ended with the scene in the rain. "I don't think I've ever had the same dream twice in my whole life."

"You know, I do remember you had those dreams when you came to live with us, Mary Jo," Terry reflected as she stacked coffee cups.

"I even remember when they started," Mary Jo said. She'd never even told this part to Terry, but the effects of last night's wine and the melancholy atmosphere must have brought it to the surface.

"It was the Christmas before I came to live with you. I was about twelve. We had a small tree set up at home, and the only thing I wanted was—can you believe this—a 'Trivial Pursuit' game. I didn't have many friends to hang out with, so I don't even know why I would want a game that required other players. I only hung out with you guys, Terry, you and your brothers." She deliberately left out Chase, who was at the Dunbar house almost as much as she was.

"Mary Jo was the resident brainiac in our circle," Terry explained to Stephanie.

"Well, all I know is things were so tight that Christmas, Mom was trying hard to make ends meet. I had a present for her—a scarf and glove set I paid for with babysitting money." Mary Jo drained her juice glass and stretched for the carton on the table before she continued.

"Mom was working the evening shift on Christmas Eve, and I figured she would put all the presents out after she got home. I had everything as ready as I could. The apartment was clean and the tree lit. My gift for her was the only one under it." Mary Jo stopped short. She had never told anyone about this but knew she needed to get it out. "Except she didn't get home at eight like she should have; she got home after two in the morning. She had gone to some of her friends' houses to hang out and watch *their* kids open up *their* presents. She finally made it home, and I gave her my gift. I really thought she was kidding me when she told me my presents were still in layaway, that she never had the chance to go get them. I was sure she was going to bring them out of a closet or drawer after a while. But she didn't. A few days later she picked them up from layaway and gave me the gifts, still in the store bags."

A tear rolled down her cheek and she didn't even bother to brush it away as she poured another glass of juice. Stephanie and Terry sat in silent empathy as they let her talk.

"Some days I never saw her at all. I was asleep when she got home, and she usually wasn't up when I left for school. By the time I got home from school, she would already be gone for work." She brushed angrily at the sliding tear now and continued.

"She never abused me. She just forgot about me, always making promises she couldn't keep. I never understood. Once, I was so excited when she told me I could take horseback lessons. I did all the legwork to find out when and where. But then she had to work evenings so I didn't have a way to get to the stables; same thing with dance lessons."

The sad story was almost more than tenderhearted Stephanie could bear. Although she had learned after her parents died that she was an adopted child, and her birth parents were also dead, the one thing she knew for sure was they had loved her dearly. Impulsively she jumped up and threw her arms around Mary Jo.

"It makes sense why you have those dreams," she offered. "Maybe they make you feel as if you are searching for something, or as if your goals are just out of reach."

"I agree," Terry added as she filled her coffee cup. "You got home from Afghanistan planning to enjoy your treasured French café and that bitching Hurricane Abby snatched it away before you even had a chance to bake in it one time."

"That's probably true," Mary Jo sniffed in agreement. "It's happened to me my whole life. I get this close." She held her thumb and forefinger an inch apart. "This close and some obstacle blocks my dreams from happening." She shook her head when Terry motioned with the coffee pot. It was time to clear her thoughts away from broken promises and unfulfilled childhood dreams before she started revealing the ones from her adulthood.

"Let's change the subject," she said with false brightness. "Stephanie, I'll tell you how Terry became my best best friend."

"Oh, please do tell." Stephanie pushed her plate away and leaned forward in anticipation. "I've only known you both for such a short time but already feel as if we could all be sisters. I want to know more about you growing up."

"We were in first grade and had some kind of parent day, where they joined their kids for lunch before a field trip. My mom wasn't there, of course. Terry's mother, Joan had agreed to be a chaperone, and Terry was proudly showing her mother the poster she'd created for 'Fire Prevention Week' which the teacher had hung in the cafeteria.

"I had a puppet in my hands, and a boy named Jeffrey Clarkson sat down at the same table. He suddenly snatched the puppet away from me, and I just sat there. Oh I wanted to hit him all right, to fight back and claim what was mine. Terry, however, had seen the incident, and as she walked near the table, stretched her arm over Jeffrey's shoulder and calmly lifted the puppet out of his hands. She walked around the table and plopped it in front of me, never missing a beat in the conversation with her mother. Jeffrey glared but made no move to try to take it again. She was my hero from that moment on," Mary Jo concluded with a smile. "I never had anyone else stick up for me like that before—or since. It's always been Terry."

"Oh, I wish I had known you guys back then." Stephanie wistfully placed her chin on her hands. "Tell me more."

"Well, all throughout school Terry was called the 'Crusader' for her passionate sense of fairness. She once approached the principal directly to protest the suspension of a student wrongfully accused of cheating and successfully facilitated that student's reinstatement to class. She went to bat for a lot of kids over the years. She still does it today, as a lawyer."

"I can see her crusading." Stephanie laughed.

"That's enough about me," Terry interrupted. "Mary Jo was our 'Warrior.' She took on the bullies as we got older, after that incident with Jeffrey." She turned to Mary Jo. "You are going to let me tell her your other moniker, aren't you?"

Stephanie's eyes darted from woman to woman, thoroughly enjoying the sibling-like exchange. As an only child, she had led a relatively quiet and sheltered adolescence.

Mary Jo rolled her eyes skyward at mention of her hated nickname. "Oh, go ahead," she said in a peeved tone, flicking her hand in defeat. "You know as well as I do that if you don't tell her now, she's just going to ask you later. And even if I don't want you to, you'll tell her anyway."

"True." Terry leisurely sipped her coffee, sensing Stephanie's anticipation at hearing the rest of the story.

"Come on!" Stephanie urged impatiently.

Terry laughed and set the cup down. "Okay. Sometimes due to her height she was called 'Princess Xena,' which she absolutely hated. But if she stepped into a melee involving someone picking on another student, it was like the parting of the sea as students respectfully stood aside to let her pass. She became a little quick-tempered too. She once knocked Jeffrey Clarkson on his ass in front of the whole school when she caught him trying to force kids half his size to eat bugs."

"Yeah, well, Jeffrey was such a jerk all the way through school. I remember a couple of times sitting on my hands in class to keep from punching him in the nose," Mary Jo muttered.

"Was that the same boy Chase and Gage went on the vandalism spree with when they were young? They admitted it but he didn't?" Stephanie asked. She remembered Gage telling her the story, how he and Chase would not tell on Jeffrey. They spent the entire summer repairing damage and reimbursing their parents for costs while he hung out at the beach with their friends.

"The same. He never got caught for anything he did." Mary

Jo stood up and gathered glasses and dishes.

"Well, as a kid anyway. He's had a few brushes with the law and just got out of jail. DUI maybe," Terry said, setting the empty juice bottle aside. "The nut doesn't fall far from the family tree. My law partner, Sandi said Jeffrey's son just got busted for petit larceny, and he asked her to take the case. It's the kid's first offense—well, first time he got caught anyway."

"I'm surprised Jeffrey came to your office," Mary Jo said.

"He didn't. They ran into each other at the pub, and he told her about his kid. They had already agreed to set up the appointment. When she gave him her card, he realized we were partners, but he seemed okay with it."

"Oh, well, let's hope he's not in denial like his parents were." Mary Jo shrugged and stood up. She didn't want to speak of ghosts or bullies or bad dreams anymore. And the two things she probably needed to discuss the most—the horrors during her tour of duty and the upcoming court case where she was being sued by her late fiancé's mother—were both tucked away in her thoughts for now. She would have to talk about them soon enough but she wanted to put it off as long as possible.

But absolutely not up for discussion anytime soon were her feelings for Chase Hallmark. Those would stay sealed in her heart—both the good ones and the bad ones.

CHAPTER FIVE

Beth Dunbar arrived at the café as early as she could, four-year old son Tanner in tow. She and her husband, Connor had spent the previous day at her parents' home, clearing their yard of branches and debris. The area in Suffolk where they lived had suffered less damage than the areas closer to the beach. Connor and several of his colleagues from the Suffolk Fire Department had helped each other out by forming a team, tackling one yard at a time for their colleagues until the individual families could manage.

With the knowledge her parents were fine, she was ready to pull her weight at the café. But now, she had a bored little boy on her hands as she wheeled into a parking space a half-block away. She gathered his backpack, her carryall, and a lunch bag with his favorite snacks and set them on the sidewalk, then unbuckled a fidgety Tanner from his car seat.

"Stay right here on the sidewalk, young man," she ordered, picking up a soft canvas cooler on the floorboard. Then she went through the routine of strapping the Spiderman backpack onto her son's back, placing the lunch bag in his hand, and throwing the carry-all over her left shoulder as she picked up the cooler with the same hand. With her free hand, she tucked Tanner's hand in hers, and they trudged to the rear of the buildings.

She noticed the extensive repair work already accomplished on the properties since the storm. With the trees cut up and moved out of the way, it looked less like a disaster area. The crews had already repaired the minor damage to the law office and apartment; however, the uprooted trees had left the parking lot in disorder, displacing the cobblestones and macadam layered on the ground over the years.

A construction crew worked on the parking lot, using backhoes to break through the layers and pile them to the side. Terry had taken Chase's suggestion to replace the uneven old surface with a smooth blacktop. Parking on the side streets was limited, and they'd all agreed the improved surface would be safer for customers once the café was back in business and the B and B operational.

Beth guided Tanner along the orange mesh fence, the little boy gawking with interest at the machinery.

"Can I go dig in the dirt, Mama?" he asked, tugging her toward the fence.

"Not right now, little man, let's go find Aunt Mary Jo and everybody."

"Awww, Mama." Then his gaze fell on Chase, and he broke free, shouting "Uncle Chase!" Although Chase and Mary Jo were friends rather than blood relatives, Connor and Beth had insisted Tanner show respect by giving them the family titles.

"Hey, there, Tanner Bear." Chase used the family's affectionate pet name for the little boy as he scooped him in his arms for a hug.

"Uncle Chase, can I ride on the digger today?"

"The backhoe? I don't know, bud, we'll have to see what your mom says. If it's okay with her, and you mind her really well, we can check it out when my guys are on lunch break."

"Can I, Mama? Can I?" Tanner turned pleasing eyes toward his mother.

Quick to seize any opportunity and not above bribery, Beth made a deal with her son that if he played quietly while she had a meeting, he could go outside with Uncle Chase at lunch.

They entered the law office Terry shared with her partner,

Sandi Cross. She and Sandi had formed their own firm about a year ago, renting a cramped office during renovation of the new workspace. Two former bedrooms became offices; the living room served as the reception center, the formal dining room their conference quarters. A small kitchenette rounded out the downstairs.

The exterior gave the appearance of an old colonial house, but in truth it only dated back to the mid-1800s. The two other buildings on the joint property were all properties owned at one time or another by Terry's ancestors. Originally built around 1780, both had undergone extensive remodeling. During the Civil War, Union troops caused extensive damage at some point in an 1863 occupation. While Terry's ancestors chose to renovate this dwelling where the law office was now located, the other houses had been too severely damaged and were rebuilt after the war.

Beth found her café partners and Stephanie poring over some sketches, Terry marking furiously in red ink across the drawing.

"Since we are removing the small back porch, I really do think the idea to extend the wraparound all the way to the back will improve the café," Terry said, drawing lines to indicate the change.

"I do too," Mary Jo agreed. "If business picks up, we would have room to add tables back there. We could use a trellis with vines or even attach hanging baskets so the guests don't have to look out over the parking lot."

Tanner stood beside his mother, shifting from one foot to the other as he waited patiently for the grownups to notice him, the way he'd been taught to do. The women looked up from their drawings to welcome him, extending their arms for hugs. After exchanging greetings, Beth gently reminded Tanner that if he played quietly he could spend some time with Chase outside.

"Chase promised to let him see the 'digger' if he behaved, so I think that will buy me a good hour," she said and laughed as she set the bag on the table. She removed sandwiches and containers, while tilting her head to study the sketches.

"How are things at your parents' house?" Terry asked, peeking under the lid of one of the plastic bowls.

"All the debris has finally been cleaned up. The guys chopped the fallen tree into large sections which Dad intends to split into firewood. He predicts a cold winter after the sweltering summer we had. How do things stack up here?"

"Well, the insurance company cut the checks." Mary Jo leaned forward and picked up a sandwich. "We're cleared to dig up the old parking surface so it can be leveled and repaved. As soon as we agree on café repairs, they'll work on that. I want to try to get it open by the end of the week."

"If Chase and Mary Jo can agree on the sketch," Terry chimed in, pushing the sketch toward Beth.

"Why, what's up?" Beth peered at the plan.

"There's no problem with extending the porch to the back," Terry said. "As pig-headed as Mary Jo thinks Chase is, we're lucky to have him as a friend. We're getting materials at cost and I'm sure some discounted labor, all at priority service."

"He's pig-headed," Mary Jo insisted. "Look, Beth, I want something simple on the back porch. Instead of a set of narrow steps from the patio area down to the parking lot, I want to have steps graduated in length so they are widest as they reach the bottom. We can place planters along the edge of each step but still have plenty of room for people to walk by them." She sketched so Beth could see her vision.

"Don't forget to include a ramp for handicapped access. You'll have to add one with the new construction." Beth tapped the sketch where Mary had drawn the proposed addition.

"Oops, good point." Terry spoke as she looked at Mary Jo. "We all forgot that."

"No problem." Mary Jo grabbed another of the photocopied drawings and started drafting new lines. "We run the ramp to the right and designate the two parking spaces directly in front of it as 'handicapped.' We move the steps and run them from the left. There is a common landing as they meet in the middle and enter the patio area. I can have a little spot here for a row of mint or parsley or something. Or maybe plant daffodils or tulips for the spring." She slashed her pen across the page and held up the design, which Beth and Terry studied.

"I like the concept," Beth said after a moment. Because the café had always been Mary Jo's dream, one that Beth had recently invested in, she deferred to most of her ideas or suggestions. "Now, on the practical matters, how long will it take to get operational? Every day the café is closed we lose money, and no one gets paid."

"Well, Chase said you should be back in business before the end of the week." Terry removed the wrapping from a sandwich and checked the contents. "With everyone pitching in to help remove the debris, his crews could get right into the nuts and bolts of repairs—no pun intended."

"Okay. I'll get started on this," Mary Jo snatched the drawings and stood up. "I guess I'll go deal with Chase."

"He's outside," Beth mentioned.

"And Mary Jo, forgive me for saying," Terry added. "You've got to stop being so prickly with Chase. If he says the sun is shining, you say it's not."

"And your point is?" Mary Jo stood with her hand on the doorknob.

Terry raised her hands, palms forward. "Just saying."

"Hmmph." Mary Jo turned on her heels and went out the door.

Beth sighed as she selected a sandwich wedge, and said thoughtfully, "Do you think she'll ever forgive him?"

"It's been how long now? Nine or ten years?"

"About that long."

"When is someone going to clue me in?" Stephanie asked.

"All we know is they had a blow-up back then and she's refused to talk about it," Terry said. "Chase is just as close-mouthed. She went into the service shortly after. Then she met Jay, and she has rarely crossed paths with Chase ever since."

"I haven't given up on them, Terry." Beth frowned. "I think they're still in love."

"I do too," Terry agreed. Her cell phone rang, and she checked the screen before pushing the answer button.

"Hi, Mom, what's up?"

* * *

Mary Jo and Chase reached a surprisingly quick and friendly agreement on the design of the back porch, and he left to secure the necessary permits. When he came back, his crew was on their lunch break. True to his promise, he took Tanner out to show him the machinery, placing the smallest hardhat he could find on the little boy's head. The bright yellow safety helmet wobbled, but Tanner grinned from ear to ear as Chase took him in his lap and let him work the controls.

Beth watched from the sidelines, one hand pressed to her stomach. She trusted Chase implicitly—but that was still her baby out there among all that macho machinery. Tanner's laugh rang across the lot as they back-scooped a load of dirt and moved it to the side, the whoops of delight nearly drowning the beeping as Chase put the equipment into reverse.

"Boys and their toys," Mary Jo said caustically as she joined Beth.

"Can't you two bury the hatchet?" Beth said in exasperation.

"I'm deciding on that," Mary Jo answered, turning to go back into the office. "I'm just trying to decide whether it'll be between his shoulder blades or through that thick skull of his."

She marched toward the café in choppy stomps.

Beth shook her head in a combination of amusement and frustration and turned her attention back to her son. She wasn't going anywhere until he was safely by her side.

* * *

Throughout the afternoon, the construction crews made

significant progress on repairs to *Pâtisseries à la Carte*. One crew extended the wrap-around porch, including the required ramp and built the steps matching Mary Jo's very detailed—and determined—specifications. Another team finished repairs to the roof. Soon painters would arrive to prime and paint the raw lumber on the railings, although plywood covered broken glass in windows not yet been replaced.

Mary Jo was impatient, though, and had to do something while she waited for the work to be completed. Beth was inside, taking an inventory of the kitchen to see what she needed to purchase, a task Mary Jo happily passed off. She surveyed the small stretch of fresh dirt around the new porch. It was a space between the curb and the steps, stretching six feet long and a foot wide. Just large enough for a few rows of mint or outdoor herbs, a backdrop of spring flowers would fill the space nicely.

Planning for colorful flowers to surround the café in springtime, she'd recently purchased a variety of bulbs, still in her trunk since before the storm. She retrieved the garden packets along with tools and selected a mound of soft dirt in front of the newly-built stairs.

For several minutes, she enjoyed the mindless task of popping small corms into scooped-out holes, knowing fruition would come with the first blooms of tulips, daffodils and crocuses in the springtime. As she plunged the trowel deeper and scooped out another mound of dirt and clay, a shiny flicker caught her eye. She stared into the pile on the metal blade, then shook it loose. Her gaze caught a tiny twinkle as the dirt fell at her knees, but when she ran her fingers through the dirt, they came up empty.

She dug into the ground with a vengeance, then pulled off her gloves in an annoyed gesture and flung them aside, plunging her hand into the soft dirt. She felt around, her fingers encircling a clump tangled in metal.

It's bad enough you have nightmares in your sleep, now you are imagining shiny lights in dirt and clay. What's next, ghosts in the window? She glared defiantly at the upstairs window of the Bed and Breakfast as if daring a ghost to appear—her heart skipping a beat as a pale face materialized at the dormer window and looked down at her.

Just like that time so many years ago.

Tanner startled her as he skipped out onto the fresh new patio. "Mama says I'm bugging her, Aunt Mary Jo. Whatcha doing? Can I bug you?"

"You sure can, buddy," Mary Jo said with a laugh as she absent-mindedly shoved the clump in her jacket pocket and glanced toward the now-empty window. "I'm looking at some places where I want to plant these bulbs, so they will grow into nice flowers in the spring."

"Can I look in your tool bag?" He plopped down the four steps, jumping with both feet on each tread until he reached her. He squatted beside her and peered into the small leather bag holding her hand tools. "What are these things?"

"Okay, this one is called a hand fork, and I use it to break up lumps that the backhoe dug up when Chase's crew tore out the big rocks in the dirt."

"Yeah, Uncle Chase let me ride wif him in the backhoe today and I scoop-ded the dirt and dumped it out."

"Yes, I saw you. Did you have fun?"

Tanner nodded. "Yeah! Hey! This little shovel is just right for me."

"That's called a trowel. I can use it to break up the dirt, and dig small holes to put the bulbs in. You see that other thing beside it, the one that looks like a tube with a handle on it? I can use that to make holes too, and I just drop the bulb in, like this." Mary Jo demonstrated by twisting the cylinder-shaped blade and handing a crocus corm to Tanner. He dropped it into the hole, pushed a pile of dirt over it and stomped before reaching for the tool bag again. She grimaced but would dig it out later.

"And this one is—'The Claw!'" Tanner removed the cultivator from the bag, pretended it was an extension of his arm and growled. "Aargh, 'The Claw' is gonna get you."

Mary Jo laughed and pretended to shrink away from the

"monster."

"Hello, lady," Tanner called out suddenly. Mary Jo turned to look in the direction he was pointing, and her jaw dropped.

Standing between the café and the Bed and Breakfast, a shimmering form materialized until she could clearly see the young girl dressed in a colonial outfit. White ribbons laced the front of the maroon bodice above a rose-colored skirt topped with a white pinafore. Strands of auburn hair twirled along her cheek. She carried a basket draped over her arm, a loaf of bread peeking out from under a white cloth.

"She's Nickel's sister," Tanner said casually. "She's bigger than me and Nickel. I can't say her name right. It's Marie Jo-fess maybe."

"You can see her, Tanner?"

"Sure, she's right there, Aunt Mary Jo."

"Does she talk to you? In your head, like Nickel?"

He shrugged. "I don't know." He started digging holes with the cultivator, no longer interested in the scene around him.

Mary Jo's eyes never left the apparition as she asked, "Who are you?"

"Dig deep, Mary Jo." Mary Jo couldn't see the girl's lips move in the image but she could hear a voice loud and clear in her head.

"Dig deep, Mary Jo, and you will find your heart."

When Mary Jo's cell phone rang, the image disappeared into sparkling fragments and faded from sight. Willing the apparition to return, she ignored the ringing until it stopped.

She stared. *What else could happen in my life?*

CHAPTER SIX

The aftermath of Hurricane Abby created a booming business for contractors, and Chase Hallmark's company could hardly handle the calls from residents. Mary Jo had surprised him with a swift—and amicable—decision on the repairs in time for him to obtain permits that day. His men completed the extended porch and made significant progress on other repairs.

Although exhausted, he'd had a late dinner at the pub in Olde Towne. Because he drank two beers, he'd hung out with a few friends, shooting pool until he was ready to drive home at midnight.

Conversation in the noisy bar centered on the remains found behind *Pâtisseries à la Carte*. Once word got out about discovering skeletal remains, the story grew from a single set of old bones to a mass burial by a serial killer. Patrons resurrected old ghost stories and circulated new ones over mugs of beer and pizza.

By the conversation flowing around him, it was clear to Chase that rumors were spreading like wildfire, and he found himself putting them out. *No, there were not three bodies under the tree. No, there were not five. No, a whole family was not buried there. Yes, the city was safe; no, there was not a serial killer on the loose. No, the houses were not haunted; no, he'd never seen a ghost.*

Chase was sick of the stupid questions and was glad to make his getaway from the equally stupid people who were asking. He briskly strolled a few blocks along High Street, noting the posters advertising "The Ghost Walk" on the front windows of closed shops.

An annual event in Olde Towne and popular for more than thirty years, the Ghost Walk consisted of walking tours, usually held the third Friday in October. Guides led walkers past many of the old houses and mansions in the historic area, where costumed actors relayed the stories and legends of reported ghost sightings and hauntings.

Chase remembered the tours with fondness. Over the years growing up he had often joined the Dunbar brothers, Gage and Connor, on the treks. Once the three boys reached their teen years however, they sought more terrifying experiences in settings that emulated scenes from horror movies. Any event with severed limbs and grizzly settings was high priority.

And though he never admitted it when conversation turned to sightings of ghosts, there was that one occasion when he thought he had seen an image in the window of the house Mary Jo and Terry were now turning into a B and B.

They were all teenagers, accompanying the Dunbar family on a Sunday visit to Terry's elderly great-aunt Ida. He and Mary Jo snuck out to the backyard to smoke cigarettes, and he happened to look up in time to catch a hazy light shimmering and what looked like the form of a girl at the window.

He tried to play it nonchalantly, asking Mary Jo if the window looked crooked. She'd glanced up, angled her head several ways and said it looked fine to her.

He was glad he had not mentioned to her that a possible spirit watched them.

As they grew older, even on the nights when he and the Dunbar brothers were trying to scare the crap out of each other with ghost stories, he never, not once, told anyone.

He zipped his jacket against the crisp air which, along with the potted mums on doorsteps, signaled the impending arrival of autumn. When he approached his truck, he noticed a couple of red laser lights dancing along the sidewalk as the shadowy figures of three boys darted between vehicles. They made silly little woo-woo sounds, so Chase imagined they were checking out the latest haunting of Olde Towne.

He circled the three houses and found everything in order. No ghostly face stared down at him from the B and B.

He spared one glance up at the apartment above the law office. Already aware that Mary Jo and Terry were staying the night to keep Stephanie company, he felt the women were safe.

He rubbed the heel of his palm over his heart as he returned to his truck. Relief was not the sensation he felt there—it was a stab of something.

Indigestion—or regret? He wasn't sure.

* * *

At five thirty a.m., Kyle Avery packed his car with parcels of genealogy supplies. The lanky history professor stacked crates of books, two plastic cases of hanging files filled with documents he had been gathering, and cardboard tubes containing poster-sized family trees in the back seat. In the trunk, he situated his electronic equipment: cameras, scanner, laptop, and portable printer. He added a bag of office supplies, then a package holding three pairs of reading glasses. He seemed to lose a pair a week.

He remembered at the last minute that he needed clothes and toiletries and went back into his apartment to pack a suitcase.

Genealogy can get complicated. He threw shirts into the suitcase, recalling how he first connected with Stephanie, due to common names they shared in their online family trees. The information he provided to Stephanie enabled her to confirm her lineage back to her colonial ancestors Étienne and Clothiste.

He and Stephanie shared other family connections. Although they were not blood relatives, his third great-grandmother Annette Wyatt was the second wife of a fourth great-uncle of Stephanie's—at least he thought that was the relationship. Without the charts in front of him, he was never exactly sure.

Absent-mindedly tossing in a dozen pairs of white socks, he rehearsed the history again in his head. Sometime in 1870 or so, this Annette had helped one of Stephanie's other ancestress trace her roots in order to be eligible to join the Daughters of the American Revolution. Those roots went all the way back to the time of the American Revolution and a French soldier fighting for the Americans named Étienne de la Rocher, and his French Canadian wife, Clothiste.

His attention drifted to his chance meeting with Joan Dunbar, the woman who had hired him to research her family tree. During an encounter with Stephanie when he visited the area for Labor Day weekend, the Dunbar siblings joined them. He mentioned the families he was researching, and Terry revealed her mother's maiden name was Wyatt and had a great deal of family history that could prove useful, setting into motion the meeting with Joan.

Within a few minutes of conversation, she hired him on the spot to research her family.

Armed with her records, he returned to his home in Maryland and got to work, finding the research fascinating and amazingly easy to document.

Then, in her last email sent just before the storm, Stephanie told him she had uncovered more information on relatives and was anxious to get in touch with him. After the storm hit, he tried unsuccessfully for two days to reach her by cell phone. When he finally made contact, the reception was terrible. Before they were disconnected he managed to tell her he would be on his way as soon as the roads were clear to travel to Portsmouth.

He had discovered information for the Dunbar family which he needed to deliver in person, but he first had to meet with Hannah. Based on her decision, he could determine how much or how little to convey about the rest of his discovery.

An image of the willowy auburn-haired Mary Jo flashed

into his mind, and he wondered what she would think of the news he would deliver to her; but he was more interested to know what the vivacious Terry Dunbar would think.

He shook his head to clear that thought away. He was so out of her league—way out.

He leaned sideways to catch his reflection in his bureau mirror. For years, colleagues told him he resembled a young Harrison Ford. His university students often loaded his desk with apples reminiscent of the scene from the first Indiana Jones movie. At certain times, like now, he did see the similarity. He'd remembered to shave but he would need to get his shaggy brown hair trimmed soon. Stroking his smooth face, he remembered the toiletry bag and tossed the battered leather pouch in the suitcase.

He wore a polo shirt and khaki pants, thinking business-casual more appropriate for the meeting with Hannah. He'd only met her one time, at the Dunbars' Labor Day cookout, but he remembered her vividly. He chuckled at the image of the tiny woman, barely five feet tall, straight and thin as a drinking straw. Tanned skin wrinkled as a prune covered her spindly arms and legs. She wore her snow-white hair cut short, and it stuck out in small spikes on top. For the cook-out, she wore a "Maxine" character t-shirt with a picture of the cartoon crone and the phrase, "I may seem a little gruff, but once you get to know me you'll know you were right," purple flowered Capri pants and purple Crocs. In that brief encounter, he observed that the old lady had an acerbic tongue but clearly loved the family.

Absent-mindedly he went back to packing and threw in a pair of khaki shorts and some jeans, then on second thought, added a pair of dress pants and a shirt to match. It never occurred to him he might need a pair of dress shoes as he closed the suitcase and headed for his car.

Then he remembered to check behind himself and went back inside to make sure he had turned off all of the small appliances. He'd been known to burn up a coffee maker or two in the past because he'd forgotten to turn them off when they were empty.

He glanced at his watch just before he put his car into gear. Six a.m.

By noon at the latest, he would be delivering his surprising news to Hannah.

* * *

As Stephanie made her way to the kitchen at six, she glanced toward the open door of the spare bedroom. The bed was already made, the room unoccupied. The bathroom door stood partially open to an empty room.

The only other person in the apartment was a huge lump on the couch, buried under a mountain of afghans and pillows. The one reason she could be sure it was Terry underneath all that was the mane of chestnut hair spilling out in wild waves. Terry Dunbar was not a morning person.

Stephanie quietly pushed the button on the coffee maker and tiptoed out the door to stand on the small landing. She guessed that Mary Jo had gone for a run, and indeed could see the tall woman jogging back toward the building, her long strides eating up the pavement.

She runs like a gazelle! Momentarily envious of the grace and elegance the other woman exhibited in her movements, she was about to call out when Mary Jo stopped short, and then broke into a run toward the back of the café. Stephanie scrambled down the wooden stairway that was a temporary replacement for the one destroyed in the hurricane and caught up to Mary Jo, now standing in the parking lot with arms akimbo.

"What is it?" Following Mary Jo's frowning gaze, Stephanie turned to look at the buildings and her eyes widened in disbelief.

Someone had spray-painted pentagrams and other cult symbols across the plywood covering windows and doors on both the café and the Bed and Breakfast. "The witch is dead," splayed in red paint across one side of the houses, the words

67

oozing blood-like drips. "Ding dong" had been sprayed on another.

"What in the world?" Stephanie started. "Did they get inside?"

"I don't know." Mary Jo tightened her lips and moved toward the doors. Nothing seemed disturbed. "I didn't see that when I went out this morning," she added. "I just headed straight out the other side to run down to the seawall. It wasn't even noticeable until I came into the parking lot and looked toward the building."

"It must have been kids."

"Yeah, most likely. Look, they sprayed all along the sides too." She stepped over the stacks of wood stored by the repair crews and led Stephanie along the remaining portion of the wide wraparound porch. More graffiti marred the siding, along with another pentagram painted on the front door.

"Should we call the police?"

"I don't know, it seems pointless, and I'm sure they have too much other stuff to deal with. But I want to get this crap cleaned off before we have more onlookers come to gawk."

"I'll go get some cleaning supplies."

"Thanks. There's paint we can use to paint over the markings. Would you bring the key to the B and B with you? Terry keeps it…"

"Yes, I know where. You want some coffee? I just started the first pot—we'll need lots."

"I do indeed. Looks like another long day ahead." While she waited for Stephanie to return, she surveyed the latest setback to her plans and shook her head.

Is something trying to keep me from my dreams?

In spite of the morning sun beaming down, a shiver washed over her body.

Stephanie returned a few minutes later, carrying tumblers in each hand and cleaning buckets in the crook of each arm. She handed one of the tumblers to Mary Jo and said, "Terry is on her way down. I told her what happened. That's the fastest I've ever seen her move in the morning. She hates mornings with a passion."

Mary Jo smiled. Such was the sign of good friends.

Indeed, it was only a minute later when Terry herself scooted down the steps, and marched across the yard, her stride almost as long and as angry as Mary Jo's had been. She glared at the graffiti as she gave her friend a hug.

"Looks like we have another task ahead of us," she said grimly, echoing Mary Jo's earlier lament. "Did you call the police?"

"It seems silly to bother them, nothing can be done."

"They don't have to come out for this. We can make a report over the phone. I think we should have it documented. With all of this commotion after finding that skeleton, we need to report everything." She pulled her phone from a back pocket as Stephanie handed Mary Jo the ring holding keys to the lot's three buildings.

"I could try to scrub that graffiti off of the siding while you paint to cover the marks on the plywood," she offered.

"All right, Steph. Thanks so much. I sure hope this will be the last of my bad luck."

"Me too! I want *Pâtisseries à la Carte* back in business. My fridge is almost empty."

They laughed lightly, but neither moved while they listened to Terry give a short and concise synopsis of the scene to someone at the police department. Then the two women followed her as she walked around the porch to record the defacement. She told the unseen report-taker she would photograph the damage and vandalism. With a tap of her thumb, she disconnected the call, snapping pictures as she circled the vandalized buildings, Mary Jo and Stephanie in tow.

"All right, it's documented. I'll get a copy of the report later if we need it." With a final click of a button, Terry slid the phone into her back pocket and pushed up her sleeves. "What can I do to help?"

"Don't you have to work today?"

"Yeah, we're opening two hours late. I don't have anything in court today, but I'm going to start work on your case."

"Oh, crap, I forgot about that for a moment." Mary Jo's resigned sigh seemed to echo between the buildings as they walked back to the parking lot. "So, my bad luck still isn't over yet. Maybe I should leave the spray paint on the B and B, and let her clean it if she wins."

"Della's not going to win, Mary Jo, so put that out of your head. She can claim most of Jay's property, and you've already agreed she can have it. We have the records we need so she can't touch either the café or the B& B."

"I know, Terry. I just want it over with." Mary Jo straightened her shoulders and spoke with determination. She'd had her sulk last night. She was in fight mode now. "I'm going to get a can of white paint from the B and B so I can cover the graffiti on the wood. You can help Steph scrub the siding, if you don't mind."

As her two friends filled buckets with water and detergent, Mary Jo went to the B and B. She stood there for a moment, one hand resting on the knob of the back door and one pressed to her stomach.

The Della to whom Terry had referred was Della Strong, the mother of Mary Jo's late fiancé Jay, who had died suddenly about eighteen months earlier when she was home between deployments. Only thirty-two years old and in seemingly good health, Jay had gone to bed with a headache. When Mary Jo went to check on him before dinner, she found him unresponsive. She called 911 and screamed into the receiver that she needed an ambulance, dropping the open phone on the bed as she started CPR. Paramedics arrived and continued working on him before they placed him in the ambulance, a distraught Mary Jo following in her car.

She paused again as she placed the key in the lock. Her thoughts drifted from the Bed and Breakfast back to the scene at the emergency room, the memory of that evening as clear as if it had just happened. She'd called Jay's parents and his sister on the way, and they met her at the hospital, where they received the sad news together. Due to his young age and apparent good health, an autopsy was required, but the doctors seemed to think it was a heart attack.

"How could this be?" Della had cried. "He was too young to have a heart attack." She turned to Mary Jo, her tone accusing. "Did you ever take him to the doctor for anything?"

"No, he was always fine. He had a physical a year ago but the doctor didn't indicate he had any problems."

They had no immediate answers and had to wait for the autopsy's results, which eventually confirmed he had suffered a heart attack in his sleep.

Hand still on the key, Mary Jo shook her head, trying to clear her mind of the images that held her transfixed.

When she opened the door and stepped inside, a blast of icy air brought her back to the present. Her breath came out in small puffs of vapor. The room was cold, almost freezing, as if an air conditioner had been left running on high. She checked the thermostat. The arrow pointed to the "off" position, but the thermostat read forty degrees.

How could that be? Even with the cooler nights since the storm, the outside temperature had probably not dipped below sixty.

Other than the cold sensation, she found nothing amiss in the house. She located the paint cans stored in a corner, grabbing one without even looking at the color. She picked up some rollers and went back to the café, where Terry and Stephanie had already managed to remove a great deal of the markings off the siding. The building would still need a new coat of paint to cover the dull smudges left behind that no amount of scrubbing could eradicate.

"Can you two take a break and go with me to the B and B, and tell me if you see anything out of the ordinary?"

"Why? What do you mean?" Stephanie asked.

"Just go inside and tell me what you notice."

Both women dropped their scrub brushes and followed Mary Jo. She waited outside and let them go in. A moment later, they reappeared, puzzled looks on their faces.

"It seems okay in there." Terry frowned. "What's up, Mary Jo?"

"When I came in here a few minutes ago this place was uncomfortably cold, and the thermostat read forty." She stepped back into the kitchen, where the temperature now seemed normal. When she checked the controls, the gauge pointed to sixty-five.

She turned to her friends. "When I first came in, this place was colder than it should have been. I even thought the air conditioner might have been running, but it was in the off position. The thermometer said forty. And now here it is, back to normal."

Stephanie shivered. "It's like the time I was locked in the attic up there, and it was so cold until you guys arrived and the door opened." Just before Hurricane Abby struck, she had gone into the Bed and Breakfast's attic to look for some boxes of files that Terry and Mary Jo had stored there. The door had mysteriously locked behind her. Both her cell phone and flashlight stopped working, and the overhead electric light failed to function. Icy cold air had enveloped Stephanie, but as soon as the other two women arrived, the warmth immediately returned, and things functioned normally.

"I don't need this on top of everything else," Mary Jo spat out. She still had not told anyone about the image she had seen yesterday. "It's my imagination. Let's just get out of here."

She stormed out of the kitchen, and the others followed.

Upstairs, a cold mist glided across the floor, dull gray crystals of ice forming behind it and disappearing almost as soon as they took shape.

* * *

By the time Chase Hallmark's construction crews arrived at seven-thirty, Terry and Stephanie had scrubbed off the most obvious markings on the siding, although the outline of the symbols still leached through. In the meantime, Mary Jo had painted over the markings on the plywood and had started working on the back door.

"What happened?" Chase walked up behind her, causing

her to jump.

"Jeez, do you have to sneak up like that?" she snapped, setting the paintbrush aside in annoyance.

"Yeah, well, good morning to you, Miss Sunshine," Chase snapped back. He and Mary Jo sidestepped each other like two caged tigers, glaring.

Sensing the tension, Stephanie took a casual position between them, anxious to head off an argument before the claws came out.

"We found graffiti sprayed all over the sides of the café and back here, Chase." She waved her hand between the two buildings, and his gaze followed. "Terry made a police report, and we were just cleaning it all off before it attracts more gawkers."

"I noticed some kids along the street last night about midnight," Chase said. "I walked around to make sure everything was okay here but didn't notice any markings then. They must have come back afterwards."

"Well, we've covered most of it," Stephanie continued.

"We're going to finish the patio today, Mary Jo." Chase turned to her, his voice a little softer. "We should have everything done so you can get the interior ready to reopen."

"Thank you," Mary Jo said stiffly. No matter what conflict they had between them, Chase would do quality work at the lowest price he could give her. She swallowed her pride and asked him to come with her so she could show him what she wanted.

Terry motioned to Stephanie and whispered, "Let's follow. I know them too well. Something is bound to lead to a disagreement before too long."

* * *

Hannah Jensen stared at her reflection in the mirror. Almost sixty-eight now, her weathered face showed every bit of her age. Usually she didn't care; she earned every damn wrinkle and was proud of them. She had survived the loss of her husband during the Vietnam War three months after their marriage, a double mastectomy six years ago, and a lot of heartache in between.

But she did primp a bit today, even if what she had to work with wasn't the most beautiful face in the world.

Kyle Avery had phoned her earlier to let her know he had made great time on the drive to her place and would arrive any minute.

She knew some of the facts because he had to ask so many questions to be sure he was on the right track. He would bring all of the evidence he had collected and let her review it, to make up her own mind about what she wanted to do.

She turned at the buzz of the doorbell and took a steadying breath, resisting the urge to stick a cigarette in her mouth. She opened the door to find the lanky former professor waiting, a briefcase in his hands.

"Hi, Mrs. Jensen, thanks for seeing me."

"Come on in, Mr. Avery, and call me Hannah."

"Only if you call me Kyle."

"All right, Kyle. Let's sit at the kitchen table. Before we start, can I get you something to drink? Iced tea?"

"Tea would be nice, Mrs.—Hannah. Thanks."

Hannah bustled with a tray and glasses and set them on the table.

"Do you mind if I smoke at times, Kyle?" she asked, reaching for an ashtray and her ever-present cigarette case. "I think I'll need it."

"Help yourself."

"Thanks." She poured tea into glasses for each of them, lit up a cigarette and took a drag, careful to blow the smoke away from Kyle.

"So tell me," she said. "Do you really think my son has found me?"

CHAPTER SEVEN

CLOTHISTE
Portsmouth Virginia 1781

Clothiste was delirious with fever, and the pain in her shoulder seared as if someone had branded her with a hot poker. She opened her eyes, and through blurred vision recognized the maid Lizzie and the neighbor, Doctor Rowe, standing beside the bed. When she tried to sit up, he held her back.

"Please, Madam, please don't move," he said.

"My daughters? My father-in-law?" She clutched his arms.

"I don't know anything about your daughters, Madam. They were gone before I got here. Phillip is recovering as well."

"The soldiers?"

"Two soldiers were killed outside the house, Madam. You were attacked by robbers, and they shot you and Phillip. The soldiers came running, and two were shot dead by the robbers before they fled."

Clothiste became agitated and tried to rise. "I must go. I need to find my children."

The doctor motioned for Lizzie to help him. He placed some drops into a cup and nodded toward the pitcher on the nearby table. She picked it up and poured water until the doctor indicated enough. He put it to the lips of the woman on the bed.

Even through the pain, the fever and the anxiety, an unpleasant memory nagged in Clothiste's mind, and she tried hard to think of what it could be. She swallowed the liquid put to her lips, and by the time it trailed down her throat, she remembered and tried to push the cup away.

She remembered—it was the same way her stepmother-in-law had once tried to poison her.

* * *

That night, Lizzie slipped down the steps of her small room over the outdoor kitchen and glanced toward the main house, windows darkened. She slipped into her shoes and turned the big key in the lock on the door. In the silence the click sounded like a gunshot. With another quick look she dashed into the dark.

She could only meet Louis for a minute, to report on the conditions of his mother and grandfather—and to tell him she had found Nicole's doll, along with scattered pages from his journal. Lizzie had hidden them away until she could take them with her.

If things had been different tonight, she would have been leaving this household forever.

But she would have to stay here a little longer—she would not leave the injured Clothiste in the hands of that wicked woman.

MARY JO
Portsmouth, Virginia, Present day

"Thank you, Kyle," Hannah rasped out. After the single puff, she'd let the cigarette burn to ash in the glass tray, and hadn't smoked at all during the time he spoke. For nearly two hours, she studied the charts he unrolled on her table. He showed her each relative document or photograph, explaining how he came across each item and its significance to her.

"You can keep those papers and pictures, Hannah, I've got copies," he said as he gathered the rest of his materials.

"Thank you," she repeated. "I'm okay with telling the family about my son but I'd like to hold off just a little. While you talk to Mary Jo, I'll call Joan. Maybe she'll get the rest of the Dunbar clan together, and we can tell the others at once. I'll let you know when I do."

"I'm ready whenever you want. Right now I'm heading to the hotel to check in. You have my number, call me at any time."

Hannah stretched her arms up to give Kyle a hug. He towered a good fourteen inches over the tiny woman and bent low to return the embrace.

As he got into his car, he hoped Mary Jo would accept her news this well.

Before driving away, he punched in her telephone number and waited for her answer.

"Hello, Mary Jo? This is Kyle Avery, we met last week at the Dunbars' house? I'm doing family tree research for Joan."

"Oh, yes, hello, Kyle. How are you?" Kyle's unexpected phone call puzzled Mary Jo and she shook her head to concentrate on the conversation.

"I'm fine, back down in the area to share some research with Joan. While I was fact-finding for her, I came across some information that might be of interest to you. Can we meet somewhere, and I'll explain?"

"What is it in reference to?"

"I'd rather tell you in person. Is there some place we can meet privately? There are a lot of facts to clarify."

"Well, sure. Where are you?"

"I'll be downtown at the Sea Siren's B and B."

"You're not far from us. Do you know where Terry's law office is? I'm sure we can use her conference room."

"That will be great. I'll be there in twenty minutes."

"All right. I'll see you there." She hung up the phone in bewilderment.

Now what?

* * *

Upstairs in Stephanie's apartment, Terry gave the all clear for Mary Jo to use the conference room in the law office. She was as intrigued by the mysterious phone call as her friend and offered to stay with her, but Mary Jo declined, adding, "Let me find out what this is all about first."

"Maybe you had a rich ancestor who left you a fortune," Stephanie chimed in. Having recently started her own ancestry research, she had already discovered the many strange twists and turns the search could bring.

"I doubt that," Mary Jo said with a laugh. Then she sobered. "I had a surprise visitor yesterday." And although she had planned to keep the incident to herself, she relayed the brief sighting she had.

"Nicole's sister?" Stephanie frowned, struggling as something tugged at her memory. "I know Nicole's married name was Lebeque, but I don't think her maiden name was Jofess, like Tanner said." She grabbed one of her notebooks and began flipping pages.

"Here it is!" Stephanie cried out triumphantly. "In the translation of Clothiste's letter, the one I found during the hurricane, it mentions—and I quote—'Marie Josephé, I suspect, would rather be fighting battles than washing the clothes or cooking, but I believe if she could have her way on the battlefront, the war would be won the next day!'" She shook the notebook. "Marie Josephé's description fits you to a T, Mary Jo. And Tanner could logically have mispronounced her name. He always called Nicole 'Nickel.' And as crazy as all this sounds, I didn't start seeing Nicole until I was with Tanner."

"Well, I don't have time for this woo-woo shit." Mary Jo rolled her eyes toward the ceiling. "I should never have told you. Now I'm going to clean up before I meet Kyle," She headed for the bathroom, paused and turned around. "Steph, if you don't mind company one more night, can I just hang here and I'll get out of your hair tomorrow?"

"Of course! With all that's been going on, I'm glad for the company."

"Thanks." Mary Jo slipped into the bathroom and wearily shut the door behind her, leaning against it with her eyes closed. She was glad to be with her friends. She didn't know what news Kyle had in store for her, but she was pretty sure she would not want to be home alone tonight.

Back in the living room, Stephanie studied her ancestry charts, running her fingers line by line. Something was nagging at the back of her mind; she just couldn't put her finger on it yet.

* * *

Nothing like nightfall to bring out the ghost hunters. Mary Jo glanced at the crowd as she walked down the stairway and into the law office through the back door. A group of spectators, slightly larger than previous nights, gathered on the sidewalks nearby. Mesh fencing and mounds of bricks and macadam displaced by the backhoe added some semblance of a barricade, along with prominently placed "No Trespassing" signs. There was nothing to physically prevent anyone from entering the yard, but the signs and fencing created an effective psychological barrier—at least in her opinion.

Kyle arrived a few moments later. They shook hands formally, and she locked the door behind them.

"Are you settled in at the Sea Siren's Porch? That is a cute place, isn't it?"

"I only had a moment to look around, just long enough to get checked in and come here. I like it better than a hotel, though. I was surprised to see so many people milling about when I got here."

"That crowd out there seems to get larger each night since those old bones were found," Mary Jo remarked as she brought two bottles of water to the table.

"So I hear. Have the police told you anything?"

"No, not yet. We should hear something soon. I think once they established that the bones were very old, it was not such a priority, and it may take longer to reach a conclusion. Do you want coffee or anything? I can fix something."

"No thanks. The water is fine. I just need to set up some

charts and spread out these documents." He pulled papers from his briefcase. "I'm sorry if I sounded mysterious on the phone. It's just easier to explain genealogy with visual aids. It helps prevent system overload when it comes to identifying who is a maternal or a paternal great-great grandparent or who is one's second cousin twice removed."

Mary Jo held up one hand. "I don't understand any of it, but I am curious about what you have found that has to do with me."

"Well, as you know, Joan Dunbar asked me to research her family tree. Her maiden name was Wyatt. It so happens that an ancestor of mine is related to her family by marriage, not by blood. This third great-grandmother helped Emily, Stephanie's third great-grandmother, trace her roots all the way back to a French soldier who fought during the American Revolution. There may also be a connection to Joan's Wyatt side."

Mary Jo nodded. She knew this much already.

"Well, anyway, you may know that I contacted Stephanie when she put her family tree online. A program is set up to provide automatic alerts whenever there is a possible link to someone in another person's tree. You just have to check out the facts, which may or may not lead to new information."

"Okay." She still wondered what this had to do with her.

"I came across Stephanie's tree and noticed she was looking for someone I already had in my files, so I contacted her. When enough of the clues matched up, they lined up with the branch of her family tree that dates back to Nicole and her parents Clothiste and Étienne."

"Okay," she repeated.

"Once we made that connection, Stephanie and I began researching to determine her link to a particular Wyatt tree. Joan gave Stephanie a box of old family letters to look through, and she found references to her Nicole."

He shuffled until he had a family tree chart in front of him.

"I won't go into all the details now, but we know Stephanie's Thomas Wyatt had brothers named Frank and Arthur. I'm not related to Arthur, but to his second wife. Now,

Thomas and Frank's wives were cousins." He showed Mary Jo a grid on the chart. "This level is the generation of Thomas and Emily, Stephanie's ancestors, and beside them Frank and Celestine, who was Emily's cousin." She nodded, and he drew a line to a third name to the left side of the chart: *Louisa*.

"I know this is a lot of information, but bear with me as I spell it out. It helps me stay straight." He kept his right forefinger on the name of Louisa while he slid his left along other names. "There was a cousin to Frank and Thomas named Edward Wyatt. Interestingly enough, he married Louisa, who was also a cousin of Emily and Celestine."

Mary Jo tracked her finger along the same path as Kyle, and shrugged. "Nothing sounds familiar."

Kyle continued. "As I said, the cousin's name was Louisa, and I believe she is also a descendant of Clothiste and Étienne, the eighteenth century couple, but I don't know how yet. Edward and Louisa both lived in New Hampshire, and it seems they married against her father's wishes. Apparently her family wrote them off. They came to Virginia about eighteen seventy and Celestine and Frank helped them settle nearby, but after that their trail seemed to vanish. Are you still with me?"

"Yes, but I don't see how it relates to me." As if in a subconscious attempt to delay Kyle's response, she fumbled with the cap of her water bottle.

"I'm getting there, but I wanted to explain all of this first. You see, it's always trickier to track down the women in families because of their married names. Louisa and Edward had a daughter Edith, who married and had a daughter Anna Linda. Anna Linda, rather late in life, also had a daughter, whom she named Anna. This second Anna gave her son up for adoption in nineteen sixty-six. Her husband was killed in Vietnam, she was without money, estranged from her family, and she didn't feel she could take care of a child alone."

Kyle rummaged in the loose documents, brought out a copy of an email, and slid it toward Mary Jo. "Anna's son has been trying to find his birth family since he found his adoption papers a while back, which provided him with her basic information. Then he found her parents' names on this online tree I'd created for the Dunbars. I made contact with his birth mother, and she's given me permission to tell you this. You know this Anna by a different name, a nickname she was given to differentiate her from her mother."

Mary Jo glanced at the charts again as Kyle took a sip of water before continuing. Nothing stood out as pertinent information.

"Mary Jo, you know her as Hannah Jensen."

"Our Hannah?" Mary Jo sat upright, totally unprepared for this news. "I know she is a distant cousin of Joan's or something, but I never even knew she had a child."

"No one did. She was barely seventeen when she married Billy Jensen, just before he got drafted into the Army. He went through basic training, and then his unit went to Vietnam. He was only nineteen and was killed a month after his unit arrived in Da Nang. Hannah was pregnant by then. She never knew if Billy even got her letter telling him."

He stopped and sipped some more water, giving Mary Jo the chance to absorb what he'd told her so far.

"Hannah quit school to marry, had no job skills, and no real way to care for her baby. It never occurred to her to check with the Army to see if she or the baby would be eligible for benefits. She was too young, and similar to the history of some of her own ancestors, estranged from her family, so she had no one to turn to. She had the baby alone and gave him up for adoption."

"Wow. What a story."

"So, after she was satisfied it was her son who'd located her, she called him, and they talked for quite a while. They plan to meet soon. She'd named him William Jensen Junior, but his name now is Wayne Eugene Teller. He retired from the Navy and lives in San Diego." Kyle stood up and stretched, then sat back down, and dug through his papers for another letter.

"Wayne grew up in Portsmouth, and one summer met a girl who was visiting from Richmond. She was supposed to spend the school year with an aunt due to conflict at home. She and

Wayne had a serious summer fling, but her parents forced her to return home in October. He promised to write to her right away. He wrote, but she never answered. Then his family moved to San Diego where he's lived ever since."

"This sounds like something from a *Lifetime Network* movie or something." Mary Jo spoke lightly but a slow burn was seeping into her stomach. Kyle handed her a paper.

"Read this, please," he said softly. "Wayne sent me this with the documents for Hannah."

She looked at date of the typed letter. It was a month old.

Dear Wayne,

I am sorry this letter comes to you so unexpectedly and so late in life. I just found you on the Internet and decided to write to you. I can't even ask how you are. There are too many years between us now. But I have something to tell you.

That summer after we met I waited for your letters. I had given you my address, but never thought to get yours. And Lord knows, we didn't have the Internet to search for people back then like we do now.

I learned a few months ago that my own mother intercepted your letters so many years ago, and kept them hidden from me. She destroyed them! For years I was afraid you had forgotten about me because you thought I was a loose girl who slept around. My parents sure let me know that's what their opinion of me was. I ran away from home and tried to find you, but by then your family had moved away to the West Coast.

You were my first and—as it turns out all these years later—only lover.

I will come right out and tell you why I am writing now.

I was pregnant. You were gone. I stayed in Portsmouth, found a minimum-wage job and had my baby daughter alone.

I've never been a very good mother. I never abused her, but I didn't take good enough care of her either. I didn't know how, really, but she was always so smart, so independent, it was easy to let her care for herself.

When Mary Jo's hands began to shake, Kyle knew exactly which part she was reading.

I named her Mary Jo.

I worked the evening shift for years. Sometimes I stopped by a friend's house on the way home, just for adult company. I did this again one winter evening, thinking Mary Jo was safe and asleep at home. Then an ice storm hit, and it was so treacherous, I stayed at my friend's. I figured I would go home at the first sign of daylight. But during the night, a fire broke out in the apartment. Everyone got out safely, but because I wasn't there, Child Services was called.

They were going to put our daughter in foster care, but she created such a disturbance, they contacted her friend's parents. She often stayed overnight with the family, and they treated her well. They agreed to take her for the night and then applied to become her permanent foster parents. She wanted that, and to be truthful, after twelve years, I couldn't do it anymore.

I was diagnosed with lymphoma just before the fire. I never told her. I've not had much contact with her since she left. I didn't do her justice growing up, why should I mess up her life any more than I already have? She grew into a fine young woman, no thanks to me, and is in the Army now, in Afghanistan. I don't even have her address.

I was in remission for years but the cancer is back, and I may have a year to live. I beat the odds the first time and went years longer than the five-year estimate. Who knows, I may beat this again.

I hope this letter reaches you and does not cause you any distress in your personal life.

I will always treasure our summer together, and I try not to think about what might have been if my mother had given me your letters.

My phone number is here. Call me if you want.

Patricia

She looked up, the paper still quivering in her hands, tears threatening to brim over. "Wayne Teller, who is really William Jensen Junior, is my father? She would never tell me who he was. She just said they couldn't be together when I was born. He's not even listed on my birth certificate."

Kyle sat beside her and took her hand. "I have thrown a lot at you and Hannah today."

Mary Jo's eyes widened. "Kyle—is she—is Hannah really

my grandmother? All these years we've been practically living under the same roof, and I didn't even know she's my grandmother? She taught me to bake my pastries! Does she know about this now?"

"Yes. That's why I went to her first. I figured it was all going to come out with this ancestry business sooner or later, but it was up to her to decide what to do with her news. She wants everyone to know, and she wants you to call her as soon as you can."

"And my-my father? Does he want to get in touch? And my mother? I have to find her, Kyle. I haven't spoken to her in years. I…oh my God, Kyle, I've had so much thrown at me this week, I'm in shock. I…" Mary Jo threw her head onto her arms and for the first time in years, began to cry uncontrollably.

"Can I call Stephanie or Terry for you?" He patted her shoulder, unsure what to do.

"No, no. Not yet." Her reply muffled against her arms but he understood what she said. He just sat there with one hand on her racking shoulder. She raised her hand and covered his, holding tightly.

She had a lot of tears to shed.

* * *

After gaining her composure, Mary Jo asked Kyle to stay with her while she completed three brief phone calls.

First she called Hannah, her froggy-throated voice croaking through her own tears as she cried along with her new-found granddaughter. Mary Jo let her know she was fine, loved her, but needed to make some other phone calls.

"Can I tell Stephanie and Terry tonight, Hannah— Grandma? I'm staying with them, and I think I need to talk."

"Go ahead, honey," Hannah answered, blowing her nose. "We'll talk in person tomorrow."

Mary Jo called Wayne Eugene Teller next, but got an answering machine. She wasn't sure what to say so merely left the message that she was Patricia Cooper's daughter and for him to return the call at his convenience.

Finally, she called the phone number Patricia had sent in the letter to Wayne. Her heart skipped a beat as she recognized her mother's voice answering with a cautious "Hello?"

Through thick tears and a tight throat, Mary Jo gained her strength and said, "Mama? Mama? It's me—Mary Jo. I love you, Mama." Her mother cried and apologized; Mary Jo cried and accepted. She promised her mother she would come see her the next day, and they hung up.

She rubbed her temples and sighed.

"Thank you for standing by me while I made those calls, Kyle. This is the most unbelievable day ever," she said. "I've always had a special fondness for Hannah. I know she appears cranky and gruff when you first meet her, but she was so good to me when I used to come over to see Terry, and then when I came there to live. How did she seem to be doing with your news?"

"She is doing very well, considering. She did have some idea in advance because I had to verify facts after her son contacted me, to see if they were indeed mother and son. She took one drag off her cigarette and then didn't smoke for another two hours."

"Really? I've never known her to go longer than it takes her to get through a meal. All of this is so amazing."

"I've heard of similar cases, believe it or not. There was a brother and sister somewhere out Midwest. I think she was a store greeter, and he shopped there all the time. Over the years they came to recognize each other on sight and even exchanged casual chit-chat a couple of times. Then one day he's doing ancestry research, and it leads to her."

"Thank you once again, Kyle."

"Not a problem, Mary Jo. Are you going to be all right? Can I give you a ride anywhere?"

"No, thanks, I'm staying with Stephanie so I only have to go upstairs to the apartment." She helped Kyle gather his papers. They straightened the chairs around the table, and she secured the door behind her as they stepped onto the small back porch.

Kyle offered his hand but in a very uncharacteristic move, Mary Jo flung her arms around his shoulders and hugged tight. She clung to him for a moment, said thanks again, and headed for the stairs to Stephanie's apartment, oblivious to the crowd gathered at the parking lot's entrance.

In a few short sentences, some significant voids in Mary Jo Cooper's life had just been filled. As she trudged up the steps, she realized she still had two more significant problems to resolve before her life could turn a corner.

She had to face her late fiancé's mother to settle matters in court.

She had to face Chase Hallmark to settle matters of the heart.

* * *

A curious crowd, larger than the night before, milled around outside the mesh fence, talking and taking pictures. Vehicles drove down the street slowly, passengers hanging out of the windows as they snapped pictures with cell phones and cameras.

Two girls in one of the cars called out they could see faces in the upstairs window of the Bed and Breakfast. A boy in the crowd shouted he saw lights flashing there. The crowd murmured and pointed. Every now and then, a catcall or whistle pierced the night. When occupants of another car tossed a couple of bottles into the street and the glass shattered, a nearby resident called the police. Two officers in a patrol car stopped, urging people to move on.

Chase Hallmark sat in his truck parked on a side street, where he had a good view of the three properties. It bothered him that he had not been able to prevent the vandalism the previous night. He remembered the kids he had seen with the laser and wondered if they were behind it. Would they try something else?

He knew Stephanie's fiancé, Gage, was working the eight p.m. to eight a.m. shift at the fire station, but Mary Jo and Terry were staying with her again, so she was not alone.

The crowd of onlookers grew larger after the patrol car disappeared. Chase grabbed the door handle, ready to see if Mary Jo would come out and talk with him for a while. Maybe they would never get back what they once had together, but perhaps they could get their past behind them and be able to be in the same room without shooting eye daggers at each other. He needed to square things with her once and for all.

If he asked in front of their friends, the stubborn woman might not take his head—or any other part of his anatomy—off.

Then he caught sight of Mary Jo and that Indiana Jones-looking guy Kyle coming out of the back door of the law office. Mary Jo flung her arms around Indie and then one of the onlookers stepped into the street to take a picture, blocking his view. He craned to peer past the photographer; Mary Jo was already heading up the steps to the apartment. Indiana Jones was nowhere in sight.

Chase was royally pissed that he couldn't drive yet. Two vehicles full of people had stopped in the middle of the street and hemmed him in. The occupants got out and mingled with the gawking crowd. He checked his watch. It was after ten, and the crowds only seemed to get larger.

What the hell do these dumbasses possibly think they're gonna see?

He was about to get out of his truck and confront the drivers when the spotlight of a police cruiser shined in and around the unoccupied vehicles blocking the road. The patrol car paused behind the second vehicle, and the driver tooted two light honks on the horn. The two absentee drivers immediately jumped in their cars and drove away. A few people broke from the cluster and started to walk toward the intersection.

Chase shook his head and jammed his truck into drive. He would come back later and check the property. He had a gut feeling something was going to happen.

He looked one more time at the darkened building.

That embrace haunted him more than any ghost ever could.

* * *

Stephanie and Terry were waiting for Mary Jo when she finally reached the door of the apartment, their faces anxious.

"What happened? What did Kyle want to tell you?" Terry pounced first. Friends for over twenty years and as close as sisters, Mary Jo didn't mind. She'd expected it.

"Let her get in the door, will you!" Stephanie admonished in exasperation. Although the newest member of the trio, she was as comfortable with the other two as if they had always known each other.

Terry playfully waved her hand at Stephanie in the way she would swat an annoying fly and grabbed Mary Jo by the arm. "Mom called me and told me the news Hannah got from Kyle about finding her son. But she wouldn't say whether she had any knowledge of what Kyle told you."

Mary Jo sighed and scrubbed her hands over her face. Normally she didn't like to talk about herself, preferring to stay in the background and let other people talk. But with the latest news just dropped on her, and the pain and regret she detected in the voices of the two people she talked with tonight, she could not hold this in. She had to make a number of decisions in her personal life—including a face-to-face meeting with Chase Hallmark.

"Let me change. Then—I have a lot to tell you."

* * *

Three boys stood under the dim streetlight as they eyed the house in the middle and formed their plan. Real skeletons and rumors of ghosts and haunted houses were just the right combination to incite adolescent males to mischief.

Early signs of Halloween already stimulated their curiosity. The temporary holiday store had just opened, packed to overflowing with ghoulish costumes and gory displays. Colorfully gruesome signs advertising haunted forests and pumpkin patches popped up around the city. Graffiti full of pentagrams and cult symbols only increased their interest in the reportedly haunted house.

The trio huddled like football players around a game ball, arms across shoulders and heads together. One held his hand to the center, and the other two slapped their hands on top. They agreed they would meet back in this spot at midnight and go into the haunted house. They broke their hands apart and let out a whoop.

They ain't afraid of no ghosts!

CHAPTER EIGHT

Mary Jo had a short dream this time. Only the childhood Easter egg hunt repeated itself in her subconscious. It was short and distinct, but different from the previous one.

In this version, the rain had already scattered the other children, but she remained behind, digging with her hands through the mire. Suddenly a girl in colonial clothes appeared, dangling a basket of Easter eggs from the crook of her arm. As Mary Jo stared, the rain stopped. The Easter eggs turned into sparkling red hearts that the ghost sprinkled like fairy dust.

Resembling a ruby snowfall, the twinkling shapes fluttered downward and disappeared into the earth, which was no longer mud but dry and freshly turned. Mary Jo held her hands out, and some of the falling hearts passed through her fingers before fading away.

"You have to dig deep for your heart, Mary Jo. Dig deep." The apparition spoke aloud in a voice that tinkled like bells and faded away.

Mary Jo awoke with a start. She half-expected to see the ghost in the room, but she was swathed in darkness, with only the small green light shining from the clock face.

12:30. The glaring green numbers seemed to mock her.

She turned over and tried to go back to sleep, but the flurry of little red shapes came to mind. She sat up and turned on the light, brushing her hands over her face.

The dream actually made sense to her. That morning, she had finally told Terry and Stephanie about the appearance of the colonial ghost.

Kyle had told her heartbreaking stories that evening.

Through an emotional phone call, she took the first step to making amends with her mother, digging deep within herself to make the move.

How ironic my thoughts seem to parallel what the ghost said, to dig deep to find my heart.

She shook her head to clear the thoughts. "Geez, you're thinking about the ghost as if it were a real live person delivering a message," she grumbled out loud. She stood abruptly and rummaged through her backpack, withdrawing a slim gold-plated cigarette case containing half a dozen Winstons. She had quit smoking years ago, but during her deployment to Afghanistan she had taken it up again, although only smoking one or two a day. She'd nearly kicked the habit a second time, ignoring those last six remaining in the box.

She drew one and snapped the container shut with an abrupt flick of her wrist. Her thumb rubbed over the simple initials carved on the well-worn front.

MJC.

Chase had given her the case on her eighteenth birthday, a month before her graduation, when they were too young to care about the harmful effects of tobacco. They had often shared a smuggled cigarette, careful to avoid the non-smoking Mr. and Mrs. Dunbar. Hannah had caught them several times, lecturing them about the negative impact while lighting up one of her own. When they pointed out the obvious, her snarky reply was always, "Do as I say, not as I do."

Mary Jo grabbed her old red Bic lighter and the gold case from the stand, and then fumbled in the dark for her Ugg boots and a sweatshirt. She slipped out of the bedroom, feeling her way down the hall so as not to disturb her friends. With eyes accustomed to the dark, she could make out Terry's lumpy form on the couch, soft snores gurgling from under the covers. Resisting the urge to laugh out loud, she considered going back for her cell phone to record the sleep sounds Terry refused to admit occurred.

She couldn't do that to her old friend though and instead groped for the door lock and flicked it open, the sound resonating like a gunshot in the silence. She stopped in her tracks, hand frozen to the doorknob. Terry stirred and rolled under the covers but did not wake.

How many times did I sneak out like this to meet Chase?

For a moment Mary Jo felt like a teenager again, the guilty adult reaction mixing with the exuberance of youth as she eased the door open and slid outside into the crisp autumn air.

She placed her booted toe against the bottom of the door to control its movement. It closed silently as she hoped, with an almost imperceptible click assuring the lock was in place.

Fall had definitely arrived; this was by far the coolest evening yet. She pulled her sweatshirt tighter around her neck and sat on the top step, tucking the cigarette in the corner of her mouth without lighting it. It was one thing to have resumed the nasty habit in Kabul. It was an entirely different thing to resort to it now that she was safely on home turf again.

So she would sit in the cool night air for a few minutes and hope that the peaceful moment would enable her to go back to sleep.

Her mind didn't register the sounds right away. Intermittent thuds, a muffled voice or two, scraping sounds; all drifted across the parking lot, so hushed she could barely discern them.

The thuds became louder, and boys' laughter echoed nearby. It dawned on her then that the sounds were coming from the house next door. She shot to her feet with the agility of a gymnast and dashed down the steps. Muffled high-pitched shouts drifted across the yard, followed by a resounding crack of wood as two dark figures bolted from the back of the B and B, sprinting to the rear of the parking lot, dodging machinery and dirt piles like athletes on an obstacle course.

"Hey!" she shouted, skipping the last three steps as she jumped to the ground and dashed in the same direction. She made it to the sidewalk to try to head them off but could see neither figure. She was sure the runners had trudged right through the mesh fencing to escape.

Shouting emanated from the rear of the house, and she headed back in that direction, pushing past the splintered back door and into the kitchen. Blinking from the bright illumination of overhead lights, she found Chase in the doorway between the kitchen and dining room, holding a struggling young teenager by the collar of his shirt. The gangling youth swung at air and tried to kick, shouting, "Let me go!" but he was no match for the strong adult construction worker.

"What happened here?" Mary Jo asked. Chase did not have to answer as her widening eyes took in what had indeed happened. Her gaze glanced over vulgar words spray-painted across doors. Behind Chase she could see that several of the dozen cans of paint that had once been stored in the corner had been thrown against walls. Two cans had broken open, spilling contents across the hardwood floors. Others had remained intact, and the culprits used them effectively as projectiles to puncture sheetrock panels.

"I caught the little bastards in the act, but two of them got away." Chase tightened his hold on the squirming teen. "What's your name, boy?" he demanded. "And who are your pals?"

"I ain't telling you nothin'," the boy snarled.

"Call nine-one-one, Mary Jo."

"I don't have my phone with me."

Chase reached in the side pocket of his cargo pants and slid out his own cell, tossing it to Mary Jo. She caught it deftly and started to punch in the three numbers for police response.

All of the wind suddenly seemed to seep out of the youthful offender, and his legs buckled. He resembled a scrawny scarecrow dangling from Chase's outstretched arm, toes barely touching the ground. His face was pale now, eyes bulging in fear.

"Please don't call the cops, lady. I'm already in trouble. My dad will kill me."

"Seems you should have thought of that before you went on this little spree." Chase growled the words, turning the boy around and forcing him to make eye contact.

"Man, I know, I know. I'm sorry. Please don't call the cops."

"You best spill your guts, boy," Chase said coldly. "Who are you, and who were your friends?" He loosened his grip enough to drop the boy to a flat-footed stance; his other hand firmly clamped the boy's upper arm.

"I-I can't tell, mister."

Chase had a flashback to his teenage years, when he, Gage and a so-called friend had gone on a vandalism spree. He and Gage had confessed when the police showed up, but refused to rat out their accomplice.

His stepfather was thankfully out of town, but his mother had come to the police station with Mr. Dunbar. Back at the Dunbars' house, the boys had come clean about everything except their friend's involvement.

Charles Dunbar spoke with the victims, who accepted his plan for restitution. It kept the boys out of court and satisfied the neighbors, who were less than pleased that the lead culprit—Jeffrey, the neighborhood mischief-maker—was going to get away with the crimes.

Chase and Gage had spent the summer repairing damage and earning the money to repay for the broken windows and slashed tires. Years passed, and they were well into adulthood before they finally revealed the extent of involvement of the third collaborator.

"You have three seconds to spit out your name, kid, or we're calling the cops." Mary Jo found her voice, shaking with rage as she spoke. She took a step toward the boy as she counted. "One—two…" Her nearly six-foot frame cast a shadow on the boy as she moved closer.

"It's Kevin—Kevin Clarkson, lady."

"Clarkson? Are you Jeffrey Clarkson's son?" she demanded.

The boy nodded. Mary Jo and Chase made eye contact. And life came full circle as Jeffrey Clarkson's son sat at their feet.

"Yes, ma'am. He's my dad."

"The nut doesn't fall far from the family tree, does it?" Mary Jo muttered grimly.

"Guess not. Sit." Chase commanded sharply, and the boy slid down the door frame into a boneless slump on the floor.

"What's his number?" Chase held out his hand, and Mary Jo returned the phone.

Kevin rattled off the number. He glanced at the two giants standing guard over him, then toward the door. Any chance for escape was effectively blocked, he realized. Even the woman looked like she could easily kick his ass. Those soft boot things she wore looked like they belonged on Sasquatch—an observation he wisely kept to himself.

Ten minutes later Jeffrey Clarkson arrived at the Bed and Breakfast. He stepped inside and surveyed the damage his son had helped generate.

He shook Chase's hand and hers. It had been years since Mary Jo had seen him.

"Kevin was supposed to be spending the night with a friend because they're out of school tomorrow. Where are Mark and Tommy?" Jeffrey asked his son, who kept his gaze down toward his feet.

"He's says he's not telling," Mary Jo interjected.

"What the hell is the matter with you, Kevin?" Jeffrey knelt down beside his son. "You just got charged with petit larceny and have to go to court on that."

"We only came down to see if there were any ghosts here." Kevin shook his head and rubbed his eyes to stave off tears. Reality was setting in. "We heard about the skeletons and me and Mark and…" He stopped as he realized his slip-up confirmed one of the partners in crime.

"Me and the guys heard the house was haunted and thought it would be cool to check it out. Once we got inside, we…" He buried his head in his arms.

"You guys had the lasers and were out last night too, weren't you? Did you spray the graffiti on the houses?" Chase asked.

"Yes, sir."

"I had a feeling something else was going to happen in here tonight," Chase said in an aside to Mary Jo. "I saw these guys the night before out with their lasers. When we had the graffiti this morning, I figured they might try some more mischief."

"I saw the news coverage of the bones and onlookers around the site and wondered when some wise guys would do something stupid. I just didn't expect my kid to be one of them." Jeffrey scrubbed his hands over his face. "Look, Chase, I'm a single dad now. I'm not going to make the same mistake my dad did when we pulled our stunt years ago. I got off scot-free, and I turned out like shit. I want better for my kid, and I'm here to apologize for him," he said humbly, "and do whatever it takes to make it right. Something I failed to do myself when we were young."

"Let's don't worry about the past now, Jeffrey."

"If you want to call the police, that'll be fine with me. I know who else was involved, and I'm sure their parents will want to know." At his father's words Kevin broke into quiet sobs, his face still in the crook of his arm.

"It's not up to me, Jeffrey. It's up to Mary Jo."

"Well, Terry is part-owner too," Mary Jo said slowly, "and she's a lawyer, so she may just want to call the cops."

"I understand."

"But…" Mary Jo raised a finger and continued. "I can tell you that the solution Mr. Dunbar arranged for Chase and Gage worked wonders on keeping them straight. I might consider a similar agreement."

She knelt beside the boy. "Here's the deal, Kevin. It's late now, and I want to go back to sleep. We're going to talk to your pals and their parents later this morning. We'll let them know you didn't tell, but we identified them through other sources. If the parents go along with the plan, the three of you will be working to pay for the damage you caused. Otherwise we're calling the police. Understand?"

"Yes ma'am." He squirmed under her glare.

"Thanks, Mary Jo." Jeffrey motioned for his son to stand up. "Just tell me when you want us to meet you. I'm working evenings at the shipyard, so I can be here anytime you say."

"Can you meet us here at nine, Jeffrey?"

"We'll be here."

"I'm just glad I caught them when I did," Chase said. "No telling how much more damage they would have done."

"But, Mister Chase," Kevin interrupted, "That wasn't what stopped us. We were already running out when you got here."

"What do you mean?"

"It was the ghosts, Mister Chase. They stopped us."

CHAPTER NINE

The adults stared.

"Ghosts, Mister Chase," Kevin repeated, squirming under their piercing looks. "Three girls, dressed in funny old clothes. We were throwing the paint around, using our flashlights to see, and then we went upstairs. All of a sudden the room turned blue, like when the television is on in the dark, you know?" He looked around at the faces of the three adults, who nodded but remained quiet. He swallowed hard and continued.

"They just appeared and scared the sh...crap out of us. We were falling all over ourselves trying to run down the stairs but they were right behind us. Then we heard the front door open. When Mister Chase turned on the living room light Mar...the other guys took off toward the back, busting out the door. He grabbed me by the shirt or I would have been gone too."

"Kevin, what kind of crock is that?" his father demanded, shaking him by one arm.

"Dad, I'm not kidding. The ghosts were standing right there! Like they just floated in the air or something." He extended his arm to point toward the top of the staircase, his hand shaking. His eyes were wide in his pale face.

Jeffrey leaned close to his son's face. "You boys been drinking?" he demanded and inhaled. Then he grabbed his son's chin and looked closely into his eyes. "Or doing drugs?"

"No, sir!"

"It's because of the ruckus over the old skeleton they dug up after the storm," Mary Jo interjected. "We've had gawkers and scavengers the past few days, and everyone thinks they see ghosts."

"Well, let me have a look at the rest of the damage Kevin and his buddies did before we leave." Jeffrey's jaw was tight. "I might just have some suggestions on what they can do to make it up." He nudged his son's foot with his own. "Lead the way and show me."

Kevin sheepishly swept his arm around the room. "We got in through the back. Mar...one of the guys pried the screen door loose, and we found the door unlocked underneath, and we could squeeze in without being seen."

"And exactly which artwork is yours?"

"Um...they started spray-painting in the kitchen. I came in here and threw one of the paint cans into the wall over there," Kevin pointed a nervous finger toward a gap in the new sheetrock, white paint splattered around the hole and the open can on the floor. "And I kicked one over there."

"Why, Kevin? Why?"

"I don't know, Dad. Just stupid."

"Yeah, well, you got that right, son. What else?"

"When I kicked that one over there, it opened and paint leaked out. So I kicked it again." A trail of white paint spattered in a semi-circle where the free-flowing paint spilled from the rolling can.

"That's pretty much all I did here. We carried paint upstairs. We were going to throw it from the top." He looked apprehensively toward the staircase, and his father pushed him forward.

"I'm scared, Dad," he whispered. "I don't want to go back up there."

"Tough shit. Up."

Kevin reluctantly dragged his feet as he climbed to the top of the stairs, eyes darting from side to side as if anticipating a return of the specters. At the top step he turned to face the three adults below him. "I was here, and the other guys were further ahead in the hallway. The girls just appeared. Dad, they were wearing those clothes like they wear in Colonial Williamsburg, you know what I mean?"

"Huh?"

Mary Jo spoke up, anxious to get things cleared up and moving. "Like the people who dress up for reenactments in the restored area?" Kevin nodded, and she turned her gaze to Jeffrey. "The history of this old house has always had ghost stories, supposedly back to colonial days. I'm sure the kids just heard some of them and imagined it."

"But Miss Mary Jo..." Kevin sputtered. "They were there. Then the room got real cold, like ice, and they went away, like that." He snapped his fingers with one hand, his eyes wide.

"And we didn't do that." He pointed to the small bedroom to the right of the hall.

Spray-painted across the door were the words, "Die French whore!"

"What the..." Jeffrey grabbed his son by the arm.

"Dad, we didn't do that. Honest! We didn't have time to do anything up here. Look, there are the paint cans right there. We were going to toss them on the walls up here, like we did below, and throw them downstairs." He pointed to the floor. Near his feet were three gallon cans of paint. Two were upright; the third tipped on its side, contents oozing onto the floor. Chase set the can upright.

"The guys shoved me to the side and ran down the steps. By then Mr. Chase was coming in the door, and he snagged me before I could get away."

"Look, this is ridiculous. I want the truth, Kevin," Jeffrey said, raising his voice. "What the hell possessed you to do any of this?" He stopped short and glanced at Chase, who met his gaze, unspoken acknowledgement passing between them. Mary Jo understood their expressions. *Didn't we do the same thing? Who knew what the hell possessed us back then?*

Mary Jo held up her hand. She was sure Kevin told the truth, at least as he saw it, but she was too tired to deal with it.

"Listen, all of you." When they looked her way, she said, "It's late. Let's just call it a night, and we'll meet in the daylight."

"Is there anything we can do now, Mary Jo?" Jeffrey's eyes held fatigue, defeat and worry.

"No, Jeffrey, really, as long as you're going to hold Kevin accountable, we can deal with it tomorrow."

"Trust me on that." He held out his hand and shook Mary Jo's, then Chase's.

"I'm sorry, ma'am," Kevin said as he offered his.

After seeing Kevin and his father out, Chase locked the back door. He didn't bother to replace the dangling screen door; it could wait until morning. He returned to the foyer and found Mary Jo on the last step of the staircase, her long legs drawn up to her chin, her forehead pressed against arms she rested on her knees.

"How much more can I take?" she muffled her words.

Then, Mary Jo Cooper, the stalwart warrior who never cried, reached the end of her limits and for the second time in twenty-four hours, sobs racked her body.

Chase didn't say a word, just dropped down beside her on the narrow staircase and slid his arm around her. She didn't move or push him away, just remained seated as her shoulders shuddered. He would hold her as long as she let him.

"I'm here, Coppertop," he said, calling her by the nickname he'd given her years ago. He rubbed her back, glad she didn't recoil from his touch. When he realized she was not wearing a bra under the sweatshirt, his stirring body betrayed him.

Get a grip, asshole, he berated silently as he raised his eyes skyward, *this isn't the time.* But he couldn't help himself as memories flooded back to a summer nearly a decade ago when he discovered the long lean body and creamy white flesh of an eager eighteen-year-old Mary Jo. He remembered enough to know he'd said the wrong thing back then, and it had cost them their friendship. She had threatened to claw his heart out with her bare fingers and shred it to pieces before she tossed it in the woods for animals to ravage.

Ten days later she enlisted in the US Army and headed to

boot camp.

Chase reverted to the present when Mary Jo suddenly raised her head and rested it on his arm.

"I don't know how much more I can take, Chase." Her eyes brimmed with new tears. "I'm losing money hand over fist in these projects. I never even had a chance to cook in my café. I lost Jay; I had a tough year in Afghanistan; Della's suing me; the hurricane; the damage; the news from Kyle; and now this." She scrubbed her hands over her face and took in a deep breath. She turned red-rimmed eyes toward him. "And you, Chase. I have to deal with you. I've let it go too long." She touched her temple to his. His touch had ignited her memory as well, dredging its way into her weary mind.

He gently traced his hand along her jaw and caressed her neck. She pressed her cheek against his palm and with a slight turn of her head brushed a kiss there. He took her chin in his hand and tilted it upward. Half of his brain told him this was the wrong time; the other half said act now or the chance would never come back. Their last time together—their only— was full of teenaged awkwardness. He didn't want a repeat, but he couldn't prevent his hand from sliding down her back.

She bolted to her feet like an uncoiling spring and folded her arms in front of her chest. Her warrior spirit had definitely returned.

"I've hated you ever since that night, Chase," she said, looking directly at him.

"Okay." He nodded, understanding her reference without explanation. A stab of ice pierced his heart. *Definitely no need to worry about repeating anything, good or bad.* Suddenly awkward and unsure, he stepped back, his tongue tied, his body tensed as he stopped all movement.

Mary Jo puffed out a breath which fluttered her bangs. "With all that has happened this week, some things I learned tonight, and some bad experiences in Afghanistan, it's time to make my life right so I can move on. We need to talk, but not tonight. I'm too tired. Let's just lock up and deal with this in the morning." She left the light on and stepped onto the porch,

Chase following. She checked the lock on the door, and ended with, "Maybe we can talk tomorrow after we deal with the kids and their parents?"

"Okay." *Now, that's intelligent dialogue.* He chastised himself as he shifted into a wide-legged stance, his arms folded in a mirror image of Mary Jo.

"Thank you for being here, Chase." Mary Jo put her hand on his forearm and brushed his cheek with a kiss. "I appreciate everything you are doing. Goodnight."

"Okay. Goodnight." *Thank God! I'm able to speak more than one word at a time.*

She took the steps two at a time and disappeared into the dark.

He looked toward the spot where she once stood, rubbing his palm over his chest to ease the ache there, then headed toward his truck. He'd always loved her—he'd just been too stupid to ever tell her. He wanted to call her back, talk more, get past that comment she made about hating him. Get her past the hate and see if there was anything salvageable between them to try again.

But he couldn't tell her that now. If he said the wrong thing at the wrong time, he had no doubt that Mary Jo would expand on her teenage promise to rip out his heart. Except now he feared it might be his balls she would shred with her bare hands and feed to the animals.

Not knowing how to handle the situation, he walked dejectedly to his truck.

He glanced in the direction of the vandalized building. Shaken by the destruction the boys had created, he thought back to his incident that could have ended with a stint in juvenile hall. He and Gage had joined their friend Jeffrey for a sleepover. In the early hours of the morning Jeffrey convinced them to prowl the neighborhood carrying baseball bats "for protection." They tipped a birdbath in one yard, bashed birdhouses and mailboxes in others. Jeffrey whipped out a pocketknife and slashed tires on a few vehicles. Next they thoroughly trashed a small store under renovation, spraying profanity and graffiti, throwing paint.

All for no reason other than juvenile vandalism.

The boys escaped detection and slipped back into the house, moods alternating between smugness and remorse. When the police showed up at Jeffrey's doorstop at the insistence of the victims, Gage and Chase owned up to their involvement. Jeffrey, supported by enabling parents, denied he was with them.

In an unspoken code of honor between miscreants, the other two boys would not implicate Jeffrey—even when they were under the stern tutelage of Charles Dunbar repairing damaged yard articles and missing out on the fun of an entire summer to repay their debt.

It never occurred to him that Charles Dunbar had missed out on that same summer as he rode herd on the boys.

Chase started his truck and drove wearily home.

By his calculation, he would be riding herd on three boys for weeks.

* * *

Meanwhile, Mary Jo headed straight to the apartment, her words to Chase echoing in her head. She dropped to the top step.

Through six years in the regular Army and four full-time in the Reserves, through passing time and sheer determination, she had willed that night and most thoughts of Chase Hallmark out of her mind, reducing it to a wisp of recollection she could easily banish when it tried to surface.

In little more than a week, every repressed memory had come back to her as if a sledgehammer had pounded its way through her heart. Ignoring the chill of the night air that coursed through her, every detail of that long-ago July evening played like a movie in her mind.

They had always been a good fit. Both stood nearly six-feet tall, strong and athletic. They each experienced tumultuous teenage years filled with dysfunction, sheltered under the wings of the Dunbar family while fiercely protected by Hannah.

The Dunbar kids considered Chase and Mary Jo as siblings, and included them in family events all through their teenage years. Mary Jo had watched Chase grow from a gawky teen stick figure into a powerful sinewy adult with nothing resembling sisterly thoughts going through her mind.

The first times they had sought each other alone, they pretended the reason was to smoke a few cigarettes. Then years of friendship and months of dating with heavy petting collided one night in a moment of teenage lust as she and Chase fumbled in the back of his Chevy Blazer, hidden in bushes near an old farm.

Under the glow of a full moon, they made love, at first awkward with innocence but then fueled by young passion. When finished, they lay together in an exhausted heap. Mary Jo stretched her long body the length of Chase's, head nestled on his chest, her fingers caressing his collarbone. He held her close, arms cocooning her, his right hand tracing slow circles on her upper arm.

"I love you, Chase," she whispered suddenly as the scent of cucumbers from a nearby garden wafted across the summer air.

"What did you say, Coppertop?" he said absent-mindedly. His hand stopped its circular motion, and he braced himself on one elbow, frowning in disbelief. His face distorted in a sneer, the only way he could think to put distance between him and her declaration. "What? Are you crazy? I-I…"

She'd been about to repeat her words when his expression in the moonlight chilled her very soul, and she shoved him away from her. Love did not reflect in his eyes, and in mortification, she scrambled for her clothes.

"You son of a bitch! Take me home."

"What did I do?"

"Nothing." She scrambled out of the back, pulled her tank top over her head and reached for her jeans. When she realized she had grabbed his first, she balled them up and tossed them as far as she could out the back of the Blazer. She found hers and put them on, stuffing her bra and panties in the pockets.

"What are you doing?" Chase rolled out of the back of the Blazer, striking his head on the hatch as he stood up. He didn't bother to look for his jeans, standing naked in the warm breeze as he grabbed Mary Jo by the arm.

"Let go of me," she demanded and shook free, diving into the back of the vehicle and tossing anything she came across as she searched for her shoes. She winged a tennis shoe that narrowly missed his head.

Then she backed out and wheeled on him. "I didn't just let you screw my brains out, you stupid asshole," she shouted. "I've been in love with you my whole life, and you just ruined it with a few words. 'What? You're crazy!'" She mimicked his tone of incredulity, shaking her head and sneering. "Crazy? I'll show you crazy." She poked her fingernail in his bare chest, feeling the satisfying indention into his skin as she pecked several times. "Now you take me back home this minute, or I'll claw your heart out with my bare fingers and shred it to pieces before I toss it in the woods for the animals to chew up." She turned back to the frustrating search for her belongings scattered in a moment of passion she already deeply regretted.

"Look, I'm sorry I reacted that way. I didn't know…I didn't expect…" he sputtered, touching her shoulder.

She rounded on her heel and faced him, poking her finger at his nose. "Don't you dare touch me! I will never forget that look on your face, Chase Hallmark, and I will never forgive you." She pushed him away, picked up scattered shoes and purse, and marched to the front of the truck. Silent during the ride home, she was out of the vehicle before he fully stopped in front of the Dunbar house.

The next morning, she visited an Army recruiter. Her timing was perfect. In ten days she enlisted and reported to basic training at Fort Leonard Wood in Missouri.

When she made visits home while on leave, usually at holidays, she managed to avoid Chase as much as possible. For the Dunbar family's sake, they remained polite on the rare occasions their paths crossed.

She met Jay a few years later, and life was good. She joined the reserves when her enlistment ended, and took night courses to prepare for her dream of opening the café and the Bed and Breakfast.

Then Jay died too young, before they had any real life together. There was barely time to grieve before her unit was unexpectedly activated and deployed to the Middle East earlier than anticipated.

And now, because of a promise she made to a dying soldier in Afghanistan a few months ago, she would have to settle her heart with Chase.

She rose and slipped into the house, the steady rhythm of Terry's snores ensuring that the latter's sleep was still uninterrupted. In the borrowed bedroom, Mary Jo flopped on the bed, exhausted. One thought clouded her mind as she sank into welcoming sleep.

I've hated you since that night, Chase, but I never stopped loving you.

In the house next door, a dark cold mist in the attic tried to gather strength and slide across the floor, but this time a tiny beam of light danced across the walls.

The light brightened, and the mist faded away.

CHAPTER TEN

Marie Josephé
On the way to Yorktown, Virginia 1781

Soft crying woke Marie Josephé, and she stirred, her body stiff from the uncomfortable way she had curled on the hard floorboards. Nicole sat upright beside her, hand patting the older girl's dress as she searched in the dark. Marie Josephé placed a finger over the younger girl's lips and gathered her close. "You must hush, little sister. We know not what is happening outside."

"I want Mama," the child whimpered.

"You must be brave, Nicole, as Papa and Louis and Mama taught us to be. Can you remember?"

"I want to be brave, but I want mama. And I am hungry." Nicole buried her face in the older girl's shoulder.

"I know, little sister, I know." The horses whinnied outside, and the crunching sound of footsteps moved closer to the back of the wagon.

Theresé stirred and sat up. "What is it?" she whispered.

"I know not. Nicole stirred and woke me. Will you look outside?"

Theresé crawled quietly toward the back of the wagon and thrust the heavy canvas aside. A sliver of light from a lantern shined through the opening, and male voices murmured. The moon was obscured by clouds, and the pungent smell of tidal mud reached their nostrils.

"Papa!" Theresé whispered hoarsely. She scrambled over the back as *the canvas was ripped from the opening. Étienne de la Roche drew his oldest daughter into an embrace.*

Marie Josephé and Nicole scuttled around the boxes to the wooden gate at the back.

"Papa!" Marie Josephé echoed her older sister as she too flung her arms around his neck. Nicole held back, her small hands gripping the back of the wagon.

"Captain, we must unload. We will lose the high tide." The driver came to the rear and unlatched metal hooks to remove the wagon's backboard.

"We must hurry, girls, we have no time to spare here. Come, ma petite.*" Étienne reached his outstretched hands and lifted the child, who flailed wildly.*

"NO! I want Mama. Where is Mama?" Nicole sobbed and ended her resistance as she slumped into an exhausted heap in her father's arms.

"Papa." Theresé laid a hand on her father's arm while she stroked Nicole's head. "Papa, Mama is not with us. She was hurt and had to remain with Grandfather."

"Where is your mother? What has happened?" Étienne turned to the two older girls, his stricken face illuminated by the scant lantern light. Never before in their lives had either girl witnessed the anguished look that crossed their father's usually stalwart features.

"Captain, sir, we must get to the ferry." The driver lifted long slender boxes from underneath the wagon's floorboards.

Étienne whistled two short shrills through his teeth. A light flickered briefly and disappeared. "Grab my cloak and follow me, girls."

Clinging to one edge of her father's cloak as they made their way in the direction of the light, Marie Josephé started to speak but her breath hitched raggedly, and the words would not come out. Mud sucked one slipper from her foot, but she trudged on until they reached a small boat waiting on the water's edge. Unmindful of the water reaching her knees, she scurried over the side, and her father placed the whimpering Nicole in her arms.

"Take them to the ship and return immediately," Étienne ordered a man with oars at the ready. He shoved the boat on its way and turned to Theresé. "Pray tell me what happened."

As the hunched soldier rowed away in the dark, Marie Josephé could hear Theresé's voice, strong and steady, describing the scene at her grandfather's house. Marie Josephé strained to hear the hushed undertones, until her sister's voice faded, and the only sound came from the soldier's oar gliding through the lapping water.

MARY JO
Portsmouth, Virginia, present day September

The day began with the now-familiar noise of beeping backhoes, whining drills and beating hammers. Terry and Stephanie met in the kitchen, ready to start their day with a cup of coffee.

Stephanie punched the start button on the coffeemaker and asked, "Have you talked to Mary Jo this morning?"

"Not yet. She's usually up by now," Terry commented with a frown.

"I know. She never sleeps late. On the mornings she went jogging, she left the door open, and her bed was already made, so I knew she was up and about."

"I'd say it was her military discipline, but even as a kid she was up with the birds. It's unlike her to be sleeping so late." Terry tiptoed to the hall and pressed her ear against the door. She looked back at Stephanie and shook her head, mouthing the words, "I hope there's no one in there with her," before she cautiously opened the door and peeked inside. Softly she called out, "Mary Jo, are you awake?"

Mary Jo was immune to any sounds, entwined in covers as if she had thrashed through the night. Terry eased the door closed and retreated to the kitchen before she spoke.

"She's dead to the world."

"I'm not surprised. She's been through so much recently. I really admire her stoicism. I'm not sure I could get through what she's been through." Stephanie added an extra scoop to the coffee filter. The morning already called for *strong*.

"What are you talking about, Steph? You've been through your own turmoil in the recent past, and here you are all the stronger for it."

"Maybe, but my situation hasn't been anywhere near the

number of crises Mary Jo has weathered."

Terry unloaded clean mugs from the dishwasher, which she set on the counter as she used her knee to shut the appliance door. As far as she was concerned, the rest could wait. "It's bound to take its toll on her. I think something happened in Afghanistan that she's not telling us."

"Oh, no! Do you think she might have post-traumatic stress or something?" Stephanie asked as she set condiments on the table.

"I hope not. She holds things in sometimes, but she's strong. We should watch her carefully as we get through these next days, though, to make sure she is okay."

"Don't forget the news she got last night about Hannah and her father. Maybe once the café is open again and she can move forward, it will help."

Thumps outside the door warned them of a visitor climbing the stairs. Stephanie answered the knock to find Chase standing outside. He smiled at her, and she couldn't help but take in his muscular body clad in a crisp white tee-shirt tucked into faded jeans; hair trimmed and face clean-shaven. She caught the whiff of his sporty cologne, pretty sure the scent of Chanel Allure Homme Sport tickled her nostrils.

"Good morning, Chase." She moved aside and gestured for him to enter. He stepped in and glanced around. As she closed the door, she leaned in for an appreciative sniff behind his back. In her opinion, he was almost the alpha male that Gage was. She walked past him, pulling a chair from the dining table and gesturing for him to take a seat. When he did, her mood sunk as she remembered the last time he came to the door. "Are you here to tell us we have reporters snooping outside again?"

"Morning. No, I wanted to let Mary Jo know the culprits were gathering, if she wanted to come downstairs now. Hey, Terry."

"Hey, Chase. What culprits?" Terry handed Chase a mug of coffee.

"She didn't tell you?"

"Tell us what? We haven't talked to her. She's still sleeping."

Chase let out a breath, Terry and Stephanie dropping into opposite chairs as they waited for him to talk. He relayed the events of the night before, and ended with the explanation that the boys who had vandalized the house had arrived with their parents.

"Oh, wow!" Stephanie pushed her coffee cup away, shaking her head. "We never heard a thing last night. We just checked on her a moment ago because she's always up so early. We were going to let her rest."

"We asked Jeffrey to meet at nine o'clock. I guess he got everyone moving earlier. It's only eight-thirty, and they're waiting in the parking lot."

"Well, he's handling it better than his father did when you guys went on your spree," Terry said caustically. She reached for her cell phone and determinedly punched in a number on speed dial. "Hi, Becky, it's me. Are you in the office yet? Okay, will you open the conference room? I'll be down in a minute...Yes, I'm upstairs...Oh, yes, please. Make pots of coffee. Thanks."

She hung up, unperturbed as she reached for her coffee and sipped; nothing kept her from her morning kick. She turned to Chase. "I'll get Mary Jo moving if you will direct the little hoodlums and their parents into the law office. Tell them I'm not convinced we shouldn't call the police. Let them sweat a little bit first."

"Thanks. And thanks for the coffee." Without touching the cup she had placed before him, he scooted the chair back and stood.

Terry asked, "How is your afternoon looking, Chase? Hannah wants everyone to meet at my parents' house today if we can. She received some news yesterday that she wants us all to hear at once. Hannah wants you there. Did Mary Jo tell you anything about it last night?"

"No. Is that what that professor who looks like Indiana Jones came for last night?" He stood rigidly, one hand on the

113

doorknob, obviously annoyed.

Stephanie hid a smile behind her hand.

Terry repressed the urge to do the same at the look on Chase's face, and said, "It's part of the reason. I'll find out an exact time and let you know."

"Okay, just give me a call. I need to get this vandalism mess straightened out."

After he left, Terry said, "I saw you noticed his annoyance about Kyle and Mary Jo?"

"I almost laughed out loud. Do you remember how Gage had a moment of jealousy that day we all met in the café, and he called Kyle 'Indie' as well."

"He does look like a young Harrison Ford, doesn't he?" Terry stood in place, her face pensive. Only Stephanie's habitual finger drumming broke their otherwise statue-like postures.

"Terry, I can't help but feel as if something monumental is going to happen." Stephanie suddenly slid her hand up to her throat, touching the antique tear-shaped diamond pendant she had recently started to wear, as if seeking comfort. The necklace seemed to tickle against her skin, and her emotions bounced between apprehension and reassurance.

"Me too," Terry agreed. She headed down the hallway to wake Mary Jo, her own hand reaching to touch the old-fashioned cross at her neck. Without thinking, she fanned the chain to repress that odd sensation tingling warmly on her skin.

* * *

Mary Jo drove to Hannah's house at three. It was their first chance to meet as granddaughter and grandmother, and she wanted it to be just the two of them. Joan Dunbar had called for the family summit to begin at five o'clock. Terry had canceled her last appointment of the day, and her two firefighter brothers were able to adjust their schedules to be there on time.

Once the full news came out about the relationships, the

entire family would be involved.

Earlier that morning, she, along with Chase and Terry, had resolved the matter of the vandalism with the vandals' parents, and she would relate the entire story to the family at one time. She had spoken with her mother again, promising to visit the next day. She had not yet heard back from Wayne Teller—her father—and she was disheartened.

As soon as the tires of her car crunched on the gravel driveway, Hannah flung the door open, her short toothpick legs reaching the last porch step at the same time as Mary Jo's toes touched the bottom of it. The extra height the step offered put the wizened old woman closer to Mary Jo's eye level, and she held her arms out, bundling the younger woman close.

Hannah had offered the same gesture a thousand times over the years, first when Mary Jo visited Terry on childhood sleepovers, and later when she came to live with the family in foster care. Racked by guilt for giving up her only child, she had always hoped she made up for her actions by offering kindness to the two friends who grew up with the Dunbar children.

"Hannah—Grandma." Mary Jo smiled wanly. "It will take me a while to learn to call you that."

"All this time we were practically under each other's noses." Hannah hugged her tightly, adding with a wry chuckle, "Well, I was always under your nose; you've been taller than me since you were twelve." She drew back to look at Mary Jo, worried at the strain showing in her granddaughter's face. "Come on in, baby girl."

* * *

Chase pulled into the long driveway leading up to the restored plantation house Charles and Joan Dunbar now called home. The large brick house, two stories high with several dormer windows on the third floor, nestled in the woods. Tall brick chimneys sprouted at either end. A quaint row of wicker rockers lined one side of the covered wrap-around porch, openly inviting guests to "sit a spell."

He still felt a rush of pride any time he looked at the building now restored to its former antebellum glory. Charles' trust two years earlier in giving Chase the contract to refurbish the dilapidated old home had been the career-defining moment for his fledgling Hallmark Construction business. Chase would be forever grateful to the man who took time and patience with him during his troubled youth. To this day, whenever he smelled fresh wood carvings, the scent transported him back to the moment he stood in awe and apprehension of Charles' old workshop, listening to instructions on how to operate the tools needed to rebuild mailboxes and birdhouses.

A crack of knuckles on glass startled him, and he whipped his head to see Gage grinning at the car window, Stephanie beside him. Obviously pleased he caused Chase to jump, he pulled the door open and said, "You gonna sit all day in the truck and admire your handiwork, princess, or are you coming in for dinner?"

Annoyed, Chase scrambled from the truck and ignored his friend's out-stretched hand as he made an exaggerated move to hug Stephanie.

"What are you doing with this loser?" he asked, slipping his arm around her shoulder and turning her toward him. "Come run away with me, and I'll give you the moon."

Stephanie played along with the joke, grabbing Chase by the shirt and pulling him in. She inhaled deeply and said, "Hmmm—that sporty Allure smells awfully good on you." She sniffed again, then batted her eyelashes and leaned in as if to kiss him on the lips, at the last moment turning to brush his cheek. "But the firefighter has already sparked my heart."

Chase gave her a good-natured hug and nodded. "You better go put him out, he's looking burning mad."

She slipped her right hand through his arm, the other in the arm of her fiancé and steered them toward the porch, saying, "Peace, boys."

As they climbed the wide steps, anything but peace existed

inside the house. Tanner thundered to the door, preceded by the two barking Irish setters.

"Uncle Gage! Uncle Chase!" He tore the door open to run with arms outstretched. The dogs tumbled past the child and made a beeline straight for a tentative Stephanie, nearly knocking her over as they put their paws on her shoulders and scrambled to lick her face.

"Down, boys, down." The dogs totally ignored her timid cry, slurping in their excitement to greet her.

"Down!" At the sound of Gage's deep command, the twin red setters plunked on their rumps.

"Did you notice the fireman accomplished that, not the carpenter?" He winked mischievously and swaggered in the door, swooping down to reach his nephew, who locked his arms around his uncle's neck, his legs around his waist. "Now if we could just teach that command to little boys." He peeled the clinging boy loose and tossed him over his shoulder like a sack of potatoes.

Tanner laughed as he hung upside down, his tiny fists pummeling Gage's back pockets. "Help, help, someone help me!" he gasped between chortles.

"I've got ya, buddy." Chase pried the little boy from Gage's back, stuffing Tanner's upper body under his arm as Gage spun around and held onto his feet.

"He's mine." Gage pretended to start a tug of war.

Chase obliged, yelling, "No, he's mine!"

"No, he's mine." A third voice chimed in, and another pair of hands reached out for one of the boy's flailing arms. Connor Dunbar, younger brother to Gage and father to Tanner, joined in the melee as he took his son's right arm, and Chase held the left.

Now the little boy faced upward as he stretched into a three-point letter "Y."

"Look, we've got us a wishbone." Connor pretended to tug one way while Chase pulled the other, all the while Tanner's high-pitched squeal sent the dogs into a new round of barking. He tilted his head backwards and glanced into Kyle Avery's upside-down face staring at him in confusion.

"Help me, Mr. Kyle," he pleaded between giggles.

"Here, Kyle, take a foot." Gage turned his hip in Kyle's direction as he wrestled with the wriggling feet.

"What? What? Oh." Kyle blinked for a moment before he realized he had been invited to join the game. He took a foot, and the little boy sagged for a moment until the men backed up slightly and held him by four points.

"Well, what have we here?" Charles Dunbar joined the fray.

"It's me, Grampie!"

Pretending not to hear, the elder Dunbar poked the squirming center mass, making Tanner giggle harder as the four men swung him gently from side to side. "Why, I think this must be my new hammock. But it's kind of lumpy." He turned as if to sit on the swaying form, but Tanner yelped between laughs, "Grampie, it's me!"

Charles peered down, shaking his head as if seeing his grandson for the first time.

"Why, how'd that happen?" He caught the little boy at the waist and rescued him from the playful clutches of the men his grandson adored as heroes.

"Will you hooligans please reduce the testosterone level in here?" Joan called out. She stood arms akimbo, one hand gripping a dishtowel. Her current and future daughters-in-law stood at her left side; her own daughter the right. All wore various expressions of astonishment on their faces, but Stephanie's face registered the most wide-eyed look. As an only child, she'd never experienced the outbursts of activity that always surrounded the Dunbar family.

"What's toss-trone, Grammie?" Tanner flopped on the floor as the dogs rolled over him.

"What you and all these men have inside you," Joan answered firmly.

"And hool-gans?" Tanner shrieked with laughter as he tried to dodge the lapping tongues.

"Is that lasagna I smell?" Knowing how to shift his mother's attention, Gage drew in his breath in a comical sniff.

He turned to scoop her into his arms, nestling his cheek on her shoulder as he cooed, "I love my mommy."

"Will you stop?" She laughed and swatted playfully as he nuzzled her neck. "You're still a hooligan and just for causing all of this commotion, you and the rest of your crew can set the table—after you add the leaf to it."

"Aw, Ma," Gage whined, dragging his feet as he shuffled away in exaggerated movements of dejection. He pointed to Tanner, "Come on, short-stuff, you got us in this mess. You can help. Go get the napkins."

Joan ignored her son as she hugged Stephanie. As usual, when they touched, a spark of static electricity seemed to pass between them.

"One of these days we have to find out why we send off shocks when we meet." Stephanie laughed. "We should channel that and sell it as excess energy to Dominion Power."

Joan nodded in agreement as she turned to hug Chase— without the startling little snap.

"That smells good, Momma D," he said as he gathered her close. He had always appreciated how Joan had first recognized the signs of abuse he and his mother suffered at the hands of his stepfather, saving, if not their lives, certainly their sanity.

"How's your mom?"

"She's good. She's in Dayton for a conference. She's giving some lectures on e-coli prevention. I think."

"We'll have to get with her when she returns."

A new wave of commotion erupted as the barking dogs headed for the front door.

"Heaven help us." Joan flipped the dishtowel over her shoulder and headed for the door. At her command to "Sit!" both dogs flopped on their rumps, tails thumping wildly as they ogled Hannah and Mary Jo bearing large dishes.

After she greeted the newest arrivals, Joan called over her shoulder to her husband, "Be sure to have plenty of chilled wine, Charlie. This is going to be a night of epic announcements."

* * *

Family time had always been important to the Dunbars, and when Joan and Charles renovated the old plantation house, they allowed modern concessions only to the huge combination kitchen and family room area, and the bathrooms. The rest of the house resonated with authentic Southern charm. The formal dining and living rooms saw use only during holidays. The massive antique mahogany table could easily seat twelve, but its dark wood was currently buried under boxes of photos and documents Kyle needed to conduct Joan's ancestry research.

The "hooligans" had dutifully added the extension leaf to the kitchen table and set it. With a little shifting, they were able to make room for twelve place settings, aided by Tanner's haphazard positioning of napkins. Stefanie brought out the Caprese salad plates while Terry positioned baskets of bread at each end. Gage emptied chilled wine into carafes and carried them to the sideboard.

The extended family engaged in various side conversations, nibbling on antipasto trays while adhering to Joan's directive against discussing the repair work to the Portsmouth properties.

Connor, the youngest Dunbar child, tapped his wineglass until all eyes were on him. He cleared his throat and said, "Beth and I have one announcement to make before we sit down." He stood near the dining bar and drew Beth to his side. He indicated his wine glass and added, "Time for a toast." She held a glass of ginger ale in one hand and Tanner's pudgy fingers with her other.

Quiet descended upon the room. He raised his glass and announced, "We just confirmed we'll be having another baby in April." He leaned in to kiss his wife before raising his hand in toast.

"Hear, hear!" Charles hugged his wife with one hand as he touched his glass lightly to those of his son and daughter-in-law.

"Hear what, Grampie? I don't hear anything." Tanner inquired, head tilted as if listening.

"It's just a saying, Tanner Bear," Connor explained, "to congratulate us on your new baby brother or sister."

"I want a brother!" Tanner dashed forward to clink his spill-proof cup to his grandfather's glass.

Beth shook her head, glancing lovingly as her son whooped around the room, touching glasses and repeating, "Brother, brother."

She touched her tummy. "We told him yesterday, hoping he wouldn't remember and blurt it out before we could tell you all. We shouldn't have worried. Once he got here nothing could distract him from the dogs."

Hugs, tears and slaps on the back consumed the next few minutes as the excited family converged on the couple.

Joan spun on her heels, an ecstatic smile on her face. "I didn't expect that piece of news!" She laughed, wiping away tears, stepping aside so Hannah could offer her congratulations.

"And of course, let's wish Terry a happy belated birthday. Hurricane Abby ruined our plans for a surprise birthday party, but we'll have cake tonight instead and plan something for later."

"Thanks, Mom, everyone." Terry nodded and smiled. Even she had lost track of her birthday because of the hurricane.

Finally, the family sat down, and Charles blessed the meal. As the food plates passed from person to person, Stephanie reached for Gage's hand, squeezing lightly. The parents sat at opposite ends of the table, Joan closest to the kitchen and Charles nearest to the ice buckets and drinks on the sideboard.

The younger members had fallen into four natural couples. Stephanie and Gage shared the same side of the table with Connor and Beth, Tanner tucked between Charles and Connor with his special plate of "bis-ghetti" in front of him.

Directly opposite, Kyle had dropped into the seat beside Terry; Chase and Mary Jo had taken the last two seats at the end. Hannah sat tucked between Mary Jo and Joan, and the three women lightly touched shoulders or patted hands as they passed dishes around.

Finally, Mary Jo spoke first, describing the vandalism the boys had wreaked upon the Bed and Breakfast. She omitted their claim about seeing ghosts as she reached for her wine. "We met with the parents this morning, and they were very amenable to settling this out of court. One of them is Jeffrey Clarkson, Gage and Chase's ringleader in their own 'eve of destruction' years ago."

"Oh, my goodness." Joan's hand went to her throat. "That's full circle."

"What goes 'round." Terry agreed. "Anyway, Jeffrey is determined not to make the same mistake his parents did, letting him off. All three boys are going to work with Chase to clean up their mischief. And Mary Jo left out the part where they claimed they were scared off by ghosts or there might have been even more damage," Terry said casually as she buttered a slice of bread.

"They were bad boys, weren't they, Daddy?" Tanner asked, tapping his father's arm as he searched his face for confirmation.

"They sure were, Tanner. Real bad boys." Connor wiped sauce from his son's cheek, then leaned until they nearly touched nose to nose, pretending to growl. "And you better not try a stunt like that when you grow up."

"Not me, Daddy!"

"So, what do you have in mind for them, Chase?" Charles said. "And would you pass the Caprese salad? The rest of you can eat the lasagna, the bread, and the antipasto. I'm in for the savory taste of fresh basil leaves sandwiched between slices of juicy red tomatoes and creamy white mozzarella." His eyes brightened as he took the plate and surveyed it.

"No, no," Joan interrupted. "I want to hear about the ghosts first. What happened?"

"They scared the boys, Grammie," Tanner said as he popped a spool of spaghetti into his mouth, slurping the strand noisily.

The adults looked at him in amazement, including Beth, too stunned to remind him to eat properly.

On a number of occasions recently, Tanner had been present when Stephanie, and later Mary Jo, had visits from the ghosts of young girls. When he spoke of his friend "Nickel" they assumed he talked about an imaginary playmate he created out of boredom. Stephanie eventually recovered clues which helped determine that "Nickel" was the spirit of an ancestress named Nicole, whose sister Marie Josephé now made ghostly appearances to Mary Jo.

"Tanner," Beth spoke carefully. "You haven't been to Portsmouth today. How did you know the ghosts scared the boys?"

Tanner looked at his mother quizzically. Sauce smeared his face, and he held his fork in one hand, a small meatball speared on the tines.

"Aunt Terry just said so, Mama," he said matter-of-factly as he popped the whole sphere into his mouth.

"Out of the mouths of babes." Beth laughed nervously. She ruffled her son's hair, visibly relieved. "I know those old family properties have a long history of reported ethereal beings, and I've come to accept them as a way of life in this family. But I absolutely will not accept their reaching out to my son when he's away from Portsmouth."

"Little pitchers have big ears," Charles cautioned, nodding toward Tanner.

"And we need to remember that when discussing certain…other-worldly beings," Joan admonished. "Now, let's finish dinner. We'll hear Kyle's news over dessert."

CHAPTER ELEVEN

Kyle strode toward two flipcharts tucked in a corner of the room, rubbing sweaty palms on his jeans. Over the years he had lectured to groups of several hundred, taught classes for dozens without a qualm; yet today, the ten pairs of eyes watching him intently sent his nerves into overdrive.

Placing one of the charts at an angle to the table occupants, he cleared his throat and flipped the page, displaying a genealogy tree.

"Since Labor Day weekend, I've been digging through as many of the records Joan provided as I could."

With his right hand he pointed to the bottom of the tree, where he had printed "Joan" in large capital letters. He trailed his left up the chart, the eyes of his audience members moving until his finger stopped at the name cards displaying "Frank and Celestine Wyatt" at the top.

"I haven't found the information I had hoped would provide Joan's ancestry beyond these two Wyatt great-great grandparents. We don't know anything about the families who preceded them, and for now there's no need to go into the details of the generations between Joan and these ancestors."

An accomplished lecturer who could turn a flipchart with barely a rustle, Kyle fumbled as he tried to turn to the next page. With an awkward jerk, he managed to pull the paper over, and pointed to the new graph.

"This is Stephanie's chart, which she put online when she started her search. We belong to the same forum, so a message alerted me because we have common names in our trees. To make a long story short, it so happens that an ancestor of mine is the second wife of a Wyatt, and she actually was the one who helped Stephanie's third great-grandmother trace her roots all the way back to a French soldier during the American Revolution."

He repeated his earlier gestures, one hand pointing to Stephanie's name at the bottom, and the other pointing to the name Nicole.

"Is everyone with me so far?" His gaze skipped around the heads nodding in rapt affirmation.

"Once we made that connection, Steph later discovered references to her ancestress Nicole in some of the papers she found during the hurricane. I think everyone here is already aware of that?"

As the extended family nodded again, Terry leaned forward on the table, propping one arm to rest her chin in her hand, wavy chestnut hair cascading to her bent elbow. Her movement distracted Kyle. Averting his eyes from her stare, he wrestled the page over the back of the stand, paper rustling nosily as he accidentally tore it in half. He pushed his glasses up his nose and turned to face the listeners, avoiding looking in her direction. "Um—okay. I know this can be boring if you aren't familiar with it, and I apologize for that."

"I've already threatened to disinherit my children for not having enough interest in their family history," Joan interjected. She looked around the table, a mischievous twinkle in her eyes. "This could well be the defining moment of whether or not I change my will."

Her three children straightened their shoulders and placed their folded hands in front of them, in exaggerated movements resembling students called to attention by their teacher.

"Now that we have their undivided attention, please continue, Kyle."

Not quite sure if the matriarch of the family was joking with her children or not, he continued. "Well, we determined that a descendant of Stephanie's Nicole married a Wyatt." He brushed his hand over the appropriate names located in the center of the chart. "Two female cousins, Emily and Celestine married two Wyatt brothers, Thomas and Frank respectively, in the mid-eighteen-eighties. By the names alone, I was pretty sure they're the same relatives in Joan's family, and the dates match up to support confirmation."

Still posturing in student mode, Gage straightened and raised his hand "If that's the case, then my mother's family and Stephanie's are descendants of the same distant grandparents at some point, right?"

"I suspect that is going to be the case."

"Then that makes us some sort of cousins or something?" He looked at Stephanie with consternation on his face. "But we're engaged! Isn't this bad for us?"

Kyle and Joan burst into laughter as she stood to speak.

"Well, if we confirm the Wyatt brothers are my family, and if their wives share the same great-grandparents back to—say Nicole, or her parents—" Joan walked around the chairs to stand behind her son and future daughter-in-law, placing her hands on their shoulders. "Then we are related through two different sets of ancestors. The relationships are so diluted by generations there is nothing to be worried about, Gage. Much of the world can trace their roots back to common ancestral grandparents if they go back far enough. We may have links to two of the same sets eventually. And that's not all that uncommon either."

Although already aware of this genetic fact, Stephanie sat in stunned silence. For the first time, she realized she could be related, albeit very distantly, to her own fiancé and his mother! She reached to pat Joan's hand resting on her right shoulder, and the familiar spark of static shot not only through the two women, but to Gage as well. He jumped, but the women did not.

"Maybe that explains this jolt we get." Joan patted their

shoulders again and walked around the table to stand between Hannah and Mary Jo.

Paper rustled again as Kyle flipped to a third chart.

"This brings us to our final connection. This relationship we are sure of, because Hannah and Joan already know they are distant cousins."

This time, Mary Jo leaned forward, tenting her fingertips in front of her mouth. She scanned the list until her gaze fell on the blank space where her name should have been written on the chart.

"These Wyatts who lived during the Civil War era were a prolific family," Kyle continued. "There's also a third link. A cousin, Edward, married Louisa, who happened to be a cousin of the brothers' wives." Once again, Kyle pointed to the pertinent names on the chart. "At the moment I still can't trace past their generation to find the common ancestors, if any, of Emily, Celestine, and Louisa. It's only Stephanie's tree that we can track directly to the seventeen-hundreds."

He pointed to a name. "Hannah is a direct descendant of this Edward and Louisa Wyatt. And as I can see everyone's eyes are glazing over, I won't even tell you how many cousins once removed she and Joan are," he said with a laugh. "Suffice it to say they are definitely related. And she has given me permission to tell you the rest of her story."

Collective eyes turned toward Hannah, who nodded at Kyle and held hands tightly with Joan and Mary Jo.

Over the next few minutes, Kyle relayed Hannah's story from her young marriage and widowhood to the baby boy she had given up for adoption.

"Hannah's son has been doing his own research as well. When I created the online tree for Joan, he got an alert for a possible match for ancestors. He contacted me. I called Hannah and confirmed enough info to know they were mother and son. He sent the paperwork, and I brought it all to Hannah yesterday." He tapped on the name Wayne Eugene Teller (née William Jensen, Jr.) printed underneath Hannah's given name of Anna Trimbolt.

Tears ran profusely down Hannah's craggy face, and she blew her nose.

"To wrap up the story, there's another twist." He glanced at Mary Jo, who sat stalwart as usual, with perfect posture. When they made eye contact, she nodded for him to continue.

"William Junior was adopted and raised as Wayne Teller. He had a summer relationship with a young girl visiting from Petersburg. She became pregnant and tried to contact him but he had moved from the area. She stayed in Portsmouth, had the baby and raised the child alone. She's ill now, but through the wonders of the Internet, she located his information and sent a letter to tell him about his grown daughter."

The room fell silent as Kyle picked up a marker and added the name Patricia Cooper beside William/Wayne's name. Without fanfare, he drew an arrow to the next blank line, where he wrote the words "Mary Jo Cooper" and circled the name.

Mild pandemonium surged around the table as everyone talked at once, getting up and gathering around both Hannah and Mary Jo.

"Hannah is Mary Jo's grandmother?" Connor asked, still a bit confused.

"Yes." Beth took his hand to lead him to the chart. "I'll show you here."

"Have you talked to your son?" Terry asked, hugging each of the women when they stood up. When her mother had called her the day before, it was with Hannah's permission to tell her that Wayne Teller had found his mother. She'd learned the rest from Mary Jo later the same evening.

"I have. He lives in San Diego and hopes to visit soon."

Gage stepped in front of Mary Jo and Hannah. "How ironic to have both of you under our roof and to not know we were all related." He greeted his newly-identified cousin with a kiss on the cheek before he turned to scoop Hannah into a bear hug.

Stephanie stepped up next. "I'm here if you need to talk," she whispered in Mary Jo's ear. "I've been in very similar shoes."

"I know you have, and I may be taking you up on that offer, Steph. Thanks."

Amidst the ongoing chatter, a cell phone vibrated on the kitchen counter, followed by a lively music segment from "March of the Toreadors" in place of a ringing tone. Mary Jo snatched her cell and glanced to see an out of area number flashing on the screen. She poked her finger in one ear as she pushed the talk button and held the phone to her other ear.

"Hello?"

"May Jo Cooper?" a pleasant male voice asked.

"This is she speaking," she answered cautiously.

After a momentary pause, the caller cleared his throat and identified himself.

"Mary Jo, I'm your father, Wayne Teller. I just got back from out of town and found your voice message on my home phone. Can you talk?"

"Yes, sir." Mary Jo's heart thundered in her chest as she broke from the huddle of her now-real family and stepped outside to have her first-ever conversation with her father.

* * *

By ten o'clock, the conversation stimulated by the startling revelations wound down. Many hands made light work, accomplishing the after-dinner cleanup in record time. The various family members prepared to go their separate ways. A snoring Tanner nestled in his father's arms as his parents accepted another round of congratulations about the new baby; everyone again hugged the newly-discovered relations.

Terry walked to her own apartment over the garage to pack fresh things to take back to Stephanie's. Gage and Stephanie left for Portsmouth, and Kyle headed back to his hotel. Chase remained behind, he and Charles discussing the flurry of work his company had garnered after Hurricane Abby.

Joan convinced Hannah since they were both too wound up to sleep she should spend the night so they could chat into the wee hours after Charles went to bed. She extended the offer to Mary Jo, who declined, stepping onto the wide porch, jangling keys.

"Thanks, Mom D, but I've spent so much time at Stephanie's apartment this week I've neglected to do things around my own place. I have to see my mom tomorrow. We have a lot to catch up on. My father, Wayne, asked me to call while I'm with her. We had a nice chat, and I hope you don't mind if I wait until tomorrow to tell you about it. I'm exhausted."

"Are you sure you're okay?" Hannah studied her closely.

"I am, Han-Grandma. Just tired."

Joan and Hannah hugged her, then walked with her to her car, where they hugged her again.

"I'm never going to get home at this rate," Mary Jo said with a laugh as she got in. She popped the key into the ignition and turned.

Nothing happened except for a weak click.

She tried again. Click.

On the third try, she got nothing.

"Hmm, maybe it's a sign to stay." Joan bent down and looked in the window. "Is it the battery? *WHOA!*" She cried out with a sudden squeal as Charles stepped behind her, circling his arms around her and kissing her neck.

"You loon!" she laughed and swatted his shoulder. "Stop with the flirting and find out what's the matter with Mary Jo's car. It won't start."

Mary Jo turned the key, producing only a telltale click. She stuck her head out the window and told Charles, "It's my battery, I think."

"Pop the hood and we'll look. Have you got a flashlight?"

"I do." Chase spoke from over Charles' shoulder. Mary Jo had not been aware of him standing nearby until that moment. He strode to his truck and rummaged through the toolbox on the back, returning with a high-powered flashlight.

The two men rattled under the hood, Charles periodically telling Mary Jo, "Try the ignition now." The best results were weak clicks that soon stopped altogether. Chase moved his truck nose to nose with the car, leaving its engine running while he got out and attached jumper cables to both vehicle batteries.

"Try now," Charles called. Mary Jo turned the key. They repeated the maneuver three more times without success.

"Looks like the battery's shot," Charles declared as he slammed the hood.

"You can take my car," Joan offered.

"Or Chase could drive you home," Hannah chimed in, discreetly nudging her cousin in the ribs.

Before Mary Jo could nix the idea, Chase agreed.

She bit back a caustic refusal and instead mumbled a curt "Thanks." It wouldn't do to get into an argument in front of her grandmother and the Dunbars.

Following another round of hugs and goodbyes, the two younger people clambered stiffly into Chase's heavy-duty truck and drove down the quiet lane.

Watching the departing vehicle, Joan draped her arm through her cousin's as they stood close together and said, "Good thinking, Hannah."

"Maybe those two stubborn mules will face their demons tonight and clear the air."

"I hope so. And now we know where Mary Jo's mule-headedness comes from." The two women bumped hips and laughed as they watched the taillights fade around the bend in the road.

As Chase maneuvered the vehicle through the dark, Mary Jo hunched her left shoulder and angled her body toward the door, creating a mental barrier between her and Chase, who kept his face forward.

At different times, each imperceptibly flicked their gaze toward the other.

Fifteen minutes later, Chase pulled in front of Mary Jo's house and cut the engine. They sat, stiff and still, for a full minute.

They started to speak at the same time.

"Thank you…"

"Mary Jo, I…"

"Sorry, you first," they said in unison.

Silence.

"Thanks for the lift, Chase."

"No problem. Will you need a ride to pick up your car tomorrow?"

"No, thanks. I'll call Han-my grandmother. We're going to visit my mother."

Chase broke the silence this time. "What a strange turn of events. Who would ever have guessed she would turn out to be your grandmother? She always scared the hell out of me."

Mary Jo smiled but did not speak as she reached for the door handle.

"Maybe that explains something else." Chase gave a half-chuckle. "You're her granddaughter—and you always scared the hell out of me, Coppertop."

With an almost indiscernible shake of the head, Mary Jo clenched her jaw and closed her eyes, her grip on the handle tightening. When it came to Chase these days, she was no longer torn between fight or flight. She had no fight left in her—and now that she was home for good, there was no escaping him anyway. She needed to confront their past.

"Will you come in, Chase? We need to talk." Without realizing she had been holding her breath, she let it out in a heavy sigh, causing her bangs to flutter. Her stomach swirled with turmoil, warning her she was heading for another heartache.

Chase nodded as his heart flip-flopped and dropped with a thud. Words he had wanted to hear for so long filled him with hope—and dread. Suddenly apprehensive at the possible outcome of their conversation, he followed her up the short walkway and wondered if he should bolt.

Inside the foyer of the tidy bungalow, Mary Jo flipped a switch that turned on a pair of lamps sitting on end tables flanking a couch. She gestured toward the couch, and asked, "Do you want anything to drink?"

"Got a beer?"

"As a matter of fact, I do."

As Chase settled in one corner of the couch, she got two beers from the refrigerator, handing one to him as she sat at the opposite end.

The awkward silence was deafening. He leaned forward, propping his elbows on his knees as he popped the top, then ran his fingers around the rim without drinking.

"Chase, I…"

"Mary Jo, I…"

"You go first," they said in unison.

"Sounds like bad dialogue in a low-budget movie." Chase winced as soon as the words escaped, but Mary Jo appeared lost in thought.

"Let me go first," she said decisively, setting her beer down without taking a sip. She held out her hands and shrugged helplessly. "But I don't know where to begin."

"Then let me." Sighing, he pushed the untouched beer to one side and angled his body toward her. She sat straight, staring at the wall.

"I was a stupid ass that night, Mary Jo," he began.

"I spoke out of turn…"

"Listen, Coppertop, I started this so let me finish." He scooted a little closer, and with two fingers turned her chin so they faced each other.

"That night, I screwed up. Everything happened so fast, and I wasn't ready to admit I loved you. I didn't even know that I did. We were only eighteen, what could we possibly know?"

Mary Jo started to speak but Chase slid his forefinger over her lips. Despite her best efforts, tears brimmed. If she blinked, they would roll down in streams, so she focused her gaze on the wall again.

"I asked myself that over and over—what could we possibly know about love?" Chase said.

Unable to keep silent any longer she shot to her feet and whirled on him, forefinger poking the air. "We made love,

Chase. It was more than physical to me, or it wouldn't have happened."

"You don't need to poke me with that finger, I well remember it." He stood also, palms up, then dragged them through his hair in frustration. "I'm screwing this up again, but what I'm trying to say is that I ruined a beautiful moment and shouldn't have let you go that night. Instead, I ran like the coward I was. By the time I came to my senses, you wouldn't answer my phone calls. When I went to the house, Terry said you weren't there. Next thing I knew, you were on your way to boot camp."

She shrugged, anger overpowering the tears. "What did you expect? I went to the recruiter, and the timing was perfect."

"I wrote you letters, and you returned them unopened."

Repeating the shrug, Mary Jo sat again and turned her attention to her beer can, wiping condensation with her thumbs.

"Hannah kept me posted on where you were and how you were doing. I didn't tell her what happened between us, and she didn't ask, but she suspected something occurred."

Mary Jo set her beer down with a thud, a small spurt foaming over the rim. "I didn't tell anyone either."

Chase nodded and said, "Then our paths didn't cross for a long time. I'd hoped to see you that one Christmas Eve a couple of years ago, when you were on leave, and Mom D insisted everyone come by. I dropped in for the holiday dinner, planning to take you to the side and try to make peace. But you came home with your fiancé, and I knew there was no chance." Chase sighed and took a half-hearted swig of beer. He pushed the full can to the center of the table, and continued. "I came to his funeral. Your mom and I sat together. I wanted to tell you how sorry I was, but it seemed…" He lifted one shoulder.

"I didn't know you were there. Either of you. Thank you for that." Propping her elbows on her knees, Mary Jo brushed her hands across her face as she shook her head. "It was a hard time, and so much death since then. So many in Afghanistan."

She stood and paced, wiping her hands on her jeans, then

turned abruptly and sat back down. "About three months ago, I made a promise to a soldier as he lay dying in my arms. He asked me to deliver a message to his family so they could find consolation—something I haven't had a chance to do yet. I am going to do it first thing tomorrow morning. And he also made me promise to make peace in my own life, which I've been trying to do. I've reached out to my mother, and I'll see her tomorrow afternoon. I will make peace with her, something I should have done long ago."

Mary Jo closed her eyes and swallowed hard. A tear shimmered in her eye as she faced Chase. "Now I'm reaching out to you. I need to forgive and forget." She knew by his expression that her words pierced his heart, and hers softened a little.

Chase slid to one knee in front of her, taking her hands in his as he looked her straight in the eye.

"Mary Jo, I'm sorry about everything. How I handled that night, the hurt I caused. I can't get that time back. I'm sorry. And the other night, when you told me you'd hated me ever since we...we..." Chase couldn't find the right words and struggled on the best way he could. "But believe me when I say this now. I loved you then, I was just too stupid to say it. I'm still in love with you now. Forgive me, but please don't forget me."

Mary Jo's tears fell now, as if the floodgates opened, and she buried her face in his shoulder. "We've lost so much, Chase."

"Can we get it back, Mary Jo? Can we?" He lifted a hand and held it uncertainly near Mary Jo's head.

"I don't know, Chase. Let's take it a day at a time." Mary Jo closed her eyes.

"That's all I ask." He dropped his hand to her shoulder. She didn't flinch. "I better go."

"Stay?" The single word was not a command or a demand, but an appeal. She rose from the couch and nudged his knee with hers, until Chase swung his legs onto the couch and reclined on his side. Mary Jo stretched in front of him, her back to him. Chase settled against the cushioned back and wrapped his arm around Mary Jo while he nudged his sneakers off with his toes.

Before the shoes hit the floor, she gave in to exhaustion, leaning against his arm as she drifted into sleep.

The rain pelted the glass in the windows as lightning flashed in the distance.

Back in Portsmouth, crowds had long given up on hanging around the site of the mysterious bones and drifted to their homes, disappointed that no apparitions had appeared. Calm settled in the dark night enveloping the three properties.

In the pocket of an old jacket Mary Jo had left hanging on a peg in Stephanie's apartment, a tiny red heart pulsed ardently before the glow faded away.

CHAPTER TWELVE

LIZZIE
PORTSMOUTH, Virginia 1781

Lizzie roused from a deep sleep, startled by voices in the scullery below her bed loft. Pots clanged together, and the sounds of a heavy barrel being rolled across the wooden floor drowned out the murmur of conversation.

Bright morning light filtered in the tiny louvered window above her head. Alarmed that she had overslept, she threw back the covers and slipped barefoot across the floor, stepping gingerly on the treads of the narrow stairs until she could peek down into the kitchen. Penny, the wild-haired Irish woman who sometimes came to help cook large meals, was pointing to a bundle of carrots on the wooden block table. Beside her, a young girl of perhaps twelve stood in rapt attention, fear emanating from her wide-eyed stare. Blond curls escaped from her cap and framed thin cheekbones. The apron she wore reached her ankles and nearly obscured the shabby dress underneath. The worn leather shoes on her feet were too large.

"Penny?" Lizzie gathered her thin nightgown tight around her legs and traversed the final steps.

"Lizzie?" Penny whirled in surprise. "I thought you had gone? The missus said you were dismissed."

"No, not yet. I was helping to care for Mr. Roker and the lady."

Penny shrugged. "Makes no never-mind to me. The missus told me to show this new girl how to cook, and here we are." She turned to the terrified girl and pushed her slightly. "Go on, child, wash these carrots."

Lizzie scurried upstairs, dressed, and returned to the kitchen. Tendrils of curls escaped from the white cap on her head. She darted across the small yard to the back of the house, entered through the main kitchen and ran toward the parlor, nearly slamming into Abigail, poised at the end of the staircase with cold eyes fixed on the maid.

"You have been dismissed, Lizzie. Your debts are paid, and your services are no longer desired."

"Yes, ma'am, but I wished to help care for the mister and his daughter-in-law."

"She is not here. Her family has come for her and taken her away. I am taking care of my husband."

"But…" Lizzie took a step toward the staircase, but Abigail stepped further into the room.

"Leave this house now. Your services are no longer desired." Abigail pinched her lips into a tight line and glared at Lizzie.

The younger woman nodded and spun around on one heel to dash out the way she had entered. Outside, she leaned against the door, pressing her hand to her stomach. Would not Louis have sent word that his mother was safely away from the household? Perhaps Étienne somehow made the arrangements without his son's knowledge.

Louis! I must reach Louis!

She grabbed her skirts and headed for the market at the four corners, where she often met him, sometimes in the company of his colleague and fellow spy James, at pre-arranged times, to exchange information. On occasion, their paths crossed unexpectedly in the area, and they used nods or eye movements to signal for each to go stand near the apothecary identified by the mortar and pestle on the sign. It was James who had helped save Phillip Roker the night of the shooting.

"Please be there today, Louis, please!" She murmured the words under her breath as she ran along the street.

At the market, Lizzie's gaze scoured the intersection, looking for the red-coated uniform of soldiers to stand out from the bland coloring of citizen's clothing. A flash of red caught her eye as two soldiers exited the courthouse, but her shoulders sagged, as neither looked familiar.

Two more soldiers walked into view, headed toward the market, and her heart nearly stopped as she recognized Louis' friend James, walking with a soldier she did not know.

How might I get James' attention? Lizzie waited by the farmer's stand, hoping James would glance her way. He was engaged in conversation, and it appeared they would walk past the market without stopping.

Lizzie looked over her shoulder at the merchant engaged with a customer. As James and his companion neared, she grabbed the corner of a small crate containing apples and overturned it, sending the fruit rolling.

The merchant yelled, "You clumsy fool," as he came around his table and pushed her aside. Although the movement only caused her to wobble, she saw the soldiers stop in their tracks, and she used the opportunity to fall to a heap, with a light cry, watching as two red blurs moved closer to her.

James reached her side first, shoving the merchant roughly as he passed. "Are you hurt, miss?"

"I'm sorry. I knocked the crate over." She blinked into James' eyes, with a slight incline of her head in the direction of the apothecary.

"A simple accident, miss. I am sure the merchant will understand."

"How can I sell these, now, bruised and broken?" The man's face flushed red at his spilled produce as he stooped to retrieve loose apples.

"Gather them, and I will pay you for the damaged ones," James said. He pulled Lizzie to her feet, nodding imperceptibly toward the usual meeting place.

When the merchant quoted an exorbitant price for the basket of apples and became engaged in a heated argument with James, Lizzie took the moment to scramble away. She raced to the apothecary shop around the corner and slipped into the doorway.

Her ears thundered with the beat of her heart, and she clutched at her throat. Around her, people passed without regard for a simple maid standing in the hot sun.

Moments later, she heard the familiar slap of a scabbard against a soldier's calf, the clink of metal and footfalls, then James turned the corner. She stepped forward with anxiety, and they collided. He steadied her.

"We only have a short time, Lizzie. I left my colleague bartering with the merchant. I told him I wanted to see if I could catch up with the pretty but clumsy little maid."

Lizzie smiled thinly. "James, how fortunate to see you. I came in hopes of seeing Louis, but when I saw you, I had to attract your attention. My aunt has turned me out, and I've nowhere to go. I've paid off my debts to her, but thought I would be of use nursing Phillip and Clothiste. My aunt tells me she has no need for me to remain, that the family came for Clothiste."

James frowned. "Was she well enough to travel? Who came for her?"

"I know not, James. I was awakened this morning when Penny brought the new girl in. Poor child. Nevertheless, it is for Clothiste that I worry. She was so ill before she was shot, but she is safer with her family than with Abigail."

"Étienne must have sent for her. His connections are truly amazing. Louis has benefit of these connections, and I am sure he will arrange to get you safely away and to the camp. Wait for a message."

Lizzie nodded, fear clutching her heart. "I must hide in the kitchen so that she does not see me. Will you be in danger if you do this?"

"Darling Lizzie, fear not." He smiled, but it did not reach the grim look in his eyes. "We are in danger every day. But so are you. I will get a message to you somehow. If we know you and his mother are safe, we can concentrate on our own dangers."

"Dear James, stay safe." Lizzie rose on tiptoes and kissed his cheek, then bolted away.

James turned to the side of the building as his colleague rounded the corner, carrying a basket on one arm and munching an apple he held in his free hand. He raised the hand holding the half-eaten apple and pointed toward Lizzie's fleeing back.

"Scare her off with your face, mate?" he asked.

"So it seems." With a casual move, James placed his hand under his colleague's elbow and steered him in the opposite direction.

MARY JO
Portsmouth, Virginia, present day September

It was the war dream again. Mary Jo, dressed in a tattered colonial dress and apron, stood on a battlefield, surrounded by smoking cannons. She shoved a ramrod down the barrel of one as a soldier on the other side fired a musket into hazy puffs of smoke rolling past. The soldier, dressed in a blue jacket and tan breeches, clutched his chest. In the way that dreams have of changing scenes without the figures moving, Mary Jo was no longer standing at the cannon but now knelt in mud beside the soldier.

A heart-shaped blotch of blood stained his jacket as she cradled his head in her lap, rain pelting their faces. She stroked the man's cheek, but his features remained obscured.

Although Mary Jo and the soldier remained in place, the backdrop distorted, as if someone swept a paintbrush over a canvas scene behind them. The landscape changed to desert sand. Her colonial clothing was now replaced by the tan desert BDU's of a modern American soldier. Dust rolled around her and the figure she held.

Rain washed the blood from the soldier's chest, covered now with a plain white shirt. His facial features became clearer, and May Jo saw that she was holding her late fiancé in her arms.

He looked at her and smiled, before he closed his eyes and his form faded.

"Jay, Jay, come back!" she screamed. Booming gunshots drowned her words, and she stared down at her empty arms.

As if someone shook out a tapestry, the scene fluttered and changed once more. She knelt beside a Humvee, this time holding a soldier bleeding from a head wound. Guns boomed as smoke rose around them. He turned his gaze to Mary Jo and clutched her sleeve.

"I'm leaving, Mary Jo. Fix my momma's broken heart for me—and yours too."

"No, no, Madison. Don't leave." Mary Jo's dream image shouted, but it was as if the wind swept in and carried the words away. She bent over the dying soldier and kissed his forehead. She drew her head back, and the scene shifted again. The military vehicle faded into a yellow backhoe, retaining the turret and gun instead of a boom and backhoe bucket. More gunshots boomed in the background as the booted feet of a dozen men sloshed through the mud past Mary Jo and the soldier. The soldier's features blurred and took the form of Chase's face. He wore a crisp tee-shirt that remained stark white in spite of the mud and rain obscuring the rest of the image. His vacant stare told Mary Jo he had died, but she didn't know why.

Rainfall increased. Rising waters covered Mary Jo's legs, inching over Chase's shoulders and lapping at his cheek, yet his tee-shirt remained dry and white.

"Chase, stay, please stay," she screamed over the roar of guns, floodwaters nearly covering them. Her vision blurred.

"Mary Jo! Wake up!" The garbled words broke through her consciousness, and she struggled to open her eyes.

"Mary Jo?" Chase's voice came through loud and clear. She had the sensation of raising her head through the blur of water to clear vision and sound, and realized they were lying on her sofa. She was on her back, Chase beside her, scrunched on his side, his back pressed into the cushion. He was propped on one elbow, gently shaking her shoulder with his other hand.

Mary Jo rolled to a sitting position and swung her feet to the floor. Blood rushed through her ears in tune with the pounding of her heart. Chase stretched his arm and turned on the table lamp but remained in place, his hand on her shoulder.

"Are you okay? Do you want some coffee or anything?" he asked.

"No, I'm fine. It was just a dream."

"That was no dream, Coppertop." He brushed a tangle of hair from her face and tucked it behind her ear. "But that *must* have been some nightmare." He rubbed his chest where her elbows had landed several thrashing blows.

"It's the storm." Mary Jo pressed her hand to her stomach. "Thunder like we're having now brings on these awful war dreams. I haven't had one like this in a while, but this was particularly weird. It started out with me standing beside a colonial cannon, then a Humvee, and ended up with me by a backhoe fitted with a turret and gun."

"Dang. What a variety pack." He tried to keep his voice

light, and refrained from describing the anguished cries that had escaped.

Mary Jo smiled wanly. "You could say that. First, I was on a Revolutionary War battlefield, in colonial clothes, loading the cannon. The backgrounds scenes changed in this floating, filmy way, as if someone shook a cloth, and the design changed with each flick. I was holding a dying militiaman, then his face changed to Jay's, then to that of a soldier in my unit, then…" Mary Jo stopped and clapped her hands to her face, the image of a dying Chase vivid in her mind. She leaned back and stroked his knee with her left hand, as if to convince herself he was all right.

He covered her hand with his. "I never knew much about what you did in the Army, except for updates from Hannah. Do you want to talk about it?"

She shook her head. "There's not much to tell. Thanks for asking, though." His touch comforted her, but at the same time sent an unexpected shock of arousal coursing through her. She lay back down on her left side, her back to his chest, and he wrapped his free arm around her. She sensed that Chase felt it too. His fingertips caressed her collarbone, but he didn't move otherwise.

The disturbing images of the dream drained from her mind as her awareness of Chase overcame her. His light touch and the whisper of his breath against her cheek stirred a warmth that settled into a burning knot low in her belly.

Without a word, she rolled over and faced him, their long frames molding together on the narrow cushions. She rested her hand on his shoulder, then slid it to his neck. He stilled the gentle stroke of his fingers at the base of her throat, tiny prickles of electricity seeming to radiate onto her skin.

Mary Jo took in the lingering fragrance of his cologne, mixed with the cotton scent of his tee-shirt. She moved first, tracing her fingers along his neck. Then she slipped two fingers inside the neckline of his tee and rested them against his skin, eyes closed.

Chase glanced at her but didn't budge. He'd bungled

everything the last time they were this close; he was taking no chances. It was up to her.

Her features softened, the stress line between her eyebrows disappearing, the grim set to her mouth easing. Her breathing became slow and even, and he thought she had fallen asleep. He studied her face. Despite her fair coloring, she had unusually dark eyelashes, contrasting against the porcelain white skin. Behind those closed lids were clear blue eyes the color of sapphires. Light freckles scattered across her nose, and he resisted the urge to brush a kiss across the delicate bridge. Mary Jo shifted slightly, and he wondered if he could maintain his resolve to remain still. Every nerve in his body was on fire.

When her eyes fluttered open, staring sapphire blue into his, time stood still.

Mary Jo's gaze never wavered. His grip tightened on her hip, but he remained still as they continued the locked stare. Her eyelids shuttered halfway and dropped to his mouth. She angled her chin, brought her lips close to his, and stopped, her gaze drifting back to his. She slid her fingers behind his neck and brought their lips together.

The heat surprised them both. Not the heat of burning passion, but the warmth of tenderness. She slid her hand toward her hip where his rested and slipped her fingers through his, then drew their clasped hands to her chin and cradled them there.

She was lying on her right hip and nudged her left leg between his legs. He followed her lead and twisted his body so he could lay flat on his back. She shifted and settled on top of him, their nearly-identical lengths covering every available inch of sofa.

Slowly, Mary Jo leaned in for another kiss.

This time the warmth of tenderness ignited the passion that had been ignored but never truly dampened. She drew her knees alongside Chase's hips and rose to a sitting position.

His hands slid along her thigh and rested at her hips, the slightest pressure sending tingles of anticipation along her spine. They locked gazes again, uncertainty conflicting with obvious desire all but sparking out of Chase's eyes. His want empowered her, triggering a feral response deep within her that warred with an inner voice urging caution or her heart would be broken again.

Mary Jo mentally told the voice to shut the hell up. She tugged at her shirttail and pulled her blouse over her head, tossing it to one side. Chase moved into a sitting position, and she ripped the tee-shirt over his head, flinging it in the other direction, keeping their eyes locked in the mesmerizing stare. He inched his fingers toward her waist, and she clamped her hands over his.

This was her ride.

Chase stilled his hands, yet his fingers tightened their grip on her thighs as she straddled him with sure, seductive moves. She placed her palms at his waist and rubbed her hands upward, along his taut stomach, over his chiseled chest until she stopped at his collarbones. She wore a plain white cotton bra and smiled inwardly as his gaze dropped to her small breasts. When his eyes widened before returning to hers, his reaction was every bit as satisfying as it would have been had she worn a lingerie store bra.

Trailing her fingers along his torso, she straightened and stopped her fingers at his waist. Slowly, deliberately, she slid the tip of her right index finger into the waistband until it stopped at the web and traced his skin from one hip to the other. His muscles jumped in response.

When her traveling finger returned to the center, she brought her left hand to his belt. Her movements were smooth and unhurried as she slid the belt strap out of a loop, paused, then flicked her wrist until the flap released from the prong. She slipped the flap through the buckle, and unbuttoned his jeans, then stopped, her knuckles brushing his stomach as she toyed with the waistband.

The woman is torturing me. Chase's eyes remained riveted on Mary Jo's clear blue eyes to keep his gaze from falling to her small, firm breasts. In the second it had taken her to pull her blouse over her head, he had just enough time to glimpse the swell over the top of each cup of the simple white bra. He wanted more.

When his hands began a slow roam up her hips, she clamped her hands over them and directed him toward the waist of his jeans. Their combined sets of hands worked the jeans past his hips to his knees.

She slid her right foot to the floor, bracing herself as she used her left leg to push his pants to his ankles, where he kicked out of them. She raised up, skimming the other leg across his crotch until her foot touched the floor. She stood near his hips, staring at him.

Chase stared, unblinking. *Good grief. She can't be going to stop now.* His gaze shifted as Mary Jo hovered beside the couch, gaze still locked on his. Thumbs tucked at the waistband, she paused, then tilted her head to one side, a sly smile, almost a smirk, appearing.

Inwardly, he groaned and wondered if she had just made a fool out of him. *After all these years, I deserve this.*

He blinked and looked at her once more. His heart thumped against his ribs.

The expression on her face convinced him he had not been made a fool.

Mary Jo's hands trailed the waist of her jeans and her fingers flicked the button open. The zipper slipped down the track with a whispery "zzz" as she separated the two sections. She shimmied out of the jeans and let them pool at her feet, and then she cast them aside with a flick of a foot.

Chase propped on one elbow and extended his hand to Mary Jo. She removed the last of the cloth barriers between them and straddled him once more, hands planted on his chest.

He could hold back no longer, and his hands began another slow roam up her torso. This time, she let him continue.

The warm passion erupted into an inferno. Their movements, their pace, their kisses ignited into raw heat, as bodies touched and tongues waltzed.

They crested the summit together, with shock waves more

powerful than the boom of thunder, and fireworks more brilliant than the lightning flashing outside the windows. Their bodies rocked until they fell together in a spent heap.

They remained still for minutes, Mary Jo with right knee bent beside Chase's hip, the left stretched along the length of his leg. She nestled her head on his chest and closed her eyes. He reached for the afghan on the back of the couch. He draped it over them and wrapped his arm around her shoulder.

Neither had spoken since he had asked her if she wanted to talk about the dream.

No words had been needed.

CHAPTER THIRTEEN

Mary Jo opened her eyes to find herself still wrapped in Chase's arms and his brown eyes with gold specks watching her. Neither spoke. She closed her eyes, resting her forehead against his, then eased from his arms into a sitting position. She reached for her cell and checked the time.

"Five-thirty! I need to get a move on. I'm supposed to be in Colonial Heights at nine, but I have to shower, then get the car fixed and drive up there."

"Look, I can go to Wal-Mart and pick up a battery for the car while you shower. I'll come back, take you to the Dunbars home, put the battery in and get you on your way."

"That would be good, Chase. Thanks. Let me grab my purse."

"I'll buy it and get it from you later."

"Thanks," Mary Jo repeated. "I'll be ready when you get back."

* * *

At seven-thirty, Coldplay blasted from the CD player as Mary Jo eased her car onto Route 58. She needed music—the louder the better—to keep her mind off of not only the difficult visits ahead, but also her night with Chase.

She headed toward the home of Madison North's mother in Colonial Heights. Signs of the wrath of Hurricane Abby littered the route. Fallen trees still dotted the landscape. Sections of severed trunks stood stacked along the edges of the road, a testament to the diligent work of road crews clearing the way for traffic.

Several houses along the drive bore orange or blue tarp coverings on the roofs, making Mary Jo all the more grateful for the personal connections that enabled her café to be repaired so quickly. The further west she drove toward Route 460, signs of damage decreased until she had driven out of the hurricane's path of destruction.

She stopped for a bathroom break outside Petersburg. Up to that point she knew where to drive, and now used the time to punch in the address on her GPS.

Her fingers itched to hold a cigarette, but she ignored the urge and followed the irritating voice giving directions to Mrs. North's residence.

Mary Jo parked in front of a neat Cape Cod home. She rubbed her stomach to settle the churn and got out of the car. She straightened her shoulders before trekking along the short walkway, barely noticing the tidy lawn and billowy flowerbox on the windows before taking the three steps onto the stoop.

Before she could lift her hand to reach for the brass knocker, the interior door opened. A diminutive woman with smooth mocha skin smiled as she unlocked the storm door and pushed it open. She held it wide and beckoned for Mary Jo to enter.

"I'm Madison's mom. Thank you for coming, Sergeant Cooper." As she closed the storm door, she extended her hand, but instead drew the younger woman to her in a fierce hug. The usually reticent Mary Jo embraced her with the same fervor. A good foot shorter than Mary Jo, the woman hugged like Hannah.

"Please call me Mary Jo, Mrs. North. I've returned to civilian life now." Mary Jo winced, afraid the words would be painful to the mother of a fallen soldier.

Mrs. North patted her arm reassuringly and directed her to a neat living room filled with family photos covering the walls and every spare inch of tabletop. "I was an army wife for thirty years, my dear, and on some occasions I accompanied my husband when he visited the families of our fallen soldiers. Come here and have a seat. Would you like some coffee or tea?"

"Tea sounds wonderful, Mrs. North."

"Make yourself comfortable, dear. I'll be right back."

While waiting for Mrs. North, Mary Jo's eyes focused on the military photos, particularly the wedding pictures of a smiling bride in lace gown and groom in Army dress uniform. The sandy-haired man smiled down at the petite black woman as two soldiers blocked their path by crossing lowered swords in front of the couple. In the next picture, the swords were behind the wedding duo. The groom was looking to his right at his bride, while she looked over her right shoulder, smiles evident on their faces. Mary Jo knew this picture represented the ceremonial swat on the backside the bride was given to welcome her to Army life.

"Did you know Madison's father was white?" Mrs. North asked as she wheeled a tea cart into the room.

"I did, Mrs. North. We had a running joke about our complexions. He was 'Coffee and Cream' to my 'Peaches and Cream.'" Mary Jo touched her porcelain cheek, smiling in memory.

"I called him my caramel candy. As he grew older, he thought it sounded too childish."

Mary Jo's gaze drifted to the shadow box shaped like a house. Blue with white stars filled the triangular shaped upper section. Below, red felt lined the interior of the rectangle underneath the flag portion. Various military insignia and patches surrounded the photo of the now-older soldier.

"Just nine months before he planned to retire, my husband was killed in late two thousand and three, during Operation Iraqi Freedom. Madison had just turned fourteen two days earlier, and his dad had called to wish him a happy birthday.

That was the last time they spoke."

"I'm so sorry, Mrs. North."

"It was hard on Madison. He was at a vulnerable age in high school. He had always wanted to go into the army, but after his father died, he quit his ROTC class. He got in with a wild group of kids. He didn't do drugs—that I was ever aware of—but he was into constant petty mischief." Mrs. North picked up a photo of Madison in cap and gown. "He dropped out in the middle of his senior year. I had just purchased his portrait portfolio and ordered his graduation announcements. I kept one of him in the tuxedo."

She sighed and motioned for Mary Jo to sit beside her on the couch.

"He moved in with two friends in this dump in Richmond and went to work at a fast-food joint. Then somehow, this eighteen-year-old kid with a minimum wage job managed to get a credit card with a ten thousand dollar limit. I had no knowledge of it. How could they have allowed that back then? Of course, he used the credit card foolishly, even using cash advances to pay the rent. And then he couldn't afford to make the payments." She shook her head and sighed.

"The collection calls started to my home, as Madison listed me on his credit applications. The callers refused to give me information at first, but when I told them I would consider paying for Madison, they were more than happy to give me information, even if they weren't supposed to. Imagine my shock when the amount had grown to more than fifteen thousand dollars, with fees and interest."

"He told me."

Mrs. North nodded. "I got them to agree to accept eight thousand dollars to clear the debt. I had the money to pay, but I wasn't going to let that boy off the hook. I told him he had to join the Army, get his GED, and make payments to me until the debt was paid. I told him of the shame his father would have felt, knowing what his son was doing. We battled verbally, but in the end he met with a recruiter and enlisted. I made him sign a contract for monthly payments. I thought I was doing the best for my child at the time. Every mother makes decisions she thinks are best for their child and then wonders if they are the right ones. He went away angry. The Army straightened him out, though, and he did get his GED. He even paid back the money he owed."

"Madison told me all of that, Mrs. North. He wasn't angry anymore. He often told me that it was the best thing that happened to him."

Tears rolled down the older woman's face. "For two years, he faithfully sent the agreed payment every month in a plain white envelope containing a check wrapped in a blank sheet of notebook paper. Never a note or anything written. Then I got a lump-sum payment for the balance and no word for months."

Mrs. North sighed, and a faraway look came into her eyes. She added, "Then out of the blue, I got a Mother's Day call from him. I was so happy. He could only talk a few minutes, but he said he loved me, he was sorry, and would send a long letter. I got it about two weeks later. It was over twelve handwritten pages. I wrote back to him right away, told him things I wished I had said more often instead of 'is your homework finished?' or 'pick up your room.' I never knew if he got my letter. When the team came to notify me, they could only provide the basic information."

"That is one of the reasons why I came here, Mrs. North. Madison and I worked together and were on the convoy together. He was my driver. We were taking supplies to one of the forward operating bases in the north. Our vehicles kept having breakdowns, and by the third time we stalled, we became sitting ducks. Two RPGs tore through our line from nowhere. The vehicle in front of us was decimated, and our vehicle was hit by debris. Madison was injured the worst in our vehicle." Mary Jo hesitated, unsure how much to reveal.

"Just say it, my dear. I know most of the details. I still have contacts, who gave me more than the notification team. And I learned more from the casualty affairs officer afterwards." She took Mary Jo's hands in hers. "No one could tell me whether he suffered, or what happened to him as he died. Can you?"

"I can't lie to you, Mrs. North. He did receive extensive injuries, and he was in pain. We gave him the best medical help we could, and made him as comfortable as we could. He stayed conscious the whole time. We got him out of the vehicle, and I held his head in my lap until we got him on the stretcher and medevacked. I rode beside him, holding his hand." Mary Jo reached in her handbag and withdrew a small parcel wrapped in plastic. She fought back tears as she pulled two envelopes from the bag.

"He still managed to make jokes. But then he got serious and told me to get the letter in the lining of his helmet. He said, 'Peaches, you make sure my momma gets this letter.' I told him he could give it to you himself, but he said he knew he couldn't. He wanted you to know he had gotten your letter, and he was so happy he had a chance to mend your broken heart. I promised him I would bring it to you."

"I told him he never broke my heart, just bruised it sometimes." Mrs. North tried to smile, but her breath hitched, and tears ran anew.

"He wanted you to know he appreciated everything you did for him, Mrs. North. He said, 'Tell my momma I'm sorry I was such a bonehead punk for those years. Tell her that her caramel candy loves her with all of his heart.'"

Mrs. North held the letters to her chest with one hand and put the other to her face as she leaned into Mary Jo's shoulder. Mary Jo put her arms around the older woman as sobs racked the older woman's body. Unable to prevent a tear from falling down her own face, she squeezed her eyes shut to prevent the burning liquid from pooling into another.

When her tears were spent, Mrs. North straightened and blew her nose.

"Thank you, Mary Jo. You don't know how much this means to me."

"Madison told me something else, Mrs. North, something that has changed the direction of my life."

Mary Jo related the issues she had with her own mother and

how they had drifted apart. Then she relayed what Madison said as they raced back to the base.

"After he had given me the letters for you, he had a sudden surge of energy, and he gripped my hand. He raised his head from the gurney and looked me in the eye. He said 'You make peace with your momma, Peaches. You make peace, or you will never find your heart. You promise me that.' And I promised him I would."

"And have you kept that promise?"

"I've started, Mrs. North. The other night, after I read the letter my mom wrote to my father explaining what had happened in their lives, and I learned who my real grandmother and father were, I called her right away. I will stop by today and see her, and try to mend her broken heart. And maybe I will find mine again. I have a lot of regrets about things I did."

"Can you change the past, Mary Jo?"

Mary Jo shook her head.

"Then you have to change your present, because it impacts your future. You are a good woman, Mary Jo, to do what you have done for me, and for Madison. Heal your own heart. Live happy."

This time Mary Jo nodded.

Mrs. North set her teacup aside with a delicate clink. "Would you like to see pictures of Madison when he was growing up?"

For the next hour, the two women poured through albums of the North family and their military life. When the Westminster clock in the hallway chimed eleven times, it dawned on Mary Jo that time was slipping away.

"Mrs. North, I have to head back home soon. Would you like me to stay with you while you read Madison's letter?"

"No, I'm not going to read it yet. I may wait until his birthday comes and read it then. It will be like a last present from my caramel candy."

"Thank you for the tea and sharing stories about him." Mary Jo stood and gathered her belongings, using the opportunity to wipe away a tear slipping down her cheek.

"Thank you for coming and for keeping your promise to him. I hope he is resting in peace now."

"I would love for you to visit my café in Olde Towne. We expect to be back in business next week."

"I will do that. I visited Portsmouth many years ago, before Madison was born. I'm sure things have changed."

"Hopefully for the better. We'll keep in touch."

Mrs. North walked Mary Jo to the door, and they hugged one more time. She stood on the stoop and waved. Mary Jo watched the tiny woman in the rearview mirror until she turned the corner. She pulled to the curb. She rested her head on the steering column and let the sobs come, a cathartic cleansing that healed one more small hole in her heart.

When she met her mother in a few hours, would her heart finally be healed?

* * *

Chase brooded as he became caught up in the traffic heading downtown. He rolled his shoulders several times to ease the stiffness that had settled in from his cramped position on Mary Jo's couch. Try as he might to keep her out of his head, the entire night replayed in his mind like a movie.

Lying on their left sides, she'd fallen into an exhausted sleep in his arms, with her back pressed into his front. He was painfully aware of her closeness and hoped she wouldn't feel the physical evidence of his reaction.

Somehow, he had dozed off, listening to her deep breathing as the rain danced on the roof.

As the storm rolled closer and the thunder increased in frequency and intensity, she had grown increasingly restless, thrashing when she had shouted out his name, and he woke her.

Despite her assertion that she'd just had a "dream," he was convinced she had experienced a profoundly disturbing nightmare. She'd described such jumbled scenes that he'd had trouble separating them.

He stopped for the long-holding red light at the corner of London Boulevard and Effingham Street, concentrating on the steady stream of vehicles heading toward the Naval Hospital.

Passing cars blurred as the image of her hovering over him dimmed his vision. The warm glow of the low table lamp had turned her skin a soft peach, that cotton bra covering her small breasts more exciting than lace, his body hardening at the memory. How he had resisted touching her as she moved over him was beyond him, but her every move had set his nerves on fire.

Except for that fleeting moment when she stood and smiled with that near-smirk, when he thought she had set him up, to tease him and then walk away, leaving him rock-hard and vulnerable.

He also knew Mary Jo was not the kind of woman to toy with a man. You knew exactly where you stood with her. She could either kiss the breath out of you…or slam her heart shut on you without a backward glance.

Two short blasts from the vehicle behind him brought him back to the present, and he proceeded through the green light. He glanced to the right, noticing two of his work trucks parked outside the 7-11, the crew loading up on their morning fix of coffee, sodas, and micro-waved breakfast sandwiches. A wave of pride washed over him as he admired the black logo on the white doors advertising Hallmark Construction. His life could so easily have gone south if Charles Dunbar hadn't knocked some sense into him.

No time to think about the past. He drove a few blocks, parked on the side street beside the law office, and stepped into a puddle as he got out. The rain had ended during the night and would further delay their schedule to complete the paving. He stared at the roped-off parking lot and shook his head. Heavy equipment stood idly. Puddles rippled through the muddy surface.

He stepped along the narrow trail of wood that formed a temporary walkway behind the buildings, some of the boards squishing into mud under each step. The morning weather report called for clear skies through the following week, which would give the ground time to dry so they could start on the new pavement.

His destination was the café, but he stopped at the back steps to the B and B. Once Mary Jo and Terry had reached the decision to resume repairs to the interior, they had set a goal to open for Halloween. His crew had cleaned the damage to the floors the boys caused by tossing the paint around and had replaced the destroyed sheetrock. When the delinquents arrived after school, he would personally oversee the tasks they would be assigned. A few hours of repetitive "paint on, paint off" would make an impression.

We just might get everything but the parking lot finished this weekend.

The scent of fresh-baked bread drifted to his nostrils. Surprised, he headed to the café. He knew Mary Jo was on her way to Madison's mother's home in Colonial Heights, so Hannah must have arrived. But why? The kitchen wouldn't be finished until that afternoon, and he didn't see the point in her baking until the inspectors had signed off on it.

He took the steps two at a time, admiring the finished look of the new porch. The scent of cinnamon danced in the light breeze.

Maybe I can bribe Hannah for some of whatever she is fixing.

He grabbed the doorknob. Instead of turning as he expected, the handle remained firmly in place. He jiggled the handle again, then rapped on the glass pane.

After knocking once again, he drew a ring with the building keys from his pocket. The first key he tried worked. The lock opened with a distinctive click, and he knocked again, before opening.

"Hannah?"

No answer.

The tantalizing aromas seemed to dissipate once he stepped inside the empty kitchen. Silence greeted him. His eyes darted from side to side as he surveyed the surroundings. The back of the house had received extensive damage from the tree trunk and its protruding branches. The carpentry crew had completed repairs to the kitchen. The damaged stove, countertops, and cabinets had already been replaced.

All of the cabinet doors hung open, but otherwise nothing was amiss. Chase mechanically closed cupboard doors as he walked around the room. Shelves were nearly empty, and he recalled Beth saying she would have to buy all new dishes and glassware, as well as cooking staples.

His gaze roamed the room, scrutinizing the labor that had completed the repairs in record time, and was satisfied he could find no fault with the finished work. With the inspectors scheduled to arrive that afternoon, Mary Jo's *Pâtisseries à la Carte* should open for business on Monday.

He smiled when he noticed a handful of Tanner's Minions battling Stormtroopers in a tangled heap on the counter. He picked up on of the yellow denim-clad characters and closed one eye to stare into the one-eyed goggle. Whichever Minion it was, Tanner would surely know the name. Chase picked up a Stormtrooper, flashing back to his childhood love of the Star Wars movies. He left the Minion squaring off against the Stormtrooper and stepped into the dining area.

Other than debris blown into the room by the hurricane winds, the room with it subtle French accents was ready for business. He knew this café was a dream Mary Jo had envisioned from the time she was a child. She had spent the summer before her senior year of high school in France and talked of nothing else when she came back. He had never pictured her to be content with such an endeavor.

But then, he'd never imagined she would have joined the Army either.

Since he was the reason she enlisted, he shoved that memory to the back of his mind and rounded the glass case that had miraculously made it through the storm unscathed. Overhead, where the striped awning once hung, only the metal frame remained now. The replacement awning had to be custom-made and the order would take several weeks to complete. He'd thought the idea of an indoor awning was stupid and had argued with Mary Jo about it. Once it was in place and the room decorated, he could see she was right. Seated at two-seater parlor tables scattered among the larger square sets, customers could enjoy the essence of sitting at a sidewalk café somewhere in Paris.

The tables were back in place, the television once again secured to the wall.

The dining area looked open for business.

He then walked to the small room where Mary Jo had planned her cooking shop for little kids. To a lesser degree than the kitchen, the back wall of *Le Petit Chef* had sustained some damage from the protruding tree limbs. The crew had replaced the broken window, repaired the walls, and repainted. Pegboards and shelving awaited the arrival of pint-sized cooking tools.

Yet over the scent of the fresh paint, Chase once again detected the whiff of fresh baked bread. The front door bell jingled, and he stepped back into the dining area, ready to greet the angel who might be bringing the homemade goodies into the café.

The room stood empty.

Chase walked over to the front door and found it locked in place. He tapped the overhead bell. A slight ping resonated under his fingertips. The brass signal was securely attached to the door and could only be set off when the door itself was opened.

"I don't have time for this shit this morning." Chase stomped toward the kitchen and stopped short.

"What the f...?" He tightened his jaw and glanced through narrowed eyes around the kitchen.

Every cabinet door gaped open once again.

CHAPTER FOURTEEN

Mary Jo had planned to meet Hannah at her mother's duplex near Maryview Hospital at noon, but a traffic jam at the Monitor-Merrimac Bridge Tunnel caused a short delay. She finally pulled into the driveway behind Hannah's VW bug. Further into the yard, a battered Ford Escort with a row of tall grass sprouting around the tires suggested the vehicle was sidelined with mechanical issues. The otherwise neat yard was trimmed. A small scarecrow in the narrow flowerbed surrounded by pots of orange and yellow mums gave nod to the approaching autumn season.

A heavy sensation settled in Mary Jo's heart. The simple surroundings and the inoperable car suggested her mother might be struggling with finances. A glance at the license plate confirmed her worries. The plates had expired in August.

Could Mama have been suffering financial problems while I bought a three hundred and thirty-two dollar bottle of Dom Pérignon champagne to celebrate my café?

Guilt washed over her in waves. She was not rich, but all her life she had managed to save more of her money than she spent, even with the expenditures for her enterprises. She could afford to offer her mother some respite from a limited income.

When was the last time we spoke? Before Jay died?

A new ripple of remorse surged through her. She'd sent her mother a Christmas card and a birthday card from Kabul, but no Mother's Day card. It was to Joan Dunbar she sent the Mother's Day message of love to "My Other Mother." Another memory flashed in her mind. Ironically, she had sent Hannah a grandmother's card, on which she had underlined and drawn quotes around "Grandmother."

Mary Jo shook her head to clear the thoughts and shortened her steps to slow her progress. A burning pain simmered in her stomach and she pressed against the pain, wondering if she had developed an ulcer. She raised her hand to knock on the glass storm door. The interior door was open, and she could see into the living room, where her mother and Hannah sat side-by-side on the couch. Her shadow formed an outline on the floor and both turned to the door. Mary Jo nodded and pulled the white-frame door open.

Mary Jo noticed immediately how thin her mother looked in a blue flowered blouse and jeans that hung from her frame. Beside the couch, an old-fashioned metal TV tray bore medicine bottles, a box of tissues, and a clear spill-proof glass filled with ice water. A partially-eaten cracker rested on a plate on the coffee table.

Patricia Cooper looked at her daughter, uncertainty creating worry lines as tears pooled in her eyes.

"Mama!" In three strides Mary Jo covered the distance and bent over her mother to offer an embrace.

"My baby." Patricia's shoulders shook, and her breath hitched between sobs. Her arms encircled her daughter's neck in a surprisingly firm grip.

"Mama," Mary Jo repeated, her voice breaking. She slid to her knees and placed her head on her mother's lap. Patricia stroked Mary Jo's hair, her own tears splashing on her daughter's head.

Hannah turned her head away, her bottom lip trembling, and then stretched her arm to pat Patricia's frail hand. She turned back, tears streaming, and laid her hand on Mary Jo's shoulder.

Mary Jo turned her face upward. "Mama, why didn't you tell me you were sick? Not just now, but when I was younger. It could have helped me understand so much."

"You were so young, and it was such a burden to put on a little girl."

Mary Jo raised her eyes and smiled thinly. "But, Mama—I don't think I've ever been a little girl." She nestled her cheek against her mother's knee, relishing the warmth of her mother's touch on her cheek, and prayed the heat was from love and not fever.

Patricia sighed with regret. "I think you were born a wise old woman. You grew up too fast. You never talked like a baby, forming your words perfectly from the moment you could speak. Before you were two, you could put whole sentences together. You amazed everyone with your ability to articulate."

"Yeah, well," Hannah rasped. "She's amazed us a few times over the years with what's come out of that mouth."

"Now, Hannah—I don't swear. That much."

"True. But when you do, it's a doozy." Hannah took a sip of iced tea. "And my name is Grandma, missy."

"Yes, ma'am."

"Hannah and I have spent the whole morning talking," Patricia said. "We've filled in a lot of gaps in our lives."

"And all these years, we could have been mother-and-daughter-in-law. As well as grandmother and granddaughter." The normally taciturn Hannah's eyes welled with shimmering tears.

Tears rolled freely down Patricia's cheek as she leaned over her daughter's form. "So much time has been lost. I should have tried harder, instead of bundling my child off to live with another family." Her teardrops rained onto her daughter's cheek.

Mary Jo raised her head. "Mom, you stop that right now," she commanded gently. "There are things we all wish we could have done differently in our lives, Mom. We can't change the past, can we?"

Patricia and Hannah both shook their heads.

"Then we have to change how we handle our present, because it impacts our future." Mary Jo paraphrased Mrs. North's words and drew comfort from the other woman's wisdom, but the self-recriminations crept in. "I could have visited you more often. I could have sent more than a Christmas card and birthday card each year. And I should have always sent you cards at Mother's Day, because you were always my mother. I should have made more of an effort to keep you in my life."

Patricia held up a hand. "Now *you* stop that right now. Your life was better than I could have given you at the time. If we're going to move forward, we'll all have to do it together. You can't be criticizing yourself at the same time you're telling me to put the past behind me."

A sudden weight lifted from Mary Jo's shoulders, replaced with worry about her mother's health. She rose to her feet and sat beside her mother.

"I want to know about your health, Mom. Can you talk about it? What is your prognosis?" May Jo was never one to mince words, but she spoke gently.

"Well, I have to have more tests." Patricia sighed. "I have indolent non-Hodgkin's lymphoma. When first diagnosed, I wasn't even thirty years old. Most patients with this type are older. But an indolent cancer spreads slowly. I went through treatment alone. I didn't want to tell anyone."

"Why, Mama? Why?"

"Growing up in my family, cancer was a shame, something to be kept secret, as if it were a crime to develop this insidious disease. I remember my mother's unmarried sister developed cervical cancer. They said God was punishing her for having sex outside marriage, although she denied she had ever been with a man. Then she suffered through a mastectomy, which at that time was a humiliating event for a woman. And reconstruction was considered vanity, so she withdrew from life. When I told my own mother about my cancer, she said I was getting my just due for getting pregnant."

"But can we do something for you?"

Patricia smiled at Mary's Jo's inclusive "we" and said, "Thank you, honey. I have to undergo some more tests next week. If it has spread outside my spleen, my prognosis may not be so good, and I may have less than a year. If it is contained, it may be a better forecast."

"I'll be here to help her," Hannah rasped.

"Not if you don't quit filling your lungs with that tobacco." Patricia shook her head in exasperation.

"I've cut back." Hannah rolled her eyes skyward.

"I bet you have." Patricia scooted to the edge of the couch.

Mary Jo held out her hand in alarm. "Should you be up, Mom?"

Patricia laughed as she smoothed her baggy jeans. "I'm sick, Mary Jo, but I'm not dying yet."

"I talked to my father last night." *Was that only last night? So much has happened.*

Tears welled in Patricia's eyes. "I know. He called me again this morning. We're catching each other up with our lives."

"We didn't talk very long, just enough to break the ice and make plans to talk again today while I'm here."

"Life might have been so different for all of us if we'd not lost contact." Patricia's blue eyes, so like her daughter's, clouded, and her gaze grew distant. Then she shook her head. "But let's dwell on that another time. Are you hungry? Hannah—correction, your grandma—brought lots of goodies."

"I am, now that you mention it."

Patricia took her daughter's arm and led her toward the small kitchen, where a tray of sandwiches, a fruit platter and a basket of pastries lined the counter. The table was already set.

"We waited for you," Hannah explained as she moved the tray to the table. "Patricia and I did a lot of catching up before you got here."

"Did your visit with your soldier friend's mom go well, considering the circumstances?" Patricia asked as she took the plastic wrap off of the fruit platter.

"It did, but it was still sad."

Mary Jo had not planned on discussing the meeting with anyone, but after Hannah said grace and plates were passed, she found herself sharing the tale of one mother who had lost a child with two who had, in different ways, lost their own children.

Although Mrs. North would never see her son again, she'd found the closure she needed to have peace.

Hannah, who had given her son up for adoption so he could have a better life, still had the chance to meet him.

And Patricia, who had lost her daughter because she had been afraid to tell her she was sick, would have that child at her side for however much time she had left.

Another wound in Mary Jo's heart closed.

* * *

In the B and B, Chase knelt on one knee and rubbed 000 grade steel wool in light strokes, following the grain of the wood as he worked away paint traces. The cans the boys had overturned during their vandalism spree had been sitting on a tarp, so the spilled contents had spread more on the protective covering than the actual floor. Still, two spots the size of dinner plates had seeped onto the old wood floor.

The original oak floors had been uncovered when the renovations had started. The work crew had taken up the 1970's gold shag, only to find hideous green-speckled linoleum underneath. Once the cracked and brittle flooring was removed, they found wood floors in remarkably good shape. When fully restored, the old home would return to its former glory.

After the crew had cleaned the paint spilled during the vandalism, Chase had undertaken this part of the repairs himself. Nothing gave him satisfaction like the look and smell of a finished wood product. Even before the boys had gone on their binge, he'd planned on the floors being the project's masterpiece. He added a bit of pressure to eradicate a sliver of paint caught in a grain.

Good thing this floor hadn't been finished yet or those little bastards would be rotting in juvenile hall.

Although his hands were busy, he thought of the gaping cabinet doors in the café. Those doors were in perfect balance. He'd inspected his lead carpenter's work himself and approved it in order to send him to another job. So, when he found them open, he knew it was not a result of poor workmanship.

He'd walked around the kitchen shutting doors, and returned to find them opened again.

He couldn't explain it, and he damn sure wasn't telling anyone about it.

His mind drifted from the task at his fingertips, as he thought of Mary Jo. His fingers eased their pressure on the fine steel wool as they moved across the wood, and his eyes dimmed as his memories drifted to their morning encounter.

The vibration of his cell phone in his shirt pocket startled him out of his reverie. He grabbed the phone and recognized Connor's number appearing on screen.

"Hey, douchebag," he greeted. Although Connor was a few years younger than Chase and Gage, he was often the third branch of the trio growing up, bugging the crap out of Terry and Mary Jo.

"Hey back, dog breath. You need any quality workers in that fly-by-night company you own?"

"Yeah, I could use some capable part-timers. Do you know where I can find any?"

"Well, it so happens I know of an expert carpenter who is burning up some leave and might be willing to work for a loser like you. Might bring some credibility to your operation."

"Yeah, yeah. It doesn't have anything to do with needing money for a new baby on the way, does it?"

"There is that. I'm here now. Beth brought the groceries for the café. We just got here and managed to find a parking space right in front. As soon as I unload it for her, I'll allow you to put me to work."

"Bring your scrawny ass over and see if you have strength

enough to lift a hammer." As Connor chuckled, Chase heard Tanner in the background, yelling, "Can I, Daddy? Can I please?"

Connor's voice muffled as he turned his head away from the phone and told his son to simmer down. Returning to the mouthpiece, he said, "There's some weird kid over here named Tanner who wants to come see you."

Tanner's laughter pealed in the background.

"What's put ants in his pants?" Chase asked.

"He's got this pirate's spyglass and thinks he can see to China with it. He wants to go up in the room with the window seat and look for ships on the high sea."

Chase laughed. "Send him over here while you help Beth. He might even be able to see down to the river from the upstairs. Drop him off at the front door of the B and B."

"Thanks."

Moments later, whoops of delight preceded the stomps announcing Tanner's arrival on the porch. Chase spread the canvas tarp over the spot he'd been sanding and opened the door.

"Uncle Chase!" With the exuberant energy of a four-year-old, Tanner rushed in. Chase waved to Beth and Connor with one hand as he scooped Tanner up with the other.

"Hey, man, didn't I just see you last night, all covered in 'bis-ghetti' from head to foot?"

"No, it was just my face. Bis-ghetti always slurps my face when I do this." The little boy puckered his lips and sucked in as if he was inhaling a strand of pasta, smacked his lips and gushed. "Look at my 'Pirates of the Caribbean' Cap'n Jack Sparrow spyglass. I bet I can see China from here. Can I go upstairs and look?"

"Sure, but I don't want you to open the window, you have to look through the glass."

"Yeah, I know." He drew his lips into a pout. "Mama already said that too."

Chase ruffled his hair. "That's because you have a smart mommy."

Tanner lifted the spyglass in Chase's direction. "I see your nose. It's big."

"Can you see any boogers?" Chase turned his head from side to side.

Tanner burst into a fit of laughter, then turned the spyglass toward the chandelier, then the parlor. He zoomed in as Chase reached down to gather his tools, then whirled and tilted his head back to direct the spyglass up the stairs.

"Hello, lady!" he shouted as he stomped on the first step. Over his shoulder he called, "Marie Jo-fess is here, Uncle Chase."

Chase took a quick look to see who had come in the room. No one had entered.

He turned his gaze toward Tanner, nearing the top of the stairs, and his jaw dropped as he watched the boy pass through the blue shimmering figure of a teenage girl in a colonial dress and turn the hall corner.

The figure looked directly at Chase. She held a basket in one hand and floated down two steps as she stretched her hand toward him.

"Help her find her heart."

She didn't speak the words; he heard them in his head.

Then Tanner's blood-curdling scream reached his ears, and Chase bounded through the haze as he took the steps two at a time.

CHAPTER FIFTEEN

Marie Josephé
On the way to Yorktown, July 1781

"Frère Jacques, frère Jacques, Dormez-vous? Dormez-vous?"

Marie Josephé sang in a low voice as she rocked Nicole in her arms. Her soothing voice and the gentle sway of the rowboat calmed the younger child. As passing clouds cleared the moon and new ones shadowed it, she had a glimpse of the ferry boat's outline some three hundred feet away in the river. A flash of light that quickly disappeared guided the rowing soldier in the correct direction. He did not speak to the girls.

"I was bad, and I hurt mama," Nicole whispered with a sob.

"Little sister, what are you saying?" Marie Josephé hugged Nicole to her chest. "A bad man hurt mama, not you."

"I took mama's necklace and hid it. And then she could not come with us."

"You must not say that, ma petite, *for it is not true. Mama was hurt by the bad man, not you. Louis will take care of her for us and soon bring her to camp. She will want to know you are a brave little girl, so you must not cry. Will you try to be brave, and when we see her again I shall tell her how courageous you are, just as our father and our brother are."*

"I will try, Marie Josephé." Her voice hitched, but she sat straighter and wiped her eyes. "Will you sing for me again? When you sing, I feel

better."

Mari Josephé wrapped her cloak around Nicole and sang.

"Frère Jacques, frère Jacques, Dormez-vous? Dormez-vous?"

MARY JO
Portsmouth, Virginia, present day

With Journey's song "Lights" blasting on the radio, Mary Jo tapped her fingers on the steering wheel as she sat through a second red light at the intersection of London and Effingham. The exodus of traffic from the naval hospital to the north and the shipyard to the south created brief but annoying traffic jams. She sang along with Steve Perry crooning about his "ci-tay."

Third car from the intersection, she glared at the green light in frustration as drivers on Effingham continued to run against their red signal for several seconds. Traffic was bumper-to-bumper, a signal the downtown tunnel was backed up.

"I bet if *I* ran a red light, there'd be a traffic cop waiting on the other side," she muttered irritably. She was ready when her intersection cleared and moved forward with the traffic. The light had already turned yellow as she scooted under. In her rearview mirror, she noticed two more cars had followed behind her.

A sudden blast of a siren shrieked over Steve's voice, and her eyes reverted to the rearview mirror. A police car zipped across London Boulevard and continued north on Effingham Street toward the hospital.

She breathed a sigh of relief. If the police vehicle had pulled them over, she figured the other drivers were more in the wrong than she was because they drove through the light after her.

As she turned onto her street, she paraphrased the last line of "Lights," singing at the top of her lungs, "Hell, yeah, I want to be home in my ci-tay."

She parked on the street and left the engine running while she folded her arms over the steering wheel and rested her head. The last note of the song faded away, she fumbled for the key and turned off the ignition without raising her head. She sat in silence, her ears ringing slightly.

All through the day, blaring music had kept her mind off the day's events. Every time her memory fluttered the images of her nightmare, or of turning to find herself wrapped in Chase's arms, she notched the volume a bit higher to stay focused on her driving.

Now, in the first quiet moment she had allowed herself, Chase's face came to mind. Her heart thumped at the memory of the searing warmth she'd experienced when they had shared their first kiss in ten years.

But she wasn't ready to think about him. As she had done all day, she pushed his image to the back of her mind and concentrated on the three small buildings to her left. She wondered what had drawn her to the Olde Towne district.

Why had she come home to her ci-tay?

Portsmouth had not been her home for the better part of ten years, since she had joined the army. After boot camp in Fort Leonard Wood, Missouri, often called "Fort Lost in the Woods of Misery" by the soldiers because of its rugged terrain and particularly hot summers and cold winters, she was stationed at Fort Meade, Maryland. While on active duty, she was deployed for a year in Kosovo before returning to Fort Meade. She had every intention of making it a career and planning for her dream of a French bistro when she retired. But during a short visit to the Dunbar family in Suffolk, she met Jay during the Peanut Festival. They shared a few dates and kept in touch through emails and phone calls. He made a few visits to Fort Meade, and she spent more and more of her leave days on return trips to see him in her hometown.

She decided not to reenlist after six years, but transferred to a reserve unit in Virginia. She moved in with Jay and began looking for a suitable place to house her French café.

Then Terry called to tell her of a dilapidated old house

about to be put up for sale in Olde Towne. It was only two doors away from a place Terry had inherited and was planning to renovate into a law office. Mary Jo jumped at the chance to see the building. The exterior of the building was in good shape, but the interior needed a complete renovation. She negotiated a deal before the agent had even placed a "For Sale" sign on the property.

The ink had barely dried on the sales contract when the third property, the house in the middle, became available. Once its potential as a Bed and Breakfast developed in Mary Jo's brain, she couldn't shake it, but she couldn't afford another mortgage. She approached her old friend with the suggestion to go into business together. Terry immediately jumped at the chance. They formed a partnership, purchased the third property, and drew up plans.

Then her life fell apart.

Jay's unexpected death had thrown her for a loop. Confusion over his insurance and bills had initiated bad blood with his mother, compounded by her quest for property that belonged to Mary Jo.

During her year-long deployment, she had witnessed the deaths of several soldiers, most profoundly Madison's. Planning for the new business endeavors had given her the distractions she needed to look forward to her future.

Then Hurricane Abby struck, ruining her dreams. The mystery of the skeleton and ghostly appearances, along with the vandalism, added to her strife.

She punched the steering wheel. How much more could she take? Surely she had hit rock bottom and had to be climbing back up.

Her café was repaired and ready for business. She'd found a grandmother and a father she never knew existed; she'd fulfilled her promise to Madison and made peace with her own mother.

And damn it all to hell—she had fallen back in love with Chase.

A flutter of movement at a window on the B and B's top

floor caught her eye. She imagined she saw a figure by the window, and then the glass became clouded by a silvery gray plume.

Connor and Beth burst from the door of the café and darted up the steps to the B and B.

Fire? FIRE!

Mary Jo scrambled from the parked car and darted into the road without looking. She stopped short as brakes squealed behind her. She turned a wide-eyed stare as she put her hands up in apology to an SUV that had screeched to a halt two feet from her hip. The driver shot her the bird.

She ignored the insult as she bolted across the road, up the steps, and through the door. She could hear Tanner wailing upstairs.

"What's the matter?" Mary Jo yelled. The only odor she detected was the smell of paint and cleaning chemicals as she pounced up the steps. She realized it could not be fire, Connor would never have allowed Beth to enter a burning building.

In the largest bedroom, Beth and Connor knelt beside a panicked Tanner who gulped for breath as tears raced down his cheeks. Chase stood to one side, phone in hand.

"What happened?" she asked. The slight odor of a struck match reached her nostrils. "Has Tanner been playing with matches?" There was no sign of burnt material anywhere.

Chase held out his hands. "I don't know what happened. He came up here to play and suddenly screamed bloody murder. I came up and found him standing by the window seat, crying and shaking. The room was ice cold. I called for Beth and Connor."

Beth dropped to the floor and cradled the child in her arms, rocking gently as Connor rubbed his back.

"Tell us what happened, baby," she cooed in a soothing voice as he buried his face in her shoulder.

He whimpered. "I was playing wif my spyglass. I got freezy cold. And the room got froggy, and it tried to eat my feet. And it stink-ded."

"What do you mean by 'froggy,' buddy?" Connor asked.

"Foggy, I think he's trying to say." Beth said. "Let's get him out of here. Connor, call Terry, see if she and Stephanie can meet us at the bistro." Beth started to get up but the little boy wrapped his arms further around her neck. With one hand under his butt to brace him, she crooked her elbow as she got to her knees, and with Connor's steadying hand under her arm, rose to her feet.

Mary Jo marveled at the silent communication between the parents. Without a word from her, Connor seemed to know exactly what she needed him to do so she could stand without breaking her comforting hold on Tanner.

Beth led the way out of the room, followed by Connor punching numbers in his phone. Mary Jo stepped forward to tag along when Chase grasped her arm to hold her back.

"I think it was one of your colonial ghosts," he murmured.

"What are you talking about?" Mary Jo jerked her arm free and looked around.

"Tanner had that pirate telescope and was heading up the stairs when he said 'hello, lady.' I thought someone had come in and turned to look, but didn't see anyone." Chase paused for a moment, then rolled his eyes skyward as he huffed out a breath. "This is gonna sound crazy, but when I looked at him as he ran up the stairs, this shimmering figure appeared." He made rippling motions with his hand. "Tanner ran right through her. She floated a few steps, said 'help her find her heart,' and poofed away. She didn't speak the words, but I heard her in my head somehow."

"That sounds like the same image I saw a few days ago."

"You saw her? When?" Chase frowned at Mary Jo. "Why didn't you say something?"

"Why would I tell you about it? And are you telling me you believe in ghosts now?"

"No…yes, maybe. She just floated down the steps. Then Tanner screamed."

Mary Jo folded her arms and shook her head. "She's not a malevolent ghost. She wouldn't hurt him."

"Maybe she wouldn't, but something scared the crap out of

that kid."

"Then let's go find out." She swiveled on her heel to leave.

"Mary Jo, wait." Chase took two long strides and stopped beside her. They stood in the doorway, inches apart, her folded arms a barrier between them.

"About last night—this morning. Are we okay?"

She remained still but stared into the little specks of gold dotting his brown eyes as they widened in concern.

Finally, she moved her right wrist and traced her fingers across his chest, resting her palm on his heart.

"We're okay, Chase. Let me go to Tanner." She brushed his cheek with a kiss and glided toward the stairs. Chase leaned against the doorjamb, his gaze following her as she walked out of his sight.

Chase remained in place, staring at the steps where he had seen the young girl earlier.

He scrubbed a palm over his chest where Mary Jo's hand had rested, but the thump he felt this time caused no pain. Eyes closed, he blew out another deep breath and let his memory drift to her in his arms.

Behind him, fingers of gray mist slithered across the floor, one tentacle racing ahead and curling around his foot.

A second tentacle had reached Chase's foot.

One house away, in the pocket of Mary Jo's jacket, the still-undiscovered item pulsed as it glowed hot as a red lava rock the size of a man's fist.

The power of love triumphed over hate. The misty claw shattered silently, scattering into dirty particles that faded into the air.

Chase straightened and glanced around as the faint odor of burning matches reached his nose.

Eerie emptiness shrouded him. He strode toward the door without a backward glance.

* * *

Outside, Stephanie and Terry nearly collided as they raced from different directions, both too concerned about Tanner to notice the slight heat radiating where their necklaces rested against their skin. They entered the café and joined Tanner's parents.

For five minutes, Beth and Connor quietly questioned their son to no avail. Conversation reached a crescendo as the adults tried to piece together what had happened.

"Hold it, everyone!" Terry's firm voice commanded her friends' attention, and the din in the bistro dining room quieted as they turned to Terry.

"One at a time. We need to find out what happened." She sat in a chair opposite Beth. Tanner's whimpers had quieted but he remained motionless, a vacant stare in his unblinking eyes as he nestled against his mother's shoulder. Connor stood behind the chair and stroked the back of his son's head.

"Tanner," Terry asked gently. "Can you tell us what happened?" Her nephew looked at her but remained silent, casting his glance downward.

"All I know is that Tanner yelled and saved me," Chase said from the doorway. He'd arrived unnoticed and remained in the shadows, but now moved closer to the chair. The little boy's back straightened and he flicked his eyes toward his surrogate uncle.

Chase nodded as he knelt before the little boy and handed him a Minion he had picked up out of the toy pile. Tanner grabbed it and clutched it to his chest, eyes on Chase, who continued talking. "I heard you yell, so I knew to be very careful when I came in the room, but you made everything go away, and I didn't see anything. That was real smart of you."

"Yeah, I didn't want you to be scared, Uncle Chase." Tanner straightened into a sitting position.

"I didn't see what it was, Tanner. I only saw the lady on the stairs. Did she scare you in the room?"

"No." Tanner shook his head with emphasis. "She likes me.

She's Nickel's sister. But Nickel doesn't come to see me anymore." His expression grew sad.

"I wasn't scared by that lady on the steps either." Chase repeated. "But do you think you could tell me what you saw in the room so I won't be scared next time I go in there?"

"Well…" Tanner's voice took on an adult tone as his face scrunched in contemplation. "Well, I saw Marie Jo-fess on the stairs but she didn't come in the room wif me. Then I was looking all around wif my spyglass." Feeling better, he squirmed from his mother's lap and plopped his feet on the floor. "I was looking like this." He mimed moving the spyglass around the room. "Then the frog came around my feet." He swirled his finger in front and to the sides, then he held his nose. "It smelled like the stinky-pooh bridge."

"The what?" Chase stifled a laugh.

"It's what he calls the Monitor-Merrimac if we are crossing it and are downwind of the coal piles." Beth explained. "And by 'frog' he means 'fog.' Right, baby?"

As Tanner nodded, the other adults laughed, collective tension easing.

"It's a little clearer now, in more ways than one." Chase stood.

Tanner, his fear forgotten as he relished the role of being hero to his honorary Uncle Chase, continued, "I was scared a little bit, but I wanted to save Uncle Chase so I scream-ded real loud, like this." He scrunched his face, eyes shut tight as his mouth opened, and he gave a shrill screech.

"Whoa, okay, buddy." Connor ruffled his son's hair. "Thanks to you, no one will ever be scared in there again."

"Can we go now? I'm hungry. Can we go to McDonald's?" he implored his mother.

"Can we, Mom?" Connor added. Beth rolled her eyes as father and son double-teamed her.

"All right. But you know how I feel about fast-food. You have to promise you'll eat all your salad and vegetables every day for the rest of the week."

"Yes, Mommy," the father-son duo said in unison. Tanner

giggled and hugged his father's leg.

"I have to put these things away first, baby." Beth rose from the chair. In an aside, she muttered to her husband, "You were no help." Connor winked at her and she couldn't hold back a smile.

"You guys go on and take our hero," Mary Jo offered. "We'll put stuff away."

"Uh-uh." Beth shook her head, brown curls bouncing. "Just leave it on the counter. I'll put it away tomorrow, so I can know things are in the right place. Once you guys wreck it when you start cooking next week, you're on your own."

"All right, sounds like a plan. And we can discuss…" Mary Jo inclined her head toward Tanner, who was stuffing Minions and Power Rangers in his pocket.

"Definitely. And that place is off limits for…" Beth mirrored the incline toward her son.

"Agreed."

The next few minutes consisted of hugs and farewells, and more praise for Tanner's "heroics."

By the time his parents ushered him out of the café's front door, he was bouncing along beside them, happy chatter mixing with the tingling laugh of the overhead bell.

The four adults stood in silence.

Stephanie spoke first. "You handled that perfectly, Chase. You turned it from a frightening experience to a positive one."

"I didn't know what else to do, but we needed to find out what scared him."

"Well, it worked." Terry kissed his cheek. "I didn't know you had it in you."

Chase shifted his stance uncomfortably. "I just wanted to help. I love that little guy."

"We all do. But Chase, did you say you saw one of the ghosts on the stairwell? Tell us more," Stephanie urged.

Chase glanced at his watch. "I've got to get to the B and B. The hooligans are supposed to report for clean-up detail. There's not much daylight left, but they'll be scrubbing graffiti, scraping paint, carrying out debris, and whatever menial torture

I can dream up."

"Why don't you all come to the apartment afterward? Gage should have his last night of twelve-hour shifts tonight, so he'll be coming by before he reports in. We can catch everyone up in one conversation. We can throw dinner together." Stephanie turned a questioning look toward Terry and Mary Jo. "Can't you guys?"

"Sure." Terry laughed as she hugged Stephanie. "We can scare something up—can't you, Mary Jo?"

Mary Jo growled low in her throat. "You two are *très drôle*."

Three pairs of hopeful eyes turned toward her, waiting.

"All right, already, quit standing there looking like abandoned puppies. I'll scare something up." She rolled her own eyes skyward, scrubbing the idea of soaking in a bubble bath to relax the day's tension away.

Maybe time spent relaxing with friends would produce the same desired effect anyway.

CHAPTER SIXTEEN

Mary Jo popped a CD into the player mounted under the kitchen cabinet and punched the play button. She needed music, the louder the better, to keep thoughts of ghosts and frightened little boys out of her mind.

"Loud music has sure saved my sanity today. I'm surprised to see you are an Eagles fan, Stephanie," she said over her shoulder as familiar chords introduced the mesmerizing tune of "One of These Nights."

"That's Gage's CD. I was into the Backstreet Boys myself. That Brian was a cutie."

"Tell me why," Mary Jo shouted over the lead voice of Don Felder. She threw back her head and laughed, Stephanie joining in as they set to work.

By the time strains of "Hotel California" blasted around the room, the aroma of buttery garlic filled the air. The two women choreographed their way around each other, Mary Jo moving from countertop to stove while Stephanie raided cabinets and drawers. China clinked as she stacked plates on the counter, followed by wine glasses.

"That smells so good." She sniffed appreciatively as Mary Jo lifted the lid of a pan and added a touch of white wine. "What do you put in this? I need to learn how to cook interesting meals for Gage."

"It's easy, really." Mary Jo shrugged and replaced the lid. "I coat the shrimp in a seasoning of olive oil, chopped fresh garlic, cracked red pepper, black pepper, let it marinade a bit, sauté in butter and more garlic, add some white wine. Add parsley. Add some more wine. Prepare a pasta or rice side dish, a green leafy veggie and voila! *C'est fini.*"

"That sounds so easy." Stephanie lifted the lid of a smaller pan and poked the wooden spoon around in the simmering spinach.

"Stir, woman, don't prod." Mary Jo laughed. "How have you survived without cooking?"

"Takeout, mostly." Stephanie dropped the spoon in the ceramic holder, and began arranging grape tomatoes and sliced cucumbers on a small dish.

Strains of "New Kid in Town" blared on the CD player, and she smiled. "That song makes me think of Kyle. I'm glad you called him to join us, Mary Jo. I'm sure he doesn't know his way around town that well to find the best spots to eat. Does Terry know he's coming?"

"No." Mary Jo shrugged but mischief sparkled in her eyes as she turned the heat on under a pan of water to boil linguine.

"Are you matchmaking?"

"No."

"Liar."

"Well, it's just so she won't feel like a fifth wheel. You and Gage, me and Chase..." Mary Jo stopped.

"You and Chase? Have you resolved your differences?"

"Hand me that bottle of olive oil. Did you know a few drops of olive oil will help keep pasta from sticking while it is cooking?" Mary Jo shook a few drops into the pan.

"I didn't. How interesting. Don't change the subject. Did you guys talk last night after we left?"

Mary Jo huffed. When "Heartache Tonight" started playing, she punched the eject button, and the CD whirled to a stop.

"Did something bad happen? I'm sorry, Mary Jo. I don't mean to pry." Stephanie switched the dial from CD to the radio. The same Eagles song drifted from the radio through the speaker, and she grimaced as she looked at Mary Jo.

"Screw it. Leave it on, Steph. We're just gonna sing our own lyrics. There's no heartache here tonight."

"Agreed." So for the next four minutes, the two friends danced around the tiny kitchen in time to the music. Mary Jo spun in circles with a ceramic dish of pasta while Stephanie whirled in the opposite direction with a pitcher of tea.

Stephanie bopped to the table and set the pitcher down. Tea sloshed from the container as she stopped short of four pairs of eyes watching in amusement.

"Oops. Don't look now, M-J," she called over her shoulder, "but we have an audience."

"You guys are just in time." Unperturbed, Mary Jo skipped over to the table and set the plate down. She spun on one foot and danced toward the kitchen, shimmying as she passed Stephanie, who mirrored her moves.

Terry snickered. "We got here one by one, and we've been watching you guys for a full minute. Someone's been in the cooking sherry."

"No, we haven't been drinking." Stephanie pirouetted to a stop in front of Gage. "We're just relaxing. And I'm happy this is my baby's last night on twelve-hour shifts." She flung her arms around his neck and kissed him.

Mary Jo and the rest of the group exchanged more mundane greetings, and welcomed Kyle. Stephanie broke from her embrace with Gage and directed them to their seats.

"We're jumping right into the meal so we can call it an early evening. Kyle, you sit here, Terry, there," Stephanie said. She nudged Kyle to the seat on one end of the table, which placed her to his right and Terry to his left. "Mary Jo will be at the other end of the table. Chase you can sit to her right; Gage will sit beside me. I know in a formal setting, Gage and I should be at the far ends of the table as the hosts, but I always hated the separation of married couples…or in our case, engaged."

Mary Jo returned to the counter area and picked up the cruet set.

What a difference a day makes.

Only twenty-four hours earlier she would have been annoyed with Stephanie's obvious attempts to pair the couples by her seating arrangements, but today her mindset—and heart—could accept it without irritation. As she set the condiments on the table, she leaned toward Gage and said in a stage whisper, "When did she become so bossy?"

"I think it lies underneath, like a dormant volcano," Gage's exaggerated whisper returned.

"I'm within hearing, people," Stephanie admonished as she sat down. She bumped shoulders with Gage, and they leaned together for a kiss.

"It really smells good in here." Kyle sniffed with appreciation. "I was just trying to figure out what was close to the Sea Siren for dinner when Mary Jo called."

"Well, I figured with your research and all, you might want to know what's been going on with the modern day descendants and their ghosts." Mary Jo dropped into the empty seat beside Chase. Their long legs bumped at the knees, and the contact sent a warm shiver of electricity up her thigh.

Stephanie, you chose well—you little matchmaker.

The group lowered heads, and Gage offered grace. Then conversation and wine flowed.

"Before we begin, has anyone checked with Beth to see how Tanner is?" Stephanie asked.

"I did," Terry answered. "She said he was fine, still talking about how he saved Chase from the dirty ghost."

"Dirty ghost?" Kyle asked.

"Apparently he means this apparition was not shiny like his others. The colonial girls seemed to shimmer in a blue haze, but this image was in a gray mist," Terry said as she poured tea into a glass. "We didn't get a chance to hear everything from you, Chase, so fill us in." She held the pitcher above Kyle's glass, and he nodded.

"On everything," Mary Jo interjected.

With a sideways glance at her, Chase sighed, then relayed the events, including seeing the fluttering ghost as Tanner raced through her up the stairs.

"Are you sure she said 'her'?" Mary Jo asked. "When she appeared to me, she told me to dig deep and find *my* heart. She said 'your' but she meant for me to find my heart."

When she saw the puzzled looks on the men's faces, she explained about Marie Therèse's appearance in the back of the *Pâtisseries à la Carte* building and quoted the specter's message.

Chase shook his head. "No, she said 'help *her* find *her* heart.' She didn't appear malicious or anything."

"So far none of us have seen an evil presence like Tanner did today," Mary Jo said.

"Don't forget, Stephanie had that encounter during the hurricane," Terry reminded her.

"Oh, yeah, that's right, when the ghost tried to pull her out the attic window."

"So let me catch up," Kyle interrupted, holding up the index finger on his right hand. Then he slipped the thumb and index finger of his left hand into his shirt pocket and fished out a small notepad. In one smooth move, the remaining fingers latched onto a pen from a slot on the same pocket. He clicked the pen and looked up as he added, "I know about the hurricane and Stephanie's encounters." He scribbled. "And, Gage, you had a brief sighting of Nicole's ghost one time, right?"

"Yeah, when the power was off during the storm, and I couldn't find a flashlight," Gage answered. "Whacked the shit out of my shin on the coffee table when she spooked me."

Kyle raised his eyebrows and nodded, then jotted more notes. "And today, Chase saw the older girl that Mary Jo has seen?"

"We assume so," Mary Jo stated.

"These spirits are getting stronger for some reason. They are restless, and the good ones, those of the young girls, are appearing more frequently. Maybe they can sense that some kind of resolution is close."

"I haven't seen Nicole's ghost since I found the white diamond teardrop," Stephanie said, touching the jewel at her throat. "I saw her that last time standing near the fallen tree. I had the feeling she was saying goodbye."

Kyle scribbled some more and said wistfully, "Dang. I'd love to see a ghost."

"Well, hang around here long enough and you will." Terry laughed.

"That was a good thing you did for Tanner up in the room, Chase," Mary Jo interjected thoughtfully. "By telling him his screaming kept you from being scared. He could have really been traumatized, but you made him feel like a hero."

"As long as Tanner is okay, that's all that matters." Chase reached for the salad plate. "Could we talk about something else for a change? Like the good news that the café is done?"

The somber mood lifted as the welcome news cheered the table's occupants, and discussion turned to a grand re-opening celebration.

* * *

At twenty minutes to eight, Gage pushed back from the table, leading the others to follow suit. "I hate to break up the party, but I've got my last night shift ahead of me. I've got to scram. Mary Jo, thanks for a great meal."

"What about me?" Stephanie teased. "I sliced the cucumbers."

"And a fine job you did." He kissed the bridge of her nose and then called out goodnights that were echoed by the others.

"I agree." Terry reached for her purse. "Steph," she continued, "if you let me slide on helping with the cleanup tonight, I'll do dishes the next two times we eat dinner here."

"Deal," Stephanie answered.

"Stephanie, you answered too fast," Mary Jo interjected. "She's going to get off scot-free. You don't cook that often, remember."

"Busted." Terry laughed. "I'll take everyone out to dinner tomorrow night. We'll celebrate breaking free of the clutches of Hurricane Abby. Are you available tomorrow night, about seven?"

The others looked at each other amid choruses of "Sure" or "Yes."

"Fine. Let me work on some details, and I'll call you all tonight. Right now I've got to get home and find something to wear for court tomorrow. It'll be a madhouse, first day back to full business."

Kyle joined Terry at the door and patted the notebook in his pocket as he nodded toward Mary Jo and Stephanie. "Thanks to you both. And this ghost business is fascinating stuff. I've got some theories, but I need to look into some of those documents Joan has given me."

"Can I drop you off at the Sea Siren?" Terry offered.

"It's only a few blocks, but…well, sure, I'd appreciate that." He shook Chase's hand, and brushed his lips across the cheeks of Mary Jo and Stephanie before following Terry, who blew a kiss to the others as she turned away.

Chase stood by the table and made a half-hearted offer to stay and help clean. The chorus of "No way!" from the two women prompted a look of relief on his face. He glanced at Mary Jo and asked, "Did your car run okay with the new battery?"

"Not a bit of problem. Thanks for the help this morning. I'll catch you tomorrow. I'm going to stay and help Stephanie clean the kitchen."

"All right. Steph, we're going to replace the staircase with a permanent structure in the morning. It'll take a couple of hours, so you won't be able to go in or out."

"That's fine. I'm going to be working on genealogy stuff tomorrow."

"Okay. I'll be going. Thanks to you both, that meal was fantastic." He kissed Stephanie's cheek, but let them linger a bit longer on the other woman's.

"See ya, Coppertop," he whispered, his breath brushing across Mary Jo's temple. He stepped through the door, and disappeared into the dark.

Stephanie closed and locked the door behind him, as Mary Jo began collecting dishes from the table.

"Oh, hell, no." Stephanie took three quick strides, yanked the plates from Mary Jo's hand, and set them on the counter.

"What?"

"These dishes can wait. I'm putting on a kettle for tea, and you're going to tell me exactly what has gone on today. Everything, including what kind of *help* you got this morning." Stephanie pushed her toward the hall. "As a matter of fact, you're staying the night. I left the yoga pants and tee shirt in the bedroom after I washed them today. Go get comfortable. You're spilling the beans tonight."

Mary Jo stood her ground, clenching her jaw and glaring down at the smaller woman, who merely cut her eyes in return. With a shake of her head, the tired redhead blew out her breath and stomped toward the bedroom. At the door, she turned and called over her shoulder, "And don't think I didn't notice your seating arrangements, Miss Matchmaker."

Stephanie's infectious laughed followed her into the room.

Ten minutes later, the two women took up opposite ends of the couch, the soft strains of Kenny G's instrumentals providing a soothing background. A tray on the coffee table bore white ceramic mugs of steaming tea flanking either side of a whimsical teapot shaped like a panda.

Stephanie raised her mug in the CD player's direction. "To Kenny G. What is that quote that applies to music? 'Music soothes the savage breast?'" She draped a large afghan over her knees, fluffing the other end toward Mary Jo. "Or is it 'savage beast?'"

"I've heard both. Tunes have soothed me throughout this long, difficult day." Mary Jo folded her legs under her and covered her knees with the afghan.

"So." Stephanie sipped her tea. "Spill the beans, Mary Jo. What help was Chase giving you this morning?"

"You get right to the point, don't you?" Mary Jo blew a cloud of steam rising from her cup, but her lips curled in a smile. She was not sure how much she'd reveal, if anything, but concluded that if anyone could draw the full story from her, it would be Stephanie. Her comforting demeanor was an exact opposite to Terry's take-charge steamroller approach that tended to put Mary Jo's back to the wall sometimes.

Mary Jo described how her car would not start, how Chase took her home, and how she invited him in to talk.

And before relaying the day's other events, she shared a story she had not shared with another living soul.

She explained what had caused the rift between her and Chase and why she joined the Army.

Untouched tea grew cold in the cups as Mary Jo talked, and Stephanie listened.

Then Mary Jo described the encounter with Mrs. North, followed by the visit with her mother. Occasionally her voice lowered to a point where Stephanie had to ask her to repeat something, but overall Mary Jo recited without interruption, except for Stephanie's words of support as they discussed Patricia's health issues. She ended with a report on the traffic jams she encountered before finally arriving in time to learn of Tanner's encounter with the ghost.

Shivers rippled through Stephanie in spite of the warm blanket. "Mary Jo," she said with a shake of the head, "I thought the day I found the key to the bank box and my mother's letter was the most horrible day imaginable, but yours today probably beats it all. And I'm glad you told me. I hope you feel better."

"I do, Steph. Sometimes, I wish I didn't hold so much inside, but I've been this way since I was a kid." Mary Jo stood and stretched. "I've never told anyone about me and Chase, or Afghanistan, not even Terry. She would never rest if she knew these things. She's the good-hearted one of the bunch, and she would want to fix things, make everyone happy. She probably would have, too, if I'd ever shared with her. But it's my battle."

"Well, that may be, but yours is a heart of courage. I'm so glad you are resolving so much turmoil in your life. I don't know many people who could have been through what you have and still face the world."

Mary Jo shrugged and smiled wanly. "Still, I'd appreciate it if you wouldn't tell anyone what I've told you, not even Terry."

Stephanie tightened her lips, making an exaggerated motion of turning a key in a lock over them, and then tossing the imaginary key over her shoulder. Mary Jo smiled and reached a hand to pull Stephanie to her feet.

"And speaking of Terry, that reminds me," Stephanie said and laughed. "Did you notice how she watched Kyle's every move? I think she's got a crush on him."

"I think she's had her eye on him since she practically clawed my eyes out for glancing his way at the Labor Day picnic."

"He doesn't have a clue, though, does he?"

"No, he doesn't. But somehow, I think the eloquent voice of our lawyer will get through to him."

"I think you're right." The two friends exchanged hugs and good nights before they retreated to their rooms.

Mary Jo brushed her teeth and settled under the covers, fully expecting to endure a night of tossing and turning in her bed as she recounted the day's events over and over in her mind. Chase's image burned into her brain, the memory of their lovemaking overshadowing every other experience she'd encountered.

She reached for her cell phone, scrolling until his number appeared. Her thumb hovered over the green receiver icon. The screen darkened. She tucked the phone at her side and closed her eyes, the little square of green reflecting behind her eyelids.

For a change, the attic next door remained calm as restless spirits settled in their places of indeterminate state.

CHAPTER SEVENTEEN

That was the best night's sleep ever!

Mary Jo lay for a moment, then opened her eyes.

"I had the best night's sleep ever!" She spoke out loud as she kicked back the covers. She could not remember the last time she slept an entire night without waking up because of dreams or thoughts.

Facing a full morning to get the café ready for a grand reopening, she decided to forgo a jog and roused from the bed. In and out of the shower and dressed in record time, her damp hair pulled into a ponytail, she made the bed and straightened the bedroom and bathroom.

Heading down the hallway, she couldn't recall the last time she'd hummed a tune without a radio blasting in her ear.

"Good morning, Stephanie." The scent of fresh brewed coffee reached her nostrils and she inhaled deeply. "Bless you for being an early riser."

"Morning, Mary Jo. You look so much better."

"I feel good, better than I've felt in a long time. I'm pumped today. The café should be finished and C-O'd today. I want to get everything ready for reopening on Monday."

"C-O'd? You sound like Gage. I can't keep up with all of these acronyms."

"Sorry. It means 'Certificate of Occupancy.'" Mary Jo

explained. "It's when the inspector completes a final examination of the repairs and approves the finished work so we can do business again. Hopefully, it will be inspected today. We're probably ahead of the pack in that regard. I don't know what I would have done without the priority treatment Chase gives the Dunbars. What are you doing today?"

"Now that repairs are almost done, I might tackle another batch of Joan's old family letters, see if I can find more clues to the ghosts."

"Well, I'm leaving that woo-woo shit to you. I'm going to the café. Can I take some coffee with me?"

"Yeah, there are some insulated tumblers in the cabinet over the dishwasher." Stephanie dragged her chart from the corner and studied the graphs. She started filling in notes from the conversation around the table. She was so engrossed, she did not answer when Mary Jo called out "Goodbye."

Crisp fall air greeted Mary Jo when she stepped out onto the stairwell. As she breathed in the refreshing coolness, she shivered in her thin sweater and remembered the jacket she left hanging on the door. She stepped back into the apartment to lift it from the hook.

"Feels like fall has fallen," she called to Stephanie

"That's nice," Stephanie mumbled, scribbling furiously on the chart without glancing up.

Mary Jo laughed as she shut the door again. She skipped down the steps and caught sight of Chase at the rear of the B and B, directing two workers as they stacked graffiti-riddled plywood to one side.

She took a sip of coffee, eyes fluttering over the locked lid as her gaze drank in the sight of Chase's tall, lean frame, dressed in his signature jeans and white tee. His tawny hair spilled in jagged layers over the collar of his denim jacket.

As if a lion had just caught the scent of his mate, he turned his head and looked directly at her.

Her heart skipped a beat as they locked eyes over the rim of her coffee mug. Without breaking the smoldering stare, she lifted the cup and nodded in salute.

"Good morning." Her voice was a mere whisper in her throat.

Chase kept his gaze riveted to hers as he sauntered over. He covered the few steps with the feral ease of a jungle cat, all but rippling with sex appeal.

"Good morning." He angled his head, studying her face.

Mary Jo swallowed hard and cleared her throat. She looked down at the cup and thrust it toward him, trying to create a barrier between them.

"Coffee?" she asked.

"No, thanks."

"Is that bread I smell? Is Hannah here already?"

"Can you smell it too?" Chase jerked his head toward the bakery and frowned.

"Yes, the scent is just drifting toward me."

Chase caught her elbow and pulled her toward the café.

"None of my crew can smell it, but I can. I've asked them two different times when the scent wafted through the air."

She took a deep breath. "I can smell it."

"Me too. But Hannah's not here. The same thing happened yesterday."

"What do you mean?" She stuck her jacket under her free arm and matched his stride. "What's all the big mystery?"

"Let's go inside, first, and see what we see. Then I'll tell you."

They crossed the new porch and stopped at the door. Chase tried the handle. It held firmly in place. Both reached into their pockets and pulled out keys at the same time. Chase was quicker and unlocked the door first.

He narrowed his eyes as he looked around the room. All of the cabinet doors were closed. Mary Jo hung her jacket on the back of the door.

"Mary Jo, look," Chase said. She glanced over her shoulder to see him pointing toward the counter.

"Look at what?"

"These figures." He pointed to the countertop, where rows of yellow Minions stood on tiny feet, squaring off against a herd of Stormtroopers. "When we left last evening, they were in a pile, except for two. Now, every figure is standing upright."

"I don't understand."

"Okay, this is freaking weird. I'm beginning to doubt my own sanity." He scrubbed his hands over his face and explained how he had smelled the scent of bread the day before and thought Hannah had arrived. He described finding the cabinet doors open, and shutting them, inspecting again although he knew the workmanship was excellent.

"I saw the stack of figures and fiddled with them for a moment. I left two of the toys facing each other and left the rest in that pile on the counter. I looked around the other rooms, saw they were empty and nothing was out of place, and then came back into the kitchen. The cabinet doors gaped open again. I shut them all, thinking I was losing it, and went over to the B and B. Then Tanner had that episode, and they brought him back here. Remember when I handed the toy to Tanner?"

Mary Jo nodded.

"I picked it up while everyone was talking to him. I had ducked in here and took a quick look around, expecting to see the cabinet doors hanging open again. But everything seemed in place, so I got the toy to calm him down." Mary Jo opened her mouth to speak, but he held his hand up. "I know what you're thinking—Tanner must have moved it. He hadn't entered the café, because he dashed straight over to the B and B with his spyglass as soon as they got here."

"I don't understand this. How can that be? Maybe Beth or Connor...?"

"No. Don't you remember? They stayed in the dining room with him until he calmed down. Then Beth said not to put the groceries away and..."

Their gaze met, and in unison, they shifted their attention to the counter where the groceries had been stashed, noticing for the first time that the corner was clear of any food items.

"No freaking way." Mary Jo stomped over to the cabinets

closest to the corner. The canned goods, bottles, and containers Beth had purchased now lined the shelves in neat rows.

"When we left, all of these dry goods were stacked over there." Mary Jo pointed to the empty nook.

"I know." Chase nodded. "What the hell is going on here, Mary Jo? I feel like we've stepped onto the set of 'The Twilight Zone' or something."

"Tell me about it. Why are we—you and I—suddenly seeing these ghostly figures the Dunbars have been seeing their whole lives? Is it because I am in some way related to one of them, the way Stephanie was to her Nicole?"

"But I'm not related. It's been weird the last couple of days." Chase folded his hands across his chest, his stance wide-legged and defiant. He looked toward the ceiling, shook his head as if making a decision, and said, "I've seen that girl once before."

"Who?"

"That ghost or whatever the hell she is. The ghost Tanner seemed to pass through yesterday. Years ago, we came with the Dunbar family to visit their old Aunt Ida. We were smoking. What were we, about sixteen then, sneaking out by the magnolia to smoke? I looked up in the window and saw her."

"You never told me."

"Oh, yeah, like what was I gonna say, 'Hey, Mary Jo, look at the ghost in the window?'"

Mary Jo's eyes widened in recollection. "I know the time you're talking about. You asked me if the window looked crooked—or something like that. You saw her then?"

"Yeah. I never told anyone. When you said it looked fine to you, I never said anything."

"I saw her that day too." Mary Jo fiddled with a toy on the counter. She was suddenly conscious of Chase, the scent of his cologne mixing with the crisp laundered smell of his cotton jacket.

"Say what?" Chase stared. "You told me the window looked fine."

"Well, duh. What was I supposed to say? 'Oh the window looks fine except for some hazy face staring down at me?' I didn't know you saw her too."

"And all this time I thought I was bat-shit crazy."

Mary Jo laughed. "Let me ask you something. Just suppose I had said I did see a face in the window. Would you have admitted you had seen it too?"

Chase mulled it over as he stepped toward Mary Jo and took the toy she had been twirling in her hands. He placed it beside the others and stared at her. "Probably not. I do remember we kissed that day, too, where the magnolia branches made that space like a little room underneath."

She crossed her arms in front of her and raised her shoulder in a nonchalant shrug, then shook her head. "Funny, I don't seem to recall that." She stepped backward and bumped into the counter. The whiff of his cologne sent a tickle through her body as he pressed closer.

"I seem to remember it distinctly. Although maybe it was another time. We snagged quite a few kisses under that tree that summer." He slid his hand up her shoulder and cupped the back of her neck, but hesitated.

She lifted one hand to toy with a button on his jacket, conflicting emotions crossing her features. "Perhaps we did. But the tree is gone now and the memories with it."

"Do they have to be?" Chase tipped her chin up and brought his lips to within an inch of hers.

She had every intention of turning her face, of telling Chase the other night had been a mistake. She had every intention— but the warmth of his touch seared through her, and she gave in. Palms on his chest, she touched her lips to his.

The kiss was soft, yet seemed to hold the heat of a thousand candles. Mary Jo's bones turned to quicksilver, and she was sure she would have melted into her shoes had it not been for the supporting cabinet behind her.

A pulsing jolt at her hip shocked her, and her arms stiffened. She and Chase pushed apart. He reached to his side and withdrew his cell phone from its case on his belt. It vibrated again as he looked at the dial.

He touched his forehead to hers.

"Text message. I'm needed."

Mary Jo straightened her shoulders. She slipped past Chase and yanked open a cabinet door. "I've got work to do in here anyway."

"Yeah. Yeah. Um—you gonna be all right in here?"

"Of course." She kept her back to him, ignoring the sensation of his stare boring into her shoulder blades, as she moved jars from side to side until she heard the door close behind him.

She slammed the cabinet door shut and rested her head against it, palms on the counter for support. Rekindling her feelings for Chase created an unexpected obstacle in an already complicated situation.

Will my life ever be normal again?

She shook her head to clear thoughts of self-pity and rummaged through drawers until she found a pencil and notepad. She marched into the dining room, slapped the pad on the table and dropped into one of the ice cream parlor chairs. With furious strokes, she began scribbling notes.

If ghosts were going to continue to invade her space, then she was going to use it to her full advantage.

Halloween would be a perfect time to open the B and B.

Hallmark Construction had about six weeks to get it ready.

With her back to the kitchen, she did not see the beam of light pulsating from her jacket pocket.

* * *

By four o'clock, Mary Jo had several piles of neatly printed lists stacked by category. She had declined lunch offers from Stephanie and Terry as she planned out a week's worth of specialty pastries to be offered in the café during grand reopening week.

Afterward, she made a list of the few tasks necessary to finalize her separation from the Reserves after her leave was up. She'd burned some of her remaining leave to handle the hurricane disaster.

Next, she concentrated on tasks for the Bed and Breakfast. She already had an idea about color schemes for each room. On Saturday, she would hit the stores to select paint, maybe find appropriate furniture for each room. She made a note to ask Terry if she could forage for accessories. Attics in both the B and B and the law office were full of items stored during the renovations. She especially wanted to look for an ornate silver tea set Aunt Ida once had. It would look perfect atop a sideboard in the parlor.

The bedrooms were smaller in size due to adding bathrooms for each, as required by code, but she would look through tile and fixture catalogues for bath accessories. Terry had no interest in this aspect of the partnership, handling the legal and financial issues instead.

Terry's position as the legal expert reminded Mary Jo of the pending lawsuit. She started a fourth list headed "Lawsuit-What I Want to Keep." Since she and Jay had never married, his parents were legally entitled to his property, which Mary Jo had no desire to keep. She had boxed his belongings and had them ready, but then his mother demanded several items that actually belonged to Mary Jo. Although Mary Jo and Terry both tried to reason with Della, she refused to accept any property unless Mary Jo turned over every item she wanted. In the end, Della had left everything on the sidewalk in front of her house. Terry and Mary Jo hauled the boxes home to wait it out.

Della made her move after Mary Jo deployed, filing a warrant in Detinue to ask the court to intervene. She had mistakenly assumed the court would grant her request based on her word alone, but the case was postponed. They now had a court date in mid October.

Acid churned in Mary Jo's stomach. She rubbed her hand across her abdomen, wondering if she had developed an ulcer, or if she even had any stomach lining left at all, thanks to the emotional roller coaster ride she'd been on. She scribbled "schedule doctor's appointment" in her to-do column and stuck the pencil behind her ear. Shoulders stiff, she arched her back to relieve the kinks and pushed back the chair to stand.

Tomorrow would be a busy day! Preparing the lists rejuvenated her spirits, and the idea of opening the Bed and Breakfast in time for a Halloween celebration intrigued her. She couldn't find a stapler or paper clips in the drawers, so she added them to her shopping list.

She glanced at her watch. It was after four o'clock. Where was the inspector?

As if on cue, the back door opened and Chase entered, followed by a man in a polo shirt emblazoned with the city emblem over the pocket.

"I was just wondering if you would make it today," Mary Jo said, extending her hand in welcome.

"This is my last inspection. Sorry for the delay, but we've been swamped."

"I understand. Will I be able to reopen on Monday?"

"If all goes well with the inspection, I'll be signing off, and you can open for business."

"I will leave you two to it, then. Chase, will you lock up, please?" Mary Jo gathered her lists and bade the two men good day.

Anxious to share her ideas, she raced toward Stephanie's apartment, slowing as she noticed the three boys huddled over sheets of plywood. They were scrubbing and sanding graffiti from the wood. The boards could have easily been painted. Mary Jo smiled inwardly at the useless task Chase had assigned them.

"Hey, Miss Mary Jo," Kevin called, a sheepish look on his face. The other two boys kept their eyes downward, moving their brushes to block out the remaining letters of a particularly vulgar word.

"Hi, Kevin. Is that the last task Mr. Chase has lined up for you?"

"No, ma'am. We have to clean this plywood and still have to come back when the yard is dry, to help with the parking lot paving."

"That shouldn't take too long. We're supposed to have dry weather all week."

The boys groaned and went back to their scrubbing.

She chuckled, drew her cell phone out of her pocket and punched in a number.

"Terry, it's me. The inspector is finishing up. I've got a million ideas in my head for the B and B. You up for breakfast and a shopping trip tomorrow?"

"I can't tomorrow. I'm taking Kyle out to my parents' house. You want to come?"

"No, I want to get my ideas organized. Also, would it be okay to use any of the old stuff up in the attic to furnish the B and B?"

"Help yourself. We really do need to see what all is up there anyway."

"Okay. Thanks. We can get together Monday. I'll have my ideas worked out by then anyway. See you."

Next she punched in Beth's number. Beth and Connor had already made plans to take Tanner to Busch Gardens. She hung up disappointed.

Walking to the street where her vehicle was parked, she dialed Stephanie next and asked if she had plans for Saturday.

"Oh, I'm so sorry, Mary Jo. Gage has the weekend off, and we're going to Williamsburg tomorrow. I'll be staying at his house for the weekend. I think I'll be moving in with him at the end of the month. You're welcome to stay at the apartment if you want."

"Thanks for the offer. I'm heading home. Don't worry if you don't hear from me. I'm going to make some flyers for the grand reopening, plus I've got some other ideas to work on."
She heard the beep of another call coming in and saw Chase's number. She put the receiver back to her ear and continued talking to Stephanie, until she was sure her "unavailable" message would have kicked in during Chase's attempt to reach

her.

For some inexplicable reason, she simply wanted to avoid him.

Mary Jo said goodbye to Stephanie and clicked the call-end button. She put the ringer on mute and tossed the phone into her bag without reading any incoming messages. Turning the key in the ignition, she checked to see if traffic was clear and eased onto the street.

She was driving now. Not the right time to answer the phone.

Once she arrived home fifteen minutes later, she did not waste a moment. Ignoring two missed calls from Chase and one from Terry, she changed her usual voicemail message to a temporary response callers would receive for the weekend:

"This is Mary Jo, I'm temporarily unavailable but don't worry, I'm just on a creative binge and won't be answering phone calls for the weekend."

Music blasting from her iPod speakers, she transferred her handwritten lists to computer files. Her analytical mind and Army discipline dictated she carefully think through her activities so she would know at a glance what she wanted to do, when she wanted to do it, and what she needed to accomplish it. While fully capable of multi-tasking, she preferred prioritizing and clearing one action at a time.

She tackled the file for *Pâtisseries à la Carte* first. Beth had confirmed the standard fare they'd developed for daily menus had been consistently popular in the short time the shop had been open, so she made no changes there. Beth had also determined they did not draw enough business on Sundays to keep the café open seven days, so she blanked that day on the schedule.

Next, she created a monthly calendar and listed the specialty pastries she planned to feature each day until the end of October. The calendars would be given out to customers to advertise the upcoming *Spécialités du Jour*. For future planning, she devised a log to keep track of the foods proven most popular with customers.

After finalizing her list for checkout from the Reserves, she placed the items she needed to take with her in her hallway. Mary Jo fingered the black leather briefcase bearing the U. S. Army seal on the flap, with her name and rank embroidered in gold thread below it. Jay had given it to her for their first Christmas together. "Congratulations, Sergeant Mary Jo Cooper," he had said proudly as she unwrapped it under the tree.

Della Strong had actually listed the briefcase as one of the items she wanted Mary Jo to hand over, and was second only to the café's glass case as items Mary Jo would fight to the finish for.

She hugged the briefcase before setting it on the floor. In spite of Chase's reappearance in her life, or Della Strong's crazy lawsuit, Jay would always hold a special place in her heart.

At the thought of the impending court case, the burn in her stomach churned under her ribcage, and she drew a packet of antacids from her pocket. Terry had assured her she would not lose the things she wanted to keep, but who knew if the judge would wake on the wrong side of the bed the morning of the trial?

She chomped vigorously on two tablets as she sat back at her computer and scratched off another task. A glance at her watch revealed it was midnight. She shut down the computer. Tomorrow, she would make plans for the B and B.

Growling in her tummy reminded her she hadn't eaten most of the day, but she had no appetite. She fixed a cup of tea and took it to her bedroom. After slipping into pajama bottoms she topped with an Army tee-shirt, she settled into bed.

But she couldn't settle yet. She threw back the covers and retrieved her cell phone.

There was one additional call from Chase after she had put the new answering message on her phone.

Her fingers stroked the keypad, and she let her finger hover once again over the green call button.

She set the phone face down and turned out the light.

From other parts of the town, Chase and Terry talked on the phone.

"She hasn't answered my calls either, Chase." Terry's reassuring voice brought a little comfort. "She's okay, that's why she left the message on her voicemail."

"It's not like her to withdraw like this." Chase ran his fingers through his tousled hair.

"Oh, Chase, it's exactly like her. She got some kind of inspiration today for the B and B, and she's on a mission. Leave her alone for a day or two."

"I just want to talk to her," he said.

"Yeah, and I am going to remind you of that next week when she starts driving you crazy arguing about her ideas."

Chase laughed. "Yeah, you're probably right."

"I am. Get some rest. You've had a busy week, and I suspect it's only the tip of the iceberg."

"All right, Terry. Thanks."

After they exchanged good nights, he hung up the phone and glanced at the fading screen.

He punched the speed dial one more time, just in case.

"This is Mary Jo, I'm temporarily unavailable but don't worry…"

He hung up the phone and rubbed his chest.

Not completely sure why, but he did.

CHAPTER EIGHTTEEN

MARIE JOSEPHÉ
Near Yorktown, Virginia, July 1781

The dawn of day streaked red across the sky as Marie Josephé pounded dough and shaped it into loaves she then placed in the cast iron Dutch ovens. One of the younger camp boys embedded the ovens in the cinders of the wood fire, shoveling hot ash onto the lids. Around the fire circle, young children waited at the fire pits while other camp followers prepared more dough that would be shaped into the first of hundreds of other loaves that would be baked before the afternoon heat consumed them.

Poor little Nicole did her share, carrying logs to the piles near the fire pits.

Marie Josephé wished she could prepare a treat for the children, but food supplies were meager and shared only after the soldiers were fed.

In spite of the harsh conditions, she preferred the austere camp to her step-grandmother's lavish surroundings. She folded a new batch of dough and punched it down with vigor.

"Is that step-grandmother's head you are beating?" Her sister Theresé asked. She pulled a ball of dough from the bowl and began kneading.

"I should not be this gentle if I could put my fist to her ugly face," Marie Josephé said. "Or my hands around her neck." She held up a strand of dough and squeezed it until the dough oozed between her fingers.

"Marie Josephé, have you no shame?" Theresé spoke firmly, although

a giggle escaped.

"Sister, I have no shame for my hatred of that woman." Marie Josephé shrugged and rolled the strangled dough into a ball.

Her father stepped into view, deep in conversation with other officers. The sisters waved, but he did not notice them as the men walked toward the general's tent. Although he appeared to listen to the man talking by his side, his attention seemed elsewhere.

"Poor Papa. He worries so about Mama that he can scarcely concentrate on his duties. Every day he waits for a message from Louis. I am afraid if he does not hear word soon, he will risk his life to go to Portsmouth to find her."

"Pray we hear something soon, Theresé."

The sisters, hands encased in dough, leaned their shoulders together and touched foreheads together before they straightened and devoted their concentration to their chores.

Marie Josephé plunged her fingers into the dough and crimped them together, once again imagining she was wrapping them around the throat of her step-grandmother.

MARY JO
Portsmouth, Virginia, present day September

Red streaks from the morning sun set the sky on fire as Mary Jo stretched muscles, her breath forming vapor clouds. When her foot touched the bottom step on her return home, a glance at her watch revealed it had taken forty-five minutes to cover a jogging route that normally took thirty-five, including her cool down.

"Getting soft, Cooper," she chided out loud, lungs still chilled from the cool air. The sun beamed in full swing now, and she looked forward to a good day ahead.

After showering, she dressed in jeans and sweater, wrapped her wet hair in a towel, and booted up the laptop. While it warmed up, she looked over her handwritten notes titled "The Bed and Breakfast," jotting down a few additional thoughts.

She made short work of transcribing her notes into a Word

document, printed a copy and hit save.

"Look out, stores, here I come!" she sang out as she shut down the computer.

Her first stops were the paint and wallpaper sections at hardware and building supply stores, where she filled a small plastic bag with color wheels, concentrating on colonial schemes. Terry had no interest in decorating but Mary Joe knew exactly what she wanted in each of the bedrooms. Next she browsed the wallpaper books for coordinating colors for the en suite bathrooms, and picked up catalogues of bathroom fixtures.

She stopped at Cracker Barrel for a full breakfast, using the time to narrow down paint choices. She spread the array of color cards across her table. One bedroom would be in shades of federal blue and navy, one in greens, but she could not decide on cream or mauve for the largest room.

"Those are pretty colors," the waitress said as she refilled Mary Jo's coffee cup.

"They are, aren't they? I've pretty much decided my other colors, but I'm having a hard time choosing between this cream color and mauve."

The waitress tilted her head and pondered. "Well, they look nice together. You could paint the walls one color and use the other color as accent."

"That's what I'm thinking, too—now just to decide which color goes where." She smiled at the waitress and left an extra-generous tip on the table.

With paint schemes decided, she attacked the linen sections of four department stores, yielding prizes at each one. In the first store, she found a chenille bedspread flocked with green tufts that perfectly matched the paint she had chosen for the smallest room, and the ideal bath linens for the blue suite. In an upscale department store, she discovered a wedding ring quilt with a beige background, the variety of blues forming the rings in perfect harmony with her paint samples. And it was marked half-price to boot.

In the drapery section, she drew her breath at the cost of

curtains trimmed with eyelet ruffles. She wanted the same white curtains in each room, with tiebacks that matched the particular color scheme. Knowing who could make them for her at a fraction of the cost, she snapped pictures with her cell phone.

Joan Dunbar might forget to use yeast when she baked bread, but the woman was a whiz on a sewing machine.

On her final stop, Mary Jo hit another sale, this time finding fluffy peach-colored towels for her own bathroom at home. The peach reminded her of Madison's nickname for her and her visit with his mother. She made a mental note to send Mrs. North a floral basket.

Trunk loaded with bags, she left the parking lot and headed for home, smiling in satisfaction as she mentally inventoried her purchases. Driving for barely a mile down the highway, she made a U-turn and went back to the mall.

She had some serious personal shopping to do.

Perhaps it was a result of her return to civilian life. She had enjoyed the discipline and structure of military routine, which carried over into her daily life. Subtle makeup, sensible clothes, clean living—nothing that would bring discredit to her service.

All her life, she closed doors behind her when she was finished with something, and opened new ones to her next endeavor. She'd made the decision to leave the Reserves and would now move forward.

In Macy's cosmetics department, she mulled over the spectrum of colors.

"You have beautiful skin," the young attendant complimented. "With your ginger complexion, this plum shade would look lovely."

Mary Jo studied the offered samples and nodded. "This is a bit different for me. I usually opt for copper tones, but this is a nice change. Why don't you suggest an entire line of makeup for me, from foundation to mascara?"

After reviewing the offerings, Mary Jo pointed out her choices. The sales clerk beamed as she rang up the purchases.

"While I'm at it, I think I'll change my perfume. What's

new there?"

Ten minutes later, Mary Jo entered the mall's main corridors, the handle of a big red shopping bag tucked in the crook of one arm. At the bath and beauty shop, she made another sales clerk happy with her purchases of oils, bath beads, candles, and scented soaps.

With the fingers of each hand now clamped around handles of several shopping bags, Mary Jo decided it was time to head out. While she walked toward the exit nearest to where she'd parked her car, her peripheral vision caught a pink sign. She kept her gaze straight ahead and took three more paces before she executed a sharp left turn maneuver and marched straight to Victoria's Secret to further tarnish her platinum credit card.

By the time she drove into her driveway an hour later, low thunder rumbled in the distance, and fat raindrops splattered the windshield. The tangy scent of the Chinese takeout she had picked up at the corner shop permeated the air as she grabbed the food and shopping bags she wanted to take inside, leaving the purchases for the Bed and Breakfast in the trunk. She unlocked the door, set the parcels on the floor, kicked off her shoes and plopped in a chair, closing her eyes to allow the quiet to consume her.

Reticent by nature, Mary Jo had engaged in lengthy conversations with more people this week than usual. Today, with the exception of store clerks, she'd managed to avoid all conversation with humans. She embraced the solitude and wanted one more day before rejoining society.

Thunder boomed overhead, and a wave of rain washed over the roof. Sighing in resignation, she pushed to her feet and placed her uneaten Chinese takeout in the refrigerator.

"You can thunder and lightning all you want," she announced to the storm as she stood. "Tomorrow will be my 'Selfish Me Day,' and tonight—tonight I *will* sleep well again."

* * *

Ten o'clock! Mary Jo bolted upright, staring at sunlight

shafting through the blinds. When she had glanced at the clock before going to bed, the dial displayed the military time of 22:03.

Had she ever slept twelve hours in a row before?

She raised the blinds at her windows. The driveway and streets still bore signs of the storm from the night before, but once her head had hit the pillow, she had no recollection of how long it lasted.

The amazing thing—for the first time in years, no wartime nightmares haunted her sleep during a thunderstorm.

Today was going to be her totally 'Selfish Me Day.' She would pamper herself as she saw fit and end with a luxurious, long, relaxing bath.

Renewed with energy, she stripped her bed and replaced the sheets with her best set in a cornflower blue cotton percale. She shoved the discarded sheets into the hamper and carried it to her utility room. Once the wash cycle started, she removed the sales tags from the fluffy peach towels and set the linens aside for the next load.

With one fell swoop, she retrieved the shopping bags full of cosmetic and bath sundries and dashed to the bathroom. Using her wrist, she swept the few cosmetics she had carried with her on deployment into the trashcan, set out the candles and bath supplies she would use that evening, and found space for the other new toiletries in her bathroom.

She readied her work clothes for the week. Black slacks, long sleeve or short sleeve white cotton shirts, depending on the temperature, her gray chef's coat with the crest she had designed with the *Pâtisseries à la Carte* emblem embroidered in black on the left breast area. Black cuffs and mandarin collar capped off the look.

With a flourish, she stripped out of her pajamas and slipped her arms into the jacket, preening in front of her mirror.

"Power suit of the kitchen," she declared out loud, twirling on her toes. The jacket hung loosely, and she realized she had lost some weight.

She studied her reflection with narrowed eyes at the dark

circles and hollow cheeks, and chided the face reflecting back at her with, "Woman does not live by bread alone."

But she had no time to stop for a meal. She returned the coat to its hanger and grabbed two bottles of nail polish.

When she had finished, her fingernails were coated in barely visible mauve enamel. Long fancy nails with bright or intense colors were not suited for her military or culinary life, and she limited her short, neat nails to neutral tones.

Her toes, however, were a different story. Hidden inside her tan ABC's—Army Combat Boots—or her street shoes, were toenails often painted wild or vivid colors.

Today's color choice was Buttercup Yellow, and she thought the name most appropriate as she wiggled her toes to study the results. The yellow-dotted digits fluttered like buttercups in the grass.

She'd have to wait a while to finish the laundry, so she flipped on her laptop. As she waited for it to warm up, she called her mother.

"Hi, Mom. I've been AWOL for the past two days. I wanted to check on how you are doing."

"I've had a good weekend, Mary Jo."

"That's good to hear. I've spent the weekend getting my mindset ready for my first real day in the café. Would you like to come down about eleven tomorrow for lunch, before the crowds hit? We're holding our grand reopening."

"I'd love to."

"Super. Should I come get you?"

"No." Patricia laughed. "I'm able to drive. I'll be there. So tell me what you have been doing that sent you AWOL?"

The daughter shared her weekend activities with her mother, the undercurrents of loneliness easing on both ends, and planting ideas in her daughter's mind.

Noticing she had received another missed call from Chase, she ignored his call, instead dialing his mother's number to invite her to attend the reopening. Once she hung up, Mary Jo scrolled through her dialing history to find the number for Mrs. North, and called to extend the invitation to her.

Might as well make a party of it. She called Joan Dunbar and invited her, adding that she could show her the pictures of the curtains she had seen and perhaps Joan could make them.

"I don't see why not." Joan responded, interest piquing in her voice. "I need a new project to keep me busy since Charlie and I are not going on our annual camping trip this October. We're postponing it so we can enjoy the fall and winter in the house. I'm debating whether to have a Halloween party or not. We do want to have an open house for Christmas."

"Your place would be great for any party," Mary Jo said. "I'm hoping to get the B and B ready in time for Halloween. We may not have any occupants, but we could certainly take advantage of the season."

The conversation lasted almost an hour as the two women discussed the latest events at the properties.

Joan promised to drop by the café at eleven.

"I haven't been downtown in ages. Some friends have opened new shops, and I want to drop by and visit them. Maybe I'll look for a shop to rent and open a little business. I've got lots of ideas."

"Great. I'll see you then."

Mary Jo tapped the red receiver icon and disconnected, then recorded a new message that she had rejoined the living and was answering calls again.

Lightly pressing her index fingernails together, she verified the enamel had dried, and she turned her attention to her final tasks of the day. She transferred wet clothes from the washer to the dryer and started a load with the new peach towels. When the last of the laundry was folded and put away, she planned to soak in a tub of bath crystals surrounded by candles and relax with a glass of wine.

She finally accomplished that bathtub mission ninety minutes later, her skin glowing with a peach tint that matched the towels still warm from the dryer. She wrapped herself in a fluffy copper colored robe and ordered delivery pizza and salad.

Her day was almost through.

Twenty minutes later, the slam of a car door signaled the pizza had arrived. She fished bills from her wallet and held them in hand as she opened the door and stopped short at the figure on her steps.

"Chase!" The bills floated from her fingers as she stared at Chase, holding the pizza box with a paper bag resting on top.

Chase pushed past her into the hall. "If I had known this would get your attention, I'd have tried this sooner instead of wasting my time leaving messages."

"Well, obviously you didn't listen when the voicemail kicked in or you would have understood the message that I didn't want to talk to anyone this weekend." She snagged his shirt sleeve and snapped, "Where do you think you're going?"

"To your dining room." Chase jerked his arm free and marched to the table. He unceremoniously plopped the box down, the salad bag tilting to one side. "You owe me twenty-five bucks. You gave the kid a generous tip."

Mary Jo picked up a throw pillow from the small foyer bench and winged it past his head. It hit the curtain and slid silently to the floor.

"Just who the hell..." she sputtered to his back, anger sending a flush creeping to her hairline.

"I know who the hell I am," Chase interrupted, whirling on one heel. "Just who the hell do you think you are? I never figured you one for playing games, Mary Jo."

She stopped short and asked, "What are you talking about?"

He set his jaw and folded his arms across his chest, his denim-clad legs balanced in a wide, defiant stance.

"You're still punishing me for a stupid mistake I made as a teenager."

"What are you talking about?" she repeated.

With narrowed eyes, Chase stepped in front of her. He jabbed his finger in her shoulder.

"The other night. You didn't seem to mind turning to my arms the next morning. I get that you had a heavy plate that day, and I didn't push it. But you've avoided me ever since. I want to know exactly where I stand with you."

"I'm not playing games with you." Mary Jo glared as she took a poke at his chest. "And don't you poke me again, buster."

Chase did precisely that, poking her in the same spot. "No games? What's with all the sexy little knee bumps at dinner, or the kiss in the café, then just turning your back and ignoring my phone calls?"

"I wasn't ignoring you, you stupid jerk. I was ignoring *everyone* this weekend. And if you bothered to remember, *you* were the one who got the text message that interrupted that little interlude in the café."

Chase opened his mouth and then clamped it shut in silence. His jaw tightened, and he shook his head, dropping his fists to his hips. His gazed drifted to her toes, and he could not prevent a chuckle from escaping.

"And what's so funny?" she demanded.

"I'm sorry, it's your toes. I just saw them. I never expected to see you with something like that on your feet. Against that green rug, they look like little buttercups in grass."

Mary Jo crossed her arms over her chest and looked down. She couldn't help but laugh at his description that echoed her earlier observation.

The tension eased like air seeping from a punctured tire, and Chase took her hand and placed her palm to the spot she had earlier poked on his chest. He didn't speak.

"I don't want to fight with you, Chase," she said. A tear pricked the corner of her eye, and she willed it not to fall.

Chase put his hand over hers and closed the gap between them.

"Mary Jo, I remember what my parents had before my dad died. I see what our friends have together. The Dunbars, Gage and Stephanie, they are happy and in love. Connor and Beth have the greatest kid on earth. If I hadn't screwed things up when we were young, maybe by now we would have had the greatest kid on earth. I want that with you. I loved you then. I realized that as soon as I let you get away. I love you now." He drew her hand to his lips and kissed her palm. "And I've got to know tonight—now. Do I have a chance with you?"

Mary Jo could feel the tempo of his heartbeat thunder under her palm, his grip tight on her hand. Her heart beat in time with his, their breaths rocked in tandem. She eased her fingers free and slid her hand to his shoulder. The close scent of his cologne overtook the light pizza aroma drifting in the air, and she skimmed her lips along the pulse in his neck.

His grip tightened, and his mouth sought hers. The kiss sent shivers of pleasure down her spine, and her tongue flicked against his. Her fingers fumbled with the buttons of his shirt, pulling the hem of his shirt loose from his belt and sliding the sleeves down his arms. He shook his wrists to help her free his arms from the cuffs. She dropped the shirt into a heap behind him and dragged her hands over the crisp white tee-shirt. Body heat warmed the cotton material between her palms and his chest. Her hands skimmed his torso as her fingers found the bottom edge of the tee-shirt, and then that, too, sailed over his head and to the floor.

"Mary Jo." He whispered her name, the raw huskiness sending a humming sensation against her lips. Chase trailed his fingers across her collarbone and let them trace the inside of her housecoat's lapel. The feel of his rough knuckles against her skin caused a sharp intake of breath, and she broke free. Without a word, she slipped her hand into his and drew him toward the bedroom.

The room was awash in soft candlelight, the aroma dancing on the air moved by the flickering wick.

"I was indulging myself in a 'Selfish Me Day,' a day just for me," she said, waving her arm across the room. The turned-back covers of the queen bed she had thought she would occupy alone beckoned the couple.

In a husky voice, she whispered, "I would like you to share my day."

She stepped backwards toward the bed, eyes locked with Chase's as she guided him to follow. When the backs of her legs touched the mattress, she lifted first one leg, then the other, until she knelt on the bed.

Chase cupped the back of her neck with one hand and with the other untied the sash of her bathrobe, stunned when he pushed the soft cloth aside and saw she wore nothing underneath. She let the wrap slide from her shoulders and pool behind her.

"You're beautiful, Mary Jo," he murmured, as his hands cupped her breasts.

When he stopped to unbuckle his belt, Mary Jo shifted to make room for him. He undressed, and they slid their bodies under the crisp sheets and melted together.

Mary Jo's secrets trumped Victoria's tonight hummed in her mind as Chase settled over her.

CHAPTER NINETEEN

LIZZIE
Portsmouth, Virginia 1781

Lizzie glanced carefully around the small yard before she glided to the outside kitchen. She had to stay out of her aunt's sight until the appointed time to rendezvous, but she had nowhere else to go. As she closed the door behind her and waited for her eyes to adjust to the darkened room, she heard muffled whimpers. She pushed open one of the small windows and peered through the stingy stream of light until her gaze fell upon the young girl from the morning, crouched in the corner. Lizzie rushed to the little girl's side, alarmed.

"Child, what is it?" Lizzie touched the child's shoulder, causing her to shrink further into the corner and sob harder.

Could Penny have struck her? *Lizzie banished the thought immediately. Penny had never shown an angry side any time she had helped with the household.*

Still, Lizzie asked, "What has happened? Where is Penny? Did she strike you?"

"She is gone. She showed me how to make a soup. But when I took it to the house, I spilled it. The m-m-missus hit-hit-hit my hands," the little girl sniveled, hiccupping a gulp of air, and then she wiped her nose. A streak of blood followed the path of her hand across her cheek.

Lizzie traced her fingers over the broken skin on the younger girl's

215

knuckles. *The child pulled her hands free and tucked her palms under her armpits.*

Lizzie's memories flashed back to her own early days as an indentured servant. Unskilled and childishly nervous, she had broken glasses or spilled things whenever her aunt was nearby. Abigail used a heavy hand against any infraction, no matter how minor. She favored a wooden stick to wrap across Lizzie's knuckles, until Phillip caught her in the act and ordered her to stop. While she never struck Lizzie again, the verbal abuse became nearly as crippling.

Lizzie left the child's side to grab a cloth, dipped it into a small pan of water. She knelt beside the little girl and pried her hands free.

"What is your name, little one?" *she asked, her voice soothing as she brushed away the streaks of blood.*

"M-M-Margaret."

"Where is your home, Margaret?"

"Richmond."

"Richmond? What brings you so far from home?"

Margaret's lips quivered. "My stepfather sold me to the missus."

Lizzie paused and inadvertently gripped the child's hands in horror. Margaret winced.

"I am so sorry, child. What do you mean, sold? Have you no family? Your mother?"

"She died. My stepfather did not want me. He says I am not his child, and he could sell me to pay his debts. Then she came to see him. He brought me here in the night and left me on the doorstep." *Sobs racked Margaret's thin body. Her breath hitched as she gasped in air between sobs.*

Lizzie clenched her fists in anger, her jaw tightening until a vein bulged. She gulped and breathed out until her muscles relaxed. She picked up the damp cloth and wiped the streak of blood from the girl's cheek.

Her mind raced as she tilted the little girls' chin, stroking away a tear with her thumb.

"Child, you must listen to me and do exactly as I say. Whatever the missus tells you to do today, obey her. If you hear the bell ring, you run to the back door as fast as you can. But you mustn't tell her I am here, do you understand?"

The child nodded.

"When I leave here tonight, you shall go with me. You shall be safe."

MARY JO
Portsmouth, Virginia, present day September

The grand reopening of *Pâtisseries à la Carte* resulted in more business than Mary Jo could have anticipated. Both Joan and Stephanie pitched in to wait tables and clean up. For two weeks, the shop sold out of nearly every *Spécialités du Jour* as well as most of the standard menu. Customers made inquiries about placing orders for Christmas catering.

On the Monday of the third week back in business, Mary Jo spent the morning in court waiting for her case to be called. Terry had explained it was not the actual trial date, but an appearance before the judge. Terry could not represent her because she had interests in the property and would be a witness, so she had hired a friend to handle the case in court.

When the case was called, Della did not join Mary Jo and her lawyer in front of the judge.

The bailiff handed a note to the judge, who read it. He frowned. They overheard him tell the bailiff, "This should have been brought up here sooner."

The judge glanced over his glasses at Mary Jo standing with her attorney, Briley Gavin.

"Ms. Cooper, I regret you were not notified earlier. Mrs. Strong had to leave court due to a family illness. However, I am setting the hearing for two weeks from today, at ten o'clock. I'm allowing one hour to hear it. Does that work for all present?"

"Yes, Your Honor," Briley said.

He smacked his gavel and called next.

Terry joined Briley and Mary Jo as they pushed the swinging doors at the bar and headed down the aisle past people in the gallery.

Once outside, Mary Jo hissed between her teeth. "She did that on purpose."

"Well, the judge should have been notified sooner so we could have been called," Briley said. "But even if she had shown, the case would not have proceeded today anyway. Now that the date has been set, we'll be ready for her games."

"I just want this over." Mary Jo pressed her fist under her ribcage. "All I want is that display case, my briefcase, and the Redskins jerseys. She can have everything else."

"You'll be fine, Mary Jo. It's a shame you're being dragged through this, but we'll get this over with."

"Thank you, Briley. I appreciate everything." Mary Jo hugged him.

"I'll call you later, Bri," Terry said, brushing her friend's cheek with a kiss.

Briley nodded and jutted his chin toward a couple waiting on a bench. "I see my clients for my next case. Catch you later, ladies." Briley joined the couple.

Mary Jo and Terry exited and walked to Terry's convertible.

"She's going to keep playing games, Terry." Mary Jo jerked the passenger door open and flopped in the seat.

"She may, but the judge won't put up with it. The good thing is we have the date set on the docket. This will be over soon."

Mary Jo pushed two fingers over the area of her solar plexus, but said nothing.

"Are you all right? I notice you keep doing that." Terry exited the parking lot and drove in the direction of the café.

"I had a physical after we got back from deployment." Mary Jo rubbed again.

"You may have an ulcer. You need to get checked for H. pylori. You could have gotten contaminated water overseas."

"I will. I'll get it checked." A few of her colleagues had been diagnosed with stomach ailments related to helicobacter pylori.

"See that you do. I'll be nagging." Terry stopped in front of *Pâtisseries à la Carte*, and added grumpily, "I'll be glad when the parking lot dries out enough to get finished."

Mary Jo waved and ran up the steps. Beth was just flipping

the "Closed" sign.

* * *

By the end of the week, business slowed but maintained a steady pace.

After the initial busy weeks, Saturday morning moved at a snail's pace. Mary Jo took the quiet time to assess the log she had devised to track her daily food sales. Croissants sold out every time they were on the menu, with éclairs a close second, so she and Beth decided these would be offered daily instead of as a specialty. Some desserts, such as *mille-feuille*, also called Napoleons, and *macarons*, were very popular as take-out orders from office workers who bought them to share with colleagues. By the end of October, they should be able to establish the best-sellers from the treats to be offered on occasion.

The parking lot remained muddy and unpaved. Despite the earlier prediction for a dry spell, rain fell every few days, rendering the ground too wet to complete the grading, but a new forecast of sunny weather for ten days promised to alleviate the problem.

Mary Jo usually closed the café promptly at two o'clock, cleaning and preparing for the next day after the doors were locked.

"Wow, this is the first Saturday we haven't had anyone come in by ten o'clock," Stephanie remarked. She sat at one of the ice cream parlor sets, coloring with Tanner.

"It's slow all over Olde Towne," Mary Jo said. "Busch Gardens opened Howl-O-Scream, and the area is full of fall and craft shows drawing foot traffic away from the historic streets. We should close early."

"Can we go to Busch Gardens, Mommy?" Tanner dropped his crayons and scooted from the chair to the table where his mother played solitaire. "Can we?"

"Oops, sorry about mentioning B-G," Mary Jo said.

Beth laughed and tweaked her son's nose. "It's okay. We've

created a monster with this little guy. He can't wait to ride the Loch Ness Monster. He thinks he'll grow tall enough overnight to reach the height marker."

"But I am bigger, see, Mommy." He ran to the room Mary Jo was setting up as the cook shop for kids, *Le Petit Chef.* He pressed his back against the door frame where several pencil lines were drawn, and he put his hand over his head to show he was taller than the last mark.

"I see you tiptoeing, Tanner." Beth laughed. "You're still not big enough."

"Aw, Ma," Tanner drawled as he shuffled back to his table.

"He sounds just like Gage and Connor did when we were kids," Mary Jo said, laughing. "*Aw, Ma,*" she mimicked, dragging out the syllables as she walked toward the display case, dragging her feet and hanging her head.

"You captured their Neanderthal gait perfectly." Beth laughed.

Mary Jo removed a tray of éclairs from the case and turned it sideways, as if somehow customers would be attracted by the change. "Boy, I'm glad I only made a dozen éclairs for today."

"No, you made too many," Stephanie interjected. "Every one of them is calling my name."

"Mine too." Mary Jo plucked the tray from the case and brought it to the table. She turned toward the kitchen and called over her shoulder, "Anyone for coffee?"

The bell over the front door jingled, and Terry walked in. As the heads of her three friends turned in her direction, she stopped short.

"What?" Terry asked.

"Nothing," the others said in chorus.

"You three looked like lions about to pounce on prey. Then I see this crestfallen look come across your face when you realize it's me coming in."

"We thought you were a customer," Stephanie explained.

"You know, that's the second time that's happened to me." Terry grabbed an éclair and took a huge bite.

"What?" Mary Jo asked.

"I enter this establishment like any other paying customer and get greeted like the fair-haired stepchild."

"You're not a paying customer," Mary Jo reminded her as she set four coffee mugs and a full pot on the table.

"Oh, yeah, that's right, I'm not." Terry shrugged and polished off the éclair. She licked chocolate icing off the fingers of her left hand while she reached for a second pastry with her right.

The friends engaged in casual conversation as they decimated the supply of delicate treats.

The front door opened again, and the women turned toward the door.

Della Strong entered the dining area with her sister Georgette.

"Shit," Mary Jo muttered under her breath, jaw clenched.

Della swept her hand across the empty room. "I see you're doing a booming business as usual, Mary Jo. Every time I come in here, it's like this."

"What do you want, Della?" Mary Jo stood up and walked toward the red-headed woman.

"I come in peace." The woman raised her hands, palm out, but her tone dripped with sarcasm.

"Yeah, right," Terry mumbled behind the rim of her coffee cup.

"What do you want?" Mary Jo repeated.

Della brushed past and stroked the glass case. "You know everything I want. But if you want to settle out of court, I'm willing to let you keep a few things in exchange for this display case."

"Forget it, Della. I think you'd better leave. I'll see you in court."

"Oh, that you will." Della hitched her handbag over her shoulder and joined her sister.

Hand on the door knob, she turned and added, "Oh, I almost forgot, Mary Jo. I do have one thing for you." Della reached into her bag and fished out a small box, taking a few steps back into the room to extend her hand toward Mary Jo.

"I found this in Jay's things. I thought you'd like to have it."

Mary Jo accepted the box tentatively and lifted the lid. A silver bracelet with garnet stones nestled on cotton.

"It's not mine." Mary Jo shook her head and handed the box back.

"I thought he might have purchased it for your birthday before he died." Della lifted the lid. "Aren't these rubies?"

"Looks like garnets to me. Garnets are January stones. My birthday is in July."

"Oh? Wait. Jay's old girlfriend's birthday was in January. Oh, I am so sorry. Oh, dear. This is just awful." Della snapped the lid on the box and replaced it. "He always had such feelings for that girl. They should have never broken up. He must have been thinking of her when you were together."

Terry snorted.

Della turned and stepped near the table where Terry sat. "Ah, Terry, how are you, dear? I didn't notice you. When I saw the graffiti on the building that the witch is dead, I thought it meant you."

Terry kept her head straight and raised her coffee cup to an inch before her mouth. She flicked her other wrist in Della's direction, and said, "Rubbish. You should get going, Della, before someone drops a house on you."

Della opened her mouth, but her sister tugged her arm and drew her closer to the door.

"Let's go, Della. You can see them in court."

"That we will." Della called over her shoulder as she let her sister lead her. She slammed the door behind her, sending the bell into an angry peal.

The four women remained silent, Mary Jo standing, fist on hip. Through gritted teeth, she hissed, started to speak and remembered Tanner. She switched words and said, "Witch."

Tanner scampered from the table and skipped to Mary Jo. "Was she the witch from the Wizard dove Oz?" His words ran together as he spoke the title in the way it sounded to him.

His childlike innocence broke the tension. The women laughed. Beth patted his head. "No, honey. Sometimes she just behaves like one. Are you okay, Mary Jo?"

"I'm fine. I just want this over." Mary Jo marched to the door and flipped the "Closed" sign to face outwards. The lock clicked under her fingers. She walked back to the table, adding, "That was perfect, Terry, almost like that quote from *The Wizard of Oz*."

"Childish, probably, but I felt better." Terry shrugged and swallowed the last of her cold cup of coffee.

"It was perfect." Mary Jo repeated and patted Terry's shoulder. "You've seen that movie so many times, you could probably quote it verbatim."

"We all could, I'm sure." Beth jumped up to clear the table.

"Leave it, Beth. You guys go on. I'll clean up."

"You sure?"

"Yes. I'll be done in no time."

Beth called to Tanner. "Hey, little man, let's clean up your toys, and we'll see if Daddy's done working with Chase. We might make it to Busch Gardens today after all."

"Yay!" Tanner tossed crayons haphazardly in a box, scattering a few on the floor in his excitement. He rushed to give the women hugs, and then grabbed his mother's hand, shouting, "Come on, Mommy! Let's go!"

Quiet settled in the room after mother and son left.

"Whew. That boy is something else." Terry leaned back in the chair.

"I hope I have a child just like him," Stephanie said.

"You're not pregnant, are you?" Mary Jo and Terry asked in unison.

"No," Stephanie laughed.

"Have you guys set a wedding date?"

"Not yet. Maybe in December. We're going to look at wedding rings today. We just want a small ceremony. I don't have that many people to invite, so we'll keep it close friends and family. Gage wants to see if his parents will let us hold the reception at their house."

"Mom would love that. She decks the halls from top to bottom, so you'd have your venue already decorated."

"Catered by *Pâtisseries à la Carte*, of course," Mary Jo interjected.

"*Mais bien sûr*! Gage is working with the Hallmark crew today too. I'm going to see if he can spring early."

Terry jumped to her feet. "And on that note, I have to go and look through dusty old family records with Kyle."

"Oh, quite the genealogist, now, aren't you?" Marry Jo teased.

"A woman's gotta do what a woman's gotta do." Terry grabbed her purse and slung it over her shoulder.

"Well, since we are calling it an early day today, I think I'll go through the attics and see what's available to decorate the B and B. The furniture should start arriving next week."

"Mary Jo, is that a good idea, to go up there alone?" Stephanie frowned.

"Of course. Our little conduit to the other world is probably on his way to Busch Gardens, so the ghosts will be sleeping. I'll be fine."

Mary Jo shooed her friends toward the kitchen, their laughter trailing as she shut the back door behind them. She made short work of the few dishes that needed washing, wiped down the table they had used, and boxed the éclairs to stash in the refrigerator.

She glanced around the kitchen for any remaining tasks, and her gaze dropped to the coat rack hanging on the back door.

"Well, I'll be damned." She stared, lifting several aprons from the peg to reveal her fall jacket. "I've been looking for this for weeks. Someone just stacked the aprons over it on the peg, and I guess I didn't notice."

She picked the jacket up. The material seemed to vibrate under her fingertips. She turned it over and dug in the left pocket, withdrawing a crumpled tissue. She tossed it in the trash and searched the other pocket.

The tiny electric shock pierced her index finger as it touched something in the pocket. Her fingers circled the object, warmth radiating up her arm. She withdrew her hand

and uncurled her fingers, revealing a dirt-encrusted lump and strand of metal.

The memory came back to her. She had found the old jewelry piece the day she and Tanner had dug in the dirt. She had shoved it in her pocket and completely forgotten about it when the colonial ghost made her appearance.

In the attic of the Bed and Breakfast, dirty gray mist slithered across the floor, tentacles winding around boxes and containers. The tips turned white with frosty rage, circling around a leather case jammed under a chair rung. A layer of ice formed over the chair and valise.

Mary Jo's palm tingled where the jewel nestled. She stepped over to the sink, opening the faucet for a gentle stream, and rubbed gently. Caked mud and dirt diminished under the flow, revealing a thin gold chain, several links twisted into knots, and a small pendant. She wiped the last of the mud and stared at the heart-shaped ruby, light pulsing from the core.

Next door, as if doused by fire, the ice cracked away and disappeared.

CHAPTER TWENTY

LIZZIE
Portsmouth, Virginia, July 1781

Resisting the urge to look outside, Lizzie fanned her face with her apron as she waited behind the door for Margaret to return from the big house. Twice, she had heard her aunt's raised voice drift through the open windows, followed by the crack of a slap.

Only after the first slap did the child cry out.

A thump resounded from the main house. Lizzie peeked from behind the partially open door and glanced toward the rear of the house.

Too small to carry a basket of laundry down the steps, Margaret pulled one end by the handle as the other end bumped each step. The child strained in a backward walk as she hauled the wicker basket with her. She yanked too hard and lost her balance, the container landing on her ill-fitting shoes.

Lizzie could do nothing but watch until Margaret crossed the threshold. She entered the kitchen backwards, heaving the basket over the step, the momentum propelling her onto her behind.

Lizzie swooped low and stretched a hand to help pull the wicker container into the kitchen. Margaret tugged one more time until the laundry basket cleared the door's path. Lizzie slammed the door shut and rushed to the little girl's side. Tears stained her cheeks, the right one still bearing the outline of Abigail's hand.

"Tell me what happened."

"I did not move fast enough. She threw the sheets on the steps and told me to gather them. She came down and slapped me, and said I must have these washed and dried on the line or she will thrash me with a reed."

"Do not worry. I will help you." Lizzie dumped a pail of water into a basin and handed the bucket to the child. *"Pump as much water as you can carry and hurry back."*

As the child delivered water, Lizzie scrubbed the bed linens, rinsing and wringing them out before tossing them into the basket.

"We will wait some time, because she will know you cannot work fast. Do you see that pole that holds the rope where the clothes will hang?"

Margaret nodded.

"Pull it free so the rope sags. You will be able to reach the line and hang the sheets. Afterwards, you will have to hook the post back under the rope and push it so that the sheets do not drag on the ground. Do you understand?"

Margaret nodded. *"'Tis how I did the laundry for my stepfather."* She dashed from the scullery and struggled to unhitch the rope wedged in a split in the wooden pole. At last she freed the line and dropped the pole.

Lizzie watched, her heart heavy. Lizzie remembered her years of servitude, and realized that Abigail's trip to Richmond had only been a ruse to find an indentured servant to replace Lizzie.

No child should endure such a life.

She untwisted the wet sheets and shook them as best she could in the cramped space, piling them loosely in the basket so it would be easier for Margaret to hang them.

"Go now and work as fast as you can. Bring the empty basket inside, and we will fill it with the rest. She will not come in here, but she may walk outside to check on you."

Margaret nodded and dragged the basket outside the steps. Lizzie could hear the child's loose-fitting shoes slapping the ground and the grunts as she struggled to toss the sheets over the line. Soon she returned with the empty bin.

"The sheets sag nearly to the ground. I must push it back, but now it is heavy."

"You must try hard."

Margaret skittered outside. Lizzie slipped to the other side of the door to peek around the frame. Margaret struggled to lift the line, growling as she gave a mighty heave.

An arm of a red coat took the pole from the child's hand. Lizzie poked her head further around the door frame. Her breath hitched at the sight of the soldier.

Louis stood beside the girl, smiling down.

"What have we here, a damsel in distress?" Louis spoke in a loud, jovial tone. He lifted the pole and tucked the rope in the wedge. With one heave, he raised it until the sheets hung clear and then he lodged the pole in the dirt. The bed linens flapped in the breeze, acting as a shield between him and the main house. He whistled once, low and sharp, and then flicked his wrist in the direction of the door.

A round object flew past Lizzie and landed with a thud. Paper anchored around a rock.

Lizzie puckered her dry lips but she could not force a whistle in response. She dashed across the room, hoping Louis would catch the movement. She grabbed the projectile and unrolled the paper wrapping to read the message. "Tonight, 12. Here."

She wet her lips and managed a single tweet.

"Tweet, tweet." Louis' double whistle signaled he understood. He said a few more words to Margaret. She waved goodbye and found space to flop one more sheet over the rope.

Lizzie leaned back against the wall. Her heart rocked the wall of her chest.

It would be a long wait until midnight.

* * *

Lizzie opened the door a fraction, just wide enough to enable her to hear a signal from Louis. She sat, back pressed against the kitchen wall. Margaret curled beside her, shoulder propped against the butter churn. Lizzie covered her with her cloak.

A streak of lightning illuminated the interior. The church bell tolled, its eerie clang echoing in the night. Margaret buried her face in her arms.

Thunder muffled the twelfth peal.

The door opened on a squeaky hinge.

"Louis?" Lizzie whispered.

"Lizzie?"

"Here, Louis." She pushed Margaret to her feet and scrambled to her own. Lightning outlined his form in the door, and Lizzie grasped his arms, meeting his waiting lips.

He broke the embrace on a clap of thunder. "You must come now."

"I have to take the child with me, Louis."

"'Tis not room enough, Lizzie."

"I will share my space with her. Louis, please, I cannot leave her behind. I prepared her, she knows that whatever happens, she must remain still and quiet."

Louis scooped Margaret in his left arm and said, "Lizzie, take my sleeve. We must leave now." He placed his other hand over his scabbard to reduce the clink, and led Lizzie to the left of the big house. They ran in the shadows, southward, until they reached the churchyard where a wagon waited. The horse whinnied and lurched forward. A man held the horse's bridle, stroking its muzzle until the animal settled.

"Climb in the front seat with James, Lizzie," Louis ordered. "I will settle the child in the back, under the canvas."

"I will be good." Margaret wrapped her arms around Louis' neck and pressed her cheek against his.

He squeezed her thin shoulders and thrust her over the side. "This corner has some space where you can curl. Goodbye, little one."

"Are you not coming?" Lizzie reached for Louis' arm.

"Not yet. James is deserting His Majesty's Army tonight. I shall remain for a while to detract."

James clambered into the seat and picked up the reins.

Louis extended his arm and the men shook hands.

"Be safe, my love," Lizzie leaned down and pressed her lips to his.

Louis tucked a canvas cover over Lizzie's legs and said, "I shall follow soon. I must see my grandfather before I leave." He stepped back and swatted the horse's flank. Illuminated by a streak of lightning, the wagon lumbered forward, swallowed by the night shadows.

Thunder boomed, warning that the storm rolled closer.

He pivoted on one heel and ran toward his grandfather's house, the first drops of rain pelting his face.

MARY JO
Portsmouth, Virginia, present day September

The tingling gradually diminished, along with the light. Mary Jo studied the stone, racking her brain. What had Stephanie once told her about three jewels mentioned in an old letter? She withdrew her phone, dialed Stephanie's number, hanging up at voice mail. Almost immediately, the "March of the Toreadors" tune blared in her hand. Figuring it was Stephanie returning her call, she punched the answer button without looking at the caller ID.

"Hi, Steph," she began.

"Nope, it's me."

She smiled at Chase's voice.

"Want to come over tonight? About seven? I'll pick up some beer and pizza. We can just chill out. You got any éclairs left?"

"How did you know I had éclairs today?"

"Tanner said you did." He laughed. "They came by to pick up Connor and he said you all were eating them when the— and I quote—wicked witch came in."

Mary Jo threw back her head and laughed out loud.

"I like the sound of your laugh, Mary Jo. You should do it more often."

"Thanks for making me laugh, Chase. I'm finishing up here. I'll see you at seven."

When he said goodbye and hung up, Mary Jo could swear she smelled his cologne.

The heart-shaped jewel she held in her other hand flickered with light, warm in her palm.

She set the phone on the counter and raised the stone to the kitchen light.

The tiny sparkle she had noticed was now gone. She held it for several seconds, waiting, but only a necklace remained.

She wrapped the necklace in a paper towel and tucked it in her pocket. She grabbed her keychain and locked the café. With the key to the Bed and Breakfast ready in her hand, she stepped up to the back door and unlocked it. With hand on the knob, she paused.

Would freezing cold or mysterious figures greet her?

She pushed the door open and crossed the threshold, greeted only by the scent of fresh paint and comfortable temperatures.

Chase's crew had nearly completed the renovation. Once the electrician installed the last of the light fixtures and the chandelier for the parlor, the work would be finished.

The tiny kitchen glistened. A door to the left led to the suite of rooms she had originally planned to utilize when guests were present. She could live there permanently and let her mom move to the little house instead of the cramped apartment. Their relationship had warmed considerably, and with the recent news that her mother's cancer was in remission again, they spent more time together.

The feel-good sensation followed her as she roamed through the house. The small dining room was fully furnished. Terry had discovered the table set at an antique shop in the rustic crossroads of the Suffolk community of Driver, and had managed to bargain the price with the seller. Mary Jo trailed her fingers on the cherry surface of the matching buffet and walked through the arch to the parlor.

Two small end tables flanked the bay window, framed with the ruffled curtains Joan had created. The rest of the parlor was woefully stark, as if a woman wore an elaborate hat and shoes, yet stood in a slip as she decided on which dress to wear.

It was time to get serious about the rest of the furnishings.

She skipped up the stairs, her footfalls echoing on the wood tread, and peered into each of the bedrooms she identified by eras.

The Colonial bore three light blue walls. A canopied bed frame, awaiting a new mattress, stood in front of the fourth wall, a darker slate blue. A slate wingback chair she had discovered in an Olde Towne shop on High Street made up the only other furniture in the room.

In The Antebellum, chair railing divided the walls in half, with a lighter green on top and forest green below.

She smiled at the third room, The Victorian. She'd considered cream for three walls and a shade of mauve for the fourth, but Terry had quickly squelched this choice. In the end, they had agreed on a wallpaper design of cream background dotted with tiny mauve roses.

They had not yet named the Bed and Breakfast, having nixed every suggestion so far. Mary Jo touched the tissue resting in her shirt pocket, but no inspiration sparked from the ruby heart.

"Okay, Nameless Inn," she said aloud. "I'm going treasure hunting to get you dressed up nice." She opened the door to the attic stairs and peered up. Streaks of light from the dormer windows crossed like swords, dust mites dancing in the beams. Her fingers flipped the electric switch. The crossed beams and mites disappeared in the synthetic illumination.

Mary Jo opened the door outward and pushed it against the wall, using the toe of her shoe to push a rubber wedge under the door. Stephanie had once been trapped in the attic when the door jammed behind her. Soon after, Terry had bought the wedge to avoid any future entrapment, whether natural or otherworldly.

With each step Mary Jo took upward, the smell of old wood and cloth reached her nose. At the top, her gaze swept the crowded floor. Boxes and trunks competed for space with old suitcases and small furniture.

The roof pitched low, and she had to stoop under the low beams to look around. She found her first treasure immediately—a Victorian-era globe oil lamp that had been electrified for more modern use. She set it near the steps.

She knelt before a steamer trunk. The protective lining still exuded the scent of cedar. Filled to the brim with clothes of bygone eras, the trunk blocked a second, more elaborate steamer trunk that she remembered the Dunbar kids were once convinced was a pirate's treasure chest. She cleared a path and pushed both trunks against one wall under the roof peak. Era-appropriate clothing might provide quaint accents in each room.

Or we could have a Halloween party and use these as costumes! Mary Jo grabbed for the phone in her back pocket to tell Terry of her find. About the same moment she patted the empty pouch, she had a flashback of setting it on the counter while she studied the necklace.

"Dammit," she muttered out loud. She tapped her shirt pocket, the touch of the soft wad reassuring her that at least the necklace was still safe.

Her gaze dropped to a dressmaker's dummy. *Perfect!* She cleared a path through clutter and freed the padded form. Hefting it under one arm, she bumped her way down the narrow steps to the Victorian Room, where she settled it in one corner.

"The woman who used this form must have been tiny," she remarked out loud. The pink satin covering the form showed signs of distress at the seams, exposing a wickerwork frame underneath. Black satin trim had turned purple. It would be a perfect accent piece, dressed in appropriate period clothing. She envisioned it standing near a cheval mirror, with a frame that enabled the mirror to swivel. A feathered hat hooked on the frame would complete the look.

Up the stairs she bounded again and assessed the rest of the room.

She didn't know quite where to begin. She and Terry had each been anxious to start renovating their own properties and needed to start with empty rooms. They had used this building as a catchall. When Chase's crew started work on the Bed and Breakfast, they eventually relegated the entire contents up to the attic.

There was no rhyme or reason to the storage. Most of the antique items came from the attic of Terry's Aunt Ida's house. Terry was ultra-modern and at the time, had little interest in the possible antiquities she had inherited. A few old boxes had been left behind when the house was sold. Mary Jo now wished she had emptied the attic before resuming the renovations after the storm.

A dingy silk lampshade caught her eye. It topped a brass table lamp with ornate claw feet supporting the base. Small holes permeated the shade, and as she reached for it, her finger caught in one, and the fabric disintegrated. Dust fluttered, and she sneezed.

Other than a line of pit marks on one side, the brass looked to be in good shape. She removed the shade and set the brass base beside the globe lamp, then laid a gilt-framed mirror on its back and pushed it to the door. Sconces, clocks, and other bric-a-brac joined the pile as she selected from the muddle.

Two matching ladder-back chairs stood at opposite ends of the room, separated by clutter but easily identifiable as a pair. A third unmatched chair with a higher back sat at the center of the room, surrounded by loose clutter, old shoes, and boxes. The ladder-back chairs offered possibilities, and she picked her way over to one. A stack of old leather-bound books—perfect for accent shelves in each room—covered the seat. She carried the books to line up by the stairwell. Once she wrangled the chair free from the clutter, she lugged it to The Antebellum, and darted back upstairs.

Another trip downstairs, this time carrying the two lamps, moving carefully so the top globe of the Victorian lamp did not wobble. She opened the door to the small linen closet and set the lamps on the floor. Next she jogged up for the books, using the mirror for a tray. Clocks and sconces made up the last delivery. She added the treasures to the closet.

Her legs wobbled a bit on the trek up. *I should call in the troops for reinforcement.* She automatically reached for her phone again, but realized that even if she had it, her friends were occupied elsewhere.

"All right," she said out loud, arching her back to stretch out a kink. "I'll do this another day when I can get the whole gang here. I'll just grab that other chair and call it a day."

The second chair was embedded deeper in the clutter. She leaned over boxes and tugged the upper rung of the back.

Something was wrapped around one of the legs and held it

fast. She pushed more things out of the way and peered under the seat. The leg was wedged in the leather handle of a wooden box about the size of a carry-on suitcase, itself jammed at an angle that rendered it immovable. There was little wiggle room to dislodge the chair.

Beads of sweat and aggravation pearled on her forehead as she shoved a mound of clutter en masse, freeing the case. The leather handle loosened its tight grip and she hefted the chair. Somehow as she lifted it, the leg caught the handle again, causing the trunk to shift with it.

She rocked the chair forward and backward to free the leg from the handle, managing to wiggle it only an inch in either direction. Temper got the best of her as she clenched her teeth and grunted "Aaargh!" before yanking the chair toward her. The leather handle maintained its stranglehold on the leg, rising in the air with the chair until it broke free. It landed with a thud, its contents jangling. The wood cover split. The momentum propelled Mary Jo backward, but she maintained her balance, pulling the chair across the clutter toward her. The chair legs caught loose materials and knocked over small items before it cleared.

"Bastard chair!" She spat the words out, now pissed.

She slammed the chair on its legs, resisting the temptation to toss the troublesome piece down the steps.

Instead, she hefted it against her hip and sidestepped down the stairs. The legs first scraped one wall, and as she adjusted her stance, the legs scraped the other side. Reaching the bottom step, she bumped both sides of the doorframe before she cleared the stairwell and set it beside its mate.

Mary Jo pushed at a strand of hair sticking to her damp forehead. "Bastard chair," she repeated, and trudged upstairs to see what she had knocked over.

The room had chilled considerably. She glanced toward the small window at the evening sky swallowing the last shreds of daylight.

She dragged the box to the stairs and sat on the top step, pulling the case onto her lap. Bound with leather hinges, the case looked innocuous enough. She pushed the lid back. The velvet lining held the cracked wood pieces together. A flap of velvet covered the contents.

The smell of tarnished silver mixed with the sulfur of a burnt match drifted to her nose. She lifted the flap of cloth.

The box was filled to the brim with silver items tarnished black.

Oh, my, this must be worth a small fortune.

Smaller items rested on larger items. She recognized a wine sommelier's *tastevin*, but not three other flat cups. Though somewhat similar but with deeper bowls, she thought they had probably been used for soup. She picked up a salt cellar. The tiny spoon slid out and landed on the base of a candlestick, one of two matching pillars resting on their sides. Discoloring muddled the design of ornate etchings on the base and stem.

She wedged her index and forefingers into a pincer, trying to reach the spoon without dislodging the rest of the contents, but it slipped further between the candlesticks and settled on the velvet.

She growled low in her throat as she pushed bowls, a snuffer, and a chafing dish to the side.

In the cleared space, the folded note was visible; she could see the trace of ink bleeding through the back. She withdrew it, flipped it open and read out loud.

Dear Frank,
Great-Grandmother had a terrible episode last night. She says this silverware is haunted and frightens her. She wants it destroyed, but it is much too valuable to destroy. The candlesticks especially seem to frighten her. Can you please hide it all with your things until—?
Thank you,
Cousin Louisa

Mary Jo picked up the remaining candlestick and gasped as her fingers immediately stuck to the frozen stem in an ice-cold burn. A vapor formed as she exhaled. She drew in her next breath and coughed at the metallic-sulfuric smell. Her eyes watered.

She forced her eyes open, blinking in disbelief at the streak of vapor passing in front of her face.

The gray mist pooled at her hips, a tentacle slithering across her lap. She jolted to her feet and shifted, her feet landing on the third step from the top, her back facing the door below. The abrupt movement sent the box and contents cascading down the stairs.

The haze trailed down the first tread, a form taking shape. Mary Jo kept her gaze locked on it as she eased her right foot to the next riser, stepping down when her foot planted firmly on the tread. Feeling her way to the next step, she moved again, repulsed yet entranced by the slithering cloud.

Mary Jo backed down to the next step, kicking aside one of the silver bowls that rolled by her foot. A muffled voice in the distance shouted her name. She tried to call out, but her throat constricted with the putrid taste of tarnished metal.

Soundlessly, the shape whirled vertically, lengthening into the upper torso of a faceless female. Arms formed, and the specter extended one palm in a pushing motion.

Instinctively, Mary Jo swung the candlestick, rippling the mist.

The figure's tentacle-like arms retracted. The faceless head elongated and bent at the neck. A cavernous black mouth appeared, and the head jutted forward, nose-to-nose with Mary Jo. It hissed once, shrunk back into a shapeless form, then disappeared like smoke up a vent.

The burning sensation in her hand eased, and she let the candlestick fall. The heavy metal struck each wooden riser with a clunk and rolled onto the hall below her.

"Mary Jo!" Chase shouted, boots pounding the floor as he raced from the stairwell to the attic door.

Her lips formed the name "Chase," but no sound came out. She stepped down another step, a candlestick rolling under her shoe.

This time she lost her footing and pitched backwards.

Chase caught her under the arms just before she hit the floor.

Even with Chase breaking the fall, Mary Jo had the wind knocked out of her.

"What the hell just happened?" Chase knelt beside her, supporting her shoulders against his thigh.

Mary Jo pushed into a sitting position and craned her neck to face him.

"The ghost came after me, Chase." She shook her head in disbelief. "I know it sounds crazy. I was fine, digging around up there for stuff for the B and B. I found an antique chest full of old, discolored silver things. The room got cold. This fog started drifting toward me. It swirled around my legs and startled me. I lost my balance when I was backing down the stairs. You got here in the nick of time." She rose to her feet and pulled him to his.

They both stared up at the empty stairwell. The only signs anything was amiss were the scattered silver pieces and the broken chest.

She threw her arms around his neck and held. "How did you know to find me?" she asked.

"I kept getting your blank text messages. I must have gotten ten in a row. When I called and got no answer, I drove right over here. I went to the café first; found your phone, but not you." He handed her phone to her. "When I didn't find you there, I came here. Why did you text me instead of calling?"

She shook her head in puzzlement and spread her hands.

"Chase, I didn't text anything, and as you can see, I didn't have my phone with me here."

He pulled his phone from his pocket and scrolled to the text message screen.

Mary Jo's number appeared in line after line. He punched the text icon after each number. Each showed a blank screen.

They stared at each other.

Then Chase's phone chirped with the sounds of text

messages from Stephanie and Terry. "Mary Jo is sending blank texts. Is everything all right?"

Chase texted back, "All is well. Mary Jo is with me, crazy episode but she'll call you tomorrow. Her phone is turned off for now." After punching the send button, then the off button, he turned to Mary Jo.

She said, "Chase, let's just make sure everything is okay upstairs and get out of here. I don't want to tell anyone about this yet, okay?"

CHAPTER TWENTY-ONE

Attorney Briley Gavin opened the tall double doors leading to the courtroom, metal hinges grinding with a low moan. He gestured for Mary Jo and her group to enter.

A court bailiff spoke in low tones to a clerk sitting at a seat to the far left of the judge's bench in the otherwise empty courtroom. The deputy nodded to Briley and resumed talking.

Briley directed Mary Jo and Terry to the first row of benches on the right side. The rest of the party, consisting of Stephanie, Hannah, and Joan, filed into the next row. They chatted casually, voices low. The murmur reminded Mary Jo of her grammar school days, when students chatted until the bell signified the start of the lesson. She sat motionless. Terry and Briley exchanged a few whispers.

The cumbersome doors in the back groaned whenever other patrons of the court entered. Three times, the collective heads of the room's occupants turned and glanced toward the new arrivals before reverting to their business.

Della strode in beside her sister Georgette, with a younger woman walking just behind them. The three continued talking as they walked up the aisle.

Mary Jo redirected her gaze toward the front of the room, resting it on the American flag stationed behind the judge's bench, to the left of the chamber door. The flags of the

Commonwealth of Virginia and the City of Portsmouth lined the wall to the right of the door.

When Della and her group stepped into Mary Jo's peripheral vision, Mary Jo turned her face toward the right wall to look at a photo gallery of former court judges.

An almost imperceptible buzz sounded near the chamber door. The bailiff straightened and announced, "All rise."

The clink of keys and rustle of papers accompanied the audience's movements as their feet collectively hit the floor. The judge entered the courtroom through a door behind the bench and sat in his high-backed leather chair.

The bailiff announced the judge, then took up a post at one corner of the bench, to the judge's left, and called, "Be seated."

"Strong vs. Cooper," the clerk said in a low voice, handing the judge a folder.

"All parties in the matter of Strong vs. Cooper, please stand," the bailiff said.

"Mrs. Strong?" Judge Forrest raised his eyes over his bifocals and peered at Della, who nodded. "Are you represented by counsel?"

Della answered, "No, Your Honor. I was told I don't need to have an attorney."

"That's correct, you are not required to have an attorney if you so choose. Please have a seat at the table in front of the bar. Are you ready to proceed?"

"Yes, I am."

He shifted his gaze toward the trio in the front row. "Ms. Cooper?" Mary Jo and Briley stood. "Are you ready to proceed?"

"We are, Your Honor," Briley responded.

The judge shuffled papers and faced Della.

"Mrs. Strong, you have filed a warrant in Detinue for property that you feel belongs to you and which you say Ms. Cooper has in her possession. Have you and Ms. Cooper attempted to resolve this matter yourselves?"

"Your Honor, Mary Jo refuses to return my son's property. My son moved out of my house when he went to live with

Mary Jo in sin, but then he died unexpectedly, without a will. I'm his next of kin. I know my son, Judge. He would have wanted me to have his property. She has things I gave him and…"

The judge interrupted her gently. "My condolences on the loss of your son, Mrs. Strong. I have three children of my own, and I cannot comprehend the pain of losing one. But we are not quite ready to begin yet, Mrs. Strong. You'll have your chance in a moment. Do you have witnesses that you will want to call?"

"Yes. My sister and her daughter." The two women sitting with her stood.

"Mr. Gavin, do you have witnesses?" The judge turned toward the defense.

"One, Your Honor," Briley answered.

"All witnesses in this case step forward and be sworn in."

Mary Jo walked around her table and stood in front. Della did the same on her side. The three witnesses formed a line between the two litigants.

"Raise your right hands." The bailiff instructed. When all were in compliance, he said, "Do you solemnly swear to tell the truth, the whole truth, and nothing but the truth, so help you God?"

"I do," the women answered in unison.

Judge Forrest said, "All witnesses will wait outside until your name is called."

Terry turned first and headed down the aisle. Della's witnesses followed behind her.

Della directed her gaze at the women sitting in the gallery. "Why don't they have to leave?" she demanded, pointing at Stephanie, Hannah, and Joan.

"Mrs. Strong, you cannot speak out of turn," the judge cautioned. "This is a public proceeding. If other people are not witnesses in this matter, they may remain as spectators." He slid his glasses further up his nose and shuffled papers.

Della and Mary Jo returned to their seats. Mary Jo winked at her support team before she sat down.

"Before we proceed further, I have some questions. There are thirty-nine items listed on the Bill of Particulars. I would prefer that we not have to deal with a line-by-line accounting if there is any chance of reaching an agreement on any of these items. Mr. Gavin?"

Briley spoke first. "Your Honor, my client has attempted to return a number of these items to the plaintiff, who refused to accept them."

"I want everything," Della snapped. "I told her I wasn't taking anything until she gave me all of it at once."

"Mrs. Strong, I will repeat my caution to you. Do not speak out of turn. I will tell you when to address the court," the judge warned. He turned back to Briley.

"Your Honor," Briley continued. "My client is more than happy to return all of the items except numbers three, four, six, and…" He paused and consulted a paper he was holding. "Six and twelve."

Judge Forrest nodded. "The court accepts that thirty-five articles are not in dispute, and will proceed in the matter of item number three, a Washington Redskins football jersey, item number four, a Washington Redskins jersey, item number six, a black briefcase with Army emblem, and item number twelve, an antique wood and glass case. Mrs. Strong, do you accept that Ms. Cooper will return all of the other items, except those four, which will be the focus of today's case?"

"I want it all, Your Honor," Della repeated.

The judge scribbled something. "The court recognizes that's why you're here, Mrs. Strong. If Ms. Cooper does not dispute the other items you have listed, the court will decide on only those last four items today," he explained patiently. "I will hear what you have to say first. Then I will hear Ms. Cooper's side before I make a decision. Do you understand that this will be the procedure today?"

"Yes," Della said.

"All right, then. Tell me your side."

"Your Honor, my son dated another girl for eight years. When they broke up, he immediately began seeing Mary Jo. I always suspected she had been cheating with him before she broke Jay and Sue up..."

Mary Jo heard Hannah hiss an annoyed "tsk" under her breath.

The judge moved his microphone and interrupted. "Mrs. Strong, you will have to leave out any personal opinions you may have had and stick to the facts of the case. Explain why you think these particular four items belong to you."

"Well, they moved in together, her and my son. She got him to open a joint bank account, and he was putting all of his paycheck in it. I don't know what she was doing with all of his money. He was always broke, and he asked me to buy things for him when he didn't have the money to get things for himself."

Hannah gave a raspy grunt under her breath. This time the judge heard her and glanced in her direction. Hannah cleared her throat, making Mary Jo smile inwardly.

"Tell me about the football jerseys, Mrs. Strong."

"Ever since he was a kid, he's loved the Washington Redskins. About six months before he died, he asked me for money to buy two official jerseys. One was short sleeved, one long, and I gave him almost two hundred dollars for them. They're selling for twice that amount now. If she wants to keep them, I want the value of the shirts from her."

A slow burn ignited in Mary Jo's stomach. Jay had given her those shirts as a birthday present. Della made him sound like a spendthrift who squandered his money on frivolous purchases.

"When did your son buy these jerseys?" Judge Forrest asked.

Della blew her breath in a long exhale, then said. "I don't remember."

"Do you have receipts?"

"Nope, Your Honor. I just know they can be sold online for twice the amount I paid."

Judge Forrest made a notation, then stated. "It doesn't work that way, Mrs. Strong. Fair market value is not what you paid for the item when you bought it. It is not how much it will cost you to replace the item. It is how much a stranger would pay for that same item at a yard sale. Do you have anything else to say about the jerseys?"

Della shook her head. Mary Jo wondered how the judge did not lose patience with her.

"What about the briefcase? You have this valued at six-hundred dollars?" He raised his eyebrow.

"Yes, it was some fancy-schmancy designer bag."

"It must have been. I didn't pay that much for my briefcase. It says it has an Army seal on it. Was this your son's?"

"No, he bought it for *her*." Della waved her arm in Mary Jo's direction and turned with a glare.

Mary Jo met her eyes, stare never wavering.

Della looked away first, turning back to the judge.

"If he bought it for her, Mrs. Strong, it's his gift to her. Why do you want it?"

"I gave him the money for it." Della's voice pitched higher with each syllable. "I want that money back."

The judge scribbled again, asking if she was ready to move on to the display case.

Della nodded.

The judge shifted in his seat. "Answer my questions with a yes or no, please," he said.

Della nodded, then said, "Yes, Judge. Jay and I were together. I wanted to buy some antiques and needed him to bring his truck. He said he was out of gas so I bought him a tank. He said she was buying something for her bake store, and he didn't have any money."

For the first time, Mary Jo broke her disciplined posture and shifted impatiently. *Shut up, bitch. That's not true.*

"Well, I couldn't find anything I wanted, but in this one store Jay found this antique case. It was wooden, with a rounded glass front, and had a refrigerated section. He wanted to buy it for her shop and asked me to loan him the money. But I also told him I wanted that case if he and Mary Jo ever broke up. I didn't think they would last long, you see."

This time Hannah muffled her derisive snort with a cough.

"Where is this case now?"

"She has it in her café. I'm sure she'll be closing down. The food's terrible."

"Mrs. Strong, I'm going to remind you this one last time, to keep your comments related to your case. Now, you say this case is valued at five thousand dollars. How did you determine the value? "

"Your Honor, I looked up a similar case online, and that was the price they listed."

"The same thing applies here, Mrs. Strong. It's the fair market value a person would expect to pay at a yard sale. Do you have anything further for the court?"

"Just this photo I have, Your Honor. Of the display case I want back." Della rummaged through her purse, removing wallet, tissue, and clanging keys. She pulled out a photograph and got up to walk around her table. Briley held his hand out for the picture, and Della whisked it from his reach.

"That's for the Judge, not you," she snapped. She took another step forward, and the bailiff blocked her path, holding his hand out. She slapped the picture in the palm of his hand and stepped back behind her table. She slid the chair back with an angry scrape. The judge whispered something to the bailiff when he brought the photo to the bench.

Mary Jo's gaze followed the bailiff's steps, wondering if all eyes in the courtroom were riveted in the same direction. The bailiff leaned close to Della's ear and whispered something. She straightened her back.

"What can your witnesses add?" the judge asked.

"They know that I wanted that case."

"If that is all you wanted to call them for, I will accept that, and we can continue."

"Yes, Your Honor."

"Do you have anything else to add?"

Della shook her head, adding, "No, sir."

The judge angled his head to Briley, "Do you have any questions for the plaintiff?"

"Not at this time, Your Honor."

The judge excused Della.

Mary Jo was called to the stand.

The judge reminded her she was under oath.

After Mary Jo complied with Briley's request to state her full name and address, he asked, "Ms. Cooper, please tell the court how these items came into your possession. Let's start with the Redskins jerseys."

"Jay and I had been engaged for about a year. We had just moved in together. He gave those to me for my birthday."

Briley handed her a photograph. "Are these the jerseys?"

"Yes. They have the number eight on them because that's the date of my birthday, July eighth. We used to joke that he looked like the player who wore that number."

"These are women's jerseys, correct?"

"Yes."

Briley showed the pictures to Della, who shrugged, and then he handed them to the bailiff, who took them to the judge. Briley continued speaking as he walked back. "You and Jay had a shared checking account, correct?"

"Yes."

"And you both contributed money and wrote checks from this joint account?"

"That's correct."

Briley picked up a paper and handed it to Mary Jo. "Please tell the court what this is."

"This is a check Jay wrote to his mom—Mrs. Della Strong—for one hundred ninety-seven dollars and ninety-nine cents, dated July tenth, twenty-twelve."

"Is there a notation in the memo section?"

"Yes." Mary Jo read, "'To mom for MJ jerseys.'"

"And who endorsed the back of the check?"

Mary Jo turned it over. "Della Strong."

Briley showed the check to Della, who shrugged.

"I'd like to introduce this to the court, Your Honor," he said, handing it to the bailiff.

"Now, Ms. Cooper, this check was dated July tenth. Please

explain to the court the significance of that date."

"Jay wrote the check after my birthday to keep the jerseys a secret. He had his mom place the order instead of using our account so I would not see the sales before my birthday and ruin his surprise. He paid her after he gave them to me."

Briley went through a similar line of questioning regarding the briefcase Jay gave her for Christmas. Once again, Mary Jo produced a check Jay wrote to his mother after the holiday.

"The last item in question is the pastry display case in this photograph." He showed it first to Mary Jo, then Della, before handing it to the bailiff to take to the judge.

"How did this case come into your possession, Ms. Cooper?"

"Like Della said, Jay was with her and located it at an antique shop. He knew I had been looking for something like this for the café, so he texted a photo of it. I loved it. He didn't have his bank card with him because he had damaged the electronic strip and was waiting for the new one. The store manager agreed to knock off three hundred dollars if he bought it right then, so Della paid for it. Then I gave her a check for fifteen hundred and ninety dollars, which included sales tax."

Briley passed a paper to Mary Jo, and she repeated the check details, ending with Della's endorsement on the back.

"Explain to the court why you have not returned the other property to Mrs. Strong."

"I was deployed shortly before she made her request. Everything had been put in storage, and my friend, Ms. Dunbar, located Jay's property and took it to Della. She refused it, saying she wanted everything. Ms. Dunbar returned the items to storage. Then Mrs. Strong filed the civil case, which was continued until I completed my deployment in Afghanistan."

"Thank you for your service to our country, Ms. Cooper." The judge studied the last check the bailiff handed him, then said, "Mrs. Strong, if you have been reimbursed for these items, I'm not quite sure why you feel they belong to you as part of your son's estate."

"I was with him when he bought these things, Your Honor. I told him I wanted the case if they ever broke up."

"That may be, but once you were paid for the case, it belonged to Ms. Cooper."

"Your Honor, she doesn't deserve these things. She left my son alone while she was traipsing around playing G. I. Jane, she…"

"That's enough, Mrs. Strong," the judge warned.

"But then she…"

"Mrs. Strong, if you say another word without me asking you a question, I will hold you in contempt of court. Deputy, call the witnesses back in."

The door hinges grated like the protests of a tired old man as the women opened the door and returned to their seats. Briley scribbled something on a legal sheet and slid it to Terry, who had slipped directly behind him. She glanced at it and nodded.

"In this matter, the Court accepts that the defendant has agreed to turn over all other items on the Bill of Particulars, and you have agreed to accept them, whether or not you agree with any decisions of this Court regarding any other part of this litigation."

"I do, Your Honor, I understand. I just don't want her—or her—" She pointed to Mary Jo first, then Terry. "I don't want either of them to come near me."

"Your Honor, my office has possession of the items and will arrange delivery," Briley said.

The judge nodded. "In the matter of items three, four, six, and twelve, I find that the plaintiff has no claim for these items, and the Court finds for the defendant. These items will remain the property of the defendant. Case dismissed." He tapped his gavel. "The court will take a fifteen minute recess."

"All rise," the bailiff announced. The spectators in front of the bar and in the gallery rose to their feet, and the judge disappeared behind his chamber door.

Della slapped her hand on the table and gathered her

papers. The bailiff walked over. She glared but remained quiet. She slung her purse over her shoulder and passed the row where her sister and niece waited. They filed out behind her, and the bailiff followed them into the hallway.

"We'll wait here for a minute, give the deputy a chance to clear the doorway," Briley said, shuffling papers together.

Mary Jo breathed out a sigh of relief. She dropped to her seat, leaned her elbow on the table and rubbed her forehead. Her loved ones gathered behind her, talking at once.

Hannah's distinctive voice rasped, "She's lucky she didn't piss the judge off."

"I'm sure that's why he sent the bailiff to her," Briley said. "In all fairness, people who come to court for the first time are often not aware of the protocol. That's why attorneys try to prepare their clients beforehand, or even groom them to behave with a certain decorum. She didn't want to have an attorney, so the judge took that into consideration. He was more tolerant than usual out of sympathy for her loss, but she was getting on his nerves. That's probably why he took a recess."

"I think he was very genuine and showed his concern when he said he couldn't imagine what it would be like to lose a child." Joan stood behind Mary Jo and patted her shoulder. "What's next for Mary Jo?"

"Well, Della has ten business days to file an appeal. I doubt that she will, but we'll have to wait to be sure. In the meantime, my office will handle the transfer of the property. But I've got to head out for a case in Chesapeake." He shook Mary Jo's hand and grabbed his briefcase.

Mary Jo pushed the chair back from the table, scooping papers. "Thanks, everyone, for coming to…" she said as she turned around. Her jaw dropped. "Chase! When did you get here?"

"I slipped in when Terry came out."

Mary Jo rarely demonstrated her emotions in public, but her voice cracked when she said, "That means a lot, Chase."

"I was worried, especially after the incident in the attic."

Choruses of "What incident?" and "What happened?" followed.

"Let's get out of here," Mary Jo said with a shake of her head.

* * *

Mary Jo refused to discuss it in the parking lot. "Let's go to the café."

"I've got lunch waiting," Hannah said, and hugged Mary Jo.

Chase declined, and Mary Jo told the others she would join them shortly.

"I'm glad it's almost over for you, Coppertop," he said when they were alone. They stood face to face, resting their shoulders against the door of his truck. "Sorry about blowing the lid on the ghost story."

"It's okay. I was going to tell them today." Mary Jo smiled. She slid her palm over his heart, comforted by the steady beat under her fingers. "Thanks for being there."

"Glad to be there. I just wanted to tell you I'm going to be gone for a few days. My mom's been thinking about putting her place in Nag's Head up for sale, and she has a buyer unexpectedly lined up, a relative of a nurse she works with. They'll be going down there for the Columbus Day weekend, and want to look it over then. There are a few things I need to fix first, so I'm going down with her. I'll be back Friday. I'd like to take you to dinner Friday evening."

Mary Jo nodded, then touched her forehead to his. "I'm sorry you had to hear what she said about me and Jay in the court room."

Chase placed his hand over the one she pressed against his heart. With his other, he touched his fingertip under her chin and lifted her face. He pressed his lips to hers.

Her own heart soared.

* * *

Ten minutes later, she joined the others waiting patiently at *Pâtisseries à la Carte*. She carried a box containing the silver with her, but left it unopened as she placed it on a nearby table.

Over lunch, she held their attention as she described the odd events in the attic.

"I can't believe you didn't tell us right away," Terry chided.

"Don't nag me, Terry, I just didn't want to deal with it. It was over, and I was safe."

"You should have told us," Stephanie interjected. "I remember my horrifying incident during the storm, when the evil ghost tried to pull me from the window."

"And you couldn't call anyone, yet you dealt with your episode just fine, Steph." She grimaced, and added, "I didn't mean that to sound so harsh. I just didn't want to deal with all that woo-woo shit literally getting in my face at the time."

She scooted from the table and brought over the box, opened the lid and lifted the velvet cloth. "These were originally in the old case I dropped down the stairs."

Joan leaned forward and remarked, "I don't think I've ever seen these before."

"There was so much stuff crammed in Aunt Ida's attic, and I was so impatient to start the renovations, I never really looked through stuff. We just had the movers pile it all upstairs in the Bed and Breakfast." Terry fingered a candlestick.

"They seem so innocuous, now," Mary Jo said. She picked up the *tastevin*. "I know these are valuable, and not for use in the B and B. But I wondered if I could have this *tastevin*?"

Terry shrugged. "Sure, you can have it. You know I'm not into antiques. You and Mom talk over all that other stuff, decide what you want to do with it."

"I know just where you can take all of this, get it cleaned up, and appraised." Joan touched the rim of the tarnished *tastevin*. "In fact, I was going there after lunch, I'll be glad to check with the owner. She does beautiful work."

"I'd like to go with you. But there are a couple of other things." Mary Jo unfolded the note and read the contents.

"Now we're going back to our genealogy and all of Kyle's

discoveries for a moment. If I remember correctly, Louisa would be in my line of ancestors, and Frank would be the cousin of her husband Edward...I think."

"Let's keep the ancestors out for the moment," Terry declared, taking the note from Mary Jo. "Who is the great-grandmother and why did she seem frightened by these candlesticks?"

Stephanie snorted as she peered over Terry's shoulder. "That would make her an ancestor, Terry."

"Yeah, yeah." Terry waved her hand impatiently. "But why would candlesticks frighten someone? And what does 'until' with a dash mean? The great-grandmother must have been old. Were they waiting for her to die?"

"These may be mysteries we will never solve," Joan said as she took her turn reading the note.

"That's still not all." Mary Jo unfolded the necklace from the tissue now protecting it.

Stephanie gasped and raised her hand to her throat, touching the small diamond hanging from her chain. "That's a ruby heart," she declared as she pointed to Mary Jo.

"It needs to be cleaned and the chain repaired, but I'm pretty sure it is a ruby." Mary Jo explained how she had found the clump in the dirt, putting it in her pocket and dismissing it until she found it in the jacket weeks later. Then she added, "But, Stephanie, didn't you once tell us something about reading a letter, which said the mother gave each of her daughters a necklace? The diamond teardrop, the ruby heart, and the cross with sapphires?"

"I did. And what I'm about to say is already giving me goose bumps, Mary Jo." Stephanie shivered. "In Clothiste's letter, she described each of her daughters' personalities, and said the heart necklace represented her daughter of courage. That daughter was Marie Josephé. I didn't realize it until now, but look at the similarities you share with her. You have almost the same name. You speak fluent French. You like to bake. And, like her, you are the epitome of courage."

Mary Jo looked down at the necklace, sudden warmth

tingling her hand. She said nothing, wrapping it back in the tissue. She tucked it back in her purse and said, "Joan, I'd really like to go with you to that shop today."

"I need to go there as well," Terry added. "My necklace caught on a sweater and damaged one of the circles surrounding the cross. I can have it fixed. I've worn it so long, I don't like to be without it."

"Let's go make a jeweler very happy today," Mary Jo said as she stood and indicated the door.

CHAPTER TWENTY-TWO

CLOTHISTE
Portsmouth, Virginia 1781

Pain seared through Clothiste's body, and her shoulder pulsed with the sensation of someone thrusting a burning knife in and out of her bone. She shifted restlessly and forced herself into a sitting position. She stopped midway, eyes closed until the swimming sensation passed. In spite of the sultry night and the fever coursing through her, she shivered. The room felt as though a freezing air had drifted through.

Lightning ripped across the sky, followed by the distant rumble of thunder. Another summer storm approached.

Questions rattled her brain. Was this the second night after the shooting or had more time passed than she realized? Were her daughters safely at the camp and under her husband's care or did harm befall them?

Perhaps Phillip would know! Was he awake?

She slid her legs over the edge of the bed. Her feet touched the floor, the jolt of cold piercing her skin as if she had stepped barefoot into snow.

The freezing sensations passed, and her flesh burned again with fever. She grabbed the poster at the foot of the bed, then shuffled to the closed door, leaning for strength as she listened before turning the knob. Grateful the door opened without a sound, she rocked in place until she had gained her balance.

Another streak of lightning shredded the sky, furnishings in the

255

hallway forming ominous shapes before disappearing in the dark. The church bell tolled twelve times, the final peal engulfed by the next roll of thunder. She turned to the right, sliding her hand along the wall for support and guidance as she crept to Phillip's room.

A thin light flickered from the partially-opened door to Phillip's bedchamber, but no sounds emerged. Clothiste gripped the doorjamb as she pulled herself into a position to peer into the room.

A crack of lightning lit the room.

She stifled the gasp escaping her lips at the scene before her.

Phillip lay on his stomach, unmoving, face to one side facing the doorway. In the flickering candlelight, Clothiste could see his eyes were shut. The wicked one stood poised at the head of the bed, holding a pillow as she leaned toward her husband. She pressed it to his face.

"Stop!" Clothiste thought she screamed, but the voice echoing in her head sounded distant. She reached a hand forward and slumped against the doorframe. A low growl of thunder revealed that the storm edged closer.

"Stop!" She found the strength to shout.

Abigail whirled, her features lined with shadows from the meager light.

"You fool!" She dropped the pillow on the floor and stepped toward Clothiste, spittle spraying as she rasped, "How I hate you. You have caused nothing but trouble."

"You were trying to kill him." Clothiste's voice returned to normal as anger surged through her.

"My husband will never walk again. He would not want to remain an invalid." Abigail took slow, deliberate steps toward the younger woman.

"You cannot just kill."

"Of course I can. I shall kill twice tonight." Abigail pursed her lips in disgust. "But I see I should have started with you."

Clothiste backed into the hall. She felt a sharp jab against her back and realized she had stumbled into the edge of a small hall table.

A flash of lightning crackled outside of the hall window, illuminating the wicked one's pinched face. As Clothiste steadied herself with her good arm, her hand brushed against a candleholder. Another thunderclap boomed, muffling the sound of the candle falling as she forced the unlit taper to the side. Her fingers closed around the base of the silver stand.

"I tried already to kill you, you know." Abigail's lips curled into a

thin smile. "Subtly. Little drops of laudanum here and there in your tea or soup, so no one could detect anything. I should have emptied the bottle and rid myself of you long ago."

"Why do you hate us so?" Clothiste asked. "We have done nothing to you."

"Are you not a woman of French blood? That is all I need to hate you." Abigail stepped closer. "But Phillip—I thought I had won him over. He was as English as I—except for the vile blood in his veins. He called on his solicitor to discuss changing his will. Did you know that? Your daughters will get it all. I will get nothing. But I will not let that happen. I will kill you now, and then him."

A sudden burst of strength came over Clothiste, and she swung the candlestick with all the force she could muster. The distance between the two women was greater than she judged, and the square base grazed her stepmother-in-law's jaw before Clothiste lost strength and dropped it.

Abigail's shriek pierced the quiet, and she lunged in rage.

Clothiste's limp arm flailed at her side as she grabbed Abigail's throat with her good hand. Abigail broke free and pounced, knocking Clothiste into a sitting position on the short hallway table. Clothiste's head cracked against the wall as she drew her knee to her chest and thrust her foot into Abigail's stomach. Abigail shuffled backward from the blow. Clothiste struggled to step around her toward the bedroom, but Abigail recovered quickly and clutched at her from behind, striking the injured shoulder.

Clothiste flinched and spun around, using her good hand to rake her nails across Abigail's neck. The two women locked in a ruthless embrace, bounced against the wall, spinning back across the hallway to the opposite wall, and into the short banister at the top of the steps.

The wood splintered but held.

Lightning flashed simultaneously with a burst of thunder that shook the house as the two women teetered near the stairwell. They leaned to one side, clawing at each other, their balance shifting as they changed directions.

The next thunderclap drowned out the thud down the steps.

MARY JO
Portsmouth, Virginia, present day October

257

Terry parked her Maserati behind the Bed and Breakfast and stepped onto new sleek black asphalt, her pink fuzzy slippers a contrast to the dark surface. Next week the pavers would stencil parking stripes, completing the last repair to damages caused by the hurricane.

She popped the trunk and grabbed an oversized plastic sack containing four sets of sleeping bags and pillows. Grappling through the rear door of the Bed and Breakfast, she caught a whiff of apples and cinnamon. She squished the contents of the bag until she could see around it, and her gaze fell on the aroma's source—a tray of freshly baked mini apple turnovers.

Mmmm, chaussons aux pommes! "Oh, thank you, Hannah," she said aloud as she maneuvered between the counter and the work island, taking care not to bump the food trays with the cumbersome bag. Her eyes took inventory as she passed the dining room table. Petite éclairs and miniature cream puffs filled each layer of a pretty three-tiered stand. Other trays bore fruit and cheeses.

Mary Jo's treasured bottle of Dom Pérignon chilled in a glass bucket containing a mix of ice and water.

A grown-up pajama party! They were going to have such fun tonight.

Terry squeezed the bag to force it through the doorway to the parlor and stopped short as a rapid chill overcame her.

Devoid of furniture except for four air mattresses, the room was freezing. A thin sheet of ice crackled over the glass panes, dimming the light filtering in. The walls took on a dull gray aura. Puffs of vapor followed her jerky exhales as she glanced around, her feet rooted to the spot.

In the kitchen, the back door slammed shut. Voices and laughter filled the air, followed by clangs of metal and glass dishes. The cold had only lasted a few seconds. As suddenly as the arctic blast had penetrated the room, it dissipated. The last of the evening sun filtered through the window, and Terry's breathing returned to normal.

She sensed Mary Jo behind her but remained unmoving,

staring in the room.

"Terry? *Terry!*" Mary Jo raised her voice and shook Terry's shoulder. At last Terry turned, her mouth gaping.

"What is it? What happened?" Mary Jo grabbed the bag from her.

Stephanie rushed in, a maroon housecoat covering her plaid pajamas. "I heard yelling," she said in concern.

Terry directed her gaze toward Stephanie, a frown appearing between her eyes. "I just had one of those 'frozen-in-time' moments you and Mary Jo have had. The kitchen was fine when I passed through it, checking all the goodies." She dropped to one of the air mattresses on the floor and pulled her jacket around her pajamas.

"Are you okay?" Stephanie dropped beside her and put her arm over Terry's shaking shoulder.

"I am. It's just that the room was like a freezer for a few seconds. The windows had a thin sheet of ice glazing over them, as if frost had frozen on them. I actually heard it cracking, the way ice does when you drop a cube in a glass of water. And the room lost color, like a cloudy black and white picture. And it felt—evil." She shook her head. "But when you two came tramping through the kitchen, it disappeared like that." She snapped her fingers with a crisp jerk.

"Maybe we shouldn't stay in here tonight," Stephanie suggested.

"To hell with that!" Mary Jo spat out. She held her hand out to Terry and pulled her from the awkward mattress to her feet, then repeated the move with Stephanie. "If you don't want to stay, that's fine with me. But I plan on being here all night, drinking champagne and eating decadent food." She shook her fist toward the walls. "And I dare whoever you are to appear."

"I'm staying, Mary Jo," Stephanie said firmly. "But, geez-Louise, don't encourage the damn thing to show up."

"Whatever is here, we three together are stronger than it." Mary Jo stomped toward the plastic bag, grabbed a rolled sleeping bag and tossed it onto one of the air mattresses.

"Screw ghosts. I claim this corner."

The other women each selected an air mattress and rolled out sleeping bags.

The back door banged again and Beth called out.

"In here," Mary Jo answered.

Beth entered the room dressed in a pink housecoat, arms laden with flowered cloth bags, and said, "Hi, girls. I've got our beauty supplies all ready." She stopped when she saw their faces. "What's wrong?"

"Hi, Beth." Terry hugged her sister-in-law and grabbed a navy blue sleeping bag, trying to appear nonchalant. "We're fine now. I just had a near-ghost experience. We're selecting our sleeping corners now. I was just about to make yours up." Without leaving an opening for Beth to ask questions, she fluffed a navy bag with a plaid liner and added, "Mom says these haven't been used in ages. Not since the boys were teens and had some campouts in the back yard with Chase."

"Eww." Stephanie wrinkled her nose and tossed her bedroll aside. "Who knows what they did in those things? I don't think I want to sleep in this. Unless it was Gage's." She peered at the name written in bold marker on the label and held it out. "Look, it *is* his." She sighed, a dreamy sparkle developing in her eyes as she hugged the sleeping bag to her.

Terry bopped her with a pillow. "Dingbat. Mom and Hannah laundered them for us. Can't you smell the Downy?"

Beth looked inside her forest green sack. "Look, I have Connor's."

"That leaves Dad and Chase."

"I have Chase's," May Jo began, then bit her lip, hoping her friends failed to notice she hadn't even looked at the label.

But notice they did. Terry pounced first. "How did you know which was his?" Her eyes narrowed. "Don't tell me you did the deed with him in it?"

"No." Mary Jo's voice wavered unconvincingly. She tossed her pillow at Terry. "Get your mind out of the gutter, woman."

Stephanie swatted a pillow against Mary Jo's backside and said, "Oh, no, you're not getting off the hook that easy. Did you or didn't you?"

"No, we didn't," Mary Jo insisted. Then she half-smiled. "But we did do some heavy making out in it one night."

"You slut!" Terry feigned shock.

"Like you didn't know." Mary Jo sent a pillow careening toward her oldest friend, who expertly dodged it. The cushion caught Beth on the back of the head.

Beth jerked around, brushing hair out of her eyes. "All right, if I didn't have a bun in the oven, I'd let you have it," she threatened with a laugh, shaking a pillow at Mary Jo. Then she patted her stomach and added, "And on that note, ladies, my baby says she's starving. Let's raid the kitchen now, and you can tell me what happened."

Feet wearing a medley of pink fluffy slippers, gray socks with black cats, maroon socks with orange Virginia Tech insignia, and tan military-issue socks shuffled to the kitchen.

Mary Jo tapped the counter. "Before we begin, we are going to pop the cork on my three hundred and thirty-two dollar bottle of Dom Pérignon and toast the grand opening of the B and B on Halloween night." She reached for the bottle. "You won't hear the traditional pop with this bottle. You waste bubbles if you pop the cork, and we are not losing one bubble in this costly delight."

"I see you have non-alcoholic wine for us," Beth said, patting her tummy again.

"I promise a new bottle of Dom Pérignon to celebrate her arrival," Mary Jo said as she flicked her wrist. The cork released with a soft sigh, and she used a small linen towel to wipe the neck.

"Oops, I almost forgot." She reached into a small cloth bag, withdrew the antique *tastevin* on a dark red velvet cord and placed it around her neck. She placed the linen over her arm and posed as Stephanie snapped photos with her cell phone.

"It doesn't look like the same tarnished junk!" Terry cried.

"The jeweler who fixed the ruby necklace repaired this as well. Beautiful, huh?" Mary Jo slid her thumb in the punt of the magnum bottle, spread her fingers along the barrel, and expertly poured an inch into each of the three flutes.

"Beautiful," she repeated. This time she directed her attention to the bubbles dancing in the flute. As she waited for the froth to settle, she opened the sparkling ale for Beth before filling the other flutes.

Terry slipped her fingers around the base of a flute and held it up. "To the success of *Pâtisseries à la Carte* and the Bed and Breakfast, for which we still need a name."

Stephanie raised her glass. "We could call it 'Clothiste's Inn,'" she suggested, in honor of the ancestress she shared in different ways with each of the other women. "About whom I have more information to share later."

"I like the sound of that." Terry and Beth said in unison.

"Clothiste's Inn it is," Mary Jo decided.

With a light touch of flutes, the Bed and Breakfast was christened "Clothiste's Inn."

In the attic, a dirty silver mist slithered around the clutter, pulsing gray steam before dissipating with an angry hiss.

After the first round of poker and food sampling, champagne gave way to cocktails. The group switched to Texas Hold 'Em and the betting grew daring. Stephanie finally won the pot, scooping chips into her lap with a gleeful laugh.

Beth spread out her supply of nail polish. The women bantered back and forth as they studied colors. Terry opted for a lilac tint, Stephanie a deep maroon to match her VT socks, and Beth a baby girl pink.

Mary Jo selected last. "French manicure for my hands, but I want that neon coral for my toes."

"I'm surprised you'd pick that, Mary Jo." Stephanie shook the maroon and twisted the cap. "You're straight and narrow right to your core."

"I've never been a girlie-girl, but I guess an inner one is trying to emerge. Which reminds me—these old Army socks have got to go." Mary Jo shrugged and tossed them in the trash. "I've always kept my fingernails subtle while in the service, but you should see the colors my combat boots have hidden."

"I think men can be surprised by a woman's toe color, don't you?" Terry asked coyly.

Mary Jo wriggled her bares toes and smiled. "They sure can." Then she blushed and looked up.

"Aha!" Terry shouted triumphantly. "You and Chase did the deed!"

"Shut up!" Mary Jo sputtered, warmth radiating to the roots of her hairline.

"Oh, praise heaven, finally." Stephanie clapped her hands. "Spill."

"Which time?" Mary Jo clamped her jaw shut. *I'll call it "Damn" Pérignon from now on.*

"Oh, more than one? Tell us about all of them." Beth rolled over on her tummy. "I can use it to cheer me up when I am as big as a house and not able to do anything."

"Well, it's obvious you've had it more recently than I have." Terry copied Beth's move, pink fuzzy feet swaying in the air. "I've been without for—let's see. Less than a year, but I'm in the double digits on the months. So details, please, before I forget how it's done."

"Don't listen to them, Mary Jo," Stephanie interjected. "I'm just glad you and Chase have found each other again."

"I'm not saying anything other than..." Mary Jo fanned her face. "Wow. And wow. And *wow*! And on that note," she said smugly, admiring the fine white lines she had just painted on her left fingertips, "allow me to finish my mani."

Stephanie's sudden squeal sent heads turning in her direction. She grabbed Mary Jo's left hand, smudging the fresh nail color and peered.

"Is that an *engagement* ring?"

Terry and Beth looked at Mary Jo's left hand.

"I didn't think you guys would ever notice," Mary Jo laughed. "I've stretched my hand outward all night waiting for *someone* to see it." She reached for the bottle of remover and added, "Although Steph just wrecked my perfect lines."

"I'm sorry. I'm just excited for you. I want everyone to find the perfect guy. When did this happen?"

"Late last night, after Chase came back from his mother's place in the Outer Banks."

"I'm so happy for you, Mary Jo." Stephanie swiveled her head toward Terry. "And what about you and Kyle, Terry? Any sizzle there?"

Terry huffed, blowing her bangs upward, and frowned. "I don't know about him. I thought I liked him, but he's such a nerd and so not my type."

"You're just piqued because he isn't swooning over you like every other man in town who isn't a relative—or a near relative." Mary Jo smirked and blew on her nails.

"Shut up, Mary Jo," Terry said. Then she added, "Although there was that one time Chase and I locked lips at one of the family barbecues."

Mary Jo sat straighter as her smirk faded. "What are you talking about?"

Terry hummed as she swirled a lime slice in her glass.

"She's just trying to antagonize you, Mary Jo," Stephanie cautioned. To change the subject, she added, "I hear Kyle might be your next tenant after I leave."

"Yeah. I'm relieved I don't have to look for new tenants. I'm kind of sorry I built an apartment there. I should have set up another business office or something. Kyle seems really interested in relocating to this area. He's finding a lot of research for his family tree, as well as Mom's. But the man is so wrapped up in writing his genealogy book and researching Mom's family tree, he only sees me as an extended branch of said tree."

"Well," Stephanie chewed on a mint leaf from a mojito. "You might have to pull a trench coat and high heels act to get his attention."

"Hit him over the head with an anvil might be more like it," Terry muttered.

For the next two hours, the women indulged in pure feminine friendship as they helped each other apply polish and topcoat, and took turns under the nail dryer Beth brought.

Despite their best efforts, no amount of cajoling by her friends could induce Mary Jo to reveal anything else. The settling of her heart was between her and Chase—although a little clarification of his kiss with Terry might be in order.

Stephanie, sporting maroon nails with an orange VT on each pinkie, stood and stretched before reaching to slide her flipchart from the foyer.

"Time for a genealogy update."

She ignored the groans from the other women and handed each a packet of papers. "Here is what I have gathered from the documents so far. And, I might add, I've compared the French and English versions, and they are pretty accurate. Whoever translated those original letters back in the mid-eighteen hundreds did a pretty good job. I just wish so much wasn't missing." She pushed her chart to the center of the floor. "I've made each of you a copy of the notes on the chart. Look it over later and see if I missed something."

Mary Jo set her booklet to the side. "I'd rather have you tell us now while I sip my champagne." She rolled on her tummy and braced her elbows on the floor to pour more liquid into her flute. After the expensive bottle of Dom Pérignon, she'd broken open a more sensibly priced bottle of champagne, but she still didn't care to waste a bubble. She stared at Stephanie, and said, "Maybe I have sipped too much. When did you become a twin?"

Laughter followed, and Stephanie rapped on the stand.

"Pay attention, class," she said in her best schoolmarm's voice, as she pointed.

Three columns lined the poster. In the first column Stephanie had posted her name. Mary Jo's and Terry's names headed the other two columns.

Stephanie trailed her finger down the column under her name. "We know from the diaries and letters that these three properties have been in Terry's family since the American

Revolution, when Clothiste's daughters Nicole and Marie Josephé spent time here.

"We've been able to document that I am descended from Nicole, and Mary Jo is a descendant of Nicole's sister Marie Josephé. Kyle and I think Terry is related to them as well, but we haven't found the proof yet." She poked at Terry's name on the paper. "Everything remained status quo until we found records of family members who lived here during the Civil War. We know all three houses suffered varying damage around eighteen sixty-three."

She nibbled on a ham biscuit, using her free hand to write and underscore the name "Nicole."

"Although I had interactions with Nicole's ghost, she only appeared to me in the apartment. And maybe I saw her once out by the magnolia tree before the storm." She looked at the other women, and they nodded. "She wanted me to find her teardrop. We also know the attic of my building is where one of the owners hid valuables during the Civil War, which they overlooked, and I found during the hurricane. Once I uncovered the white diamond, Nicole stopped appearing to me."

Mary Jo scrambled to her feet, stood on the opposite side of the chart, and poked at her own name. She drew the lid off a marker and wrote Marie Josephé beside her name.

"Although I saw a ghostly face several times, the ghost of Marie Josephé only appeared to me in or around *Pâtisseries à la Carte*. I found her missing ruby heart necklace when I dug deep enough in the garden." Warm air fluttered across Mary Jo's cheek, and she had the feeling Marie Josephé had just said goodbye. She touched the pendant, warm on her skin. "However, we don't know what triggered the other ghost's anger when I found that box of silver."

"But," Stephanie added, finger in the air. "Somehow *our* ghosts are able to help us. Mine reached out to save me from being pulled out of the window. May Jo's somehow caused text messages to reach us until Chase found her."

Terry sat in the lotus position, propping her elbows on her

knees and cupping her chin with her right hand. Using the glass as a pointer in her left hand, she alternated between Mary Jo and Stephanie. "And you've both had scary incidents in the attic of this house, encountering our unknown monster spirit. I haven't seen any ghosts around here since I was a child, but this episode tonight did spook me a little." She touched her neck where the sapphire cross usually rested. "I want my pendant back. It should be ready next week."

"I feel left out," Beth said with an exaggerated pout. "I don't have a ghost."

Mary Jo poured ginger ale in Beth's flute and said, "Well, Tanner seems to be the conduit for these spirits to first appear to us. As Connor's son, he's related to the colonial sisters in some way. So, vicariously, you have our ghosts."

"But I don't have a necklace either." Beth stuck her bottom lip out further, although her eyes twinkled.

Mary Jo jumped to her feet and held her champagne glass high.

"Ladies, may I have your attention please?" All eyes turned toward her as she lifted the velvet cord holding the silver *tastevin* from around her neck and held it up to the light so the silver sparkled.

"Beth, I bestow upon you the Association of the Sisterhood Medal of Champagne—nope, make that Ginger Ale in deference to your gentle state." With a flourish of ceremony, she draped the cord over Beth's head.

As Beth clapped her hands and reached for the *tastevin*, she cooed, "I feel like an Olympian gold medalist." Terry and Stephanie giggled.

"Sorry, champ," Mary Jo said. "It's only a silver."

Stephanie and Terry collapsed into boneless heaps, rolling from their respective air mattresses to the floor, peals of laughter punctuating the air.

The shrill of Terry's ringing cell phone pierced their mirth. "Who is calling at two in the morning?" She glanced at the dial and looked up in alarm. "It's Dad."

"Hello, Dad. What's wrong?" Her eyes widened, and her

hand flew to her heart. She jumped to her feet. "Oh my God, when? Is she okay?...We're on our way... No, Beth didn't drink anything so she can drive us. We'll meet you there...Okay, Dad. Tell her I love her."

Her voice cracked as she punched the button and turned to her friends, tears running down her cheeks.

"It's Mom. She's on the way to the hospital. They think she's had a heart attack."

EPILOGUE

Louis rotated the key in the lock at his grandfather's house, pressing his finger against the metal to muffle the click. He pushed the door inward, stepped into the silent room, and waited. He lifted the darkened lantern from its hook on the wall and set it at his feet. His hand trailed the wall until he located the tinderbox. He knelt and struck flint until he produced a spark. The tinder flared, and he lit the lantern wick.

Wooden floorboards creaked under his feet, and he paused, his pulse pounding loud in his ears. The rug under the dining table muffled his footstep, as did the parlor rug. He stepped with care toward the entrance and his boot brushed something soft. He raised the lantern to shine on the floor.

"Mother!" He whispered hoarsely and knelt by Clothiste's side. She lay in a huddled heap at the base of the stairs. In the lantern's reflection, her face was colorless, her lips blue. Blood spread down the sleeve of her gown and pooled under her injured shoulder.

She struggled to open her eyes and move her lips. He cupped her neck and tried to raise her head. He bent his ear to her face, her gasp fluttering against his skin.

"My son." She tried to raise her good arm, but could only shift her wrist.

"Don't talk, Mother."

"She tried...to kill...Phillip," she whispered, voice breaking between gasps of breath. Tears trickled from her half-opened eyes, sliding along her temples to the floor.

Her jaw slackened. A gurgle rattled deep in her throat before the life ebbed from her body.

Louis gathered his mother's lifeless form, muffling sobs against her neck.

Low groans reached his ears. He glanced up the dark staircase. He could make out a form at the top of the steps.

"Who is down there? Help me."

He gently lowered his mother's shoulders to the floor. Her blood smeared his right hand, obscuring the emerald of the signet ring on his pinkie finger.

"Who is there?" The raspy voice strengthened.

"British soldier." Louis brushed his mother's cheek with his clean hand and stood up. He held the lantern higher and began a deliberate ascent up the stairway.

Abigail was sprawled on the top steps. Her head rested on the floor, her body aiming downward. One leg stretched before her. The other twisted at an odd angle, the heel almost reaching her hip.

Louis moved closer and shined the light.

"Never mind the whore at the bottom of the steps." Abigail gasped. "Do you know who I am?" She shifted and screamed in pain. "Do your duty."

Louis stepped, careful not to touch Abigail's twisted limbs. He knelt beside her and moved the lantern close to his face.

"Do you know who I am?" he asked.

A trickle of blood seeped from a cut on Abigail's chin. In spite of the pain etched in her face, she glared insolently at Louis. "You were here the night my husband was shot."

"That is true. But do you know who I am?"

Abigail met his gaze with a sneer of contempt on her face.

Louis leaned closer and whispered, "I am Phillip's grandson. And the woman you call a whore is my mother."

He pressed his bloodied thumb and fingers to either side of her windpipe.

Her eyes widened in understanding as he pressed harder, harder.

MARY JO'S FRENCH CONNECTION

PHILLIPE DE LA ROCHER (aka Phillip Rocker) *m. 1ˢᵗ wife (unk name), m. Abigail Wheeler (2ⁿᵈ wife)*
/
ÉTIENNE DE LA ROCHER (1743-1812) m. **CLOTHISTE JANVIER** (1750-1781)
/
MARIE JOSEPHÉ ROCHER (1765-1843) *m. Thomas Harris (1760-1830)*
/
PETER HARRIS *m. Rosa (unk last name)*
/
JONATHAN HARRIS *m. Jenny Smythe*
/
LOUISA HARRIS (1847-unk) *m. Edward Wyatt[1]*
/
EDITH WYATT (1864-1960) *m. Joseph Cameron*
/
ANNA LINDA CAMERON (1907 – 1970) *m. Patrick Payne*
/
ANNA "HANNAH" PAYNE (1946-) m. William "Billy" Jensen (1946-1965, age 19)
/
WAYNE EUGENE TELLER *(nee William Jensen Jr.1964-) and Patricia Elizabeth Cooper (1966-)*
/
MARY JO COOPER (1985-) engaged to Chase Hallmark (1984-)

---

[1] Edward Wyatt is a cousin to Stephanie's third great grandfather Thomas Wyatt, whose wife Emily Long is a cousin to Louisa Harris. Edward Wyatt served with his cousins in different units during the Civil War. While researching for proof needed for Civil War soldiers' pensions, Emily establishes that she, and also Louisa, are descended from Revolutionary War hero Étienne de la Rocher, and this helps the women to also establish DAR eligibility.

TURN THE PAGE FOR A SNEAK PREVIEW
OF
VOICE OF THE JUST
THE BLUE SAPPHIRE STORY
COMING FALL 2016

PROLOGUE

Theresé and the Blue Sapphire
Near Yorktown, Virginia, August 1781

The break of dawn brought no sunlight, but more of the storms that had plagued us for days—storms that reminded me of the horrible night when British soldiers attacked and wounded our mother and grandfather. My sisters and I were forced to leave them behind, but my brother Louis remained. His disguise as a British soldier gave us hope that they were cared for.

Thunder boomed in the distance outside as the rain eased. My sisters slept peacefully. Usually it was I who woke last, but I made up for it by working late into the night, sewing or writing letters dictated by soldiers unskilled in writing.

This morning, however, I was up with my father. I prepared him a breakfast but, as he had done with too many of his meals, he pushed it to the side. He worried about his own father, but for my mother, he was nearly driven mad with concern for her safety.

My beautiful mother had been so sick that we were forced to seek shelter in my grandfather's house. But his wife Abigail, our step-grandmother, had made it clear to us we were not wanted. When grandfather discovered his wife tried to poison my mother, he arranged for us to leave immediately in a wagon. Working with the patriots, he helped smuggle weapons and ammunition to the French soldiers supporting the Americans, and we would hid in the wagon under a canvas covering.

But that night, soldiers had gunned down my mother and grandfather before our eyes. My brother Louis, a spy within the British Army, shot the soldiers and sent us on our way while he stayed behind to care for our loved ones.

We had hoped for news to reach us before now. Nearly two weeks had passed without a word, unusual given the number of contacts my father had. I feared that if he did not hear some word of Mama's condition, he would risk his life to go to Portsmouth to find her.

"Papa, please eat something," I begged as I pushed a plate of biscuits closer to him. My youngest sister Nicole and I had picked a basket of blackberries during breaks from the rain, and Marie Josephé had used them to add some taste to the flavorless firecakes we so often ate.

My father smiled and shook his head. "No, ma petit, I am afraid food is not on my mind." He rubbed his eyes and then pinched the bridge of his nose.

"Are you thinking of Mama?" I asked.

"Every moment I am awake, I think of your mama, and when I sleep, I dream of her. I long for the day when my beautiful wife and our daughters live together again in a grand house, where we can watch our girls laugh and play. To one day see you wear the pretty jewels that your grandfather and I wanted to surprise you with."

"Papa, they were so beautiful. It made Mama very happy to give them to us. Nicole thought they were the continental colors, but Mama told us how you chose each one specially for us."

I had told this story to my father a number of times but he seemed never to tire of it.

He said, "Diamond for our innocent Nicole, ruby for our brave Marie Josephé, and sapphire for our crusader, Theresé." He smiled, but the light did not shine in his eyes.

Thundering horse hooves signaled the arrival of a wagon. A driver's voice shouted, "Whoa!" as the creaks and groans of the wooden carriage came to a halt.

"Dear God, please let there be word," my father cried as he pushed aside the flap on the tent, taking no notice of the stream of rainwater that poured from the shifting canvas. I stepped to the doorway, ignoring the drips as I watched Papa stomp through the mud toward the wagon. He reached it at the same time as several other soldiers from his brigade.

I recognized James, our brother's fellow spy ensconced within the British Army at Portsmouth. He lifted the canvas covering the back of the wagon, and Lizzie, our step-grandmother's unfortunate maid, scrambled over the sides, helped by my father. Her hair dripped into her eyes, and her soaked clothing clung to her. Fresh mud clumped with dried as her hem swept over the wet ground. A small girl I had never seen before scrambled *over the wall of the wagon and immediately wrapped her arms around Lizzie. Papa pointed toward our tent and gripped James' arm in frantic conversation.*

Lizzie scurried toward the tent, the little girl in tow. I reached for a blanket and held it as she came to the door. The commotion had wakened Marie Josephé and she came to stand at my side.

"Theresé!" Lizzie threw her arms around me and we held each other, unmindful of the wet. Lizzie embraced Marie Josephé next.

"We did not expect to see you, Lizzie. How did you come to be here?"

"My aunt has released me from my servitude. This child was sold as a servant to my aunt, and when I escaped, I brought her with me."

I hugged Lizzie again, and asked, "Then have you news of my mother? Can you tell me how she is? And Grandfather?"

The color drained from Lizzie's face and she said, "Your mother? Is she not here? I was told her family came for her."

My heart sunk to my feet.

"She is not here, Lizzie," I answered.

My sister and I clutched each other's hand as cold harsh fear washed over us.

ABOUT THE AUTHOR

Author Allie Marie grew up in Virginia. Her favorite childhood pastime was reading Nancy Drew and Trixie Belden mysteries. When she embarked on a new vocation writing fiction after retiring from a career in law enforcement, it would have been understandable if her first book was a crime story. Researching her own family tree inspired her to write the True Colors Series instead. The other stories are patiently waiting their turn.

Her debut novel is Teardrops of the Innocent: The White Diamond Story, a New England Readers' Choice Award Finalist in paranormal. The second in the series, Heart of Courage: The Red Ruby Story releases in May 2016, with the third book Voice of the Just: The Blue Sapphire Story slated for release in fall 2016.

Besides family, her passions are travel and camping with her husband Jack.

Made in the USA
Middletown, DE
24 November 2021